Happy Birthday

Happy Birthday

CHRISTINA JONES

ISIS
LARGE PRINT
Oxford

Copyright © Christina Jones, 2008

First published in Great Britain 2008
by
Piatkus Books
an imprint of
Little, Brown Book Group

Published in Large Print 2009 by ISIS Publishing Ltd.,
7 Centremead, Osney Mead, Oxford OX2 0ES
by arrangement with
Little, Brown Book Group
An Hachette Livre UK Company

British Library Cataloguing in Publication Data
Jones, Christina, 1948–
    Happy birthday. [text (large print)].
    1. Astrology - - Fiction.
    2. Dating services - - Fiction.
    3. Chick lit.
    4. Large type books.
    I. Title
    823.9'2–dc22

ISBN 978–0–7531–8354–0 (hb)
ISBN 978–0–7531–8355–7 (pb)

Printed and bound in Great Britain by
T. J. International Ltd., Padstow, Cornwall

For The Toyboy Trucker — he knows why

Acknowledgments

With many thanks to all at Piatkus/Little, Brown — especially my lovely, generous and very talented editors, Emma Dunford and Donna Condon, who must have had so many sleepless nights thanks to my appalling working methods but who never once grizzled or shouted (at least, not to/at me) . . .

Also many thanks to Sarah, Adrian and Francois at Forresters for curing me of my phobia, for giving me all their expertise and technical info on the hairdressing, and — inadvertently — more than one stonking sub-plot!

Forresters, I must add, is a fantastic salon, and absolutely nothing like Pauline's Cut'n'Curl!

My grateful thanks to Thirza, Kizzy, Zillah and Mrs C for the Romany fortune telling stuff and letting me mess about with the dialect.

And, last but definitely not least, special thanks to my friends, Mags, Val and Maria who were so brilliant at supporting me through the rough bits.

CHAPTER
ONE

Outside Hazy Hassocks' drowsy midsummer church, Mrs Finstock, the vicar's wife, was energetically executing a solo version of "YMCA" to a small but seemingly appreciative audience.

Resplendent in a lilac tulle two-piece, she leaped up and down in the middle of the road, her arms waving wildly, her generous bosoms dancing beneath the glimmering fabric. Her lilac hat, a mass of feathers from some exotic and possibly protected bird, danced too, albeit to a slightly different beat.

"Is Mrs Finstock *dancing*? In the *street*? In *this* heat?" Phoebe Bowler, the perfect size ten, ash-blonde-bobbed, designer-frocked bride-to-be, sitting beside her father in the back of the rose-scented white limousine, giggled delightedly. She leaned forwards and stared at the spectacle through the blur of her veil. "Yes — she is! Oh, bless her. She's always so funny, isn't she?"

"Funny wouldn't be my word for it," Bob Bowler muttered, looking rather anxiously from his daughter to the now star-jumping Mrs Finstock. "I'm far too nervous to find anything amusing — especially the vicar's wife having one of her turns."

"Vicar's wife is she? Blimey . . ." the limo's chauffeur joined in as he slowed down and, despite the efficacy of the car's expensive air-con, took the opportunity to mop the sweat from his forehead. "Looks to me like she's found the communion wine and had a hefty swig or three. Ah — she seems to have stopped prancing — yep, she's waving at us now. Hope she don't want us to join in. Too darn hot for any of that old nonsense. Maybe she just wants to tell us something. Shall I stop, duck?"

Phoebe smiled happily. "May as well, seeing as we're outside the church and it's nearly midday, the wedding's at noon and I'm half of the main attraction."

As the limousine purred to an opulent halt, the vicar's wife stopped dancing up and down and bustled busily towards the driver's window. Her face glistened under its generous coating of Crème Puff. There were little beads of moisture in the bristles above her upper lip.

"Thank goodness I caught your attention."

Difficult not to, Phoebe thought, beaming the prenuptial smile that had been impossible to suppress since she'd woken in her parents' semi that morning. "Actually, we thought you were dancing."

"What? No, no . . ." The vicar's wife squinted into the depths of the flower-and-ribbon-bedecked car. "Oh, Phoebe, dear, don't you look lovely. Now, I don't want to worry you — but we've got a bit of a delay. We're not quite ready for you." She pulled a face at the driver. "Would you mind awfully driving round the block again?"

2

"Fine by me," the driver said with a nod. "Allus happens at every wedding. Five minutes or so OK?"

"Lovely." Mrs Finstock bared her teeth in an agitated smile. "Five minutes should be perfect."

"What sort of delay?" Phoebe's prenuptial beam slipped slightly. "Not something wrong with our planning, surely? I've timed the whole day to perfection. It's taken me months to get this show on the road. Oh, I know — don't tell me — Clemmie hasn't arrived yet. She's so useless about time. I knew I should have forced to her to be at our house with the rest of the bridesmaids instead of coming straight from Winterbrook. Trust Clemmie! I'll have to have serious words with her later."

The vicar's wife nodded vigorously. "That's the ticket. Good girl. Nothing to worry about. Now, off you pop."

The driver replaced his cap, wiped his face and the limo moved slowly away.

Phoebe got a quick glimpse of her nearest and dearest in their wedding finery, a sea of rainbow colours, outside the church, sheltering from the searing midday sun in the mellowed portals before the car rounded the bend into the High Street.

As she'd suspected, there was no sign of Clemmie in the throng.

"I'll drive back out towards Bagley, shall I?" the driver asked over his shoulder. "No point getting caught up in the Saturday shopping traffic in Hassocks, is there? Who's this Clemmie, then?"

"My chief bridesmaid." Phoebe settled back into her seat. "Or matron-of-honour I suppose I should say seeing as she's already beaten me to the altar. Lifelong best friend. Scientifically brilliant and amazingly clever, but a complete pill-brain when it comes to common sense or being organised. She'll owe me big time for this."

"Ah, but you go easy on her, duck. Everyone'll expect the bride to be late anyway, won't they? Goes with the territory." The limo driver headed away from Hazy Hassocks' main street and out into the narrow lanes surrounding the large Berkshire market village. "Five minutes or so won't make any difference, will it?"

With a sigh, Phoebe shook her head. Well, it wouldn't. Not really. But, any delay to her minutely crafted day was slightly irritating. She was never late for anything. Not ever. Possible disruptions, interruptions and disasters were all carefully factored into each of Phoebe's plans. Trust dizzy, disorganised Clemmie to be the one to mess things up.

That was the trouble with having someone like Clemmie as a best friend. Especially an extremely loved-up, newly married and even more newly pregnant Clemmie.

Secretly, Phoebe was a teensy bit miffed that Clemmie had met, worked with, fallen in love with and whirlwindly married the divine Guy Devlin within six months, and was now merely seconds later expecting their first baby, while she and Ben — having been together since school — had taken the more sedate, orderly, well-planned route to everlasting love.

4

After a fifteen-year relationship, they'd become engaged, planned the dream wedding down to the finest detail, and had decided to start a family in another year or two when they'd left their rented Hazy Hassocks flat and sensibly saved enough to scramble onto the first rung of the mortgage ladder.

Clemmie, with no regard for planning or organisation, had simply characteristically plunged in. It was all rather annoying to someone like Phoebe who rarely even decided on what to wear without consulting her astral charts and considering all the possible options at least three times.

"Nervous?" Bob Bowler broke into her thoughts and squeezed his daughter's hand.

"About Clemmie being late? No, of course not. Well, not really." Phoebe looked serenely at her father through the ice-white froth of her veil. "Par for the course with Clemmie. She's probably having morning sickness or something — as long as she manages not to have it on her frock it'll be fine. She'll turn up eventually. Why on earth would I be nervous?"

"Because it's your wedding day and I'm petrified." Bob Bowler chuckled rather shakily. "I've never been father of the bride before."

"Well, I've never been the bride before either and I'm absolutely calm," Phoebe smiled at him and reached across the rear seat of the pink-rose-strewn limousine and patted his grey-trousered leg. "There's nothing to worry about, Dad. Today will run as smoothly as any military campaign. Stick with me, kid, and you'll be OK."

Bob shook his head, running a sweating finger round the tight collar of his morning suit. "You're scary, Phoebes. Cool as a cucumber. I thought brides were supposed to be a mass of nerves."

Phoebe gazed out on the scorching blue-sky June morning as the limo swept through the glossy Berkshire lanes close to her parents' semi in the tiny village of Bagley-cum-Russet and circled once more towards the church in nearby Hazy Hassocks. Even the weather had come up trumps. As she'd known it would.

She smiled blissfully. "I'm not worried — not even about Clemmie — because everything is going to be perfect. What could possibly go wrong?"

"Don't even expect me to answer that." Bob moved his top hat from his lap to the acres of silver leather seat beside him. "I'm not going to tempt fate."

"Fate," Phoebe said firmly, "can't be tempted. Fate is on my side. And I've planned today with minute attention to detail and a time-line never before seen in the history of weddings — not to mention it being astrally charted, of course."

Bob snorted. "You and your astrology! Do you really think a deck of tarot cards and some sort of star-sign mumbo-jumbo can forecast —?"

"Absolutely," Phoebe said happily. "I used my charts to plan the exact day, time and place for this wedding. All the portents pointed to this day being the perfect one for our marriage. And after all, Ben and I know each other inside out. You wait and see — he'll be as calm as I am. We're just looking forward to it being the best wedding anyone can ever remember."

Settling back in the limousine's smoothly purring luxury, Phoebe rearranged her slim-fitting silk frock and checked her mental tick-list. Yes, it was fine. Apart from Clemmie being late, everything was simply perfect. This, her and Ben's wedding day, was truly going to be the happiest day of her life.

Seven and a half minutes later, the limousine pulled up outside the church again. This time there was no sign of the vicar's wife and the guests had all disappeared.

"There," Phoebe said cheerfully, "see? No problems. Clemmie's obviously arrived intact and they're all inside waiting. Blimey, I bet Ben's chewing his fingernails, though. I promised him I wouldn't be late."

The limo driver struggled out and held the door open. A tidal wave of heat swooshed into the car.

"Proper scorcher you've got," the driver said, as Phoebe, in her slender strapless column of silk, wriggled the pooled hem round her high-heeled white sandals and clutched her small bouquet of pale-pink rosebuds. "Still, you know what they say, duck? Happy the bride the sun shines on . . . Now — where's the photographer? You'll need some snaps of you and your dad together before you gets going."

Bob Bowler frowned towards the church as it shimmered beneath the June sun. "Yes, where is the photographer, Phoebes? I know you've got the camcorder bloke waiting in the porch to film us coming up the path, but I thought —"

Phoebe sighed in exasperation. "Why can no one be relied on? Yes, the photographer should be here —

7

maybe he was late as well. As long as he arrives for the after-the-event pics I'll be OK. Oh, well, at least we'll have it on film."

Bob smiled moist-eyed at his slender, blonde daughter in the exquisite ice-white silk dress, short veil and diamante tiara. "You look gorgeous, Phoebe, truly. I'm so proud of you. Let me just straighten your veil a bit. Now, you take my arm and we'll be off. Are you feeling OK?"

"Fine, Dad, honest. Not a tummy-dancing butterfly, trembly hand or nerve in sight."

Phoebe gave a wide beam to the crowd of Hazy Hassocks Saturday shoppers all clustered round the church gates. The Saturday shoppers beamed back. Several clapped.

"Phoebes . . ." Clemmie, tall and beautiful in a filmy dress of dusky pink, her mass of unruly dark-red hair caught up with white rosebuds, suddenly appeared from the porch and hurried down the church path. "Oh, you look so lovely . . . I'm so sorry . . ."

"It's OK. You're here now. And you look stunning yourself. Have you stopped being sick? Have you got the little flower girls under control? And has Mum stopped sniffling? And has my nan left that awful hat at home and —"

"What? Yes, but, Phoebes —"

"Don't worry, Clem — honestly. I'm used to you being late for everything. I should have factored it in on my list: ten minutes extra in case Clemmie doesn't turn up."

"It wasn't me . . . isn't me . . . Phoebe, listen —"

8

"Oh, Clem, stop fretting about it. I'm cool — now let's get on with this."

Clemmie gave Bob Bowler a beseeching look, then held out her hand. "Phoebes, come over here . . . please . . . There's something I've got to tell you."

"Not now!" Phoebe laughed. "Whatever it is can wait until after the wedding."

"No it can't." Clemmie swallowed. "Phoebes, sweet-heart . . . Oh, Lordy, there's no easy way to say this. There's not going to be a wedding. Ben isn't here. He isn't going to be here. He's called it off . . ."

CHAPTER
TWO

A month later, Phoebe slid the key into the lock of the two-storey Edwardian red-brick terraced house and felt sick. Despite the midday heat and wearing the minimum of underwear beneath her brief pink Cut'n'Curl tunic, she was bone-cold and her hands were shaking. It was the first time she'd been back to her Hazy Hassocks flat since the-wedding-that-never-was.

There had been many, many days in the past awful month that she was sure she'd never do this: would never be able to return to the flat again. How could she walk into the home she and Ben had created and see all the things she'd left so happily the evening before the wedding just sitting there as if suspended in time? How could she walk into the flat knowing Ben wouldn't be there? Knowing that he wouldn't ever be coming home again?

The sun scorched down, as it had all this glorious summer, but everything in Winchester Road looked bleak, grey and dead. Phoebe took a deep breath, praying that the neighbours weren't peering at her with prying inquisitive eyes from behind their prim nets. It was almost like being bereaved, she thought: people knew and stared and sympathised silently, but really didn't know what to say.

What could they say? Ben had left her in the most humiliatingly public way possible and everyone knew that she'd been jilted. And they all speculated on why.

As she had. Over and over again.

Taking another gulp of hot air, Phoebe tried again to turn the key, averting her eyes from the "Bowler and Phipps" bell-push beneath the one for the upstairs flat, which simply said "Lancaster".

It would be separate "Bowler and Phipps" for ever now, she thought miserably. Of course, she'd planned to conjoin the names on the marriage certificate. Phoebe Bowler Phipps, she'd said, had a really nice ring to it. Ben hadn't agreed. He simply couldn't see why she wanted to amalgamate her maiden name with his surname. Even when she'd said gently and almost jokingly that much as she'd always wanted to be his wife, she'd always thought Phoebe Phipps sounded like a cartoon character, Ben had failed to as much as smile.

Phoebe sighed.

Maybe that's why he . . . Why he . . . Well, why he did what he did. Because although she'd wanted to be married to Ben for as long as she could remember, she didn't want to be alliterative Phoebe Phipps. Maybe she shouldn't have told him. Maybe she'd really hurt his feelings. Maybe it was all her fault after all.

She fumbled with the key again.

Could she really do this? On her own? Should she have accepted her parents' offer to come with her —

just for this first visit? No, she had to start standing on her own feet, because . . . Well, because there wasn't an alternative, was there? Her mum and dad would have made it worse, wouldn't they? They'd have been kind, as they had been since the wedding day when she'd returned home and cried herself to sleep every night in her childhood bedroom, and their kindness would make her cry. And, Phoebe had decided, she'd cried enough to last her a lifetime and would never, ever cry — in public at least — again.

Or even worse, they might have launched into yet another vitriolic attack on the hapless Ben and his cold-feet jitters at best, or his cold-hearted abandoning at worst.

No, on balance, Phoebe knew, this visit to the flat was something she had to do alone. And if she managed it today, then after this first time it wouldn't be so bad — she'd just collect her bits and pieces in as many visits as it took, and go back to her parents' home in Bagley, and then she'd contact the letting agents and tell them she was moving out of Winchester Road. For good.

The key turned and she pushed the door open.

A pile of post was heaped against her flat door. Stepping over it — it probably hid more than one wedding congrats card — Phoebe walked into the carefully updated neutral minimalist living room, her pink Cut'n'Curl clogs slip-slapping rhythmically on the wooden floor.

How quiet it was in the flat. How pale. How sterile. As if all the life had been sucked out. It looked, she thought bleakly, like a neglected showroom. Not like a home at all. There was no hint of warmth, of laughter, of living, of loving.

Of Ben there was no trace at all. Her CDs, books and magazines were still there. But someone — Ben? — had been in since the-wedding-that-never-was and removed every last one of his personal items. The flat even smelled empty. A month ago it had wafted with scented candles and Ben's aftershave and her own perfume and herbs and spices from the experimental cooking sessions they'd shared. Now it had a neglected, bland smell of nothingness.

It was as if the life she'd shared with Ben — and Ben himself — had never existed.

Feeling suddenly dizzy and engulfed by loneliness, Phoebe sank down onto the white sofa. A shaft of sunlight sneaked through the cream and white embossed linen curtains and formed a glinting golden puddle on the floor. Phoebe swallowed the lump in her throat. This wasn't her home any more — how could it be? When she'd left it, she'd been laughing and giggling and Ben, accompanied by Alan, his best man, had kissed her goodbye.

For ever.

Phoebe sniffed back a threatening tear and hauled herself to her feet. No time for wallowing in self-pity — there were things to be done, tasks to be tackled, stuff to be sorted. The flat was stifling, airless, so she opened the French doors on to the garden. The only sound was the Kennet, a snaking river tributary, rippling unseen behind the high walls, making its way towards the Thames at Winterbrook.

She and Ben had worked hard on the garden, too. They'd built a little courtyard for sitting in with a glass of wine on balmy summer nights, with lush foliage and jasmine, honeysuckle and orange blossom tumbling from the high-brick walls, making a secret, sensuous oasis. A lovers' arbour.

Oh, God . . .

Phoebe turned away from the garden, determined not to cry.

Today, she'd returned to work as senior stylist at Pauline's Cut'n'Curl in Hazy Hassocks High Street after the three weeks leave she'd booked for the Caribbean cruise honeymoon — which she'd spent holed up in her old bedroom in Bagley-cum-Russet — followed by an extra unpaid week because she knew she wasn't quite ready for the ill-concealed interrogation from her regular blue-rinse-and-bubble-perm clients.

Today, she was using her lunch hour to start packing her possessions and close the door on the flat. Today she was going to try to pull her life back together.

So far the life-pulling had been a dismal failure, Phoebe thought sadly, as she listlessly tugged a holdall from the hall cupboard and pulled her coats and jackets from their pegs. Pauline and the girls at the salon had been lovely this morning, of course, and kept up a stream of bright chatter, shielding her from the more nosy clients by getting her to count conditioner bottles in the stockroom. But Pauline and the girls could do nothing to shield her from the frankly curious eyes and

14

whispers. Pauline and the girls could do nothing to shield her from her own mortification.

The whispers she'd get used to, she knew that. The humiliation might just take a little longer.

Unzipping the holdall, Phoebe then slowly consulted the "Things to Collect" list in her pink spiral-bound notebook. Even devastating heartbreak and her life falling apart hadn't managed to totally destroy her obsession with organisation. She'd listed the rooms in the flat: five; sub-divided the contents of each that a) belonged to her, b) belonged to Ben, c) were jointly owned; and sub-sectioned each of a) and c) into things she would remove on this first visit.

Pressing her jackets into a neat pile at the bottom of the holdall, Phoebe lugged the bag into the living room and made a start on the books and music.

She'd just finished pushing the CDs into every available corner, ticking them off her list, trying not to remember the myriad "our tunes" included on them, knowing she'd never listen to them again and pretty sure they'd all end up in Hedley and Biff Pippin's animal charity shop, when her phone rang.

Fishing it out of the pocket of her short pink Cut'n'Curl overall, she frowned then smiled. Clemmie. Probably wanting to know how the first morning back at work had gone. She'd have to sound cheerful otherwise Clemmie would be hot-footing it from Winterbrook to lend a shoulder to cry on. Again.

"Hi," Phoebe said breezily. "How are you? Still being sick? Poor thing . . . Still, it can't last for the whole nine months, can it? What? Work? Oh, well, you know . . . it went OK. Pauline and the girls were lovely of course, but . . . What, now? No, I'm in the flat . . . Yes, well, it had to be done some time. I'm alone. No, no, really, Clem, even if you are in Hassocks, I'm much better doing it on my own. It's really kind of you but I need to do this my way. What — tonight? Who with? Oh, right. Yes, lovely . . . Thanks. Where? OK? See you later. Bye."

Pushing her mobile back into her pocket, Phoebe sighed. Clemmie was the best friend anyone could wish for. And a girlie night out in anonymous Winterbrook — their nearest largish town — as Clem had suggested, would be nice, but it was so hard being the only single one — especially when she and Ben had been together for ever.

Phoebe swallowed. She wasn't going to think about Ben. Not now. Not ever again.

Just as she was pondering over whether she was brave enough to walk into the bedroom — which she seriously doubted — and shove a few more clothes into the holdall before returning to work, the doorbell rang.

"I really hope it's not Clemmie," Phoebe muttered to herself, heading for the door. "I've just got to get used to doing everything alone . . ."

It wasn't Clemmie.

Slo Motion, one elderly third of Hazy Hassocks' only funeral directors who lived with his cousins, Constance and Perpetua, and rather sadly ran their business a few houses away in Winchester Road, stood on the doorstep.

"I saw you arrive earlier." Slo, dressed in a heavy black serge suit despite the searing heat and with

16

cigarette burns on his waistcoat, grinned gummily at her. "Thought I'd come and say welcome home. Be neighbourly, like. Here . . ."

Phoebe peered dubiously at the lidded dish in his hands. "Oh . . . er, thank you. Um, oh, that isn't an *urn* is it?"

"Nah, course not. It's a casserole. Weather's a bit hot for a casserole I know, duck, but it's what our Perpetua allus makes for the bereaved on our first visit. Seems to cheer 'em up. It's what them telly chefs would call rustic — got lumps in it — oh, and don't let on to our Constance that you've 'ad it. She's as tight as a duck's whatsit over freebies. I've defrosted it for you."

"Thank you." Phoebe smiled bravely. "It's very kind of you. And a casserole will be lovely — but it still looks like it's in an urn. For ashes . . ."

"Ah, well, yes it *is* an urn if you wants to split hairs, but it's a fresh one, duck. Untouched by human remains. Therefore it's just a container really, isn't it? We uses them for all sorts. The gels swear by 'em for storing leftovers and what have you. Here — you take it — there's no need to let us have it back. It'll come in handy later for flowers or face cream or talc or summat."

"Thank you." Phoebe took the casserole-urn, holding it at arm's length. "I'll, um, enjoy it. Er, are the gels, um, Constance and Perpetua not with you?"

"Nah," Slo wheezed happily. "They've gorn up the Twilights to measure up a customer."

"Right." Phoebe pulled a face. The thought of the two female Motions sorting out yet another funeral at

17

Twilights — Hazy Hassocks' warden-assisted rest home for the elderly — was probably best not dwelt on. Not in her current state of heightened emotion. But at least the sad departure of a Twilighter to their eternal rest meant Constance and Perpetua weren't here to offer their own heavy-handed brand of sympathy. Every cloud and all that. "And it's lovely to see you, but actually, I'm just going back to work. I was only collecting a few of my things."

"Why? You're not leaving, duck? Oh, that's a bloomin' shame. Me and the gels loved having you here. A bit of young blood in the street livened us old uns up no end. I was right sorry about . . . well, about what happened." Slo shuffled his feet. "Can't imagine what that Ben was thinking of. Buggering off and leaving a lovely young girl like you — and you allus seemed so happy together."

"Mmm." Phoebe knew she had to change the subject. It was always worse when someone was kind. "Well, that's all behind us now — and yes, I'm moving out. I'm going back to my parents in Bagley and —"

"Damn shame!" Slo looked indignant. "You'd made a lovely little home here. Seems all wrong that you've got to leave it. Still, I suppose it'll be too dear with you on your own. Mind, you've got two bedrooms — you could allus take in a lodger, couldn't you? To help with the rent?"

Phoebe sighed. "Well, yes, I suppose I could if I was staying, but I can't live here any more."

"Because of the memories? Ah, they can be right killers — that's speaking professionally, of course." Slo fidgeted in the pocket of his waistcoat and brought out a battered packet of Marlboro. "All right with you if I sparks up, duck? Don't tell the gels, though. They thinks I packed up on New Year's Eve. Again."

"Puff away. Your secret's safe with me," Phoebe said faintly as Slo gurgled and wheezed and shuddered pleasurably with a spasm of chesty coughing. "And thanks again for popping round."

"You think over what I said." Slo inhaled deeply. "You don't have to run away. This is your home, duck, and you've got every right to stay here. Sometimes —" He broke off to cough cheerfully. "Sometimes we finds — professionally speaking again — that the one what's left behind can rebuild a nice little life for themselves among the memories once the first pain has gorn. It helps 'em. Not that your Ben has died, duck, more's the pity I says, but you knows what I mean."

Phoebe nodded. Lots of her friends — and even her parents — had said much the same thing about moving out. But staying in Winchester Road was simply impossible. Even if she could afford to pay the rent single-handedly, every inch of the flat reminded her of Ben and their life — not just the future they'd planned, but their shared history too. And how, Phoebe thought despairingly, could she ever, ever sleep in *that* bed again?

Slo sucked shakily on his cigarette, the ash tumbling down his waistcoat. "I'll let you get on now, duck — I can see you're busy — but you think on what I've said. And if you do decide to leave, then don't go without saying goodbye."

"No, I won't. And thank you again for this." Phoebe glanced down anxiously at the ebony urn which was, she now noticed, steaming slightly. "I'm sure it'll be delicious."

As soon as the door was closed and Slo had disappeared back along Winchester Road, Phoebe tipped the casserole into the sink. She felt a bit guilty, watching as it glugged glutinously and hovered in unrecognisable clumps round the plug hole. It smelled of very old mushrooms and moth balls. No doubt the Motions had made it with the very best of intentions — still, they'd never know she hadn't eaten it, would they?

Running the tap over the residue and using a fork to force the more recalcitrant lumps out of sight, she then quickly rinsed the urn, wrapped it in a shroud of kitchen roll and, still holding it at arm's length, disposed of it in the dustbin outside the back door.

The deed done, Phoebe glanced at her watch. Nearly two o'clock. Oh, Lord — thanks to Slo she was going to be late back to work and she hadn't even started on sorting out her clothes. Ah, well. At least it would mean not having to go into the bedroom — yet . . .

"Who's that down there? What are you — *Phoebe*? Phoebe!" A voice screeched delightedly from somewhere above her. "Cool! I thought you were the Bath Road yobbos doing a bit of breaking and entering! I'm up here!"

Squinting upwards, against the sun spiralling in the deep blue sky, Phoebe groaned inwardly at the sight of Mindy — her upstairs neighbour — leaning precariously over her greenery-fronded balcony.

20

"Oh, er, hi, Mindy. Yes, it's me — not burglars. Er, I can't stop, I'm late for work and —"

"Nooo!" Mindy — all stylishly layered short black hair, expensively tanned face and heavily mascared eyes — screeched. "You can't go. Not yet. I've been dying to see you. I want to know what's happening. I want all the gory details. Stay there, sweetie. I'm coming down."

Phoebe shook her head as Mindy, wearing a skimpy white bikini top and even skimpier white shorts, clattered down the cast-iron fire escape which led to the garden. Mindy — long-haul cabin crew out of Heathrow — was probably the last person she needed to share her innermost angst with right now. Mindy — impossibly slender, stunningly glamorous and wildly indiscreet — was definitely not going to be sympathetic about the jilting.

"If I'd known you were here I'd have brought a bottle of wine." Mindy immediately folded herself elegantly onto one of Phoebe's wrought-iron chairs and crossed her long, long legs and flipped her designer sunglasses over her eyes. "Phew — it's sooo hot! Sweetheart, why haven't you got your lounger out? You're very pale — you should be catching some rays."

"I'm going back to work," Phoebe said again. "I'm already late."

Mindy waved a slim hand. "Phone in sick. Take the afternoon off. We've got sooo much to talk about. So — go on — what happened? I couldn't believe it when I got back from the Far East trip and everyone told me Ben hadn't turned up. Oh, sweetheart, you must have felt such a prat!"

Phoebe swallowed. Typical Mindy — ultra-sensitive. "Honestly, I don't want to talk about it."

"Talking's good." Mindy lifted the large sunglasses and batted her eyelashes at Phoebe. "Cathartic. That's why everyone should have counselling after traumas. Did you? Have counselling?"

"No."

"Well, you should. Must. Otherwise you'll turn all embittered. Hate men for ever."

"Yes, very probably. Look, Mindy, I really don't have time to chat. Maybe later — next time I come round . . ."

"What do you mean? You mean you're not living here? Why on earth not, sweetie?"

Phoebe sighed. "All sorts of reasons. And as I'm leaving here as soon as possible, unless you're grounded for a while we probably won't see much of each other and —"

"Leaving? The flat? Moving out completely?" Mindy lowered the sunglasses again and frowned at Phoebe. "Really? Well, there's a coincidence, because I'm moving out too. This weekend in fact. So this old house will be a sad and lonely place. Where are you going?"

"Back to my parents in Bagley-cum-Russet. You?"

"A west London penthouse with a really cute Airbus pilot."

Phoebe almost smiled. "No contest there then, but I thought you and, um . . ."

She stopped. What on earth was Mindy's boyfriend called? Was he the Lancaster on the flat's name plate, or was that Mindy? No, Phoebe frowned, Mindy's

22

surname was Martin, wasn't it? She'd noticed it when she'd sorted letters from their communal post in the hall. So he was Somebody Lancaster, wasn't he? In his absence, Mindy had always referred to him as Lover Boy with a sort of erotic purr, but somehow Phoebe felt she couldn't call him that, could she?

Phoebe had only ever glimpsed him either going upstairs, or coming down, or jumping in or out of his car, and had a vague image of a tall, dark, shadowy, uniformed figure who'd waved and called hi, but she'd never met him. He'd been absent more than he'd been at home most of the time she and Ben had lived in Winchester Road, and Phoebe had guessed his cabin crew job also took him all over the world.

Then, on the odd occasions when he and Mindy had been home at the same time, she and Ben had listened with guilty enjoyment to regular rip-snorting rows, slamming doors and stomping feet reverberating from the upstairs flat. Rows and separations, Phoebe realised now, that she'd thought smugly would never happen to her and Ben in their rock solid relationship. How blindly self-righteous she'd been . . .

"Rocky?" Mindy supplied helpfully. "The divine Rocky Lancaster? Drop dead gorgeous Rocky Lancaster?"

Rocky — that was it. Phoebe nodded. She remembered thinking it was an odd name and probably the poor bloke's parents had been Sly Stallone fans or something. But — Rocky Lancaster . . . Surely she'd heard that name somewhere else? In connection with something else entirely? Not recently, but . . .

Mindy frowned. "Drop dead is what I wish he'd do — anytime soon for preference. The bastard. Everyone thought he was wonderful but — oh, sweetie, if only you knew the truth. Of course, you must have heard about him. I was so ashamed. Ah well, like you and Ben, that's all history now. I do have some pride and a massive sense of self-preservation — and there was no way I was going to stay here with him after what he did. I mean, would you, if your boyfriend —?"

Phoebe's mobile rang. She glanced at the warbling phone. "Sorry, Mindy, it's work, I'll have to answer it. Pauline? Sorry I'm late. Oh, yes I'm fine, really. I got a bit side-tracked. Yes, I'm just on my way back now. What? Two perms? Yes, I'm sure I can — right — I'll be with you in five minutes."

Damn, she thought, snapping the phone shut. Just when Mindy was getting down to the juicy details. Now she'd probably never know what foul misdemeanour Rocky had committed, would she? And she could really, really do with wallowing in someone else's misery at the moment. Bugger.

"You've clearly got to dash." Mindy uncurled herself and hugged Phoebe. "Duty obviously calls. Well, you take care of yourself, sweetheart, and if we don't see one another again, have a happy life."

"You too." Phoebe extricated herself from Mindy's Chanel-perfumed embrace.

"Oh, I will." Mindy stretched with a sleepy, lascivious smile. "And if you should be unfortunate enough to run into Rocky while you're clearing the rest of your stuff out, tell him I hope he rots in hell."

24

CHAPTER
THREE

On the other side of Hazy Hassocks, the twisting High Street with its shops and small businesses and rural roads of houses petered out into narrow lanes and endless fields. Here, Twilights Rest Home for the Elderly stood in splendid bucolic isolation.

Essie Rivers pulled aside her fawn curtains and watched as Constance and Perpetua Motion bade their farewells to Tiny Tony and Absolute Joy Tugwell.

It was a morose scene. There was a lot of limp hand shaking on both sides, with suitably grim lips from the Tugwells matching an air of all-round-misery emanating from the Motions. Strangely, Essie thought, the gloom seemed further increased by the glorious July sunshine spreading itself into every corner of Twilight's honey-flagged courtyard and carefully tended and colourful herbaceous borders.

The Motions, Essie knew, had called to make arrangements for the removal of Ada Mackie's mortal remains.

Sadly, the Cousins Motion were fairly regular visitors to Twilight. Well, Essie considered, as the average age of the residents was ninety-three and half — she and her closest Twilighter friends, Princess, Lilith and Bert, had

25

worked it out one boring wet Sunday afternoon — that wasn't too surprising, really. Anyway, Ada had reached almost 104, which, Essie thought, was pretty good going.

And, she reckoned, as she let her curtains slip back into place, if Ada was a yardstick, then it gave her at least another good twenty-three years, didn't it? And twenty-three years was simply ages, wasn't it?

At eighty and tall and slender, Essie felt as fit as she had at thirty, kept the twenty-four-inch waist she'd had at twenty, dressed in the loose-trousers-with-fitted-top style she'd adopted at forty, and maintained the glass-half-full attitude to life she'd been born with. Defying the sheeplike urge of some of her peers, she'd also eschewed the ubiquitous cauliflower-head hairdo and wore her abundant multi-toned silver hair tied up with a variety of colourful chiffon scarves.

Tony and Joy Tugwell stood on the gravelled drive, waving until Constance and Perpetua's black Daimler had disappeared. Then, assuming their professional caring expressions, they strode back into Twilight's functional single-storey red-brick sprawl.

Essie stood back from her just-open window — despite the scorching summer heat, none of the windows at Twilight opened more than an inch, whether to prevent accidents or escapes or both, Essie wasn't sure — careful not to be seen. The Tugwells loathed the inmates peering out from their rooms.

Peering out was frowned upon, just in case someone from the outside world wandered close to Twilights and spotted the residents, looking for all the world like bored caged animals on view in a zoo. Peering out made Tony and Joy turn sanctimonious. And there was no way Essie was going to give the Tugwells an excuse to turn sanctimonious. Not that they needed a reason, really, because in Essie's opinion, they just were — well — thoroughly smug and holier-than-thou.

Not that the Tugwells were unpleasant in any sort of stereotypical moustache-twirling hiss-boo baddie sort of way, of course. They weren't even the sort of nursing home managers who gave nursing home managers a bad name. Oh no, Tony and Joy Tugwell were nothing like that. They were simply, in Essie's opinion, completely unsuited to the caring professions.

Tony and Joy were totally self-obsessed, emotionally cold and without even a trace of humour.

With excellent written qualifications for their roles, they managed Twilights with ruthless efficiency. They were no doubt paid huge target bonuses to cushion their own pension plans and made a comfortable income for the local authority who owned the home, but made no allowances whatsoever for the residents' individual quirks.

However, the rest of the staff — the live-in carers for the more infirm Twilight inmates, the mostly Eastern European girls who did the cooking, cleaning and waitressing, the ex-nurses who came in from Hassocks and worked shifts and made sure everyone was happy and healthy in their roomettes — were wonderful, Essie thought.

No, despite Tiny Tony's and Absolute Joy's lack of imagination, as rest homes went it was all very well run and efficient. But being a Twilighter was like being interned in a reasonably comfortable prison for life with no possibility of remission for good behaviour.

Tony and Joy Tugwell reckoned old people were old people, full stop. Old people, Tony and Joy seemed to think, left their personalities and histories behind the minute they collected their pensions. Old people, Tony and Joy clearly felt, needed daytime telly, night-time cocoa and very little else in between.

Essie smoothed the taupe duvet over her single bed in her basic beige bedsit — or "roomette" according to the Twilight brochure — and thought, not for the first time, that if things didn't change soon, she'd probably die of boredom long before she reached Ada's benchmark.

And, as she had very real reasons for wanting to outlive her children, she simply couldn't allow that to happen.

Still, first things first — there were preparations to make for Ada's send-off. She'd have to discuss outfits with Princess and Lilith. Black or navy? A touch of pink maybe as Ada had been very fond of pink? Hats or not? It was important to have the details right for the paying of the last respects.

Like the majority of Twilighters, Ada had had few visitors. And as residing in Twilights would have taken care of any money Ada may have had, Essie knew the funeral would be just this side of pauper and there'd certainly be no rich pickings for any of Ada's family who may emerge greedily from the woodwork with great expectations.

No, Essie thought forlornly, for poor Ada's farewell it'd simply be another gloomily clad trip in the convoy of Twilight minibuses to the nearest crematorium, a rousing chorus of "The Day Thou Gavest", and back to Twilights for one of Joy's minimal ham teas.

Everyone at Twilights went to everyone else's funerals because it made a bit of a crowd for the late lamented, got them out for a couple of hours, and they could grizzle happily about the eulogy, the circuit vicar, the other mourners, the flowers — or lack of them — and the choice of finale music.

Essie, who already knew she wanted a bright and happy funeral with lots of colour, lots of flowers, loud music and a magical funeral tea provided by Mitzi Blessing's Hubble Bubble herbal catering company, wondered how many more of her friends she'd shed tears over in the bleakness of Winterbrook's crematorium.

She sighed heavily. This really wouldn't do. Ada was gone and she was wasting yet another day. The afternoon stretched away into the blue and golden heat haze. Twilights dozed and was silent in the somnolence.

Tony and Joy always reckoned a good three-hour nap after lunch was mandatory for anyone over sixty. Most of the Twilighters obliged, either in their roomettes or in front of the constantly blaring plasma-screen telly in the residents' lounge, out of a sense of duty and lack of anything else more interesting to do.

Essie, who was quite happy to indulge in the luxury of a daytime snooze but in her own time, always forced herself to be awake and visible during the after-lunch and before-tea hours. Mainly because it irritated the pants off Tony and Joy.

A sharp rap on the door jerked Essie back to the present. She frowned. It wouldn't be Lilith or Princess, or even Bert, because they all had a secret coded knock. Must be Absolute Joy or Tiny Tony, then? Not much to pick between them — and she didn't want to see either. She stayed where she was and didn't answer.

"Mrs Rivers?" Joy's voice warbled plummily from the corridor outside. "Essie? Are you asleep?"

If I had been I wouldn't be now you daft bat, Essie thought irritably, still staying silent.

With a rattling of the master key and a bit of huffing and puffing, the door opened.

Bugger. Really must remember to bolt the damn door, Essie thought sourly, as Joy's rigid auburn bouffant — à la Margaret Thatcher: The Early Years — appeared in the room a split second before the rest of her. Sadly, Joy embraced everything about her hero — blue suits, neutral blouses with pussycat bows, and a huge and unpleasant handbag for every occasion — with almost religious fervour.

"Not sleepy, Essie?" Joy's attempt at the imperious Thatcher voice still needed some work. "Tony and I noticed you at the window."

Never, Essie thought, had anyone been so inappropriately named. Joy was surely the most congenitally cheerless woman ever born.

"No."

"Would you like a tablet to help?" Joy gesticulated to the trolley she'd parked in the corridor outside Essie's door.

"No, I damn well wouldn't."

"I know Ada's passing over must have absolutely upset you, but —"

"Ada didn't pass over, pass away, fall asleep, shuffle off this mortal coil or any of the other twee euphemisms you seem to favour. She died. And yes, I'll miss her and mourn her, but no, I'm not upset. She'd had enough. She was ready to go."

"Well, I'm sure that's a comfort to us all." Joy blinked her beige lashes very quickly. "Dear Ada — a wonderful woman — we'll miss her dreadfully, but sadly her passing is all part of the rich tapestry. In the midst of life we are in death."

"Bollocks."

"Sorry?" Joy pursed thin orange lips.

"Bollocks." Essie sighed. "And sorry if that offends your sensibilities, but you're talking sanctimonious claptrap. You'll fill Ada's roomette with another unwanted and unloved oldie before the final strains of the Twenty-third Psalm have bitten the dust, the money will continue to roll in, the council will be happy and everything will continue as normal. Now, did you want something?"

There was a slight pause while Joy remembered to put on her caring face. "Just to remind you not to peer out of the windows, dear. Accidents do happen, as you well know, and a tumble from the window at your age —"

"If —" Essie narrowed her eyes "— I tumbled from that window — which is unlikely as it only opens wide enough to allow an anorexic snake to squeeze through — after my horrendous eighteen-inch fall, I'd land in a cushiony bed of soft and springy ground-covering perennials. Which is hardly likely to warrant you having to dial nine-nine-nine, or call the Motions back so that I can double-up with Ada in the hearse, is it?"

Joy's forced laugh grated like nails on a blackboard. "Mrs Rivers, dear! Essie — you're so funny."

"I know. Val Parnell missed out on a star when he passed me by, I can tell you."

Judging by the blank look in her colourless eyes, Joy had clearly never heard of Val Parnell. Essie wasn't surprised. In the days of the great variety acts, Tony and Joy Tugwell possibly hadn't been the London Palladium's target audience.

"So — now you've issued the dire warning of the open window, can I get on with going out for a walk?"

"A walk?" Joy screeched. "A *walk*? In nap time? A *walk*? On your own?"

"On my own. All alone." Essie nodded. "Totally solo. You don't need to worry — I remember all my Brownie and Guide road drill, I've memorised the Tufty Club stuff and the Green Cross Code, so I know how to cross the roads safely. Thanks to the red tops I'm fully aware of stranger danger. And as I'm still in possession of all my marbles I know I'll find my way home again. Although —" she frowned at Joy "— I use the term loosely."

Joy, who still wasn't sure if she was being mocked, shook her head. "Absolutely not — one, you should be napping; two, it's absolutely blistering out there; three, you absolutely know you can't go for a walk, unless it's in the grounds. And only then at the set time. And with someone else. You know you can't go out alone, Essie."

"This," Essie hissed, "is a retirement home, not bloody Abu Ghraib."

Joy blinked in quick-step time, clearly trying to remember if she knew what Abu Ghraib was. She gave up the struggle. "And you're absolutely my responsibility. And you know what was agreed after — well — after last time."

"Agreement, as I understand it," Essie snapped, "is a two-sided affair. I never agreed to anything."

They glared at one another in a stand-off of iron wills. Joy buckled first.

"Mrs Rivers — Essie, dear — I only have your best interests at heart."

Essie snorted. "Rubbish. *Your* best interests, you mean. You think, if there are any more, er, unfortunate incidents, and they make the press again and Twilights gets a bad name, then even the minimal fees and council-covered costs won't be alluring enough to appeal to grasping relatives desperate to offload their elderly rellies and fill your empty roomettes. And empty roomettes equal loss-making, which equals council closure, which equals you and Tony out of a job — not to mention your free flat and all those nice little extras."

Joy smoothed down her eau-de-Nil shirt and fussed with the bow. There were tiny pinpoints of colour on her cheeks. Essie thought she heard the words "leftie" and "bloody agitator".

Joy held up her hands in supplication. "Essie, I know it's been some time since your . . . little accident . . . and I know you're absolutely one of our fittest residents and that you loathe the restrictions on your freedom, but we do have to adhere absolutely to the health and safety strictures laid down by the HA and the LA not to mention the NHS and the PCT —"

Essie exhaled crossly at the acronyms. They sounded like a bad hand at Scrabble.

"Gobbledegook claptrap. Oh, go away, Joy, please. You make me angry — which might be bad for my blood pressure — and I'm not due my check-up for ages. Maybe, if you and Tony offered a bit more to interest us here, then those of us that are able-bodied and still have full mental faculties, wouldn't need to look outside for our entertainment."

"Goodness me, Mrs Rivers, what more do you want? You have a cosy home, three good nourishing meals a day, not to mention your en-suite roomette with all mod cons in your kitchenette, and you have your own telly and radio-cassette and a Teasmade. Then, communally speaking, there's the multi-channel plasma screen in the lounge, and we have Tony's bingo nights every Monday and Martin Pusey's Hoi-Pollois in once a month for a singalong. All absolutely fabulous. What more do you want?"

"Life, love and loud music." Essie sighed. "And quizzes and book groups and up-to-date films, and seeing people younger than ninety and something to exercise our cerebrums — not to mention our muscles. Why can't we have — well — classes to stretch us in every way, and hobbies and dances and entertainment? And don't —" she shook her head "— tell me that the Martin Pusey's Hoi-Pollois fall into that latter category. Most of them are older than we are and they sing the same Gilbert and Sullivan tunes — wrong words and pitifully off-key — every single bloody time. If I have to hear several batty old birds from Winterbrook being Three Little Maids any more I'll definitely spit. Is it any wonder some of us feel the urge to escape?"

"*Escape?* Twilights isn't a prison, Essie. It's your home from home. And Tony and I have never curtailed any of the resident's hobbies, have we? Well, apart from yours, of course, and that was regrettable, but under the circs we had absolutely no option, did we?"

Essie tried hard not to laugh. "No, I suppose not. I suppose in your position I'd have done the same. Although it was quite good fun at the time."

"Good fun?" Joy Tugwell looked appalled. "It could hardly be called good fun, Mrs Rivers. It was like a geriatric episode of *Desperate Housewives* — not that I watch that sort of programme, of course, absolutely preferring wildlife documentaries, but I've been told — no, I'm afraid after your little, er, experimentation, we can only encourage the more absolutely acceptable hobbies here."

"But you don't." Essie sighed. "That's the point. It's all same old, same old."

"On the contrary." Joy bridled. "Mrs Evans is constantly knitting. Miss Hollywell has some wonderful scrapbooks — and look at Mr Fiddler's bird watching."

Essie chuckled. "Bird watching? That isn't what Norman Fiddler uses his binoculars for, I can tell you. And Floss Evans has been knitting the same scarf since nineteen seventy-two and Gertie Hollywell sticks anything that isn't nailed down into that bloody scrapbook. Marmalade labels, old stamps, tissue hankies, cornflakes, baked beans . . . Oh, never mind, Joy. Forget the hobbies for the time being. We're never going to agree on them, are we? And, much as it irks me, I promise — as I've promised every day for the last few months — not to go into Hassocks or Winterbrook on my own. But surely, a walk outside in the countryside wouldn't hurt?"

"Absolutely not." Joy shook her head. The sculpted hair didn't move. "Please don't push me on this. Surely, you must realise that after your little . . . um . . . accident, you're very vulnerable. And as to your other suggestions, we are working on a tight budget here. We can't provide entertainment at the drop of a hat. We absolutely can't afford it. Make the most of what you've got, Mrs Rivers, and be grateful."

Ten minutes later, Essie gave the secret knock on the door of Lilith's roomette just along the spotless, over-lemon-air-freshenered, cream-painted corridor.

"Come on in, honey," Lilith growled. "I'm not asleep. I'm not tired and anyway it's too damn hot."

Essie smiled at Lilith, a large septuagenarian Caribbean queen, sprawled on her bed in a flowing caftan in shades of red and orange.

"You look a bit down, honey." Lilith hauled herself into a sitting position. "Not more trouble with the Tugwells? Not Tiny Tony and Absolute Joy causing you grief?"

"Not really." Essie perched on the edge of Lilith's bed. "Nothing more than the usual rubbish about not being allowed to do anything I want to do. I can cope with that."

"You can if anyone can." Lilith chuckled. "Mind you, I suppose they have a point . . . after . . ."

"Don't." Essie held up her hands. "Just don't. If you're going to remind me of the little problem with the astrology sessions, Absolute Joy has already done so. Again."

"I wasn't, honey." Lilith chuckled. "Wouldn't dream of it. That was fun. No, I was going to say after what happened to you in Winterbrook, I guess the Tugwells are desperate to make sure it doesn't happen again."

"Yes, I know, and I know what happened to me meant that you're all suffering the same incarceration, but blimey, it was ages ago. Just because I was silly enough to be trusting and allowed myself to get mugged, doesn't mean that every Twilighter is going to suffer the same fate."

Lilith laughed. "And you put up a good fight, but the Tugwells can only see their reputation — and their cushy jobs — going down the Swanee should anything like that happen again. And we don't blame you for the rules on going out alone being changed, honey, none of us."

Essie sighed. Maybe they didn't, but she did. And it had been ages ago, and surely lightning didn't strike twice, did it? Yes, she'd been wary when the gang of dead-eyed vacant-looking boys — and they were boys, Essie thought, mere children — had approached her in the short-cut alleyway in Winterbrook. But she'd moved aside and carried on walking, becoming more shocked and angry than frightened when they'd followed her and barred her way and growled at her in some sort of guttural language she didn't understand. She remembered thinking how odd it was that these English boys didn't speak the same language as she did.

And then they'd scuffled around her, and made horrible, loud, threatening noises and pushed against her and tried to snatch her handbag.

Essie exhaled. It was still frightening — even now.

And, angry at their bare-faced cowardice, she'd swung her handbag at them, swearing at them, fetching one of them a cracking blow on the side of the head.

This had made them roar with even more non-human noises, and they'd pushed her and grabbed her bag. Still more furious than frightened, Essie had called them every name she could think of and tried to grab her bag back. Then they'd all laughed at her so she'd lunged at them, and they'd pushed her again, and she'd crashed against the wall and fallen, and the boys, still laughing, had run away further up the alley — and then there'd been a lot of shouting and this huge fight had broken out . . .

38

And then the police arrived and the paramedics and she, protesting, had been rushed off to hospital and kept in overnight. She'd been shocked, and there had been a few bruises, but nothing more sinister — at least, not physically — and after a day's bed rest Essie had been sent back to Twilights and — she had to admit — treated with nothing but kindness by Joy and Tony and the staff.

She'd recovered quickly from the bruises, but the shock had taken much longer . . .

And even afterwards, at the court case, when she was fully recovered, Essie had been so cross that no one really listened to her side of the story. They got it all wrong. And those boys had laughed together and lied — lied in court, under oath — and the whole thing had been a sham. A massive miscarriage of justice. It still made her shake with fury, thinking about it.

"Honey?" Lilith's voice broke into the hateful memories. "Essie, you OK?"

"Fine. Sorry — just having a bit of a flashback. Really mustn't dwell on it. Water under the bridge as Absolute Joy would say. Now, we need to get Princess and Bert in here. We've got to discuss Ada's funeral. And, more importantly, decide what to do with ourselves to stop going gaga with boredom."

"Sounds good to me." Lilith pulled herself off the bed, mopping her sweating face with the hem of the caftan. "Stay there — help yourself to some juice from the fridge. I'll go and get the others. Have you got any ideas, then? Oh, not for the funeral, honey, but for livening up Twilights?"

"Mmm." Essie nodded, smiling. "Several, actually. After all, if the Tugwells won't allow us to go out, and refuse to provide things to stimulate us here, then we'll just have to make our own fun, won't we?"

"Essie!" Lilith paused in the doorway. "This fun wouldn't involve you starting your, um, hocus-pocus again, would it, honey?"

"Maybe." Essie smiled even more. "Maybe not. We'll have to absolutely wait and see what happens, won't we?"

CHAPTER
FOUR

The beer garden of the Muffin Man, one of Winterbrook's last remaining proper pubs with its beams, brasses and male domination, and no jukebox, gaming machines or wall-to-wall sports coverage, sweltered in the late evening heat haze. Darkness was falling, the sky had faded to a deep misty blue and moths bumbled around in the lights from the pub's leaded windows. No wind stirred the overhanging hazel trees or moved the dark-green waterfall of ivy tumbling from the crumbling walls surrounding the tiny patch of scrubby grass and its quartet of weathered trestle tables.

"Too bloody hot." Clemmie fanned her face with a beer mat. "Why couldn't I have stayed unpregnant until the winter?"

"Do you really want us to answer that?" Phoebe clunked rapidly melting ice cubes round and round in her spritzer. "Think you, think Guy, think not being able to keep your hands off each other and —"

"Pul-eeze!" YaYa held up her hands in mock disgust. "You just think yourself lucky you don't have to live with them, Phoebes. All that lovey-dovey stuff all the bloody time — it's enough to make a girl puke."

"Please don't mention puking." Clemmie winced. "I've only just stopped for today."

"Oh, you poor thing." Phoebe pulled a sympathetic face and patted Clemmie's hand. "Still, look on the bright side — it can't last for ever, can it? *Can it*? At least that's one good thing about being a dumpee — as I'll never look at another man again I won't have to go through the horrors of morning sickness."

YaYa drained the last of her gin and tonic. "Never say never."

"Never, never, never," Phoebe said defiantly. "Never in a million years. Never!"

"Whatever, love." YaYa stood up. "I can't say I blame you at the moment. Me and Ben got on OK when you were a couple, but now, if I ever set eyes on that little bastard again, he'll wish he'd never been born. Same again, girls? My shout."

"Lovely — and could you ask if they've got any olives, please?" Clemmie looked hopefully at YaYa. "Don't care what colour they are, stuffed or unstuffed — any old olive will do."

"Jesus —" YaYa pouted glossy scarlet lips "— you don't want much, love, do you? Olives? I doubt if they've got past plain crisps with a twist of salt in blue paper in this place, but for you — anything. I'll ask — OK?"

"You're a star."

"I know."

Phoebe realised that the other beer garden incumbents — all being of the Muffin Man's typical clientele variety: rustic, male, middle-aged and drinking real beer from cloudy glass tankards — were staring at them with ill-concealed lust and open-mouthed curiosity. There were some very non-pc and blush-making remarks being Berkshire-burred in their direction.

Possibly for the Muffin Man, she, Clemmie and YaYa were an eye-catching trio, Phoebe thought, especially given that the pub's only token female was an elderly barmaid called Maud.

Knowing she'd lost far too much weight since the-wedding-that-never-was, Phoebe was pretty sure she looked the hollow-cheeked and dark-eyed epitome of heroin chic in her short denim skirt and brief vest. And wild-haired, beautiful Clemmie in one of her trademark long, psychedelic frocks and chandelier earrings was arresting enough, but add YaYa Bordello — an outrageously gorgeous Gwen Stefani lookalike cross-dresser, who lived and worked with Clemmie and Guy at The Gunpowder Plot, their pyrotechnics company, in Winterbrook — and together they probably looked like something off the more debauched end of the celeb circuit to the Muffin Man's punters.

Mind you, YaYa, who had been christened Steve and was The Gunpowder Plot's accountant and PR person when she wasn't on the road with her drag act troupe, The Dancing Queens, turned heads everywhere she went.

It was funny, Phoebe thought now, how easily she'd accepted YaYa as simply another really good friend and how she found it odd that people still stared. At least Clemmie and YaYa hadn't brought Suggs — Guy and

43

Clemmie's much-adored and well-trained house ferret — with them. That possibly would have been a step too far into the weird and wonderful world of Clemmie, Guy and YaYa for the Muffin Man's regulars to cope with.

"I think the bloke with the comb-over is eyeing you up," Phoebe hissed to YaYa. "He keeps leering."

"Par for the course, love." YaYa flicked her layers of ash-blonde hair back from her shoulders. "Happens everywhere I go. I can't help being stunning, can I?"

Clemmie and Phoebe laughed. In her skintight gold pedal pushers, stilt heels and a lacy Bardot top, YaYa looked every inch the pin-up girl of any red-blooded male's wildest fantasies.

With a stage wink in the direction of the oglers, YaYa sashayed seductively into the pub.

"So," Clemmie said as soon as YaYa had disappeared, "how is it now, honestly, after going back to work and visiting the flat for the first time?"

"Weird. Oh, being back at Cut'n'Curl was OK. Everyone was lovely. And the flat? Truthfully, not as awful as I thought — but then I didn't go anywhere near the bedroom. That's going to be the killer, I think. Far too many memories in that room. The rest of the flat is sort of neutral territory, but the bedroom . . ."

"Blimey, yes. Oh, God, I can't imagine what I'd do if Guy left me. I know I'd die. Phoebes, you've been brilliant. Really brave."

"No, I haven't — inside it's still crap. Truly crap. I never thought it would hurt — really, physically hurt — so much. The pain under my ribs never goes away. Oh,

I'm sleeping better — but it's funny, it's the waking up that's worse now. You know, you wake up and for a split second you forget and then — wham! It's like a punch in the face. I may not cry myself to sleep, but I sure as hell cry myself awake. And the dreams — nightmares . . ."

Clemmie sighed and squeezed Phoebe's hand.

Phoebe squeezed back. "Thanks — and for tonight. It's lovely to be out. And for inviting just YaYa. I'm still not ready for the full onslaught of girlfriends in major sympathy mode. Especially not with both Amber and Sukie planning their upcoming weddings."

"And Fern and Chelsea pregnant — we all meet up at the same clinics — and Lulu still indecently loved-up and Doll having just produced her third baby. They do care, though, Phoebes."

"I know — they've all been lovely to me since . . . well, you know, but en masse they'd be too much."

Clemmie fanned herself again. "And still no word from bastard Ben? No news today?"

"Nothing. I still haven't got a clue why he did . . . didn't . . . well, why he did it. I think I accept now that he had someone else all the time. His parents haven't heard from him either. They still ring me most days, bless them. They're worried sick and can't understand it any more than I can. And he hasn't been in touch with work or any of his friends or anyone since that day."

"You don't think, um, that something's happened to him, do you?"

"That was an option to start with, as you know." Phoebe shook her head angrily. "But, no —

unfortunately. He might have done a runner, but he's still alive and well. The police, naturally, told his parents that he is a grown man who has left home of his own accord, so they aren't that bothered. However, his mum says they've been told he's still using his bank account and credit cards and mobile phone."

"Couldn't someone else be using them, you know —?"

"Nah. He may have disappeared off our radar but there's apparently plenty of CCTV footage of him at various cash points across the country looking healthy and normal — never in the same place twice of course. Honestly, Clem, I don't want to talk about B — , him. He's gone. I've just got to accept that he didn't want me and he decided to make that clear in the most public way possible. It's over, and I've just got to cope."

"Coping's one thing — money's something else. It's not your bank account he's clearing out is it, love?" YaYa joined in the conversation, plonking the tray of drinks on the table and winking across the beer garden at her admirer at the same time. "Here we are then — spritzer for Phoebes, orange juice and lemonade for the fecund Mrs D. — and sorry, love, not an olive in the entire pub, although they did offer a pickled egg as a substitute — and a triple g and t for me as for once I'm not chauffeuring. So —" YaYa slid her long legs over the bench and under the trestle table making the men across the beer garden all splutter into their pints "— it's not is it, Phoebe? Your money?"

"No — we had separate accounts. Even for our savings."

Clemmie shook her head. "I didn't realise. I always think that's a mistake. You should share everything. Me and Guy —"

"This isn't about you and Guy," YaYa put in quickly. "This is about Phoebe — and to be honest it's a bloody good job they *did* have separate accounts under the circs, isn't it?"

"S'pose so." Clemmie buried her nose in her drink. "Oooh, that's better . . . be even nicer with olives, though."

"Totally disgusting." YaYa shook her head. "Of all the cravings you could have it has to be olives. Olives always taste like someone's eaten them before you and —"

"Thanks. Now I feel sick again." Clemmie grinned. "And before the pregnancy I'd have agreed with you about olives — loathed them — now I can't get enough."

"She eats the bloody things by the jarful," YaYa said, pulling a face. "Day and night. With cornflakes, on toast with black cherry jam, dipped in chocolate spread . . ."

"You don't?" Phoebe looked horrified. "That's gross, Clem."

"I know." Clemmie smiled cheerfully. "One of the joys of impending motherhood, along with big knickers and burping. Anyway, back to more pressing matters — you're definitely leaving the flat?"

"Got to. I can't afford to stay there, even if I wanted to."

"And do you?"

Phoebe pushed a beer mat into the table's ancient crevices. "Yes, strangely I think I do. Going there today to collect my stuff was so scary and something I didn't think I'd be able to do, but once I'd been there for a little while it still seemed, well, like coming home. Even without B — , him being there. And to be honest, being back at Mum and Dad's is pretty awful. They're wonderful, of course, and I couldn't have managed without them at the start, but they fuss over me like I'm ill, and I'm so used to being independent."

YaYa fished a chunk of lemon from her g and t. "So — if you took over the tenancy of the flat on your own, would money be the only issue?"

Phoebe nodded.

"Well, then." YaYa sucked the lemon with obvious delight. The man with the comb-over spat a mouthful of his real ale across the neighbouring table. "Let's work on the possibilities — can you ask for a pay rise?"

"No, out of the question. I'm Pauline's senior stylist — I'm on top whack."

"What about moving on to another salon, then — in Reading or Newbury, say — somewhere bigger, better known, for more money?"

"Couldn't do it. I've always been at Cut'n'Curl, ever since school — Pauline's wonderful and the girls I work with are like a second family — I love it there. I'd never let them down. Anyway, I couldn't cope with any more changes. I need the stability that Pauline's gives me."

YaYa smiled. "Good girl — I do admire loyalty. Even if it does mean you're working for a pittance. There are more important things than money."

"But not in Phoebe's case at the moment," Clemmie interrupted. "Right, so how about a bit of mobile moonlighting? You know, like Sukie does with her aromatherapy stuff — doing home visits? You could be a mobile hairdresser in your spare time, couldn't you? I'm sure there'd be loads of people who'd prefer to have their hair done at home."

"Hel-lo? Conflict of interests, love?" YaYa raised perfect eyebrows. "Pauline would be right arsed if Phoebes nicked her clients, would'nt she?"

"Oh, yeah, guess so."

Phoebe sipped her spritzer, sweltering in the heat, resisting the urge to slide the ice cubes down her top. "I suppose I could always look for housebound customers, though. I mean, people who wouldn't be able to get into Hassocks to the salon. Maybe young mums with kids or people who can't get out for whatever reason. I don't suppose Pauline would object to that."

"OK." YaYa nodded, lighting a long foreign cigarette and blowing perfect smoke rings away from Clemmie. "There you go, Mrs D. — I'm even mindful of Junior D.'s passive smoking. So, the mobile hairdressing is one option — but, what about your readings? You know how hot you are on astrology. Can't you make it a bit of a business on the side? There are loads of people interested in all things mystic. I never miss reading my horoscope in the paper in the morning. I totally believe in all that stuff and I'm not alone. You could charge a fortune for telling fortunes."

"Oooh, yes." Clemmie giggled. "That's a great idea, Phoebes. You could make your Madame Zuleika act legit."

"No way!" Phoebe looked aghast. She hadn't as much as turned a tarot since the wedding-that-never-was. "And for the umpteenth time I've never called myself Madame Zuleika. But, I'm never, ever having anything to do with astrology, cards, charts, star signs or anything like that ever again."

"Course you are, Phoebes. It's part of you. And — blimey — no-one could have been more sceptical than me, could they? But when you did that tarot-reading session at our wedding reception, well, you were spot on, weren't you? I kept getting an upright Empress, didn't I? And you said it indicated immediate pregnancy and I said no way, but you were right." Clemmie leaned back and happily stroked the slight swell of her stomach. "And if you can convert scientific, logical, disbelieving me, you can convert anyone. I'd put in a good word for you and —"

"No." Phoebe shook her head. "No. I'm definitely an ex-astrologer."

YaYa exhaled smoke and sighed. "Shame. I loved you doing my readings, and I always thought you were dead accurate. You were damn good. You'd make a lot of money, Phoebes. Anyway, why are you giving up? Surely, it's been a lifetime thing for you?"

"Yes — and so was bloody Ben . . . Honestly, no way. Look what a disaster my — our — the wedding was. I'd planned that day using every card, every astral chart, everything I had at my disposal. I even did our tarot readings the day before — using both Major and Minor Arcana cards — just to make sure. They said it would be perfect."

They sat in silence for a moment, then YaYa leaned forwards.

"OK, so if astrology and tarots are a definite no, and mobile hairdressing is a definite maybe depending on getting the right clients and Pauline agreeing, then how about taking in a lodger for some guaranteed extra bunce? You've got two bedrooms, haven't you?"

"Don't mention the bedroom!" Clemmie said quickly. "It's a no-go area."

"Not for you and Guy it's not, love," YaYa said tartly. "You two are hardly ever out of it. And if the bloody bedroom had been a no-go area for you two I wouldn't be sent out in the middle of the night, every night, hunting down olives, now would I?"

Clemmie giggled.

Phoebe suddenly felt swamped by loneliness. Funny how it struck unannounced out of nowhere. She turned her head away in case she cried. Would she ever get used to being alone?

"OK, Phoebes?" YaYa, ever sensitive, finished her cigarette and reached across the table to pat Phoebe's hand. "Poor love. I know you feel like shit, and I wish there was something I could do to give you back your sparkle. But, being boringly practical, just think about sharing the flat. If you had a lodger, you could swap bedrooms, couldn't you? Buy a new bed and everything and you move lock, stock and eyelash curler into the second bedroom. It'd be a fresh start for you, and the lodger has your old bedroom and brings in a regular monthly income to boot. Promise me you'll think about it?"

Phoebe nodded. "I promise I'll think about it. Oh, yes — meant to say — the upstairs flat is going to be empty too. Mindy's moving out to live with an Airbus pilot. You met her a few times, didn't you, Clem?"

"Yep, very glam girl. Big mouth. I liked her. Have she and what's-his-name split up then?"

"Apparently. She said he did something really, really bad, but I didn't find out what."

"Cheating?" YaYa queried. "Or maybe something even worse — maybe she came home and caught him wearing her flight attendant's uniform complete with heels."

Clemmie and Phoebe shook their heads in mock shock.

"What?" YaYa frowned. "What? There's many a closet cross-dresser out there, let me tell you. And some of those cabin crew uniforms are pretty hot. Think Scootch, sweeties."

"Oh, God," Clemmie groaned. "Please don't start on your encyclopaedic knowledge of all things Eurovision. Or your cross-dress uniform of choice. Just don't, OK?"

"Whatever, mum-to-be-of-the-year." YaYa pouted, then giggled and poked out her tongue.

The beer garden men all groaned lasciviously.

"No, I think it must have been something far more serious than that," Phoebe said. "I get the feeling that Mindy wouldn't dump anyone for a bit of playing-away or inappropriate dressing. She was really angry and hurt — almost disgusted."

"Must have beaten her up then." YaYa drained the remainder of her g and t. "Nasty bastard. Just as well he's cleared out if you're going to be living in the flat below, Phoebes. You don't want to be sharing your personal space with a moronic cowardly woman-beater, do you?"

"Course not, but you know, it's weird, I've got this niggling feeling I sort of know something about him — Rocky Lancaster." Phoebe picked up her glass and realised it was empty. "I'd heard about him somewhere — perhaps someone mentioned him in the salon. There's so much gossip in there, I don't take all of it in. Whatever the connection is, I don't think it was good — maybe he *was* handy with his fists now you come to mention it. He and Mindy used to have some right ding-dongs upstairs."

"Last orders please!!!" roared from the depths of the Muffin Man. There was a puffing and wheezing scramble from the beer garden's tables.

"Rocky Lancaster?" Clemmie mused. "Nope — doesn't ring any bells with me. Still, we don't need to worry about him if he's gone and Mindy's found someone else, do we? And it'll give you a whole clean sweep, won't it? If you move back in with a lodger and have new upstairs neighbours at the same time? It'll be as John Lennon always says, just like starting over. Anyway, sad little Rocky Lancaster and his fisticuffs are history — we've got loads of other things to think about."

"Have we?" Phoebe, who could still really only think about the pain and humiliation and her heart being broken, frowned.

"Course we have." Clemmie stood up. "Like which one of our plans you're going to take up so you can afford to stay in Winchester Road and if we can get another drink in before closing time. No, put your money away. I'll go — I need the loo anyway."

Phoebe sat in the velvety darkness, a tiny squirm of hope wriggling inside her. Maybe she could earn enough money to move back into the flat. Maybe taking a lodger would be the perfect way to deal with the situation — and YaYa's suggestion about swapping bedrooms was a stroke of genius. Maybe, just maybe, there was going to be a sort of life after Ben. Maybe the hurt and humiliation would one day be just a distant memory. Nah — that was a hope too far.

"Excuse me for a second, Phoebes, love . . . Something I have to do."

Phoebe watched as YaYa flicked open her mobile phone, then slid from the bench seat and seductively shimmied across the beer garden to the comb-over man who'd been left alone while his chums had gone for refills.

There was a whispered conversation, a snatch of throaty laughter, a scribbling on a beer mat and then YaYa plonked a huge kiss on top of the comb-over's balding head.

"What the hell was that about?" Phoebe asked as YaYa sashayed back again. "You didn't tell him you were a *bloke* did you?"

"Course not, love." YaYa batted her inch-long Kate Moss eyelashes. "He thinks I'm the hottest thing since Samantha Fox, and who am I to disabuse him? He'll probably never wash the top of his head again."

Phoebe squinted across the beer garden. The once-leering comb-over was now beaming from ear to ear in a soppily bemused fashion.

"So, what did you write on the beer mat? Blimey, YaYa, you didn't give him your phone number, did you?"

"As if." YaYa looked shocked. "I don't do relationships, Phoebes, as you well know. And if I did, a mucky old lecher like him wouldn't be top of my to-do list. But I did tell him if he — or any of his mates — ever fancied a steaming session that would knock spots off Viagra — day or night — then all he had to was dial that number."

"But you said you didn't give him your mobile number."

"I didn't." YaYa smiled broadly. "It wasn't mine. I gave him Ben's . . ."

CHAPTER
FIVE

In the still-stifling sunset glow of late evening, her unpacking completed, Phoebe, her blonde hair caught up in a tiny, spiky ponytail, one of her dad's old shirts knotted at the waist and hanging from her shoulders, her long legs bare beneath her denim cut-offs, stood back to admire her handiwork. Less than two weeks since the brain-storming session in the Muffin Man, and here she was back in the Winchester Road flat to stay.

Having rearranged the furniture in the living room and added heaps of cushions, a virtual forest of green plants and scented candles on every surface, the austerity of her and Ben's original minimalist decor was softened if not completely eroded.

But it was in her bedroom — her *new* bedroom — that most work had taken place.

The second bedroom had been transformed into a pink-and-lace girlie boudoir thanks to YaYa's OTT style ideas and Phoebe's own predilection for everything Barbie. Clemmie, who had loudly hoped for a mural of rainbows, fireworks and bold primary colours, had thrown up her hands in horror and said it'd be fine for a ten year old but not for someone of

Phoebe's mature years, as the spare bedroom's off-white tones and minimalist decor had been replaced by a candyfloss blush of feminine frills and fripperies.

A new canopied double bed — because YaYa had insisted on it "just in case you change your mind about giving up men one day, love" and because Clemmie had pointed out the luxury of being able to sleep diagonally — a new wardrobe, new fluffy rugs on the floorboards and full-length lace curtains at the French windows completed the look.

"Tarty Lolita." YaYa had nodded approvingly. "Just the right look for someone who wants to make a complete change. Don't listen to Clem. This is such a lovely room, Phoebes, leading out into the garden. Much nicer than your other room at the front of the house facing out on to the road. And when you get a lodger, your old bedroom is all ready, all done up nicely neutral so it'd suit a boy or a girl."

While the whirlwind makeover had been totally Phoebe's choice, it had been organised by YaYa and Clemmie with noisy and wine-fuelled input from several of her other girlfriends, especially Amber and Sukie, and part-financed by her parents who had been delighted that she'd decided to pick up the pieces. The remainder had been topped up with cash from Phoebe's own savings account, which would have been the mortgage deposit in her other life.

And the changing of the tenancy agreement had been even easier.

★ ★ ★

"Oh, yeah, right." The girl in the letting agency, who had looked as though she should be at home glued to CBeebies, hadn't stopped chewing her gum. "We know all about that." She'd zipped expertly through her computer files. "We had a letter from Mr Phipps about six weeks ago, paying four months rent in advance, returning his keys and saying that, in November, the rental agreement would be changed into a sole name. Phoebe Bowler. That's you, right? We were going to contact you nearer the time, but you've saved us the trouble. You got some ID, right?"

Phoebe had nodded and produced it.

"Right." The chewing had become more frenzied. "So, the second set of keys are now yours — case you want to sub-let or anything. You're OK for that in your agreement — read it through — your risk, not ours. Right?"

"Er . . . yes . . . right."

"Mr Phipps' cheque has cleared, guilt money if you ask me seeing as what happened, so there's no problem about the advance rent, so we'll draw up a new agreement with your details and bank account to start in November and get it out to you. Right?"

Utterly bemused, with a cold chill closing round her heart because this new information meant that Ben had *planned* all this, which in turn meant it honestly hadn't been last minute cold feet, Phoebe had nodded again.

"Right. So you just sign here and here and here — we don't need any other docs from you 'cause you brought them all in last time with Mr Phipps, right?"

Phoebe had nodded like an automaton.

58

"Happens all the time." The girl had shifted her gum into her cheek. "We see it a lot here. Split ups. Easy for us to swap names on tenancies if both parties and the landlord agree and s'long as one's already on the agreement, right? And we wouldn't have had to ask you 'bout it until November, right? Not so easy for the one left behind to carry on. Mr Phipps had it all planned, didn't he? He left nothing to chance. He obviously wanted out." She'd smiled a sisterly smile. "You get on with the rest of your life, right, and stuff him."

Now, Phoebe thought, on her first solo night at the flat as she threw open the French windows to the evening air to remove the last scent of new paint from her new bedroom, she intended to do just that. Well, once she'd stopped being heartbroken and humiliated, of course.

To be honest, there was so much to think about without dwelling on the fact that Ben must have been planning to leave her for ages before the wedding if he'd been so organised with cancelling his part of the tenancy agreement. She'd pushed that to the back of her mind along with why, and why she hadn't known/spotted it/guessed, and was concentrating on advertising for a lodger, working out a new budget, getting used to life as a singleton for the first time since she was fifteen, and coping with the extra work that she'd agreed to undertake.

Phoebe had expected Pauline to be horrified at the thought of her moonlighting — even if she was just going to visit customers in their own homes who'd never make it to Cut'n'Curl anyway. Again, she'd been surprised.

"Well, blow me down." Pauline had slurped cheerfully over a dunked custard cream in their tea break. "Great minds and all that. I was actually going to put a little proposition of a similar nature to you."

"Were you?" Phoebe had carefully fielded a soggy biscuit with her spoon. "Really?"

Pauline had nodded. "I was. That awful Joy Tugwell — you know, the one who comes in for the nineteen eighties shampoo and set with the juniors of a Wednesday to save money and then grizzles about it? Well, she runs Twilights — the old folks home on the outskirts of Hassocks, you know? — and apparently some of her residents have been kicking up a bit of a fuss about wanting more to do, have more provided for them, and one of the things the ladies up there mentioned was not being able to get out to get their hair done or anything. So, apparently, to keep them sweet, Joy's asking all the local businesses, like us and Jennifer Blessing's beauty salon, if we'll do cut-price sessions up at the home."

"And you agreed and suggested me? Oh, Pauline, that's really kind of you. Thank you so much."

"Well, yes, but only if you want to, dear, you know that. It'll mean extra money for you as well as for Cut'n'Curl, of course, but the appointments will probably have to be mostly in the evenings because you're needed here during the day and —"

"That's perfect." Phoebe had swallowed the last of her biscuit. "I need something to fill my spare time, and the extra cash will obviously come in handy for me, not to mention improving Cut'n'Curl's finances, so we'll both benefit, won't we? And it'll probably be mainly wash and sets or perms, won't it? Standard stuff. When do I start?"

"Next week if that's OK with you," Pauline had said happily. "I'll let Joy Tugwell know straight away, then she can tell the residents, we'll draw up a list of appointments and get you organised."

So, Phoebe thought, as she stood in the darkening doorway, inhaling the scents of jasmine and honeysuckle from the overblown garden, listening to the shush of the Kennet gurgling on its never-ending journey, and wallowing in the absolute silence, this was her first night here alone. The first night of the rest of her life — alone . . .

Would she cope? Well, she'd give it her best shot, but it was so strange without Ben here. So quiet. So lonely knowing that he wouldn't be coming home. She felt the tears well up in her throat and swallowed them quickly.

Enjoy the evening, she told herself sternly. Be a grown-up. Pour yourself a glass of wine or two, go and sit in the garden, watch something mindless on the telly, go to bed when you want to, make the most of being alone in this blissful peace and quiet. Think positively about the future. Don't think about the past. Just don't.

Easier said than done.

Just as she turned to head for the kitchen and the fridge and a bottle of Chardonnay, the balmy silence was rudely shattered by the communal front door slamming open, a loud curse, a crashing and banging as someone thundered up the stairs, further crashing as someone tried — and clearly failed at the first attempt — to open the upstairs flat door, then, having succeeded, an even louder thundering as someone dumped things down and thumped across the floor, making Phoebe's ceiling shake.

Several other loud thumps indicated that something heavy was being dropped. Then the footsteps crashed downstairs again.

The process was repeated twice more then there was silence. Phoebe, on her second glass of wine, exhaled with relief. Sadly, the relief was short-lived.

AC/DC at ear-bleed level blared from upstairs, rattling not only the ceiling, but also the windows and the edges of Phoebe's frayed nerves.

"Noooo," she groaned. "Not new neighbours — not noisy new neighbours. No — not tonight of all nights — that's so not fair!"

While she'd changed the name on her doorbell to "Bowler", Mindy had left the upstairs one labelled "Lancaster". Phoebe wondered who the new tenants were and what the new name would read. "Noisy Bastards from Hell" would do nicely, she thought angrily, grabbing the wine bottle and glass and making for the seclusion of the courtyard.

Outside in the garden, the noise from upstairs was even worse than indoors, so, returning to the flat and gulping down another large glass of wine leaning against the kitchen sink, she waited for ten agonisingly long minutes.

The noise level increased as AC/DC's brain-splitting music was accompanied by what sounded like thirteen sumo wrestlers having a ruck.

Enough was enough.

Fortified by the wine, and knowing that if she didn't do a bit of bud-nipping now, then she and the new upstairs neighbours were never ever going to live in any sort of harmony, Phoebe ran upstairs.

Knocking on the door she realised was going to be pretty futile. No one would ever hear her over that racket. Neither would a neighbourly shout of "Coooeee!" be particularly useful.

Discovering that the flat's door wasn't locked or even closed properly, Phoebe tentatively pushed it open.

It looked as though a small earthquake had coincided with a mini hurricane and sounded — thanks to Bon Scott and the rest of his AC/DC chums — as if a volcano was erupting beneath the floorboards accompanied by mass genocide.

Mindy's once-pristine flat was a scene of total devastation. Most of the furniture still seemed to be in situ albeit rapidly disappearing beneath a sea of clothes and books and records, but all her personal trappings had disappeared, presumably to share the cute Airbus pilot's penthouse. Half-opened packing cases and large cardboard boxes were hurled everywhere, their miscellaneous contents spewing across the floor.

Phoebe, who abhorred disorganisation of any kind, looked at the living room in complete horror.

As there was no sign of the new occupants in the living room, Phoebe picked her way through the mess and turned down the stereo, reducing Bon Scott's rasping vocals to a whisper.

"Bloody useless thing," a voice muttered furiously from the bedroom. "What's happened to it now? Always cutting out . . . bloody hell!"

The owner of the voice appeared in the bedroom doorway and stared at Phoebe.

Phoebe stared back.

"Who the hell are you? Did you turn my music down? What the —?"

Phoebe blinked. The stunning owner of the voice was gloriously tall and lean, with dark cropped hair and even darker angry eyes. He was also naked apart from a pair of faded jeans.

"Sorry, yes — but I live downstairs and —"

The angry dark eyes narrowed. "Do you? I thought you'd moved out? Mindy said —"

Two and two suddenly made four. Phoebe swallowed. "You're Rocky Lancaster?"

"I am — and you're Phoebe. The jilted bride. We've never met properly, have we? Mindy said you were leaving."

"Mindy said you'd left."

"Well, she would say that, wouldn't she?"

Phoebe, suddenly hotly aware of her brief shorts and shoulder-baring shirt, swallowed. "I've moved back in. Are you moving out?"

Rocky Lancaster frowned and shook his head. "I'm moving back in too. Just sorting out my stuff. Making this my home again. So, what the hell did you think you were doing turning down my music?"

"Because it was taking the plaster off my ceiling." Phoebe frowned back. "Because I wanted some peace and quiet in the garden. Because I didn't know it was you — but mainly because I thought I'd come upstairs and say hi to the new neighbours and ask them to keep the noise down."

Rocky shrugged. "Well, OK — maybe it was a bit loud. But I was revelling in playing my music of choice, instead of Mindy's everlasting Take That, Boyzone and Westlife, and this *is* my home. And I may as well warn you, I don't simply favour AC/DC — I've got CD racks full of Deep Purple and Rainbow among others of the same ilk. I've even got some in the original vinyl so you get noise *and* distortion. Do you want to raise your objections now?"

Phoebe, whose musical tastes were much in line with Mindy's and whose knowledge of retro rockers was fairly minimal, shook her head.

"Good." Rocky didn't smile. "At least we've established some ground rules. Live and let live? Although I must admit I really didn't expect a visit from the noise police on my first evening back."

"It's not just me, though, is it? What about the other residents in Winchester Road? They probably like to sit in their gardens or have their windows open on hot nights like this and —"

"They're mostly ancient and probably deaf," Rocky growled. "Although, OK, maybe it was a bit loud. I'll adjust the volume — OK?"

"OK. Thank you." Remembering the many loud rows she'd overheard and the hints that Mindy had made about Rocky's violent temper, Phoebe edged towards the door. "And, like you say, if we're going to be neighbours, we'll just have to make adjustments as well as allowances for one another, won't we?"

"Will we? Are you warning me that you'll be playing James Blunt at full volume on a Sunday morning when I'm nursing a hellish hangover?"

He still looked, Phoebe thought, very angry and rather threatening. If, as Mindy had inferred, Rocky was handy with his fists, she really should diffuse the situation. Antagonising him wouldn't be a good idea.

"Not if I can help it, but maybe a bit of give and take . . ."

Rocky laughed. It sounded neither happy nor friendly. "Give and take? We've probably both done plenty of the former and not much of the latter in our recent relationships if the results are anything to go by, don't you think? Sorry, but I'm intending to spend the rest of my life as a selfish, self-centred, self-obsessed bastard."

Great, Phoebe thought. I'm going to be sharing the house with a violent egomaniac. Nice one, Phoebes.

Still moving slowly backwards, she'd reached the open door. "I can't blame you for feeling bitter. Mindy said —"

"I don't give a shit what Mindy said." Rocky looked decidedly unfriendly. "You really shouldn't listen to airhead tittle-tattle. No doubt you got chapter and verse about my prolonged absence being the reason she had to turn elsewhere for, er, amusement."

"No, actually, I didn't. She didn't tell me anything. And yes, I knew you were away a lot, but I simply assumed that as you were cabin crew, like Mindy, you were often working on different flights. I don't listen to gossip. I get enough of that at work."

"Ah, yes. At the hairdressers' — see, I do know something about you. I did talk to Ben occasionally when we were both waiting to be served in the Faery Glen. Anyway, for what it's worth, I'm sorry he did a runner. Spineless of him. He should have told you face to face."

"Yes, he should." Phoebe fought the urge to defend Ben's actions and suddenly wondered what other nuggets he'd passed on to Rocky about her or their relationship in the bar of the Faery Glen. "And you'll be relieved to know that I know nothing at all about you apart —"

"Apart from the fact that I spent more time away than at home and that on the rare occasions when Mindy and I were ground-based at the same time we fought like cat and dog? Come on, you must have heard the rows."

"Well, yes, but . . ."

"Mindy was hell to live with — and I wasn't much better. We should never, never have got together. Lust has a lot to answer for."

Deciding there was no answer to that remark that wouldn't land her in deep trouble, Phoebe merely shrugged. "We'll both have to make huge changes I suppose, now we're single again."

"Which I intend to stay for the rest of my life, and which also means, as far as I'm concerned, you keeping to your flat and me to mine. More ground rules — I don't want sympathy or any sort of mothering. Nor do I want a friend. Understand? We live in the same house but totally separately, and that's the way I want it to stay. Just because we've both been dumped doesn't mean —"

"Jesus! You're so bloody arrogant!" Phoebe totally forgot that she was supposed to be pussy-footing in case he punched her. "I'm quite happy leaving you entirely alone. I've got far better things to do than popping up here every five minutes to see if you've swapped AC/DC for Coldplay and slit your wrists."

"Which I well might — especially if you add Radiohead into the mix. Although I can assure you I'm not in the slightest bit suicidal at the moment. Just more than a little pissed off at having to start rebuilding my life at the grand old age of thirty-two."

Phoebe could sympathise with that one, but she wasn't going to say so. "At least we've both kept a roof over our head and a job to pay the bills and —"

"Platitudes!" Rocky snarled. "Oh, you may be OK with your little hairdressing job and your girlfriends and your doting parents, but I'm back here with absolutely sod all."

God, now he was going to get mawkish, Phoebe thought. Aggressive *and* maudlin. Great combination.

"But you've got your job, haven't you? A really great job. Travelling the world. Stopping off in exotic locations, seeing places people like me can only dream about —"

"My job?" Rocky's laugh again sounded like a slash of fury. "You really haven't got a clue, have you? I haven't been a steward for ages. I got the sack. I'm really surprised Mindy didn't delight in filling you in on all the gruesome details."

"Well, she didn't." Phoebe declined to say that Mindy probably would have done if they hadn't been interrupted by a phone call. "And I'm sorry — I had no idea you'd lost your job, I thought you were still —"

Rocky shook his head. "The real reason you've not seen me here recently is the same one Mindy used as an excuse to dump me."

An Airbus pilot of his very own? Was Rocky a closet gay? If so, YaYa may not have been so far off the mark.

Rocky continued. "Yes, as you imagined, I've been away. But not dishing out plastic meals to tourists or sunning myself on far-flung beaches. Far from it — the airline couldn't get rid of me fast enough. They somehow didn't want a steward who had been convicted of ABH."

ABH? *ABH?*

"Funny, that." Rocky didn't sound at all amused. "Can't imagine why. No doubt they probably thought I'd assault the passengers with the plastic cutlery."

"What?" Phoebe frowned again, her heart sinking to the soles of her flip-flops. "ABH? You mean —?"

"Yep. Actual Bodily Harm. Beating the crap out of someone. I've just been released from prison."

CHAPTER
SIX

As a scorching July gave way to an even more sweltering August, Essie — dressed in her regular mourning outfit of floppy black linen trousers and a black lace cardigan but with a vivid pink scarf in her hair — stood in the crowded Twilights dining room nursing a glass of tepid sweet sherry in one hand and a limp ham sandwich in the other.

Ada Mackie's funeral had gone — as Twilighter funerals went — fairly well. It had been a standard service, with flowers from Twilights and nowhere else. The crematorium had been packed, which Ada would have appreciated, because lots of the more elderly villagers from Hazy Hassocks, Bagley-cum-Russet and Fiddlesticks had turned out for the occasion.

Most of them had probably never known Ada, Essie realised, but they rarely missed a local funeral as it was looked on as a grand social occasion, a chance to catch up with old friends and enjoy a bite to eat afterwards at someone else's expense.

The majority of them had followed the Twilights minibuses back for Joy's ham-and-salad spread so the dining room was heaving.

"All alone? Are you OK, honey?" Lilith, in a long black frock and a wide-brimmed black straw hat dotted with bright pink roses, stood beside her. "Not too sad?"

Essie shook her head. "No, Ada had had a good life, really. And she'd got very tired lately, hadn't she? And the vicar was pretty spot on with the eulogy. I think she would have approved. Although the addition of that new steak house opposite the crematorium since the last funeral was a bit —"

"Don't, honey! I didn't know where to look! I didn't dare meet your eyes. I know Ada liked a laugh and she'd have seen the funny side, but it wouldn't have been respectful for us to be sniggering all through the service, would it? You'd have thought they could have been a bit more careful with their choice of words — given the position — wouldn't you?"

"Mmm." Essie grinned. "Being dead opposite the crem, a huge banner reading 'Can You Smell the Sizzle' possibly wasn't the most appropriate slogan."

They looked at one another and giggled like schoolgirls.

Eventually, Lilith wiped her eyes with the hem of her frock. "Ah, that's better. So, you're not unhappy?"

"No, honestly. I'm not standing here on my own being miserable. I'm standing here on my own thinking."

"Oh, honey, dangerous stuff." Lilith chuckled. "And are you thinking about what we discussed the other day?"

"I am." Essie smiled. "Out of respect, I didn't want to, um, do anything until Ada's funeral was over, but now I think Twilights could do with a tiny bit of livening up. Don't you?"

"I do." Lilith's splendid body shook with renewed giggles. "But whether you'll get Absolute Joy and Tiny Tony to agree, I don't know."

"Ah, I shan't be telling them *everything*, naturally. I'll just give them the more acceptable ideas. Oh, look, there's the Banding sisters over there. Must try to speak to them before they leave, but I know better than to interrupt them when they're eating. They're so barking mad they always cheer me up."

Lilith glanced across the crowded room to where Lavender and Lobelia Banding, elderly skinny spinster sisters from Hazy Hassocks, were stationed firmly by the food table with their plates piled perilously high. Apart from the gargantuan helpings of food and the fact that they were both dressed like Queen Victoria after the death of Albert, the most bizarre thing about the Bandings was the addition of neon cycle helmets decorously draped in black crepe.

"What the —?"

"Long story." Essie grinned. "But briefly — they wear the cycle helmets all the time, suitably trimmed to fit the occasion. Apparently they were once told by young Mitzi Blessing's daughter Lulu's husband Shay — still with me? — who's a paramedic, that cycle helmets prevented head injuries. Lav and Lob interpreted this as meaning they had to wear them all the time to keep safe, and have done ever since."

"Even if they're not cycling?"

"Lordy, Lilith! The Bandings have never been on a bike in their lives!"

"Lilith!" Joy Tugwell's Thatcherite tones carried imperiously across the dining room. "If you've got a moment, could you pop over here, please?"

"Go on." Essie nodded. "She's chatting to a bloke with too much hair gel and a bad suit. I think I saw him in the crem — he's probably from the council, they usually send a representative, don't they? No doubt Absolute Joy's going to wheel you out, yet again, as one of our token ethnic residents to score politically correct points. Go and do your stuff, girl. I'm going to go out into the grounds anyway. It's too bloody hot in here. Catch up with you later."

Outside, the heat shimmered hazily on the green and gold horizon. Leaving the hum of the funeral lunch behind, Essie crossed the courtyard, nodding politely distant acknowledgements to al fresco groups of munching mourners, and headed down the sloping lawns to a small spinney of holly bushes and ornamental cherry trees. Secluded and cool, it hid Twilights from view, gave a wonderful vista across the cornfields and gently undulating hills of Berkshire and was one of Essie's favourite spots.

The hateful incident in Winterbrook had, at first, made Essie wary of being alone — not that she'd ever admit it to anyone, particularly Absolute Joy — even in the grounds. But now, she occasionally craved solitude and cherished the moments when she could slip away from the institutionalised lifestyle.

74

Reaching her sanctuary, she selected a green and shaded patch and grabbed a handy low branch to hold. With minimal puffing, Essie sank down slowly on a cushion of moss. Blimey, she thought, I must be getting old. Despite her regular twenty minutes of stretching exercises every morning, that had been a bit of an effort. Her joints were creaking. She snorted. That was what came of not being allowed to go for the long, long walks she loved. And, of course, there was this never-ending heat. Much as Essie adored the hot weather, she really wished this summer-long heatwave would end. A good storm would work wonders.

Still, she thought, kicking off her sandals and stretching out her legs, this was delightful — the cool, dappled shade of the trees, the trill of birdsong, the sleepy murmur of unseen cars from the distant road, the occasional lazy buzz of a pollen-laden bee and the scent of — ? Essie frowned. What exactly was that smell?

Tobacco? Tobacco!

Oh . . . Essie inhaled greedily, the scent awakening the craving that had been buried for more years than she cared to remember. Having happily puffed away on thirty a day for the early part of her life, Essie had been forced to kick the habit for financial reasons. There were times, even now, when she wanted nothing more than a filter-tipped to go with her first cup of coffee of the day.

Naturally, Twilights was a no-smoking zone, although addicted residents were permitted to smoke in their roomettes if they had to. Most didn't. Mainly because the Tugwells kicked up such a stink about spontaneous combustion and practically stood guard with a fire extinguisher every time anyone lit up. And the poor girls who were on night duty had to double-check the rooms of smokers to make sure no one had inadvertently set fire to themselves during *News at Ten*.

Essie sniffed again. No . . . Nothing but warm grass and hay. It must have been her imagination. Either that or a "smoking ghost" — the stuff of urban myths and rural legends.

As she didn't believe in ghosts, smoking or otherwise, Essie leaned back against the trunk of the cherry tree, gazing at the fields and the shimmering cornflower-blue sky, happy to be alone with her thoughts. Now Ada's funeral was over, her plans for providing the Twilighters with in-house entertainment could gather momentum. If Tiny Tony and Absolute Joy refused to stretch the budget, they'd just have to make their own fun, wouldn't they?

Mitzi Blessing, Essie knew, had galvanised the over-forties in Hazy Hassocks several years ago. Now they had clubs and more activities than they knew what to do with, all using their own talents. So why shouldn't she, Essie, do something similar with Twilights? There were more than enough able-bodied residents who'd love a variety of mind-stretching leisure interests for their hours and hours of enforced idleness.

Lilith, Princess and Bert had come up with wonderful ideas when her plan had first been mooted. Lilith could teach Caribbean cookery, Princess — a tiny raven-haired seventy-something so nicknamed by her doting parents and never known by her given name of Doris — was an enthusiastic exponent of yoga, and Bert, bless him, had offered to share his love of macramé and origami.

For her part, Essie smiled happily to herself, she was going to really upset Tony and Joy by dabbling . . .

Long an enthusiastic amateur astrologer, Essie had, over the years, developed her natural talents for foreseeing the future into even more in-depth fortune-telling. Using tarot cards and star signs, following ancient theories and embracing newer ones, Essie had also become something of an expert in personolgy and numerology.

There had been quite a fuss when, on her arrival at Twilights, she'd given uncannily accurate readings to an enthusiastic following. The Tugwells, calling it "the work of the devil" and "tinkering with things absolutely best left alone", had banned Essie from ever dabbling again.

But that hadn't prevented her from using the mobile library van's visit to read up on her craft and study the more recent research, and then successfully secretly experimenting with Lilith, Princess and Bert and any other Twilighters who'd expressed an interest. Adding this to her own God-given talent and the folklore knowledge handed down by her Romany grandmother and great aunts, Essie was sure — quite sure — that she'd now unearthed some ancient powerful method for seeing into the romantic future.

She'd discovered the Five Questions linked to the magical secrets of birthdays. Five Questions, the answers to which gave a blueprint for everlasting love. Five Questions, which when linked to an ancient Romany chant, and as long as the birth dates were compatible, made even the most reluctant lovers suddenly fall on one another with cries of unbridled passion.

Which, she thought with a wry smile, had worked quite wonderfully on more than one occasion.

Beaming at the thought of the Tugwells wrath and itching to get started on developing her new endeavour, Essie closed her eyes in the dreamy warmth and sighed happily. All she needed now were some new guinea pigs to prove her Happy Birthday theories. After all, she knew everything there was to know about Lilith, Princess and Bert and everyone else at Twilights — what she needed was to get started on someone about whom she knew nothing.

There it was again! That smell!

Her eyes shot open. It *was* tobacco.

Essie swallowed. This wasn't a "smoking ghost" — there was definitely a flesh-and-blood someone in the spinney. She wasn't alone.

Instantly, the old terror kicked in.

"Who's there?" she demanded, hoping her voice didn't betray her fear. "I know you're there. Come out!"

There was a rustling and scuffling in the undergrowth. Essie's mouth grew dry and her palms grew damp. Her heart was rapidly double-drumming like a timpani orchestra.

The rustling became louder and nearer, a colourful oath preceded a crashing of small holly branches, and a black-clad figure clutching a smouldering cigarette stumbled into Essie's clearing.

"Bugger me." Slo Motion spat out bits of twig. "You scared the living daylights out of me, duck. Nearly had a cardiovascular back there. Didn't think there was anyone else here."

Essie laughed in relief as she recognised the undertaker. It sounded like a sob.

"Mr Motion! What on earth —?"

"Having a crafty fag or three away from our Constance and Perpetua." He indicated the smouldering cigarette. "They'll be busy networking for hours up at the 'ouse. Nothing like a wake for drumming up a bit of business. What about you, duck?"

"Just escaping for some peace and quiet."

"Well, sorry to 'ave disturbed you, like. Look — if you could forget you ever saw me smoking I'd be ever so grateful."

"Consider it forgotten." Essie gave a weak smile as her pulse reduced its frantic thundering and subsided to a more normal level. "I'm not one of the anti-smoking brigade, Mr Motion."

"Slo, please, duck." He leaned against the cherry tree. "Let's not stand on ceremony as we're both refugees from the shenanigans. Sorry, duck, I didn't catch your name . . ."

"Because I didn't throw it — but it's Essie. Essie Rivers."

"Nice to meet you Mrs — er, Miss Rivers."

"Mrs — married in nineteen forty-eight, widowed twenty-two years ago. Essie will be fine."

"Nice to meet you, Essie, duck." Slo dragged happily on his Marlboro.

Essie frowned. "Forgive me for being rude, but there's something I've always wondered about . . . your name? Is it a nickname — to go with Motion?"

Slo blew out a lungful of smoke. "Snackranim."

"Sorry?" Essie frowned some more. "Is that foreign?"

"No, duck. It's like when you uses the initials or summat. Leastways, that's what our Connie says."

"Initials? Initials ? Oh, you mean it's an *acronym*!" Essie beamed.

"That's what I said, Essie, duck. I was christened Sidney Lawrence Oliver — been Slo for as long as I can remember." With a shower of sparks, he stubbed out his cigarette on the cherry tree's trunk. There was a lot of ash residue sprinkled on his jacket. "Never sure if my old mum and dad 'ad a sense of humour or not. Probably not, comes to think of it."

They lapsed into a companionable silence.

"Why don't you sit down?" Essie patted the cushiony moss beside her. "Unless of course you have to rush off?"

"Nah, we ain't going nowhere. One funeral a day's enough for anyone, and the gels — our Connie and Perpetua — will talk the hind leg off a bloody donkey. That's right chummy of you, duck, thanks."

With a lot of wheezing, coughing, groaning and sighing, Slo eventually lowered himself to the ground. "Nice spot. Pretty view. Quiet. So what or who are you hiding from?"

"Nothing and no one really. I just needed some thinking time."

"About? Or is that a secret?"

"No secret." Essie smiled. "I was just pondering on the more acceptable face of dabbling in the unknown."

"Ah. You another witch, then?" Slo chuckled. "Black, white, kitchen or hedge? Like young Mitzi Blessing? Or little Sukie's Great-aunt Cora? Or any of them moon-bayers in Fiddlesticks? In my experience, duck, Berkshire's full of witches and not all of 'em fly on broomsticks."

"I'm not a witch. I'm . . . well, a sort of amateur astrologer, and if you're going to laugh or mock then I'm saying no more."

"Mock? Me?" Slo was clearly trying to keep a straight face. "Wouldn't dream of it. You going to tell my fortune, then? Read my palm? Or do you do the tea leaves? Ah, no, silly me. Astrology you said. That's star signs and horoscopes, innit? Go on then, duck — I'm all ears."

And because Slo Motion looked interested, and because it was so nice to have someone different to talk to, Essie told him about her plans, her experiments, her delving into numerology and personolgy and her ideas for advanced astrology.

"Bunkum!" Slo puffed when she'd finished. "Oh, I know lots of people believe in that sort of stuff, but when you deal with real life and real death, like I do, you gets pretty sceptical about . . . well, about there being anything else out there, if you gets my drift, duck. I don't believe a word of it, begging your pardon, of course."

"My pardon is begged." Essie nodded with a smile. "Which means, added to the fact that I know nothing at all about you, you'd be an ideal subject."

"Whoa! You ain't practising any mumbo-jumbo on me."

"No, no, it's nothing like that. I'd just love to try out my ideas on someone I don't know, and especially on someone who is a definite non-believer. Look, if I just ask you a few questions do you promise to answer them truthfully?"

Slo lit another cigarette, blowing a plume of smoke into the still air. "I reckons I could do that. But I got to tell you now this ain't going to work, duck."

"We'll see. Just relax, and give me honest answers to the Five Questions."

Essie closed her eyes, closed her mind to everything except recalling the questions she needed, breathed deeply and evenly, and eventually felt the steamy Berkshire countryside fade into the distance . . .

"One, add together the days your parents were born on — like the sixteenth would be one plus six equals seven. OK? Now two, add together all the numbers of the year of your birth. Right — remember those numbers and add them together. Three, add together the number of letters in your star sign. Done that? Good. Now, four, find the number of the season of your birth, with winter being number one and add that to your answer to question three. Done that, too? Thank you. And finally, five, take the second sum from the first and tell me the answer."

As she asked the questions, she heard Slo's laborious answers from far, far away . . .

They really, really weren't what she wanted to hear.

Questions over and the answers assimilated, gradually she opened her eyes. If — and it was a big if — she'd interpreted Slo's answers correctly, the outcome was rather disturbing. Was it too much of a coincidence? She must have got it wrong. Surely, she'd got it wrong.

"Thank you," she said faintly.

"Is that it?" Slo seemed disappointed. "That got me cogs turning and no mistake. Like being back in 'rithmetic lessons again. But blimey, duck, I expected puffs of green smoke and screaming genies at the very least. That might 'ave given me brain a bit of a workout but it weren't very exciting."

"It was to me," Essie took a deep breath. "Your birthday is November the sixteenth."

"Stone me!" Slo looked stunned. "Someone told you! They must 'ave!"

Essie shook her head. "No one has ever mentioned anything about you to me. I've never met you before today. We've never spoken before. But it is, isn't it? November the sixteenth?"

"Well, OK, so you've got three hundred and sixty-five days to pick from — three hundred and sixty-six if you counts a leap year — but they're damnable long odds for a guess."

"I can assure you it wasn't a guess. So, it is? Your birthday? November the sixteenth?"

"Yep. Spot on. Scorpio Slo, that's me. Crikey, that's magic, Essie, duck. Bloody magic."

Essie exhaled. She smiled shakily and nodded. It had worked! Worked on a total stranger. She really knew it was magic now.

But, it certainly wasn't the date she'd expected to hear.

"So —" Slo blinked "— this, um, magic act of yours, are you going to take it on tour? Round the halls so to speak?"

"No, no — I'm just going to liven things up here a bit. I just want to use it to amuse the other residents."

"Other residents? At Twilights? Blimey, I thought you was a visiting mourner. You're an inmate, then?"

Essie nodded, still feeling breathless and rather disturbed. "I am. This is my second year. I hated it at first. But now I'm more used to it. I've got some good friends and we're well looked after, but, oh, I do miss my independence."

Slo fumbled in his pockets for another cigarette. "That birthday stuff has fair rattled me, Essie, duck. OK with you if I —?"

"Yes, please do. I love the smell . . . No, no, thank you — I don't want one. I gave up years ago. Don't tempt me. I'll just inhale and enjoy a bit of passive smoking without anyone telling me that it'll fur my arteries, knacker my ventricles, bugger up my lungs, turn my skin to old leather and kill me before I reach sixty-five."

Slo gurgled a laugh as he lit up and sucked smoke deeply into his lungs. "Now, tell me, Essie duck. What's a clever lady like you doing incarcerated in a place like Twilights? You're a fine figure of a woman and you're clearly not gaga, so —"

"Oh, we're not all here because we can't be trusted to boil our own eggs. Some are, of course, but the majority are as fit as fiddles. Some didn't want to live alone any more, others had no bloody choice."

Slo raised his eyebrows and coughed. "You — sorry, just got to clear me tubes — you, I reckons, falls into the latter category?"

"How much time have you got? No — you really don't want to hear the whole sad story. It makes me all bitter just thinking about it."

"Better bitter out than in." Slo beamed. "And I've got all the time in the world. And after you knowing my birthday spot on from a few questions, you've got me right intrigued. Tell you what, Essie, duck, are you thirsty? Hungry?"

"Well, yes, but —"

"Wait 'ere." Slo achingly, creakingly, wheezingly, manoeuvred himself to his feet. "You can tell me your life story and we'll have ourselves a bit of a picnic at the same time. No, stay there. I've got it all under control."

Watching Slo rasp his way back through the undergrowth, Essie somehow doubted it. She'd probably have to give him CPR before long. And where in God's name was the mad old coot going to find a picnic out here? She smiled fondly to herself. He was a nice man, though, and amusing, even if he was completely barking. But, oh, his birthday. She shouldn't have dabbled. It really wasn't what she wanted to hear.

The bushes crashed and squeaked, leaves and small branches tumbled like confetti, as Slo emerged once more, this time hauling an ancient cool box behind him.

"There!" he panted triumphantly. "I never relies on the food at a Twilights do. That Joy Tugwell could starve for England. Parsimonious cow. A few dry sarnies and cheap sherry — no way to send a soul off in my opinion. Our Constance is a bit tight when it comes to vittles mind you, she'd eat cardboard if it came for free. But our Perpetua allus makes me a bit of a spread on the quiet. I brought it up here to go with me fags. Plenty enough for two."

Essie stared in delighted bewilderment as Slo painfully resumed his sitting position and, diving into the cool box, produced hunks of French bread, uneven lumps of cheese, a jar of home-made chutney, two large lopsided pork pies, several thick slices of fruit cake, a couple of apples and four cans of ice-cold ginger beer.

"It might be a bit robust for a lady like you," Slo apologised. "Our Perpetua tends towards the hearty when it comes to food."

"It looks wonderful," Essie said, meaning it. "Thank you so much. But are you sure you don't mind sharing?"

"Wouldn't 'ave mentioned it if I 'adn't wanted to share, would I? And after your Paul Daniels

86

thingamajig just now I can't think of anyone I'd rather share with. Blimey though, it's getting 'otter." Slo struggled out of his jacket and rolled up his shirtsleeves. "Right, duck, dig in."

Feeling like a child with an unexpected treat, Essie dug.

Munching happily, and with a bit of prompting from Slo, Essie gave him the truncated version of how she came to be a Twilighter. How her children, Patrick and Shirley and their spouses, had robbed her of her home. How they'd lied and fooled her and because, of course, she'd trusted them implicitly, they'd managed to get their hands on the only thing she really cared about. Her home. And then evicted her from it. It didn't matter how many times she told the story, it still angered her. How could her children — her own flesh and blood — have done it to her?

Slo was a good listener. He only interrupted to clarify a point or offer more food or ginger beer.

"This is the loveliest picnic I've ever had," Essie sighed when she'd finished the whole sorry tale, full to bursting and her thirst slaked. "Thank you so much."

"I've right enjoyed myself too." Slo wiped his mouth with a large black-edged hankie. "In fact I can't remember when I last enjoyed myself more. Lovely spot, nice food and great company — not to mention a magic act thrown in for free. Mind, that story of yours almost took the edge off it. What nasty, grasping, greedy, cheating little bastards — begging your pardon, Essie duck — your children are. If you don't mind me saying, that is."

"Not at all. I couldn't have put it better — apart from the bastards bit. They were both born well within wedlock. Still, let's not dwell on them any more. Thanks for listening, and for being a guinea pig, and for the picnic. You've turned what could have been a very sad day into a very pleasant one."

"My pleasure," Slo said, happily reaching for a post-prandial cigarette. "We should do it again some time. That is, if you wants to, which you probably don't of course."

Essie drew in her breath. Should she? After *that* birth date? But then, who was she to argue with forces far stronger than she was? Maybe it had been meant — meeting Slo, using him as a guinea pig? Maybe the whole encounter had been *meant* to show her that she was right to pursue the birthday magic?

She hesitated for a moment longer, then nodded. "Yes, I'd love to. Honestly. And next time I'll provide the picnic."

"That you won't." Slo exhaled a billow of smoke like an angry dragon. "I may not 'ave 'ad much experience with members of the fairer sex, but I knows what's what. Next time we'll do it proper. A proper meal. On me."

Essie smiled. "We'll argue about that later then. I've always paid my way. But, the Tugwells are a bit . . . Well, they don't like us going out, mainly because of me. I had a bit of trouble in Winterbrook. No, you don't want to hear about that now. You'll think I'm some sort of mad woman — if you don't already — and that my life's one long horror story. But anyway, since then the Tugwells have stopped me going into Hazy Hassocks or anywhere else on my own."

"Bugger the Tugwells!" Slo roared, dropping his cigarette in the excitement, then scrabbling in the moss to retrieve it. An entire tussock was smouldering and he extinguished it with dregs of ginger beer. "I reckons we was fated to meet, Essie, duck. And you won't be on your own, will you? I shall come and collect you proper in the Daimler and we'll go and 'ave tea in Hassocks and you can tell me more about your Happy Birthday stuff if you wants to, then I'll bring you back again. The Tugwells can't object to that, can they?"

Essie thought they probably could and definitely would. "You mean — like a date?"

Slo looked slightly nonplussed, then he beamed. "You know, Essie, duck, I think I do. Exactly like a date."

CHAPTER
SEVEN

Twilights was abuzz. Phoebe, hauling her equipment into the residents' lounge from the back of her Astra, blinked at the seething mass of chattering elderly ladies. Her first official evening appointments — two wash and sets, one cut and colour — were sitting expectantly in huge beige wing-backed armchairs. Everyone else had obviously turned up as an audience.

On first impressions, Phoebe decided Twilights wasn't anywhere near as bad as she'd imagined it would be. Although it was utilitarian bland, it was spotlessly clean, and even if it did smell overpoweringly of lemon air-freshener, it was certainly vastly nicer than she had anticipated.

"We're absolutely delighted that you could make it." Joy Tugwell's flinty eyes fought with the sugar in her voice. The sugar eventually won. "My sweet girls — and some of the boys, too — have been looking forward to it so much. In fact, we had to draw lots for this first session, everyone wanted to have their hair done tonight. You're going to be a regular visitor, Polly."

"Phoebe. And I'm pleased it's proving to be a successful venture for you."

"Absolutely." Joy beamed. "Although Tony, that's my hubby, and I really had to dig deep into the coffers to be able to provide this sort of little luxury — but then, absolutely nothing is too much for my ladies and gents. Now, we thought if you washed in the kitchen — we've cleared a space by the little veg sink — then you can do the folderols in the lounge. We've set up a nice secluded area, over there on the other side of the plasma screen, with mirrors and what have you for you to use as a salonette. What say?"

"Er, yes. That sounds great, thanks. Of course, back-washing would be preferable — I'll have to see if Cut'n'Curl can provide a suitable chair for future sessions if this is going to be a regular event — but otherwise it all seems fine."

"Lovely. Absolutely lovely. Right, let's get a move on then. Who do you want first?"

"The cut and colour lady." Phoebe squinted at her three appointees. "Then she can be 'cooking' while I shampoo the others."

"Right you are," Joy barked. "Princess! You're up first. Don't keep Polly waiting."

Princess? Phoebe blinked at the diminutive lady with the jet-black hair who leaped nimbly to her feet.

"Not really," Joy confided, gripping Phoebe's elbow and steering her fiercely towards the kitchen. "East End. Common as you like. Nickname. Huge gossip — take everything she says with an absolute pinch of salt. Right, here we are. I'll leave you to it, then and go and keep the others away from the kitchen. They seem to think this is some sort of spectator sport. They can be so absolutely belligerent you wouldn't believe."

Phoebe exchanged glances with Princess as Joy strode away to spread happiness in the residents lounge.

"Daft cow." Princess grinned, hopping up on to the stool placed beside the sink. "Nice to meet you, Polly."

"Phoebe."

"Trust Absolute Joy to get it arse about face. Now — Phoebe — what I wants is my hair dyed black again — me roots is coming through something shocking — and then a bit of a trim. And don't you go telling me that at my age I should be going lighter to match my aging skin tones — I reads *Woman's Weekly*, I knows all that stuff — but I want to be black. I've always been black and black I wants to stay. OK?"

"OK." Phoebe smiled. "You're the client here, but how about if we lift the dead flat blackness with some different shades? Blues — no, not blue-rinse blue before you bite my head off — but really vibrant blues: cobalt, royal, midnight, and some purples? We'll feed them through the black base colour then cut your hair into a style that shows them off. Does that sound OK?"

"Crikey, that sounds dead exciting," Princess said happily. "You go for it. I'm in your hands. Oh, aren't you going to wash me first?"

"No, I just thought we'd have a bit more privacy in the kitchen. We'll do the colour first, leave it to take, then shampoo you and cut the new style at the end. Ready?"

92

Princess nodded, wriggled herself more comfortably on the stool and, once Phoebe had draped the skinny shoulders with towels and a plastic shawl, she began measuring and mixing the colours in the tiny bowls, organising her brushes and combs, sorting out the foils. Working on autopilot as she separated strands of Princess's coal-black hair and starting to apply the first colour, Phoebe allowed her thoughts to drift . . .

In the week since her head-to-head with Rocky Lancaster, she'd heard him — and his music, although at a far more reasonable level — upstairs but thankfully hadn't seen him again. She'd noticed that he no longer had his previous-life flashy hatchback on the hardstanding and that it had been replaced with a rather battered green van. Knowing she should feel sorry for his straitened circumstances, Phoebe had found it very hard to raise even a glimmer of sympathy. He'd brought it all on himself, hadn't he?

Anyway, she spent enough time feeling sorry for herself — there wasn't anything left over for wasting on a violent thug, no matter how gorgeous looking.

Gradually, she was growing used to being alone in the flat. Coming home was the worst, but once she'd made something to eat and turned on the television for company, the initial loneliness passed. Almost. Well, sort of. One day, maybe, she'd even get to like it . . .

She had, feeling a bit silly and slightly guilty, immediately made sure that her flat door had a new bolt fitted and that the Yale deadlock actually worked. And she'd given up any idea of sleeping with her French windows open to the garden. She'd decided she'd rather stifle than be assaulted. Not that she excepted Rocky Lancaster to come sneaking downstairs and punch her for no reason, but it was rather unsettling knowing that someone capable of that sort of violence was living in the same house.

For this reason she hadn't mentioned Rocky's presence at all to her parents — they'd have insisted she come home straight away — and had sort of fudged the facts for Clemmie, YaYa and her other girlfriends, by simply telling them that Rocky was living upstairs alone after his split from Mindy. She'd also fielded all sorts of nudge-nudge wink-wink suggestions about two lonely souls gravitating together, by saying firmly that she was seriously off men for life and that Rocky felt the same about women since Mindy left.

Poor Mindy, Phoebe thought. Putting on a brave face when she'd been a battered live-in lover. Phoebe wished now — wise after the event — that she and Ben had rushed upstairs when they heard those awful rows. No one had guessed that Rocky — the slimeball — had been using her as a punchbag. If only they'd known what was going on. If only they'd known more about Rocky Lancaster.

It was Pauline who had inadvertently filled in some of the gaps.

"Know what I meant to tell you," Pauline had said in Cut'n'Curl while she and Phoebe were trying to comb out a too-tight perm without scalping the victim. "What with you going up Twilights soon and that. That old lady that got mugged in Winterbrook is one of the

94

residents — can't remember her name offhand but it'll come to me — but of course, silly me, you'll know all about it, won't you?"

"Will I?" Phoebe had frowned, trying to tease out a particularly frizzy curl. "Why?"

"Because the bloke what did it is your neighbour."

"Neighbour?" Phoebe had furrowed her brow and tried to imagine any of Winchester Road's elderly and upright citizens scuffling with some equally elderly lady for a share of her pension. "Which neighbour?"

"That really nice-looking bloke — just shows." Pauline had sucked in her breath as a clump of hair fell to the floor. "Sorry, Mabel, did that tug a little? Yes — where was I? — just goes to show you can't judge a book by its cover, doesn't it? Such a handsome young man — used to wear a lovely uniform — and him no better than an axe murderer with what he did to that dear old lady. Oh, Phoebe, you must know him — he lives in the upstairs flat in your house."

"I've got an axe murderer living upstairs, have I? No, I'd've noticed," Phoebe giggled. "Rocky Lancaster lives upstairs and he —" Phoebe had stopped teasing the sparse hair, feeling sick. "You mean *Rocky Lancaster* mugged an old lady?"

"Mmm." Pauline had nodded. "Been in prison. Someone said he was out now though."

"Yes, he is. But I had no idea —"

"Oh, Phoebe, you must have! Although, now I come to think of it, it was all going on while you were, um, planning your wedding. Sorry, love, know you don't want to talk about it. You were away with the fairies all the time, what with your never-ending lists and checking and cross-checking everything and on the phone to people all the time. I think World War Three could have broken out and you wouldn't have noticed."

Phoebe had felt very dizzy. Rocky was even worse than she'd thought! The lowest of the low and then some! Of course, Pauline was right, she'd been oblivious to everything else going on in Hazy Hassocks, or at home in Bagley-cum-Russet, or in the world at large while she was immersed in and obsessed with planning the perfect-wedding-that-never-was.

Maybe, she'd thought, she'd even ignored Ben during that time. Yes, she probably had. Had she been so wrapped up in planning the minutia of the wedding day, that he'd thought she didn't give a stuff about the marriage? The rest of their life together? Had Ben believed that the ceremony was far more important to her than their ongoing relationship?

Was it her fault that he'd jilted her? Was *this* the reason?

But — somehow, even worse — Rocky had gone to prison for mugging an old lady? What had he said? "Beating the crap out of someone." An *old, helpless, vulnerable* someone. How despicable was that? He was truly the worst kind of scum — a wicked, evil, cowardly thug.

She'd never, ever speak to him again — but oh, Lordy — should she even be living in the same house?

Oh, God!

★ ★ ★

"Blimey!" Princess caught a glimpse of her befoiled head in the mirror. "I look like a cross between an oven-ready turkey and that strange girl from *Star Wars*. I never have all these little tin foil things when I dye my own hair; I just slosh it on from the packet, wait for a bit then slosh it off again."

"Hopefully you'll really see the difference with this then. Right, now, do you want to stay here, or go through to the lounge to allow the colour to take?"

"I'll stay here and watch if you don't mind. You've got Patience and Prudence — twins, inseparable — next, and they're funny. No, really funny — as in peculiar, not ha-ha. They might be the most peculiar girls I've ever met." Princess met Phoebe's eyes in an adult-to-adult stare. "Know what I mean? And I says that seriously bearing in mind that there's some really peculiar people in here."

Great, Phoebe thought.

She stretched. The evening was as hot and oppressive as those preceding it. This truly was a scorching summer. The open windows showed a very pretty courtyard with vibrantly coloured flowers and long lush lawns leading to a spinney, but there was still no air to rustle through the branches.

"I'll go and give Patience and Prudence a shout then. Will they want to have their hair washed together?"

"Oh, yes. They do everything together. They've got one of the few twin roomettes in this place. I'll move over to the table, so's you've got more room."

As soon as Prudence and Patience — bent backed and droopy dressed — had twittered their way to the sink and indicated that they wanted their wiry pepper-and-salt hair washed at the same time, Phoebe, once her enquiry about water temperature being OK and receiving dual curt nods was out of the way, concentrated on honing her chatty-hair-dresser skills.

"So, have you been anywhere nice recently?"

Princess sniggered. Prudence and Patience said nothing.

"Don't bother asking them questions." Princess nodded her headful of foils like some small exotic bird. "They don't do small talk except to each other. They just say yes and no to everyone else mainly, and then only if it involves their well-being. But no, since you ask, they haven't been anywhere nice. None of us have. We're not allowed out without a minder."

"What?" Phoebe concentrated on her two-handed wash method. "Not even into Hassocks?"

Princess shook her head this time. "No. Not even into Hassocks. Tiny Tony and Absolute Joy have forbidden any of us to go anywhere — that's why this hairdressing thing is such a treat. We don't get to see many people stuck away up here."

Phoebe frowned. How awful must that be? To be old, and shut away, and not allowed to do *anything*?

"Is that in case you, er . . .?"

"Wander off and can't find our way back again?" Princess finished. "Nah. We're not doolally. It's because one of us got mugged last year — loads of bad publicity. Absolute Joy and Tiny Tony were shit scared that the council'd close this place down because we weren't being looked after properly. So it's been like a prison ever since."

Phoebe slopped rinsing water over Prudence and Patience. "Oh, so sorry, are you soaked? Um, my hand slipped." She mopped, dual-handed, then looked at Princess. "It wasn't you, who was mugged, was it?"

"No, thank the Lord. One of me mates, it was. Bless her. But it put the kibosh on all our extra-curriculars. The Tugwells have given in a bit now, and agreed that if we can't go out, they'll let us have a few things to entertain us like this hairdressing and that Jennifer Blessing to do our nails and that."

Phoebe started to massage conditioner into the matching scalps.

"And, er, the lady who was mugged? She survived, didn't she? She's OK now?"

"Oh, yes." Princess grinned. "Right as ninepence. She's not here this evening, otherwise you could have seen for yourself. She's stepping out."

Stepping out? Phoebe frowned. Stepping . . . Was that like step-aerobics? Wasn't that a bit energetic for an old person? And weren't the Twilighters banned from outside activities? How odd.

Princess chuckled. "She's gone with a beau."

A *bow*? Phoebe was even more confused. Tie? Violin? Ribbon?

Then she smiled. "Ah, I know! My nan used to do that! Keep-fit! Lots of ladies in vests and divided skirts leaping up and down and waving long ribbons. Dozens of them. I've seen the photos."

"That's nice, lovie." Princess looked perplexed. "But I don't know what the heck you're talking about."

"Stepping out with a bow."

"Whatever you say, lovie. But I hope Essie isn't wasting her evening out doing that sort of malarkey. She's gone for a fish supper with a bloke, gentleman caller, suitor. Date, would you say? Dunno what you young 'uns call it these days. Can't see either of 'em dancing with ribbons, to be honest."

"Oh, right — sorry — I misunderstood." Phoebe shook her head at the generational language barrier. "But I thought you weren't allowed out?"

"Ah, the Tugwells couldn't do nothing about it when he asked Essie out, seeing as he's one of their best business contacts and he promised to have her back here by nine o'clock on the dot. Shame you missed her really — she's been organising some other stuff for us to do. She's a laugh. You'd like her."

Essie, Phoebe thought. Now Rocky's victim had a name. It made it even more horrendous somehow.

Prudence and Patience emitted matching squeaks as Phoebe massaged a little too fiercely.

"Sorry, ladies. We're nearly done. So, she's truly fully recovered, has she?"

"Bless you, yes. And, like I said, we're allowed out if someone responsible takes us — and this is her second outing with her beau — he took her out to tea at Patsy's Pantry last week — so she's a lucky girl on all counts."

She certainly was, Phoebe thought, rinsing off conditioner and wrapping twin towelling turbans round

Patience and Prudence, in more ways than one. At least Rocky Lancaster hadn't completely ruined the poor woman's life. It was lovely that she'd found someone to go out with. Maybe, Phoebe thought, when I'm 109 and over Ben, I might just find someone else too.

But why weren't there more people willing to take the Twilighters out? Maybe she ought to volunteer?

"Mind you," Princess said hopefully, "we're always looking for other things to do up here. I've got my yoga classes up and running, Bert's doing macramé and origami — bloody boring if you asks me and most of us has got arthritis in the fingers so the results are abysmal and only end up in the recycling bin — and Lilith gives cookery lessons, but we've had all that before. What we needs is fresh blood. I don't suppose you know anyone who can put on a bit of a show or would be prepared to visit us and do things of an evening, do you?"

Pushing the treacherous thought of inviting YaYa and The Dancing Queens to the back of her mind in the firm belief that a drag act — however tasteful — possibly wasn't the sort of entertainment suitable for the Twilighters, Phoebe pondered as she combed through Prudence and Patience and juggled fat foam rollers.

"Well, my friend works for a firework company — I'm sure they'd love to come and put on a display. Oh, and a couple of my other friends belong to a cancan troupe, that might be fun."

Princess clapped her hands. "Whoo! That sounds wonderful — just what we need. You have a word with Absolute Joy before you leaves, lovie, and make the arrangements. We'd all love a bit of cancan — and fireworks! So pretty! Oooh, I can hardly wait. It'd liven us up no end. You've got some clever friends. But what about you? What do you do in your spare time? You got any hobbies, apart from the hairdressing, you could share with us, or have you got a husband and kiddies to take up your time?"

"No, none of those," Phoebe said quickly, carefully using tail combs on Patience and Prudence and fastening the rollers. "And as for hobbies . . . I . . . well, I used to be keen on astrology."

"Really?" Princess's eyes gleamed. "Now, there's a thing. See, a bit of fortune-telling was one of the things we suggested to Absolute Joy and Tiny Tony, but they wasn't happy. Mainly because we'd had a bit of a dabble beforehand and it went funny — if you gets my drift."

Phoebe didn't. Although she could imagine what sort of problems an amateur astrologer could cause. Especially among the vulnerable Twilighters. Anyway, she'd given up astrology, hadn't she? It was a lot of hokum wasn't it? Look what it had done for her and the-wedding-that-never-was.

"However," Princess continued, "that was because it involved — well, never mind, you don't need to know. But if you could suggest doing some readings, the Tugwells might see it differently, coming from outside like."

"Well, I really don't do it any more."

Princess looked crestfallen. "Oh, that's a shame. We have such a boring time up here. Please, please think

102

about it, Phoebe — it'd make a lot of lonely old souls very happy."

"That's blackmail." Phoebe grinned. "But — OK — I'll think about it."

"Whoopee! Oh, now this is a long shot, but you don't happen to do tarots as well, do you?"

"Well, yes, but . . ."

"Oh, we loves tarots! Oh, go on, Phoebe. Suggest it before you leave. You'd make us ever so happy. We all wants to believe we've still got something to look forward to before we, well, you know."

Oh, Lordy — put like that, how could she refuse?

As she blow-dried Patience and Prudence, Phoebe mulled it over. Well, she could do it, couldn't she? It wouldn't hurt, would it? Even if she no longer believed in the power of the solar signs, star signs, or any other damn signs, it would fill another couple of long, solitary evenings, wouldn't it?

"OK," she mouthed over the noise of the dryer. "I'll suggest it."

Princess clapped her hands delightedly.

Surprisingly, once Patience and Prudence had been dried, combed out, teased and lacquered, they became almost garrulous with delight.

"Lovely, lovely, lovely," they chorused in matching high-pitched voices. "The best hairdo ever. Thank you very much, Polly."

And tossing their bouncing, shining curls, they skittered away hand in hand into the lounge to be greeted with cries of delight from the waiting spectators.

"You won't have time for tarots at this rate." Princess smiled as she hopped up on the stool to have her colour checked prior to having her hair washed. "Everyone and their dog'll want you up here to do their hair. OK then, lovie, if the colour's OK, do your worst."

Half an hour later, Princess made her entrance into the residents lounge to rapturous applause. Her coal-black hair was now shot through with strands of multi-toned blues and purples and styled in a spiky urchin cut.

"Oh, my, honey!" A large lady in an emerald-green caftan, enveloped Phoebe in a hug. "You're a star and no mistake. Princess looks stunning."

"Well, I think so — and she's pleased with the result." Phoebe extricated herself from the hug. "Which is the main thing. And yes, you're right — she looks lovely."

"A huge success." Joy Tugwell forced herself between Phoebe and the caftan with single-minded determination. "Wonderful, Polly. You absolutely must come again — soon. I've taken any number of bookings for you. What say we check our diaries? Could you allocate us, say, two evenings a week?"

Phoebe, watching Patience, Prudence and Princess preening round the lounge like divas at an Oscars ceremony, nodded. The simple restyles had given them all renewed confidence. Amazingly, she'd made someone happy. In the middle of all her own misery and self-doubt, she'd made three old ladies beam from ear to ear.

"Two evenings? With proper appointments? I do like to be organised. Yes, I'm sure I could. In fact, I'd love to."

"Absolutely wonderful," Joy gushed in a strangulated hernia voice. "Hubby and I will do absolutely anything to make our residents happy."

Phoebe smiled. "Mmm, and Princess mentioned that, er, due to recent unfortunate circumstances, they, um, you were trying to organise some more activities for them here at Twilights. I wondered if, along with the hairdressing, I could perhaps suggest one or two ideas . . ."

CHAPTER
EIGHT

"Damn." Essie looked at her watch. "Look at the time — nearly nine o'clock. It really flies when you're having a good time, doesn't it? Now I'm going to be late back, and I'll have missed all the excitement of the hairdressing."

"You don't need your hair a-doing, duck." Slo mopped up the remains of chip fat and brown sauce from his plate with a thick slice of bread and butter. "I likes my gels with long hair — and yours is real pretty."

"Is that a compliment, Mr Motion?" Essie looked archly across the red and white checked tablecloth of Hazy Hassocks' Silver Fish Bar. "And is that what I am? One of your gels?"

Slo's mottled cheeks blushed becomingly. "No, well, what I means, is . . ."

"It's OK. I'm only teasing you. Thank you for the compliment — and for the meal. That was really lovely. I can't remember the last time I had a proper fish supper — with bread and butter and a pot of tea. But we really should be making a move. You know that Absolute Joy only let me out this evening on pain of death should I be late back."

106

"Ah." Slo wiped his mouth with the ubiquitous black-edged hankie. "And I needs to get outside and have a fag. Nothing like sitting back at the table and relaxing with a cigarette to round off a meal proper. This blame-stupid nanny state is ruining all a bloke's basic pleasures."

They pushed back their chairs, smiled thank yous and goodnights to the Silver Fish Bar's staff and stepped out into the dusky, sultry heat.

"Ouf," Essie exhaled as Slo fumbled with his cigarettes. "It's still baking. And where do Constance and Perpetua think you are tonight, then? Not sharing a fish supper with me, that's for sure."

"No, duck." Slo wheezed round his filter tip. "They thinks I'm doing a deal with the coffin makers. That's why I parked the Daimler well out of sight down Big Sava — there's allus someone in this village who'll tittle-tattle — and they'd give me gyp if they thought I was out with you — again. That's the trouble with our Connie and Perpetua — they've never had a friend of the opposite, er, sort, so to speak. Kept 'emselves to 'emselves all their lives. They'd think all manner of nonsense if they thought we'd been out for a meal."

Essie fell into step beside Slo. He was several inches shorter than she was, and probably because of the smoking, a lot, um, slower. He was also surprisingly good company. Since the impromptu picnic at Twilights, they'd had tea in Patsy's Pantry and this was their second — what? Essie frowned. Date? Not really. Not at all, in fact. They were just two lonely people who found they could talk easily, laugh together, had things in common and were happy and comfortable with one another.

Friends, she decided, that's what they were.

If only she could forget that his birthday was 16 November.

"Well, your cousins needn't worry on that score, need they? We're only good friends who enjoy a meal together and a chat. So, none of you ever married?"

"Nah." Slo dragged on his cigarette as they walked along the High Street towards the Big Sava car park. "Never even got close. We was sucked into the undertaking business from kiddies, allus busy, there never seemed any time for me to meet gels. The only ones I ever came in contact with were either put off by the nature of me job, or grieving — and that's not the best basis to start chatting them up, is it?"

"Possibly not. Although you're a very good listener, and sympathetic — maybe you could have won them round by just being your gentle and understanding self?"

"Kind of you to say, duck, and mebbe I could, but we was allus straight on to the next embalmment if you gets my drift. And as for Constance and Perpetua, well, they were never, well, pretty girlie gels. Our Connie would of scared the pants off 'itler, and Perpetua is a bit, well, grey and wittery and p'raps not quite the full shilling."

They walked on in contented silence. The High Street was sleepily closing down. Even the Faery Glen was quiet. There were few late-night revellers in Hazy Hassocks. They passed Beauty's Blessings and the

108

dentist's and Patsy's Pantry and Cut'n'Curl without seeing anyone. Just by the Dovecote surgery they passed another couple strolling home, and there were several people on the other side of the road near Mitzi Blessing's Hubble Bubble building and the library. Essie was amused to see that Slo kept his head down in case anyone recognised him.

He broke the silence.

"What about you, then, Essie, duck? Was you happily married?"

"Very. Me and Barney met at school, married young. He worked on the railway in Reading, I had a little job in a florist's. We never had much money, but we had a lovely marriage. God knows how we produced such awful children. We never had enough to spoil them, but they never went without, and we taught them right from wrong without resorting to punishments — and then they . . ."

"All kids is a mystery to me." Slo expertly catapulted his cigarette butt through the air with a flick of thumb and forefinger. "Different in our day, of course. You had wrong 'uns, of course, but in the main kids seemed more decent and respectful like. So, yours don't come to see you now?"

"No, never. And I wouldn't want them to, even if they suddenly remembered they had a mother. No, I served my purpose. I try not to think about it really. I've got my friends up at Twilights — they're better than any family."

"And a lot less trouble, in my experience," Slo laughed throatily. "So you've got a proper little clique of friends up the Twilights, 'ave you?"

Essie nodded. "We all arrived at much the same time and we're all in the same boat — more or less — so we sort of gravitated together. Princess has never married and has no relatives away from the home; Bert was single too, lived with his mother and two aunts — they all died within a month — so he needed looking after by lots of women because that was all he knew. I think that's why he's chums with us and not some of the other men. Bert doesn't know anything about cars or football or blokey stuff but he's great on needlework and knitting and making things with paper. And then there's Lilith . . ."

"The black lady who allus laughs and wears them bright colours? She's a bit of a card, that one."

"Oh yes, Lilith's amazing. Never miserable. Nothing gets Lilith down. She's been married twice — no children. She always says both her husbands died happy thanks to her hot love and spicy cooking — or maybe it was the other way round."

Slo chuckled.

"And now you're another friend — and I really have enjoyed tonight." Essie smiled. "I'm very grateful to you for taking me out like this. Especially after . . ."

"Ah, yes — you never did tell me about why you're all kept under lock and key, did you? You've told me about your bloody nasty kids, and about your magic astro-ma-ology stuff, but you never said —"

"No, and I'm not going to. It's all over — but I've got a couple of ideas about how to right the wrongs that were done, too."

"That don't surprise me. What've you got in mind?"

"Oh, just something that might make me — and the boy who, well, let's just say, I think my plan will do us both good. No, don't ask — I really, really don't want to talk about any of that."

"And I knows you better 'n to keep asking." Slo's laughter rasped as he cleared his throat. "So, changing the subject then, did the miserable Joy Tugwell agree to let you do your magic birthday act to cheer up the other Twilighters?"

Essie shook her head in the darkness. "No way. I didn't give her the chance to put her dainty little Thatcherite foot down. I simply didn't tell her. She's happy enough with what she knows is going on. What she doesn't know is going on won't hurt her. A bit like your Constance and Perpetua, eh?"

Slo chuckled again as they turned off the High Street and ducked down the unlit alley alongside Big Sava. Under the solitary streetlight, a noisy gang of young men in baggy clothes was visible, approaching the alleyway from the car park end.

Essie's heart started racing and her mouth grew dry. She stopped walking.

"What's up, duck?" Slo puffed. "You OK?"

Essie couldn't speak. Couldn't move. Surely it couldn't be? Not the same boys?

They were in the alley, loudly shoving and pushing. Heading straight for her. Three abreast.

She took gasps of breath, feeling her heart thundering, her palms growing damp.

The gang was almost upon them now. There wasn't room to pass. Panic attack in full swing, Essie shrank against the wall, feeling faint.

There was a shout of raucous laughter, some swearing, more laughter.

Essie felt her legs growing weak, her head swimming, her heart rate increasing.

The gang grew level.

"Evening," one of them said cheerfully as they split into single file and passed.

"Evening, lads," Slo said cheerfully back as the group headed for the High Street.

Essie whimpered and sucked in some hot air.

"Essie? Essie, duck?" Slo peered at her. "Oh, Lord, Essie. Are you ill?"

Essie shook her head. She couldn't speak. She had to take deep breaths — she knew that. One, two, three . . . breathe in, and out. Slowly.

Gradually, her pulse returned to something like normal.

"I'm OK. Sorry."

Slo held her hands in his, and looked at her, his eyes worried. "Whatever happened, duck? It's not your heart, is it? Shall we find somewhere to sit down? Oh, Lord, Essie."

She smiled weakly, angry with herself for her weakness. "Sorry, I was just being silly. It was those boys . . . They . . . they scared me."

112

"Them lads? They were OK. Just lads. Probably from the Bath Road Estate. Bit rough speaking, but friendly enough. No harm in 'em. Look, duck, we'll just stay here a moment while you gets your breath back, and when you have, we'll go and sit in the Daimler, and then why don't you tell me what the hell's going on?"

It was nearly ten o'clock when Phoebe got back to the Winchester Road flat from Twilights. Lights gleamed into the hot black night from both upstairs and down. As Phoebe always left her lights on to deter burglars she assumed Rocky, as he seemed to spend most evenings out, had done the same. Not that he needed to worry about being robbed — felons were obviously his closest friends.

The temperature was the same as it had been mid-afternoon only now the night air was even more stale and heavy. Far too hot and weary to unload the hairdressing paraphernalia, Phoebe decided to leave it until the morning and pulled her car in behind Rocky Lancaster's scruffy green van. Whichever innocent and frail pensioner he'd decided to assault tonight, she thought as she fumbled for her door keys, he'd clearly chosen to do it on foot.

God, how she despised him. He should have been thrown into prison for the rest of his life for what he'd done.

Still, the unpleasantness of living cheek by jowl with Rocky-the-scumbag apart, the evening had been a success. She'd managed to spend several potentially lonely hours out of the flat, had made Princess,

Patience and Prudence very happy and had secured Joy Tugwell's enthusiastic agreement, not only to make regular hairdressing visits on Tuesday and Thursday evenings and, more surprisingly, an initial astrology session the following Monday, but also to spread the word about Twilights needing entertainers among her friends.

"A bit of singing and dancing sort of thing might keep them quiet. Good idea. I'll leave that one with you. However, re the fortune-telling, though, Polly, we absolutely don't encourage them to, well, dabble in things that might upset them," Joy had said in a loud and patronising voice. "However, as one of our residents thinks she's some sort of cross between Mystic Meg and Russell Grant and has caused All Kinds Of Trouble In The Past, I think that inviting you to keep them happy fortune-telling wise, might be an absolutely brilliant idea. Tony, my hubby, and I don't believe in that nonsense, of course, but anything that stops them grizzling will be absolutely super. I trust you'll only tell them the good stuff, won't you? I absolutely forbid you to give them Bad News. *Comprendez?*"

Still smiling at the memory of Joy's lengthy lecture, Phoebe flicked the television into comforting burbling life. Well, the excursions to Twilights would bring in much-needed extra money — she'd decided to postpone the lodger idea until Ben's pre-paid rent ran out in November — and would mean that she now only had four evenings a week to fill. And, she thought, being among people in their latter years who no longer

114

had homes and families and who had mostly outlived their friends and had nowhere to go and no one to go there with, might just help to put her own misery into perspective.

Ignoring the newscaster who was reporting on something depressingly awful as usual, Phoebe made for the kitchen, poured a large glass of wine, chucked in a handful of ice cubes and, relishing the prospect of an hour listening to the Kennet and nothing else, opened the French doors.

"Jesus!"

She dropped her wine glass with a splintering crash.

Rocky Lancaster, wearing faded jeans and a scruffy T-shirt, was lounging on one of the wrought-iron chairs, a fat, scented, bug-busting candle flickering on the table, a bottle of beer in his hand.

"What the hell do you think you're doing?" Phoebe immediately backed away, scrunching over broken glass, wondering if she could get inside and phone the police before he lunged at her. "This is my garden. Not yours. The words 'garden flat' hold any clues?"

Rocky looked at her, his face expressionless. Phoebe thought fleetingly that it was such a shame he was a spineless thug — he was truly beautiful.

"Did you hear me?"

"The whole of Winchester Road probably heard you." Rocky took another mouthful of beer. "Don't shout."

"I am not shouting," Phoebe shouted.

"You are. It's late — and you were the one who kept on about not disturbing the neighbours with noise, I might remind you."

"You have no right —"

"I have every right, actually." Rocky put the beer bottle down. "The garden flat certainly has easier access to the garden, I'll grant you that, but we've always shared the facilities."

"That was before —"

"Before you knew I was an ex-con? Sorry, but that doesn't appear in the tenancy agreement. You should read the small print about shared amenities. And you'll cut your feet on that glass if you're not careful. Those flip-flops aren't very sturdy."

"Please don't concern yourself with my health and safety — just go back upstairs to your flat and leave me alone."

"I'm not here for your company, much as that may surprise you. We share the same roof but I don't want to be your friend. I don't want anyone. I'm quite happy with my own company, and I was here first, so tough."

Phoebe swallowed. This was so awful. This man she loathed was taunting her, goading her, and there was little she could do about it. Not usually timid, she knew that someone who had been imprisoned for a serious assault really wasn't to be trifled with.

And now, because he'd made clear his intentions of living in the flat and sharing the garden just as if nothing had happened, she suddenly knew she really couldn't stay here. If Rocky stayed she'd have to go. All her plans for building an independent life, all the laughing suggestions made by Clemmie and YaYa and Amber and Sukie, counted for nothing.

Rocky bloody Lancaster had achieved what Ben had failed to do — he'd driven her out of her home.

Phoebe wanted to scream. It was all so unfair. Perversely, having jumped through such huge emotional hoops to move back to the flat, she now wanted to live there more than anything.

The only faint glimmering hope was that Rocky wouldn't be able to afford to stay in Winchester Road. He'd lost his job, she knew that, and no one would give him another one, would they? Not with his record? So this presumably meant he was living on benefits, and surely, they wouldn't last for ever, would they? He'd have to be the one to leave.

"Nothing more to say?" Rocky raised a quizzical eyebrow. "Good."

"I've got plenty more to say," Phoebe said, far more confidently than she felt, and clutching at a million straws. "But as you won't be staying here much longer, it'll be a waste of breath."

"What, here in the garden? Oh, I don't know. I've got another beer, an empty double bed doesn't hold much promise, and the night's only just beginning."

"Not the garden — I mean the flat."

"My flat? Why on earth won't I be staying there? I've only just moved back in?"

Phoebe hesitated. Should she really be confronting him? She was the vulnerable one here. Anger and disgust overcame her sense of self-preservation. "But will you be able to afford the rent? Oh, no doubt you're on some do-gooder rehab course to ease you back into society — but when that ends you'll have to get a new job and —"

"Already got one." Rocky grinned. "They're very good like that in prison these days, as you seem to have guessed. It's not all twenty-four-hour lock-ins and slopping out. Yes, we first-timers all got put on retraining programmes. Mine was extremely useful and strangely enjoyable. I'm now a gardener. I'm surprised you haven't noticed the little green van with bits of twig on it. However, it's kind of you to be concerned for my future though, Phoebe. I appreciate it."

Oooh, Phoebe groaned inwardly. Bugger.

"Now, if you've finished your interrogation about my future income and are happy that I'll be able to afford to live —" Rocky pushed his chair back "— I'll go and get a dustpan and brush for that glass — no doubt you've got a nice colour co-ordinated one lined up in your kitchen listed under 'cleaning tools'. Mindy always said you were ultra neat and anally organised."

Thanks a bunch, Mindy.

"I'm not, and don't you dare think you're setting foot in my flat. I'll sweep it up — in the morning. I'm going inside now and locking the doors."

Rocky laughed. "Because you think I'm going to attack you? Sorry, not a chance. I'm in non-attack mode tonight. And, yes, maybe it'd be a good idea if you went in. I honestly was enjoying my own company before you arrived."

"Got used to it in solitary, did you?"

"Oh, American cop show speak, now. Clichéd. Actually, I wasn't in solitary confinement — although there were times when I wished I had been. You've no idea —"

"Don't expect me to feel sorry for you! Not after what you did."

"You know what I did, do you?"

Phoebe nodded. "I might have missed it at the time because I was, um, preoccupied with other stuff —"

"Your wedding? Yes, I can see how that would have taken precedence."

"Don't be so damn condescending!"

"I'm not being anything. I'm genuinely sorry about what happened to you and Ben."

"Really? Shame you didn't show such concern for your victim, isn't it? Oh, yes, I know exactly what you did. Remember, you told me the basics? And since then other people have joined up the dots."

"And probably coloured them in and added captions. Oh, go away, Phoebe. If you don't want to hear my side of it, I can't be bothered listening to your right-wing tabloid self-righteous opinions of my behaviour. I really want to be left alone."

Phoebe glared at him. He really was the most arrogant sod she'd ever met. And there was not a trace of remorse for his heinous crime. Dangerous, egotistical bastard.

"You can't intimidate me. You might be able to terrify weak and helpless little old ladies — like the mindless, cruel bully you obviously are — but you don't scare me."

Rocky picked up the bottle again, carefully swallowed his mouthful of beer, then looked at her. "No? That's nice to know. And I'd love to hear what you've been told about my misdemeanours. They're obviously at odds with my own recollections of the event."

"Well, they would be, wouldn't they? No doubt you think that some problem in your childhood, some imagined grievance, some dysfunctional family problem excuses what you've done. Probably your social worker told you it wasn't your fault. Probably blamed it on your parents and said there, there, and —"

"Bloody hell!" Rocky interrupted, angrily flipping the top off the second beer bottle. "You've worked it all out, haven't you? And honestly, I can't be bothered to put you right. You believe what you like. As I've said before, I'm staying in the flat, as you are, but we really don't have to spend any time together. Maybe you'd like to draw up a rota for the garden? Mindy said you had lists for everything and —"

"Bugger Mindy!" Phoebe snapped, forgetting for a moment that she was supposed to have been in sisterly solidarity with Rocky's battered ex. "And bugger you! I'm locking the doors and I'm going to bed!"

"Sweet dreams," Rocky laughed softly.

Phoebe stomped inside, slammed the French doors shut and dragged the drapes across them, her heart pounding.

Damn, damn, damn.

Now she had to go to bed — in her new pink and frilly bedroom — knowing, *knowing* that Rocky

120

Lancaster was sitting merely inches away on the other side of the glass.

"Oh, Ben!" she muttered to herself. "I bloody hate you for doing this to me!"

CHAPTER
NINE

"You've done *what*?"

Clemmie, YaYa and Suggs stared at Phoebe in triplicate horror.

"Agreed to read a few horoscopes, plot astral charts, that sort of thing."

"At *Twilights*? For all those *old* people? This *evening*? A *Monday* evening?" YaYa shook her head. "When we've come round to your lonely flat to take you out for a pint or two of Chardonnay and a girlie chat. Well, one girlie, one cross-dresser and a ferret, but you get the drift. And now you tell us you're going out?"

"And," Clemmie joined in, mumbling round her little plastic container of olives, "not just going out, but going out to play at being Madame Zuleika, which you've already said: a) you'd never do again, and b) even you don't believe in, and c) —"

"Don't call me Madame Zuleika! You've always mocked my astrology by calling me Madame Zuleika since we were at school. I've never called myself Madame Zuleika."

Laughing, Clemmie shook her head. "Dear me. Sooo touchy for a star-sign diva, dear, aren't you? OK, no more Madame Zed from me. Promise. But, seriously, Phoebes, if you don't believe in the astrology any more then I don't know why you've agreed to —"

"Oh, I've agreed to a lot more than that," Phoebe said airily, zipping her case round her solar charts and astrology books, "I've volunteered you too."

"Us?" YaYa looked askance. "We don't do fortune-telling, love. And you wouldn't catch me at any old folks home. All that air of impending death and an overriding aroma of piss and biscuits."

Phoebe laughed. "You are so out of touch — and so wrong. Twilights is lovely — well, as lovely as any sort of institution can be, the residents are as fit as fiddles, and you were the ones who said I should be looking for extra money-making activities and that I should use my gifts and —"

"Yes, love —" YaYa nodded "— but not by fleecing some vulnerable old souls of their pensions."

"The Tugwells are paying me to do the astrology stuff as part of a raft of entertainment ideas, which is where you come in. I've sort of volunteered The Gunpowder Plot for a firework display."

"Oh, right." Clemmie chewed a black olive with relish. "Oh, yeah, that's fine. Guy'll be up for that. He's always doing free shows for charity. Just let us know what you want and when and we'll be there."

"And me?" YaYa smoothed down her skin-fit turquoise sundress and preened prettily. "And the girls? Foxy and Cinnamon and the others? Some of the more tasteful numbers from our drag act?"

"You just said you didn't want to have anything to do with old people."

"That was when I thought you meant I had to tell fortunes. I'm always up for a bit of showtime stuff. We'd love to do a bit of old-time music hall or something else suitable."

"Well, I hadn't thought about it — no, actually I had, but I reckoned you might be a bit too, er, risqué for Twilights. Mind you, if you want to do something more, er, acceptable, I could certainly suggest you."

YaYa looked mollified.

"Sukie has agreed to come along with the Bagley-cum-Russet cancan dancers, so maybe you could all get together and do a show some time. Anyway —" Phoebe picked up her case "— I'll have to dash."

Clemmie sucked the last of the juice from her olives and flapped her hands. "Blimey, Phoebes, it's so hot in here — and don't tell me it's me 'ormones — I don't know why you keep all the doors and windows closed. Have we got time to let Suggs out for a quick wee before we put him back in the car?"

Phoebe nodded as Suggs scampered towards the French doors, and Clemmie opened them to let him out into the courtyard garden allowing a waft of sensuous jasmine and honeysuckle to float into the flat.

"Holy shit."

"What?" Phoebe looked across the living room. "What's the matter?"

"Nothing." Clemmie shook her head. "Absolutely nothing. But you kept him quiet, Phoebes."

"Who?"

"The gardener out there hacking away at that overgrown ivy. All bare bronzed torso and tight jeans. He's sooo gorgeous."

"And you, Mrs Devlin," YaYa said severely, "are a very married and quite pregnant woman — both courtesy of my best mate Guy — so do *not* lust over Phoebe's hired help."

"He's not my hired help," Phoebe said quickly. "He's Rocky Lancaster. He's a, um, gardener, and he's taken it into his head to tidy up the courtyard."

"That's Rocky? Wow, you never said he looked like that! And I'm not lusting, honest. I mean, I'm married to the sexiest man in the world, but," Clemmie giggled, "you have to admit, Rocky looks just like that beautiful boy who played Henry VIII in *The Tudors* on telly. He's certainly easy on the eye. And recently dumped too? Oh, did you find out why Mindy dumped him, Phoebes? If he didn't cheat on her or beat her up, she must be have been mad."

"I've no idea," Phoebe said shortly. "We don't speak much."

"And, Clemmie's right, you didn't say how cute he was." YaYa peered over Clemmie's shoulder. "Are you sure he couldn't be the one to put your heart back together again?"

"Never more sure of anything in my life," Phoebe said firmly. "Now, if Suggs has finished, I really have to go."

YaYa sashayed out into garden, tossed her ash-blonde hair and fluttered her eyelashes at Rocky who laughed at something she said.

"Oh, look!" Clemmie cooed. "He's even playing with Suggs. Gorgeous, available, drag-queen friendly and an animal lover. What more do you want, Phoebes?"

"Not him — or any man."

"All right." Clemmie held up her hands. "Back off. Only joking. Are you coping OK?"

"As before. Coping, yes. OK might be stretching it a bit. Look, Clem, honestly I do appreciate everything you're doing for me. Everyone has been brilliant, but I just have to grit my teeth and get on with the rest of my life and try not to think about, well, think. Which is why I'm doing all this stuff up at Twilights. Anything, anything at all, is better than sitting in night after night, remembering."

"Don't — you'll make me cry again. I still cry over everything at the moment, but at least I've stopped being sick." Clemmie gave her a quick hug. "Now go on — off you go. Get out your crystal ball and wow the oldies."

"So, what's this one called again?" Bert looked expectantly across the table half an hour later. "This lot of cards? And what do they do?"

"Uh? Sorry? Oh, yes — sorry."

Phoebe dragged herself back from hoping that Clemmie and YaYa hadn't picked up on the I-hate-Rocky-with-a-vengeance vibes because they'd only ask awkward questions later and then tell her she

126

had to leave Winchester Road, which she already knew and didn't want to think about, thank you.

She blinked at the spread of cards in front of her. "Oh, right — yes, well, this deck is called the Major Arcana — they're the tarots that indicate the basics of what's going on generally in your world and outside it. The others are the Minor Arcana. There are four suits of them — cups, wands, pentacles and swords — with fourteen cards in each suit, and they relate far more to you personally. I usually use both decks together to give the whole picture. Does that make sense?"

"Ah — thank you." Bert, tiny and wrinkled, his grey scalp showing through his sparse grey hair, smiled shyly at her with surprisingly lovely big brown eyes. "They're very pretty cards. I like pretty pieces of paper. I do origami, you know. And macramé although sometimes the knots are the very devil with me arthritis so I use glue. I used to do collages — with rice and dried peas — but they kept dropping off and getting in my socks so I stopped. Tell the truth, I thought this tarot thing would be a bit scary. I worried that I might get a lot of death cards."

Phoebe managed to keep a straight face as she rearranged the decks.

"No, no. Look, the hanged man and death are both in the Major Arcana cards, but neither of them foretell the end of your life. Quite the opposite — as you'll see if we turn them up in your reading. Whatever the tarots tell you, it won't be anything frightening. Is that all right?"

"Yes, thank you. I understand now. I wanted tarots, mind, not me horoscope. I knows what me horoscope'll be, I had that done once. By one of my mother's chums. She said that I was born under a black star and that I'd only bring unhappiness to everyone I met and that I'd live a lonely old age and die alone. I thought the tarots might give me better news."

"Bloody hell." Phoebe blinked. "Your mother's chum should be shot for telling you that load of rubbish. Let's see if the tarots can do a bit better, shall we?"

Bert nodded with enthusiasm. "This is going to be really exciting — for both of us, isn't it?"

Phoebe somehow doubted it. Excitement didn't figure much in her life any more. And Bert didn't look as though he and excitement had ever been close acquaintances. As tarots should be read in an atmosphere of quiet calm, the accompaniment of a crowd of Twilighters gathered round the table as an audience and all giving loud and mixed advice at the same time wasn't helping much either.

Phoebe took a deep breath, regrouped the cards and handed them to Bert.

"Right, concentrate on the important issues in your life and the things you want answers to while you handle the cards, take your time to feel comfortable with them and then give them a shuffle. Then when you're ready you pass them back to me and we'll start the reading. Is that OK?"

Bert took the cards, awkwardly at first, and began holding them, looking at them, stroking them . . .

128

Phoebe sat back and waited. An hour into the astrology session and she was feeling totally exhausted. The Tugwells had rigged up a sort of post office queuing system, and when she'd arrived every Twilighter seemed to be waiting impatiently in line, laughing and talking.

"This is your table, Polly, but," Joy had said, casting disapproving eyes up and down Phoebe's slim-fitting cut-offs and brief top, "a little word of advice. Maybe in future, a little less inflammatory dress would be absolutely advisable? My gentlemen are very elderly. We wouldn't want to give them absolutely any ideas of a certain nature would we?"

Phoebe had tried to look demure and promised to be dressed more appropriately next time.

"Good. Good." Joy had appeared mollified. "Oh, and another little word of advice. Now, don't you go filling their heads with nonsense about lottery wins or eternal youth. Give 'em a couple of minutes each and send 'em on their way. Just tell 'em what they need to hear to keep 'em sweet — and absolutely no bad news at all. I absolutely forbid bad news. Now, sit yourself down and let's crack on."

Phoebe, feeling rather fraudulent, had sat and cracked, pretty sure that whatever she told the Twilighters would be as useless as the portents that had proclaimed Midsummer's Day was going to be perfect for her wedding.

Taking a deep breath, wondering if one of her customers would be Essie, she'd dived in on autopilot.

One after another, the Twilighters, obviously used to queuing, sat at the table and were embarrassingly grateful for anything Phoebe could tell them. Actually, she'd found it had all come back frighteningly easily, and the basic horoscopes, based on star signs, cusps and planets ascending or stars waning, went down well with the participants.

Remembering her promise to Joy, and wanting to keep this a regular visit, Phoebe was careful to gloss over any of the more worrying astral omens. Strangely, she felt, despite her protestations that star signs were tosh, it went oddly against the grain to be forced down the charlatan route and having to temper her predictions to suit her clients.

However, Joy, hovering watchfully in a corner, beamed her pleasure.

So far so good.

Patience and Prudence — still sporting their new hairdos — had insisted that she read their horoscopes together as they were twins and therefore it'd be the same, wouldn't it?

Phoebe said that yes, it probably would, and was therefore a little disconcerted when Princess, wearing a blue and purple dress to match her hair, had muscled in and asked to be done at the same time.

"Two's company, three's a party." Princess had grinned. "You can handle the three of us together, can't you, lovie?"

Still with a feeling of misgiving that she really, really shouldn't be doing this any more when she didn't believe in it, Phoebe had said well, it wasn't usual, but she'd give it her best shot.

As they were all Sagittarians it was slightly less complex than it might have been, and, even as a new non-believer, she was surprised to find the predictions flowed smoothly.

Having told them the main characteristics associated with their birth sign, she'd gone into a little more detail. Sagittarians being fire signs, she'd told them, meant they'd have warm times ahead. Given the current equatorial Berkshire temperatures, this was greeted with some scepticism from Princess.

"Not just physically warm," Phoebe had improvised, "but emotionally too. You're all going to be happy and contented."

Patience and Prudence had twittered excitedly and even Princess had looked less doubtful. Phoebe, both following the charts and using the knowledge that had kept her enthralled for as long as she could remember, also predicted that they'd be facing the challenge of filling in their leisure time with even more exciting pursuits in the days ahead.

Patience and Prudence had clapped their hands and trotted off together happily.

"You mean we'll have loads of time on our hands," Princess had said, grinning at her. "Tell us summat we don't know. It's all a bit general, lovie, really."

"You have to put your own interpretation on it."

"Oh, I know — and I will. Thanks for doing this — we're having such a lot of fun, honestly. You're a clever girl, you know — hairdressing and fortune-telling — is there no end to your talents?"

Hanging on to a fiancé isn't top of my list, Phoebe had thought sadly, but she'd simply smiled.

"I think I'm ready now." Bert dragged her back to the present, handing the cards across the table. "In for a penny as my mother used to say."

Phoebe took the tarots, automatically noticing which ones Bert had shuffled to the top of the deck, which ones were reversed, which ones fell out of the pack. Another deep breath to block out the raucous chattering of the watching Twilighters and she flourished the spread of the decks across the table, drawing the cards from the top of the pack.

Bert's large eyes grew even wider as she laid the Justice, Tower, Sun and Star cards from the Major Arcana face up. The Twilighters stopped talking. From the Minor Arcana, Phoebe turned over the four, followed by the king, then the ace and the nine.

"Well." She smiled at Bert. "I think this hand is telling a very strong story."

Bert swallowed nervously.

"The first Major cards all indicate that there will be changes in your life — changes that you may not even consciously know about yet, but that deep down you've longed for."

Phoebe stopped. What was happening? She wasn't telling Bert what he wanted to hear as she'd imagined she would — she was giving him a true reading. Impossible. She didn't believe in tarots or any other form of prediction. It wasn't true. She took another

132

deep breath. "And the Minor cards are backing this up — there are going to be new beginnings for you, but new beginnings linked to the happiness of your past. It's a lovely reading. Very optimistic."

Bert beamed happily. The Twilighters clapped.

"I can go on — read more into this if you like."

Bert shook his head. "No, I'm right happy with that. Don't let's go any further. I don't understand it, mind. I had a lovely past with my mother and my aunties, but it ended when they passed on, so I never thought there was any hope for a happy future. Thank you so much."

"My pleasure," Phoebe said truthfully, as Bert shuffled away from the table.

"What did I say?" Joy Tugwell appeared like an Exocet with a handbag. "What did I absolutely say to you?"

"Er." Phoebe frowned, still amazed at how naturally the reading had flowed. "Um . . ."

"Not to give them bad news, that's what! And what have you just done to Bert?"

"Not given him bad news?"

"Absolutely worse than that! You've filled his head with nonsense about finding happiness! The poor man cries himself to sleep every night. Now he thinks his mum and his damn aunts will be coming back!"

"Oh, I don't think he — I mean, I didn't say that. He can't think —"

"Believe me, I know my residents. If you're going to be allowed to carry on with this malarkey, then for Lord's sake keep it bland. Next!"

* * *

133

Half an hour later the queue had vanished, and with it the tidal roar of dozens of enthusiastic pensioners. As the Twilighters disappeared back to their own quarters or out into the grounds to do, well, whatever old people in old people's homes did with their, um, twilight hours, Phoebe, feeling exhausted, sat back in her chair.

As far as she knew — and most people had cheerfully introduced themselves to her — there had been no sign of Essie among her astrology clients. Perhaps the poor woman was still traumatised by crowds after Rocky's attack, or maybe she'd been lucky enough to be taken out again. Whatever, it was something of a disappointment. Phoebe would have liked to reassure herself that Rocky's victim was well and as happy as possible.

"Hi, honey." A large glamorous black lady in a shocking pink caftan leaned over the table. "I've brought you some iced orange juice. Absolute Joy hasn't given you as much as a sip of anything, has she?"

Smiling her thanks, Phoebe shook her head and gulped at the juice. Her throat was parched after so much talking.

Bliss. *Absolute* bliss, she thought with a giggle.

"You were good, honey, and thank you for being so kind to Bert. He's a sweet man, but unhappy. You made him smile, which is really nice to see. I'm Lilith, by the way."

"Phoebe — and thanks so much for the drink."

"You're welcome — you played a blinder there. Everyone loved you. You'll be a regular. Which is all to the good as we're climbing the walls with boredom."

"Yes, Princess said much the same when I was doing her hair the other day. I've spoken to some friends of mine about them coming up here as well to put on entertainment, but there must be some way you can organise things for yourselves."

Lilith laughed. It was like a treacle volcano. "There sure is, honey. But we keep some of those under wraps. What Absolute Joy and Tiny Tony don't know about won't hurt them. Mind, after Essie's last stint, they've been a bit anti the fortune-telling stuff."

Essie — again. How strange. Phoebe frowned. Maybe Essie was the one Joy had said "dabbled". Poor old thing, she thought, probably reads tea leaves or something.

"Really? Then why wasn't she here?"

"Didn't want to show her hand." Lilith nodded. "Felt, if she listened to you, she might not be able to stop herself getting involved. Absolute Joy watches her like a hawk. Essie's predictions aren't, well, perhaps quite as lily white as the Tugwells would want. Joy once accused her of being in league with Satan."

The volcano of a laugh erupted again.

Blimey, Phoebe thought, a geriatric tea leaf reader in league with the devil.

"She sounds, um, fascinating."

"Ah, she is, honey. If you're going to make this a regular thing, Essie's the one you want to talk to."

In more ways than one, Phoebe thought.

"And can I do you think? Talk to her, that is? Tonight? Is she here?"

"In her roomette, honey. Ready and waiting for you."

135

CHAPTER
TEN

The cream-painted, beige-carpeted corridors of Twilights roomettes were, Phoebe thought, reminiscent of a spotlessly clean, impersonal private hospital. They had that same air of universal, corporate, frightening nothingness.

Having followed Lilith's directions, Phoebe rapped smartly on the door of number nineteen.

"Come in — I'm in the kitchen. The door's on the latch."

Should it be? Phoebe wondered. What if —?

Tentatively, she pushed the door open, was met by a waft of spicy fragrance and tried to disguise her surprise.

Expecting to find a frail and wispy old lady dressed in limp florals and worn-down slippers, Essie came as a complete shock.

"Hello, Phoebe. I was expecting you. Lilith managed to get the message to you without Absolute Joy realising, did she? Good, good. Lovely to meet you, and don't you look cool and summery all in pink and white. Like coconut ice. Come in and sit down, dear."

Hoping that she wasn't staring too much at this tall, slender elegant woman in her floppy linen trousers and dark-green lace shirt with lemon chiffon scarves in her hair, Phoebe sat in the indicated ubiquitous beige armchair.

How could bloody Rocky Lancaster have attacked this beautiful, delicate, ethereal elderly lady? How truly sick must he be?

Essie beamed from the kitchenette. "I've got a nice little bit of supper on the go — one of Lilith's recipes. You will share it with me, won't you? I'll bet a pound to a penny that the Tugwells didn't give you as much as a stale biscuit, did they?"

As Phoebe couldn't remember the last time she'd eaten, and her stomach was rumbling, she nodded eagerly. "That'd be great — as long as you've got enough."

"Loads," Essie said cheerfully, opening the fridge and closing the microwave. "It'll only take a minute to heat. Lilith made it in one of her Caribbean cookery sessions. Jerk chicken. It took on a whole new meaning, I can tell you — especially with Reggie Baker having that tic and being borderline Tourette's."

Phoebe giggled, watching Essie move round the tiny galley kitchen with graceful economic movements. Goodness, how small these places were. And so hot, and the windows only opening a crack. God, it was just like a prison.

"There we are." Essie carried two bowls of piquant chicken and rice into the room and placed them on the low coffee table. "Enjoy! Sorry to be so cloak and dagger." Essie grinned, then sat down opposite Phoebe and picked up her bowl and fork. "It's a recurring theme in my life at the moment, but there are a million reasons why the Tugwells would prefer you not to speak to me. How did the astrology session go?"

"Er, very well, I think," Phoebe mumbled round her spicy chicken. "Oh, wow, this is fabulous. Thank you so much. Um — everyone seemed very pleased with it and Joy has agreed to make it a regular Monday evening thing."

"Has she indeed? Good. And what did you do?"

"Um, well . . ." Phoebe hesitated. She really didn't want to confuse Essie with too many technical details. "Well, I just asked each of them their star signs and then gave a reading based on them and the appropriate planetary aspects."

Essie nodded. "No room for anything to go wrong there then. Clever girl. And I understand you read the tarots for Bert and that he was delighted?"

Phoebe frowned. Essie was very well informed.

"Lilith reported back straight away." Essie put her bowl down. "Would you like a drink, dear? I've got some peppermint tea brewing. Wonderfully refreshing in this damn hot weather, goes really well with the chicken and helps me keep a clear head."

"Oh, er, yes, thank you." Phoebe smiled, deciding not to say that she really wasn't a fan of herbal teas as they all reminded her of medicine at best, and Suggs' ablutions at worst. "And yes, Bert was happy with his tarot reading, although it was very brief. I could have done more, but —"

"But?" Essie asked quizzically from the miniscule kitchen.

"Well, Joy Tugwell had warned me not to go too far, and to be honest the tarots from both suits were telling the same story. Oh, sorry. Maybe you don't know much about tarots."

"A little." Essie, still busying herself with spoons, mugs and the teapot, didn't turn round. "Which spread did you use for Bert?"

Phoebe blinked. What on earth did Essie know about tarot spreads? "Well, the basic one I always use. I mean, there's only one, isn't there?"

"Bless you." Essie reappeared with two white mugs of steaming fragrance and placed them on the coffee table. "Stick with just the one if that's what you're happiest with. Personally, I favour the Romany spread. But then I would, given my ancestry. When I was a child, my Auntie Thirza was always trying to flog clothes pegs or sprigs of white heather or turn a few cards. And Auntie Kizzy used to annoy the neighbours something wicked with her crystal ball. They just amused me, but then again, my grandmother taught me everything she knew, which is why . . . No, not now. We'll talk more of her and that, later."

Was Essie joking? Rambling? Old and muddled? All of them?

"Er, right, the tarots — the Romany spread? I've never heard of that one." Phoebe picked up her peppermint tea to cover her confusion, juggling bowl and mug. "Oh, this is lovely too. Thank you."

"Another one of Lilith's recipes," Essie said, picking up her chicken again. "Much nicer than shop bought I think. Right, where were we? Ah, the Romany spread —

well, it isn't anything too complex. It's the one that's been used for generations by travelling fortune-tellers. Uses both decks, seven cards in three rows — past, present and future — you read them vertically. Very accurate. You should try it some time for a change."

Phoebe hungrily scooped up her jerk chicken and sipped her tea. Essie Rivers was no mug.

"I will — thank you. And I'll have to ask Lilith for this recipe. It's fantastic. And sorry for assuming you didn't know about tarots. I mean . . ."

"No offence taken. How were you supposed to know anything about me? We've only just met, haven't we? Although I'm sure Princess and Lilith have already told you that I have my own predilections in the predictions area." Essie chuckled.

"Yes they did, but to be honest, I thought they meant, well, you read tea leaves or something. Sorry for thinking that, and for, well, just sorry. It's obvious that you know far more than I do."

Essie settled back in her chair. "Well then, why don't you tell me what you know, and I'll tell you what I know, and we'll find out, won't we? And then I'll tell you what I'd like you to do for me. Deal or no deal?"

Phoebe, feeling that Essie deserved something — anything — to make up for the horrors Rocky had inflicted on her, nodded. "Deal, definitely."

So, in between bowl-scraping and tea-drinking, Phoebe explained about her life-long obsession with astrology, and how she had always organised her entire existence round her readings, and why, now, she felt like a fraud because she didn't believe in any of it any more.

"So that's it really. My love affair with astrology is all over — just like my love affair with Ben."

"Such a sad story, dear." Essie nodded sympathetically. "I'm so very sorry that things were so awful — still are awful — for you. And you certainly know enough to be a very competent amateur astrologer. But you shouldn't blame the stars for your problems."

"Why not? I planned it all by the stars. Charted it all. We were a perfect match. Everything pointed to the date for the wedding being perfect. How can I believe in anything any more when —?"

"Oh, you poor child. But don't blame yourself — or your readings. Look, it goes much further back than that. You were only using the very tip of the star and sun sign portents. Let me ask you something? You based everything on your — and Ben's — star signs, didn't you?"

"Well, yes, but . . ."

"And your star signs were compatible, no doubt?"

"Of course. I'm a Virgo —"

"Clever, organised, nit-picking, fussy, reluctant to change your mind. And Ben?"

"Capricorn."

"Materialistic, power-seeking, obsessed by money, ambitious and practical."

Phoebe nodded. "Yes — but we're both earth signs, so —"

"And those are just the very basic and general characteristics of those born under your signs, wouldn't you agree?"

"Well, yes, but we were compatible because of the earth sign thing. I knew that when we were at school. We *were* perfectly matched. The wedding date *was* just right. At least, according to the stupid stars. I feel such a fool now for *believing*."

Essie smiled kindly. "Right, now, if I ask you some questions — five questions — about you and Ben, will you promise to answer them honestly? First for you and then for Ben. This is important, Phoebe, so total honesty is vital even if it upsets you to talk about your Ben, OK?"

"OK."

Placing her empty bowl and mug on the table beside Essie's, Phoebe relaxed back in her less-than-comfortable chair. Essie fascinated her, but she wondered when she could change the subject away from astrology and get on to the more important issue of her being mugged by Rocky Lancaster.

Essie closed her eyes and seemed to go into some sort of trance. For a while Phoebe thought she'd gone to sleep, but then her soft Berkshire voice asked five very specific, but as far as Phoebe could see totally irrelevant to astrology, questions.

Hesitantly, slowly, doing rather rusty mental arithmetic and feeling more than a bit silly, Phoebe eventually answered them.

"Thank you." Essie, opening her eyes, smiled slowly when she'd finished. "Now, Phoebe, I can tell you that it wasn't the stars that got it wrong. Or you with your astral charting. The marriage could never have happened. You and Ben were — are — incompatible. It wouldn't — couldn't — have worked."

"What?" Phoebe said quickly, annoyed now. How ridiculous was this? What gave Essie, who didn't know either of them, the right to make such an outrageous statement simply on the strength of a mathematical conundrum?

Essie held up a slender hand. "I know what you're going to say, but hear me out, please. Your birthday is September the ninth?"

Phoebe looked at her, nonplussed. "Yes, but how on earth . . .?"

"And Ben's is January the twelfth?"

"No way!" Phoebe shook her head. "There is no way on earth that you can know that from my answers to those questions. You already *knew*."

"I can assure you I didn't. How could I? But I'm really delighted that I'm right. It goes to prove such a lot of things I've believed for ages. Now, much as your overall signs may have been compatible, your birth dates aren't. Look, Phoebe, how much do you know about personolgy? Or numerology?"

"Nothing. I've never heard of them. But —"

"Right, well, I can tell you anything you need to know, but right now let me say something else about your birth date — and Ben's. Your birth number is nine — and a Virgoan nine is always a perfectionist and overly critical of others who fail to match up."

Phoebe nodded. "Yes, but that goes with the Virgo territory. I've always wanted everything to be just so. I've always kept lists. Been organised — and yes, my best friend, who reckons I have an A★ in OCD, is completely haywire, and that drives me mad."

"And Ben's birth number is three. Capricorn threes are notoriously cautious and careful — especially when it comes to their private and personal lives. Threes will always try to divide nines. Always wants to be boss. No meeting halfway. The two together equal disaster. Seriously, dear, it was a match made in numerology hell."

"But . . ." Phoebe frowned. "But, how . . . I mean, I don't understand."

Essie looked at her. "There are far more things available to the amateur astrologer than simply following the star and sun zodiac charts. But this combination of numerology, personolgy and astrology, plus a sprinkling of Romany mysticism that I've known about all my life, eclipses — if you'll forgive the expression — anything that's actually written down anywhere. The secret magic of birthdays can —"

"The *what?*" Phoebe, still spooked by Essie's uncanny knowledge, interrupted. "What secret magic of birthdays?"

"This is where my grandmother comes in." Essie leaned forwards. "I can trust you, Phoebe, can't I?"

Phoebe, still pretty sure that Essie had had prior information about her and Ben's birthdays somehow, but more intrigued than she'd admit, nodded.

144

"Good. Now, predictions for the star signs are general, as you well know. But my grandmother taught me that if you had the gift, as she did, and you studied the planets and the personal characteristics of your, um, clients, and then asked the Five Questions — the ones I've just asked you — which relate to the birth-date numbers, if, and it's a big if, the astral magic is there for you, then the answers will give you a formula which enables you to uncover the secret magic of birthdays. The key to happiness. The key to compatibility. The ability to create happy-ever-after couples — couples who may previously not have been aware of their feelings, but who, when birthday-magicked, fall tumultuously in love. I've inherited that power and I'm sure now that with my Happy Birthday magic, I can help the right couples to get together and the wrong ones not to make disastrous mistakes."

"Like some magical astral matchmaker?" Phoebe laughed. "That's too weird for words. Sorry, but I simply don't believe it."

"No, I didn't think you would. Not for a moment." Essie sighed. "Which is a pity, as I was hoping you could become my apprentice."

"Apprentice?"

"Oh, not like Sir Alan on the telly — more the sorcerer's apprentice if you like." Essie laughed. "Or is that too silly for you?"

"Not silly, no, maybe even fascinating, but there's one huge flaw here."

"Yes, go on. Please, Phoebe, you won't insult me."

"Well, you use your, um, Five Questions, to find out when people's birthdays are. Then you announce them — ta-dah! — just like some sort of conjuring trick. But why on earth don't you just ask them when they were born?"

Essie chuckled cheerfully. "Ah, the sort of question I'd have expected from Absolute Joy and those of her ilk. Yes, of course I could *ask*. And sometimes I do. Then I'd just do a normal reading, based on the given birthday star sign. No problem. It's the magic in the questions — the Five Questions — that forms the link, and stimulates the magic in the answers, which in turn provides me with the formula. I've tried it out many times throughout my lifetime, believe me. Those who have told me their birth dates haven't triggered anything in me. I've been able to give them a normal reading, but not 'see' their suitability to the person of their choice. Those who have answered the Five Questions — well, in every, and I *mean* every case, I've been able to accurately foretell whether they will be happy in love or not. The Happy Birthday magic simply doesn't work without the Five Questions."

Phoebe shook her head. It was all too much for her to take in.

"Now listen, dear, if I said I only married my husband after I'd asked him the Five Questions, what would you say?"

"That you weren't really sure about him."

"Oh, I was. And I was very much in love with him, but I had to be sure he was the right one for me. And I got the answers I needed — the right answers. But if I

146

also told you that I'm now, er, walking out with a gentleman, and I tried the Five Questions on him too. Oh, not because I wanted to marry him, but because he was an ideal subject. And what if I told you that his answers, his birth date and birth number were exactly the same as my husband's. Which, of course, means that he —"

"That he'd make a perfect second husband."

"If I was looking for one — which I'm not. But yes, it proves to me that S — , er, my gentleman friend and I are certainly compatible. And for once, for me, the Happy Birthday magic has thrown up the same match — twice. You see, dear, this is magic, so there are no firm and fast rules."

Phoebe sighed. She so wanted to believe in this — and not just for Essie's sake. Pre-Midsummer's Day and she'd have believed every word of it. Now — well, wasn't it just too far-fetched for words?

Essie stretched. "Look, I'm flattered that you've given me so much of your time. I'd hoped you'd be all for the Happy Birthday magic, but clearly you're not. I'm glad you came to see me, it's been a pleasure to meet you. Of course, I'd appreciate it if you didn't mention our conversation to the Tugwells though. And no doubt your Monday sessions will go down well here anyway with or without the birthdayology. But let me just say one more thing. Is that all right, dear, or do you have to rush off home?"

"No." Phoebe smiled. "I'm in no rush. And there's something else I'd like to talk to you about before I go anyway. But that can wait. Please — what else were you going to say?"

"Just that if you marry — oh, sorry, awful choice of word under the circumstances — all these aspects together, you will always get the right Happy Birthday answer. If you believe what I'm saying — and you quite clearly don't — then that's fine. But is there any way that I can convince you?"

"No, not really. Sorry, but I'm a born-again sceptic."

"Mmm, we'll see," Essie chuckled. "However, just humour me for a little longer — tell me the birth date of your best friend. The slap-happy one."

"May the fifteenth."

"And is she married? Engaged? Courting?"

"Married. Very, very happily. Ecstatically so in fact."

"Right — and if I applied the Five Questions to her and her husband — if I asked you to answer them on their behalf as well as you can . . ."

Phoebe considered. "Yes, all right — I'll do that, although the first one might be a bit tricky. I'll do the best I can. But they're really happy. A perfect couple. No Happy Birthday nonsense will change that. Or my mind for that matter."

"No, of course it won't," Essie chuckled cheerfully. "But let's try. This really only works when the people involved are close by and answering for themselves, so it may well go awry, but to try and prove this to you, let's do the questions anyway. Answer for your friend first and then her husband."

Essie closed her eyes again and asked the questions. Phoebe, wondering just how long she really could go on humouring her, answered as honestly as she could on Clemmie and Guy's behalf.

Eventually, Essie opened her eyes again. "Even if you were a little out on the parental birth years, I calculate that he was born on February the fourteenth."

Phoebe felt a shiver wriggle down her spine. "You can't . . . I mean, it can't work! Not just like that!"

"So it is February the fourteenth is it? Good. A perfect partnership with the answers you gave for your friend. They'll live long and happily and always be madly in love."

"But how . . .?"

"As I've said, a combination of harnessing all the portent powers and a very important touch of Romany magic."

"So, using your formula, would everyone born on a certain day only be suited to another person born on the Happy Birthday corresponding day? Say all August the seconds would only match all December the eighteenths or something?"

Essie frowned. "Lord, dear, you do like to complicate things, don't you? But no — otherwise anyone could do it, couldn't they? You'd just have to memorise the matches and learn it off-rote like a times table, wouldn't you? Or you could just run your finger down a chart? It's not that damn easy! The Five Questions give the answers. The birthdays then present themselves in your head — if you have the gift. Every couple will have different results."

Phoebe nodded. "OK. That makes more sense — I think, but . . ."

149

"However, just to make things a bit more complicated — if I told you that the Five Questions are only the first part of the Happy Birthday magic, that the process is twofold, no doubt you'd be even more sceptical, wouldn't you? You wouldn't even want to hear about stage two of my grandmother's magic. Such a shame."

Phoebe smiled. "Don't mock me. You know I'm interested, fascinated, but this is going against all my newly found anti-astrology principles."

"But you're not averse to a bit of magic, surely? Living round here — everyone knows what Mitzi Blessing does with her herbal cooking, and the entire population of Fiddlesticks relies on the moon and the constellations to organise their lives, and —"

"And my friend Sukie has had some totally inexplicable results with her home-grown aromatherapy recipes and Clemmie made a magical firework, so, yes, mad as it sounds, I might just find Real Magic easier to accept." Phoebe giggled. "Blimey, hark at me. Now I sound almost as cuckoo as —"

"As me, dear? Well, let's find out shall we? Now, you can use the Five Questions to find out if couples are well matched and leave it at that. But if your intention is that they should really get together, then the second part of the Romany magic comes into its own. Do you want me to go on?"

"Oh, don't stop there, please. Honestly, I'm intrigued."

"Right, well, after you've asked the Five Questions and got the birthday dates, if you think the couple want to be together or if one of them believes they should, this is where the — what did you call it? magical astral match-making comes in. All you have to do is get them to hold hands while you chant the Romany spell of Happy Birthday magic and then —"

"No!" Phoebe giggled. "No way! Not the old eye of frog and ear of toad stuff!"

"Not quite anatomically correct, dear, if you don't mind me saying. David Attenborough would have a fit. And no, nothing like that at all. It's very simple." Essie closed her eyes and took a deep breath. "Although I must warn you this must, and I mean must, be used with care — once you're sure that the couple are romantically matched. Once you've used the powerful Romany chant, after the Five Questions, no one can undo the union. No one."

"OK — seriously, Essie. Carry on, please."

Essie's eyes were still closed. Her voice was faraway. "All right, dear. You just say:

"*Happy Birthday chal and chie,*
A misto rommerin will be nigh.
Dukker rokker duw not beng
Misto kooshti rommer and rye."

"It's as easy to learn as a nursery rhyme."

Phoebe tried hard not to laugh. "And that's it? And then they're together for ever — living happily ever after? You just spout Esperanto at them and —"

"It's not Esperanto," Essie said sharply. "It's Romany patois. A magical love chant handed down through the

151

generations. Very, very powerful when used in conjunction with the Five Questions. And believe it or not, Phoebe, it works. Every single time — so definitely not something to be trifled with."

Phoebe's head reeled. Whatever she'd expected to gain from meeting Essie, it certainly wasn't this. And this Happy Birthday magic — *if* it existed outside Essie's imagination and *if* the examples she'd heard weren't simply coincidences — was actually far, far more exciting than any astral experimentation she'd ever experienced.

She felt a tingle of enthusiasm, a frisson of the old passion.

Essie smiled gently. "Oh, look, dear — leaving out my ancestral stuff — let's cut to the chase. What I wanted you to do really was to ask the Five Questions — not the love chant — when you do your Monday sessions here. Not because I think the Happy Birthday magic will be any use at all to any of us in here, but just for a bit of fun. We Twilighters so need livening up. And also because Absolute Joy absolutely banned me from doing it last time. But she'd never know if you were doing it by proxy, would she?"

"Why on earth did she ban it? She seems more than happy for me to indulge in a little bit of harmless fortune-telling, even tarot-reading — so, if she was dead against astrology, surely —"

"Mmm." Essie was trying not to laugh. "But I got a bit carried away and used the whole shebang at one of my sessions. The Five Questions and the Romany chant. Several couples who'd been giving one another

152

the glad eye asked me to try it out on them, so I did. Sadly, Absolute Joy found several of them, er, at it in their roomettes when she came round with the Horlicks."

"*At it?*" Phoebe shrieked with laughter. "What? You mean — old people — really at it?"

"Really. Full X-rated stuff. And old people may be a bit slower in that department than you youngsters, but they still know all the moves, dear. Absolute Joy didn't know where to put her face — or her Horlicks. It caused all manner of ructions, as you can imagine, dear. The couples in question had been permanently Happy Birthday magicked by then and couldn't keep their hands off each other."

Phoebe giggled delightedly. "So what happened to them?"

"Oh, eventually they were found new care homes that provided them with double rooms, and I was warned never ever to dabble again. Which is where you come in. Not to create Sodom and Gomorrah in the residents' lounge of course, but just to spice things up a bit with some of my more, er, interesting methods."

Phoebe was still laughing. "But I can't . . . I mean . . . Oh, look, I may not believe that this secret magic of birthdays works, but just say it does — I don't have Romany blood, or your inborn knowledge. I'm a basic amateur astrologer, how could I make something as, well, downright spooky, as this work?"

"Oh, don't worry about that, I'm pretty sure that you were born with the magic, Phoebe, even if you've never been aware of it. And I'll teach you everything you need

153

to know about how to interpret the answers to the Five Questions and turn them into discovering the Happy Birthdays. What do you say?"

What Phoebe really wanted to say was "thank you", because for the first time since the-wedding-that-never-was she was feeling a fizzle of excitement, a frisson of eagerness about something, anything, again.

It was a revelation.

Essie leaned forwards. "Sleep on it, dear. You don't have to say yes tonight. Oh, but before you go — can I tell you that your perfect partner, your Happy Birthday partner, was born on April the first."

Phoebe laughed. "Yeah, right. Poor sod. He'd have to be an April Fool to get involved with me, wouldn't he? Look, thank you so much for the great supper and for trusting me with all this and I'll certainly think it over. Maybe I could come and see you again when I'm next here for the hairdressing?"

"Yes, yes, do that, dear. That'll be lovely. I'm sure we can work really well together. Oh, didn't you say there was something else you wanted to ask —"

A sharp knock on the door interrupted her.

"Sorry," Essie stood up. "Probably Princess or Lilith or even Bert. They usually pop along here before lights out. Excuse me a moment, dear."

As Essie went to answer the door, Phoebe sat back in the hard chair and smiled to herself. Why shouldn't she do this? It was madness, of course, but such a wonderful daft kind of madness — the sort of insane thing that she really needed to help her move on. A complete change of direction. Something silly and

154

other-worldly. Something that might just take away the dull ache of emptiness and loneliness.

". . . lovely to see you again, of course . . ." Essie's voice echoed from the front door. "And I'm so very pleased that our little plan worked." She laughed. "Really? Did she? Oh, that's wonderful. Look, I do have a visitor but the more the merrier. Why don't you come in, dear, and we'll talk about it a bit more. This way."

Phoebe, who had just decided that her answer to Essie and the Happy Birthday magic was going to be a resounding yes however daft it may be, was halfway to her feet.

Suddenly the beigely utilitarian roomette swirled dizzily around her.

Essie, beaming happily, was ushering Rocky Lancaster through the door.

CHAPTER
ELEVEN

They stared at one another in poleaxed silence. Phoebe, hotly aware of the stare, now desperately wishing she was wearing an authoritarian power suit and a polo neck instead of fairly revealing tight white pedal-pushers and a navel-skimming pink vest, just couldn't believe it.

Rocky? Here? With Essie? The woman he'd — by his own admission — beaten to a pulp.

And poor, trusting "I see good in everyone, dear" Essie was smiling.

All Phoebe's anger surged to the surface, making her want to gibber and stamp her feet with rage and then run and pummel cruel, hateful, twisted, sodding Rocky Lancaster to a pulp.

Realising that this wasn't really a good plan, she simply continued to glare at him. "What the bloody hell are you doing here?"

Rocky shrugged. "I could ask you the same question."

Essie stopped smiling and peered curiously from one to the other. "Do you two know each other?"

Rocky gave a fleeting smile as if it amused him. "Sadly, yes. Although *know* would indicate some sort of

156

intimacy or friendship. Luckily, we don't have either of those. But a passing acquaintanceship, yeah, that just about sums it up."

Phoebe, pretty sure she was going to explode with fury, clenched her fists. "Actually, and unfortunately, we live in the same house, but —" she looked fiercely at Essie "— what on earth is he doing here? Are you mad?"

"Well, since you ask, dear, a little crazy, yes, but not certifiable as far as I know. And what a coincidence, you two living together."

"We don't." Phoebe and Rocky spoke together.

"We live in the same house, but in separate — very separate — flats," Phoebe hissed. "And after what he did, you shouldn't let him come anywhere near you."

"Sorry, dear." Essie frowned. "You've lost me."

"Phoebe thinks she knows exactly what I did," Rocky put in. "She thinks I should have been hung, drawn and quartered — and then been thrown in prison to rot."

Essie shook her head. "Why on earth — ? Oh, Rocky, dear, pull up that other chair."

"Don't you dare sit down!" Phoebe spat at him. "What the hell is going on?"

"Exactly my next question." Essie frowned at Phoebe. "I think you should apologise to Rocky. After all —"

"Apologise? *Apologise?* You must be joking!"

Rocky, ignoring Phoebe, sat easily in the other armchair, sprawling his long legs across the floor, and grinned at Essie. "Phoebe thinks I mugged you. She thinks that's why I went to prison."

Phoebe was astounded by the barefaced cheek of the man. "Well, you did — right on both counts!"

Essie shook her head. "Really, Phoebe, I'm surprised at you. I know we've only just met, dear, but I thought I could recognise more than a glimmer of myself in you when I was your age. But I would never have —" She looked at Rocky. "And you, you wicked boy, you haven't told her, have you?"

"No. Why should I? She'd already played judge and jury and found me guilty. I saw no reason to try to change her mind."

"But you are guilty!" Phoebe snapped. "You know you are! You went to prison! You told me so — everyone has told me so! You can't deny it."

"I don't intend to."

"So, what's this visit for then? Another part of the touchyfeely rehabilitation process? Come and make friends with your victim? Explain that you didn't really mean it? Or is it more sinister? Did you think you'd come back to have another go? See what else you could steal with a bit of violence? I can't believe —"

"Lord, Lord, Lord." Essie smiled from one to the other. "Look, Phoebe, sit down again — no, please, sit down. I think we all need to calm down a little and sort out what's going on here."

Phoebe, still simmering, sat down and glared across the tiny, stiflingly hot room at Rocky. Rocky glared back. Essie looked from one to the other, then smiled.

"Right — peace has temporarily broken out, has it? Good." She settled herself back in her chair. "Now, both of you keep quiet for a moment and I'll do the talking."

Rocky and Phoebe continued to glare.

Damn him, Phoebe thought. Not only is he a spineless, vicious thug, he's one of those awful con-men too. So bloody good-looking, he thinks he can use some sort of charm offensive to worm his way into Essie's good books — make her feel sorry for him — and then go for the kill. Probably literally. Well, I won't let that happen. Someone has to protect her. Poor old soul. And she nearly had me believing all that stuff about Happy Birthday magic, too.

"Rocky went to prison for causing Actual Bodily Harm —" Essie looked across at Phoebe "— but not to me. He didn't touch me. He rescued me. He should have had a medal, not a damn prison sentence."

Phoebe frowned, not making sense of the words. "Sorry? I don't understand —"

"I was mugged by a gang of yobs in Winterbrook, Rocky was passing, heard the commotion and came to my rescue. He chased them, got my handbag back, made sure I was OK, called the ambulance and the police —"

"*What?*"

"True," Essie said quite angrily. "Totally true. The police took descriptions, and yes, the little bastards were all rounded up. Cutting to the chase, they went to court, we all went to court, but they lied and laughed and got away with paltry bloody sentences. *Community service* sentences. Because they were *disadvantaged* according to their solicitors, and the stupid judge

159

bought it hook, line and bloody sinker. Poor little lads — needed my money because they'd been deprived of parental love. Didn't know right from wrong because they came from dysfunctional families. Total bollocks! They're uneducated morons with no morals, no decency and damn all respect. No one —" Essie was even fiercer now "— no one listened to me. Or to Rocky. No one!"

"But why . . .?" Phoebe shook her head, a nasty feeling of having got things very wrong indeed snaking through her veins. "Why did Rocky go to prison if he —?"

"Because," Rocky said quietly, "I was a little, er, heavy-handed in dealing out, um, retribution. After I'd stopped the little bastards and got Essie's bag back — well, my temper got the better of me. To cut a long story mercifully short, one of the scumbags accused me of beating him up — which of course I did, as I cheerfully admitted."

"Nowhere near enough," Essie put in furiously. "Should have bloody killed him. The cheek of the little sod! And some bloody do-gooders who hadn't seen the attack on me, but witnessed Rocky dealing out the much-needed justice, came forward and said Rocky had launched into an unprovoked attack. So the police arrested Rocky then, and the silly CPS brought the case to court and . . . and the second namby-pamby stupid judge fell for it. Said Rocky was older and stronger than his victim. *Victim* — I ask you! Said he had to make an example of someone — that people couldn't just take

160

the law into their own hands, that we couldn't have vigilante action on the streets of Berkshire!"

"But that's mad." Phoebe frowned. "That's not justice."

"Tell us about it," Essie snorted. "Silly old git said that if he didn't make an example of Rocky, then we'd have open warfare in rural England. Dear God! Can you imagine how I felt — Rocky, the man who bravely rescued me from an entire gang of feral louts, being sent to prison, while the little buggers who'd attacked me walked away virtually scot-free."

Phoebe swallowed. Ohmigod, if the judge had got it so terribly wrong, she'd made an even bigger mistake, hadn't she?

"Essie was a great witness at my court case," Rocky laughed. "After I'd been sentenced she yelled at the judge — told him what she thought of him. Told him again what had really happened. Told him he was a doddery old leftie, woolly, blinkered upper-class tit, didn't you, Essie? They nearly locked her up too."

"Prats! Called it contempt! Contempt was only a quarter of what I felt for them. It was a bloody travesty and I told 'em so." Essie looked sharply at Phoebe. "But I'm surprised you didn't know anything about it, dear. With Rocky being your neighbour and all."

"Phoebe had other things on her mind at that time," Rocky put in before she could speak. "A lot going on in her life. Reading boring court case reports in the *Winterbrook Advertiser* possibly wasn't top of her list of exciting things to do. And to be fair, I was away from home so much on flights that she'd probably not even noticed my absence."

Phoebe nodded ruefully. Oh, Lordy.

"And of course, Rocky is only a life-long nickname, so probably a lot of people didn't realise it was me as the court and the newspapers used my real name."

Phoebe nodded again. As she'd thought — no one would be christened Rocky, would they? "What is your real name, then?"

"Doesn't matter."

"Yes it does. I think you owe me that much."

"I don't owe you anything."

"Children!" Essie beamed at them in amusement. "Play nicely. And tell her your name, Rocky. It's lovely."

Rocky glowered. "Avro."

"Avro?" Phoebe wrinkled her nose. "That's even funnier than Rocky."

"Thanks."

"You're too young to make the connection," Essie said cheerfully. "It goes with the surname — Avro Lancaster — one of the truly great planes of the Second World War. Apparently Rocky's parents were plane buffs."

"Anoraks," Rocky muttered. "Met at a plane spotting club. I think I was conceived at Biggin Hill."

"Is that why you became cabin crew?" Phoebe asked innocently. "Was it sort of congenital?"

"No it bloody wasn't! Anyway, we're digressing."

"We are," Essie agreed. "And I don't want you two spitting like cat and dog in my roomette, thank you

162

very much. Where'd we got to? Ah yes, why Phoebe might have not known about our court cases."

Rocky, Phoebe thought, looked seriously peed off at having revealed so much about himself. Hah! Good!

"Why didn't Mindy tell me though?"

"Ah Mindy, dear Mindy." Rocky raised his eyebrows. "Well, she was so ashamed of having a violent jailbird boyfriend that she wouldn't have told a soul, especially those who didn't already know. And you thought — because you must have heard our rows — that I went to prison because I'd beaten her up, didn't you?"

"Well ..." Phoebe felt herself blushing. "Yes, but ..."

"I've never touched her. Never. I'm not at all violent. Before Essie's fracas, I'd never hit anyone in my life — apart from playground scuffles. I wouldn't — couldn't — hit a woman however much I was provoked. And Mindy would have provoked a saint. However, the Airbus pilot isn't Mindy's first, um, extra-curricular activity. That's why we rowed all the time. Mindy's aspirations always lay further up the fuselage. Anything with a joystick — that was Mindy's motto."

Phoebe exhaled. Oooh, dear ...

"But why the hell didn't you tell me? Why did you let me go on —?"

"Because it amused me. You were so high and mighty. But you were scared of me, weren't you? Pretty brave too, mind. You stood up to me even when you thought I might attack you, didn't you? It was quite funny, Phoebe, watching you avoiding me, locking all your doors and windows even in this bloody heatwave, backing away from me every time we came within half a mile of each other."

Oh, God, Phoebe thought bleakly, he *knew*.

"Bad boy," Essie chuckled. "Not funny. Poor Phoebe — she must have been terrified of you."

"You should have told me. Not let me go on making a fool of myself."

"And would you have believed me? No, probably not. You'd already decided that Mindy had left me because I was a thug, hadn't you? Then you found out I'd been in prison, and then someone told you why, and you added two and two together and made it about five hundred."

They sat in silence for a moment. Phoebe knew she'd have to apologise. Oh, God — Elton John was dead right — sorry really was the hardest word.

"Sorry."

"It's OK." Rocky shrugged. "I'm glad you know the truth, I suppose. Although it'll spoil my somewhat twisted fun a bit. But, honestly, it makes no difference, does it?"

But it did, Phoebe thought. It made all the difference in the world. It meant that she'd treated him really, really badly — and it also meant that she could stay in Winchester Road.

"No, I suppose not."

"Good," Essie said, "that's sorted. Right so we're all friends now are we?"

Rocky, Phoebe thought, still looked anything but friendly.

164

Essie stood up. "I'll get us all a nice drink and you can tell Rocky what we've been discussing this evening, Phoebe, if that's OK with you? Rocky and I don't have any secrets."

Phoebe shook her head. What right had she to mind about anything now? "No, that's fine, but I'd better be going anyway, so you can tell him all about it. Obviously you and Rocky have a lot to chat about. Things to catch up on."

"Oh, this isn't my first visit. We see each other often," Rocky said. "Essie has been wonderful. She was the only one to come and visit me in prison — well, apart from some of my friends, of course — and she had to do it while pretending to have doctor or dentist appointments because the damn Tugwells had stopped her going out. I couldn't have survived without her. At a time when none of my family or Mindy came near me, Essie never once let me down. She was — is — a star."

"And now," Essie chuckled from the kitchenette, "I've pulled a few strings and, thanks to Rocky having a brilliant probation officer who actually knows the truth when he hears it, got him a job here too. As a gardener. Did you know he was a gardener, dear? I expect you did — but of course he's had to go self-employed. What with there being so many people looking for jobs given the economic migrant situation, and the majority of those don't have prison records. Rocky's doing OK, but he needs as much work as possible to get his business going."

"That was nice of you — getting him a job."

Essie clattered glasses. "It was the least I could do after everything he'd done for me. I knew the current lot of gardeners here had out-stayed their contract and Absolute Joy and Tiny Tony were looking for someone else — someone cheaper. Bert pinched the tenders for me from the office — he's a sly little devil, could have been another James Bond if his mother had loosened the apron strings a tad. Anyway, with the help of the probation officer and the new rules about the rehabilitation of offenders, Rocky and I cooked up a tender that the Tugwells and the council simply couldn't refuse, and tonight he's just told me they've accepted it."

Phoebe glanced quickly at Rocky. "Congratulations."

"Cheers."

"So," Essie continued happily, "now you're both my protégés, and you'll be seeing loads of each other — both at home and up here — without any of those silly old misunderstandings in the future. Won't that be lovely?"

Phoebe looked at Rocky who stared back at her with a sort of mocking disinterest in his eyes.

"Er, yes," Phoebe said faintly. "Lovely."

CHAPTER
TWELVE

". . . so, it's all worked out well then, duck?" Slo peered at Essie across one of the tables in Patsy's Pantry during morning coffee. "With young Rocky and now little Phoebe? I do like her, such a nice girl. She lives near me — I told her we all wanted'er to stay in Winchester Road after that silly bugger stood her up at the altar. I'm so glad it's all coming on lovely for both of 'em. And I'm so glad you've told me everything about your own problems, too."

Essie smiled. "Well, you know what they say? A trouble shared and all that. Thanks for listening and for your support. One day I'll really stop being scared of harsh voices and crowds of young men. Anyway, yes, everything else is coming on wonderfully. Rocky has Twilights on his rota of regular jobs — with more lined up — so he'll be OK. And Phoebe has more hairdressing and astrology appointments up there than she knows what to do with."

Phoebe, Essie thought, still had absolutely no idea about the talents she had, or what she could do with them, but she'd proved an attentive and willing pupil in the three sessions they'd spent together in the week since the Happy Birthday magic was first mooted.

Gone was Phoebe's early scepticism, and now, Essie thought happily, she was simply itching to get on with it.

"Sorry this will have to be so brief, duck." Slo mopped the cappuccino froth from his mouth with his handkerchief. "We've got a burial at midday."

"I think you're very brave — being seen with me in Hassocks, in the High Street, in broad daylight."

"Actually, our Constance and Perpetua think I'm checking on the last of the floral tributes for today's interment. If anyone says anything I'll just say we bumped into each other by accident and I was, er, well, I'll think of summat."

Essie smiled. "I'm sure you will. As you know, I'm supposed to be at the doctor's again — goodness knows what Tiny Tony and Absolute Joy think is wrong with me but I'm sure they reckon it's terminal the number of appointments I've had in the last few weeks."

"Right old pair of Romeo and Juliets ain't we?" Slo chuckled. "Well, not — I don't mean —"

"I know what you mean," Essie said soothingly, finishing her cappuccino. "And I find all this secrecy rather exciting. In fact, I'd find anything a bit different exciting."

"Which is why you've taken young Rocky and Phoebe under your wing, isn't it, duck? Well, I reckons that, and the fact that they're probably much, much nicer than your own children."

"Perceptive," Essie chuckled. "And probably right. But my children are far from children now. They're both heading towards pension age. Doesn't seem

168

possible, but there you go. Anyway, I mustn't keep you. I don't want your cousins on my back."

"No more you don't!" Slo said with a shudder. "They'd make a right beggar's banquet out of us being together, even as just good friends, I can tell you. It's not you personally, duck, it's business. The funeral business. As I keeps telling 'em, it'll die out with us, being as none of us 'as 'ad kiddies, but for now it's our Connie and Perpetua's lifeblood. Constance in the main, she's determined it's ours and ours alone as it allus 'as been. I've often said we should bring in youngsters to take over when we've gorn. But she won't 'ear of it. She won't have it as anything but Motions. No new blood. She's allus warned me and our Perpetua about making 'friends' if you gets my drift. She thinks that anyone coming in from outside will take away what she 'olds most dear."

"You? Or the business?"

"The business, duck. I'm sorry, Essie, but she'd just see you as a gold-digger."

Essie chuckled. "Well, that's a new one on me. I've never been accused of that before."

"Look, duck, it's not that I'm ashamed that we're chums, far from it, but —"

"It's OK." Essie stood up. "No, my turn to pay — and no need to apologise. I do understand what it's like to be watched like a hawk and have to explain my every move. And I'd hate to cause a family rift for you; I know only too well how awful that is. You go on and do your burial — and I'll make my way back to Twilights."

"Not on your own, duck. I ain't having that!"

"No, no, it's fine. I've got to pop into Pauline's Cut'n'Curl to pass a message on to Phoebe, then I'm meeting Rocky and he's giving me a lift back up to Cell Block H. It's one of his mornings. Thanks again, Slo, I've really enjoyed this."

"No more than I'ave and that's a fact. I'll see you again soon, duck, won't I?"

"Of course." Essie fiddled in her handbag for her purse. "We'll use the usual channels — one of your official visits up to Twilights coinciding with me needing a lift into the village. I love doing that! Absolute Joy would have a fit if she thought I'd hoodwinked her."

"Oh gawd!" Slo glanced through the Pantry's frilly-curtained window. "Our Perpetua! She's heading off towards Big Sava — if I nips out now she might not see me. Look, duck, I'll have to skedaddle. If we went all new millennium and got ourselves fixed up with them mobile phone thingamabobs, we wouldn't 'ave to go through all this palaver, would we? Bye, duck."

Laughing, Essie waved goodbye as Slo flew out of the door and disappeared up Hazy Hassocks High Street in the opposite direction to Perpetua.

"And that ain't seemly," Patsy huffed as she took Essie's money for two cappuccinos and toast. "An undertaker running out of here like the hounds of hell were on his heels. An undertaker should carry himself with decorum at all times. Especially when the temperature's already getting into the nineties. I wish this bloody heatwave would end — it's playing havoc with my iced fancies."

Essie, feeling there really wasn't much she could add to this tirade, accepted her change and smiled non-committally.

Right, first Phoebe, then Rocky. Slo, she thought, as she walked out into the solid wall of stifling heat in the High Street, was right. Phoebe and Rocky were exactly like the children she wished she'd produced. And they were both unhappy and confused and lost, and it was so *nice* to be able to do something to help them. And by helping them she was helping herself from dying of boredom.

With a smile of satisfaction, she headed towards Pauline's Cut'n'Curl.

". . . so, I'm now going to be a regular feature on two fronts," Phoebe shouted — three fans whirring in an attempt to cool the salon's sub-tropical temperature had the effect of a Concorde fly-past — to Pauline as she fastened the final pin curl into the thinning hair of Doreen, a slightly batty pensioner known for loud and inappropriate outbursts, on her regular cheap-day special. "Mind you, I'm still not sure about the astrology . . ."

She stopped. She wasn't sure about the straight astrology, true, but oddly she was becoming more and more convinced about the Happy Birthday magic. The accompanying patois Romany chant was something else though. Phoebe hadn't yet managed to get through all four lines without dissolving into giggles.

Still, the three further training sessions with Essie had convinced her that there might, just might, be

171

something to it. And Essie had also nearly managed to convince her that she had some sort of latent gift for using the secret magic of birthdays.

It had given her more of a boost than she'd ever believed possible.

"Well, it all sounds right interesting, anyway," Pauline yelled over the hand-dryer and fans as she attempted to straighten a bad home perm. "And lovely for us that you've got regular hairdressing appointments up Twilights. All those older ladies wanting colours — fabulous."

"Yes, well, after I did Princess, a lot of them decided to try it. Mind you, as most of them already have bubble perms, green and red streaks make them look like they're wearing acrylic fright wigs."

"Perms is making a big comeback. Everyone's going to look like early Kevin Keegans again afore long, you mark my words. Anyway, the Twilights money's good for both of us, and your extra-curriculars up there has put a smile back on your face. Oooh, sorry Mrs Wiseman — did that tug a little?"

Phoebe popped the hairnet over Doreen and led her to the trio of hood dryers which Pauline still hung on to knowing that the elderly ladies of Hazy Hassocks and surrounding villages didn't consider they been "done right" if they didn't get an ear-searing burst of heat from a "proper dryer — not one of them damn blower things".

Life certainly had been peculiar since she'd met Essie, Phoebe thought. Nice peculiar, but definitely odd. She reckoned Essie really might have some sort of

Romany powers. All she needed now was a suitable candidate or three to practise the Happy Birthday magic on and —

"Phoebes!" YaYa, dressed in a spectacularly short orange broderie anglaise sundress and sensationally high orange sandals, popped her head into Cut'n'Curl. "Morning, ladies. Pauline, I've just got to check something out with Phoebe. Is it OK if I . . .?"

Pauline nodded her head in the direction of the hood dryers.

"Don't tell me you've come to have a nice wash and set?" Phoebe smiled, handing the control to Doreen who promptly dropped it into her handbag. Scrabbling amongst the tissues, bus tokens and indigestion tablets, Phoebe retrieved it. "There you go, Doreen. Try to keep a grip on it, won't you? And don't play with it. I wouldn't want you to singe." She turned to YaYa. "I thought you and your wigs always went to London?"

YaYa patted her current style of choice, a burnished raven bob. "We do. I'm strictly a Toni and Guy girl. Wouldn't be seen dead in a place like this — no offence meant."

"Loads taken." Phoebe grinned. "And — oh, God, it's not Clemmie, is it? Not something wrong with the baby?"

"Nooo. The divine Mrs D. is still shovelling back the olives and blooming beautifully. No, it was just I was passing — actually on an olive mission to Big Sava, they're having to order them in by the pantechnicon load — and I wondered if you'd got anything firmed up for us to do a turn at the geriatrics place?"

"Twilights!" Phoebe put in quickly. "And no, I haven't, not yet. Why?"

"Oh, I'm off to do a couple of Dancing Queen gigs at the end of the week and I'd like to let the girls know if there's anything written in stone that's all. Martinique likes to get everything down in the diary soon as poss."

"I'm going up to Twilights again tomorrow. I'll ask what they've decided and give you a ring. It'll have to be decent though — nothing raunchy."

"I know, love, you've said often enough. You are getting sooo boring. So, how are things, generally?"

"Not bad. Better. Sorry, YaYa, but I can't stop and gossip now, we're really busy."

"I can see that." YaYa pulled a face as she glanced round the salon's mostly elderly clientele. "I can also see that for the first time you've got a bit of colour in your cheeks and your eyes don't look like you've been crying all night."

Phoebe just smiled.

"Oooh, and," YaYa said suddenly, "my head! I knew there was something else. Clem and Guy want to know what you want to do for your birthday. I know there's plenty of time, but we'll be into September before you know it and we do want to get something organised. So what do you fancy?"

"Nothing," Phoebe said, wincing at the silly twinge of pain under her ribs. "It'll be my first birthday for sixteen years without B. — well, on my own. I'd rather just forget it."

174

"No can do, love." YaYa winked. "We'll have to find something really, really special — a huge celly of some sort."

"Seriously, YaYa. I mean it. If I do anything at all, I'll probably just spend the evening with my parents. I'll admit I'm feeling a little bit more able to cope, but I don't look forward. I just take one day at a time. I can't even think about my birthday."

YaYa hugged her. A lot of make-up was exchanged.

"Whatever, love, but don't shoot the messenger or mess with her St Tropez. I'll expect a call from you later about the oldies show then. Be good, Phoebes. Have fun. Tarrah."

"She's a pretty girl!" Doreen roared from beneath the dryer as YaYa sashayed into the High Street. "Looks a lot like I did when I was a youngster!"

The door opened again and Essie peered round the salon and waved at Phoebe. Phoebe waved back.

"Excuse me —" Essie smiled at Pauline "— but is Phoebe available for a moment?"

"Yes," Pauline said with a mock sigh, "but clearly what she needs is an appointments secretary. She has more social life in here that I gets at the WI. Go on — have a quick chat before we start on our next tint."

Phoebe ushered Essie back towards the relative privacy of the hood dryers and Doreen. "Lovely to see you. I wasn't expecting to. I thought you weren't allowed out without an armed guard?"

"Um, Mr Motion gave me a lift into the village."

"Did he? That's nice of him. He's lovely — he lives near me. He's been very kind to me since . . . But how are you getting home? Do you want to hang on and I'll give you a lift?"

"No, dear, thank you. It's very sweet of you to offer but Rocky's taking me back. Absolute Joy couldn't object to this little jaunt, you see. Under escort for the entire time. I just wanted to pass on a little snippet of information before you next come up to Twilights so that you can make plans. Forewarned and all that."

"Ooh, has Lilith run off with Bert? Has Tiny Tony garrotted Absolute Joy with the strap of her voluminous handbag? Has —?"

"They're resurrecting the August bank holiday fête."

"Oh." Phoebe was rather disappointed. "And is that, um, good news?"

"You bet it is," Essie said fervently. "When you're an incarcerated Twilighter with nothing but boring, boring routines to look forward to, the prospect of an entire day with the place being filled with strangers and bustling with life is like, well, like finding a unicorn dancing on a rainbow just for you."

Phoebe smiled at the image. "Sounds lovely then. But how does it involve me?"

"Because Tiny Tony and Absolute Joy want you to man one of the stalls."

Oooh, Lordy. Awful memories of school fêtes and village jamborees, with terrible white elephant rubbish or whiffy jumble or tombola stalls piled with out-of-date home-made jam, filled Phoebe with a sense of déjà vu. There'd be heaps of other people's tat and hordes of villagers from every corner of rural Berkshire all scrambling to buy someone's cast-off vest at a

176

knock-down price. And then there'd be the Brownies dancing badly to an accordion, and being constantly forced to guess the weight of the cake and the name of the teddy bear and how many beans in the Kilner jar and . . .

"You're going to be our fortune-teller," Essie said triumphantly. "Won't that be fun?"

"Oh, um, yes, I suppose so. No, it will be. But, *real* fortune-telling or —?"

"Just the stuff you do normally. As OTT as you like. You know all about star sign predictions and you've picked up plenty about numerology. We could get a crystal ball or use tarots if you want. Anything. But definitely not the full Happy Birthday stuff."

"Happy Birthday to yooo! Happy Birthday to yooo . . . la-la-la!" Doreen bellowed tunelessly from under the dryer.

Cut'n'Curl stared at her in some surprise. Mrs Wiseman, her bad perm now straightened to resemble thatch, clapped.

"Ignore them," Phoebe hissed at Essie, then she glanced at Doreen. "Don't play with the controls, please. Keep it on medium."

"Punch-up at a successful séance," Doreen yelled. "Striking a happy medium."

Phoebe raised her eyebrows at Essie. "So, the fête — is this an official engagement?"

"Yes, dear. A definite. The council have agreed to stump up some funds — mainly to advertise Twilights, of course, which will bring in even more money — and they want this to be the biggest attraction for miles around. So, as well as the usual fêtey stuff, and our own efforts, and pony rides for the kiddies and a fancy-dress competition for all and getting a celebrity for the opening ceremony, the Terrible Tugwells have also agreed to let your friends do a show — the cancan ones and the bit of a cabaret that you mentioned. Won't that be wonderful?"

"Fantastic."

"So glad you're pleased, dear. I hoped you would be. When Absolute Joy and Tiny Tony told us the news last night we were all thrilled to ribbons and started making plans right away. Let's hope the weather holds, eh?"

There were far more worrying things to think about than the weather, Phoebe thought. Like YaYa and her friends, Campari, Foxy, Cinnamon and all the outrageous others, misinterpreting the nature of the booking and the age of their audience; like Bagley-cum-Russet's mainly middle-aged cancan troupe stumbling and creaking and falling off the stage; like her own fortune-telling thing reminding her of everything she'd lost . . .

"Phoebe!" Pauline yelled down the salon. "Sorry to interrupt you but I've mixed Mrs Newlove's titian. It'll be as hard as a blessed cowpat if we don't get a shift on."

"Right. Just coming." Phoebe smiled at Essie. "I'll see you tomorrow evening."

"You will. I'll just go and wait outside under the awning. Rocky's collecting me from here. How are you and he getting on now, dear? Hostilities ceased?"

178

Phoebe nodded. "Although I haven't seen much of him to be honest. We're both busy — mainly thanks to you — but yes, I've apologised again, and we're very polite to one another when we meet on the stairs."

To tell the truth, Phoebe thought, she dreaded having to have any sort of one-to-one with Rocky now. She felt, despite the fact that he'd made no attempt to put her straight, that she really shouldn't have leaped to the conclusions she had about him. It made her squirm with embarrassment just to think about it. Still, at least she no longer had to swelter in her bedroom at night. It was bliss to have the French doors open and drift off to sleep aided by a waft of honeysuckle and a cooling breeze.

"Good. That's nice," Essie said. "He's had a very rough deal. I'm glad you and he have buried the hatchet. Right then, dear, I'll let you get on."

Pauline was jerking her head in an agitated manner. The titian colour was no doubt setting like quick-drying cement.

"Just coming." Phoebe nodded at Pauline, shepherding Essie away from the hood dryers. "Bye, Essie."

"Goodby-ee, goodby-ee, baby dear, wipe the —" Doreen trumpeted.

"Leave the damn controls alone!" Phoebe almost broke into a run away from the hood dryers.

Then she stopped.

"Oh!"

The door opened again and Rocky stepped cautiously inside.

179

He looked, Phoebe thought, way, way out of his comfort zone.

He also looked completely gorgeous in his faded jeans and black T-shirt.

All the youthful Cut'n'Curl girls and the elderly customers perked up as one.

"Er, good morning." He looked at Pauline. "Is it OK if I —?"

"You wants Phoebe, no doubt." Pauline narrowed her eyes. "Every damn man and his dog wants Phoebe this morning. Mind you —"

Phoebe, suddenly realising that Pauline had been the one to add two and two together and come up with five hundred and equate Rocky with an axe murderer, dived across the salon.

"He's come to collect Essie. Mrs Rivers. That's all."

"Hrmph," Pauline snorted. "I'm not so sure that —"

Fortunately Essie had followed Phoebe towards the door and she, unaware of Pauline's bristling, was beaming at Rocky. "All ready to go, dear. This is very kind of you."

"My pleasure." Rocky still looked edgy. "Hi, Phoebe. Working your magic?"

Essie chuckled.

"What have you told him?" Phoebe hissed.

"Oh, just what he needed to know." Essie's eyes glinted with mischief. "You did say I could tell him whatever I liked. So I did. Well, glad you're happy about the fête, dear, and I'll be seeing you soon. Goodbye."

Rocky, still grinning, held the door open for Essie, then, without a backwards glance at Phoebe, left.

180

"I do hope you and he aren't getting too friendly," Pauline grizzled, briskly beating the titian rinse with a tail comb like a demented Delia Smith. "You knows he's been in prison — and what he did."

"We're not getting remotely friendly. I do know he's been in prison, yes, but it wasn't for anything like what you said it was. It was —"

"Sweet Baby Jesus!" Doreen screamed from the far end of the salon. "Me ears is on fire!"

CHAPTER
THIRTEEN

It was blissfully, fragrantly shady in the courtyard that evening, and the Kennet burbled soothingly on its invisible path behind the walled gardens of Winchester Road. After the manic day at Cut'n'Curl, Phoebe had scrubbed off her make-up, had a long, cool shower, pulled on a baggy cotton shirt over her underwear, slicked back her hair and eaten a Big Sava ready-made cheese salad straight from the carton.

Now, outside, with a large glass of iced Chardonnay, the remainder of the condensation-encrusted bottle and her favourite notebook, Phoebe was refreshed, relaxed and ready to organise the rest of her week. She'd plan one day at a time as she'd told YaYa. That way she could cope.

Making lists wasn't anal, she thought, as she scribbled quickly across the pristine page. Making lists was sensible and organised. And she was a Virgoan perfectionist, wasn't she? It was the natural thing for her to do.

Of course if she *were* to look ahead, then the August bank holiday fête at Twilights would have to have a page or two all of its own, wouldn't it? And it would be sensible to start making notes now, wouldn't it?

Nodding to herself, she turned to a fresh double page and carefully wrote "BHF/Twilights" at the top and neatly underlined it. There! Now she should have several columns and suitable headings . . .

Oooh, there were lots of plans to be made for the fête — such as should she just stick to basic astrology, or risk adding tarots? She sucked the end of her pen, doodled a bit, then scribbled some more. It amused her to realise that her doodles were all on the secret birthday magic theme. She'd scrawled Happy Birthday in various fonts, and had even written out several versions of Essie's bizarre Romany chant.

Smiling to herself at the hold this birthday magic had on her subconscious, she knew that what she really needed was a suitable guinea pig or two. What was the point of an experiment without having had a practice run? She could be intrigued all she liked, and be impressed by Essie's examples, but until she actually saw the magic work for herself, there was no way she'd really, really believe it.

If only all her girlfriends weren't already happily coupled-up. In the last few days, she'd tried the Five Questions formula out in a distant way by using the dates of every couple she knew — even her parents — and it had worked every time, producing accurate birthday dates. But as for the rest — the real matchmaking acid test of the Happy Birthday magic — unless she had a real couple of would-be lovers to try it out on, she'd still have that niggling doubt. She'd have to keep a very close eye out for likely candidates, wouldn't she?

Sipping her wine, she returned to the bank holiday fête page. And carefully drew another column. Good. Now, should she go the whole hog and borrow a crystal ball from somewhere? Should she?

The lazy, languid evening silence was suddenly shattered by a blast of Rainbow's "Since You've Been Gone".

"Bloody hell!" Phoebe craned her neck upwards. Rocky's balcony door was wide open. "Oy!" she yelled. "Rocky! Too loud!"

"What?" Rocky leaned over the balcony. "Sorry. Can't hear you. Let me just turn this music down." He disappeared for a second. "Right, that's better. Sorry, what did you say?"

"I said it was too loud."

"Is it? I can hardly hear it."

"Not now. Before —" Just in time Phoebe realised Rocky was laughing. "Oh, very funny. Just keep it down, please."

"OK." And he disappeared inside again.

Holding her breath, Phoebe waited for another ear-shattering bombardment but none came. She smiled to herself. Rocky Lancaster was becoming almost house-trained.

She resumed her lists.

"Excuse me," Rocky stage-whispered from above her head. "Can I ask you a question?"

Phoebe laid down her pen and nodded.

"Is the garden still out of bounds or would it be OK if me and my couple of bottles of Bud shared it with you?"

Phoebe sighed. She couldn't say no, could she? It *was* his garden to share and, after all, he'd done a fantastic job of lopping, trimming and honing it into shape. The fact that she really didn't want to spend any time alone with him because she felt so guilty about their misunderstandings was beside the point.

"It's just as much your garden as mine, but I'd prefer it if you keep the music down and don't talk to me."

"Blimey, you sound like my mum. Nag for England could my mum. Not any more of course. She doesn't speak to me at all any more." He started to clatter down the metal stairs. "But you're OK on both counts. Music isn't worth listening to unless it blows the pictures off the wall and I don't want to talk to you. I just want to sit in the garden and hope it's a damn sight cooler than the flat."

Phoebe moved her notebook and wine closer towards her as he flopped into the opposite wrought-iron chair. Try as she might, concentrating on her must-do lists was nigh on impossible. Well, with six foot plus of undeniably beautiful male, albeit a totally disinterested one, in close proximity, it was enough to unsettle any girl. Even one who was sworn off men for life.

"Is it work?" Rocky asked after about five minutes, staring hard at her notebook. "No, sorry, don't want to interrupt you."

"No, it isn't work. I'm trying to get organised for the next few days. Juggling my time at the salon and the stuff at Twilights and meeting up with my friends. You know — it's all part of my anal retentiveness. Something you seemed to know a lot about."

"Only from Mindy." Rocky nodded. "And she turned out to be about as unreliable as a long-range weather forecaster. You carry on."

Phoebe chewed the end of her pen and tried to focus her attention. Somehow she'd lost her momentum.

Rocky swigged his beer. "We're handling our life changes in totally different ways, aren't we? You're still sticking to being organised, whereas I'm just going with the flow. Wonder what a psychiatrist would make of it?"

"They'd probably spend weeks or months or years and charge a fortune discovering that I'm clinically obsessive and you're not."

As Rocky simply laughed at that, and then leaned back in his chair, staring at the never-ending blue sky dappled through the fragrant foliage, Phoebe wrote another heading on a fresh page.

Rocky stopped staring at the sky and, peering across the table, studied her notebook. "Does that say 'TOAT'? Is that dyslexic toast?"

"It stands for Taking Out A Twilighter."

"Ah, right." Rocky pondered, then he frowned at her. "You mean, like a *hit man*?"

Phoebe sniffed. "Not remotely funny."

"Sorry, so you mean, like finding someone who'd be willing to take them to the pub or the cinema or out for a walk or to football or shopping?"

"Exactly like that. In fact —" Phoebe flicked through her notebook "— I've made a few notes here . . ."

"I bet you have, but before you tell me about TOAT and your plans to release all the Twilighters into the wild, can I ask you something else?"

Phoebe nodded. They lived in the same house. They may as well speak to one another. It had been very civilised so far, although it amused her that Rocky was the one who'd said he didn't want to talk to her. Maybe, she thought, he was just as lonely as she was; just as lost in an empty flat; just as in need of a friendly human voice at the end of a hot, tiring day.

"Why do you use a notebook and pen for all your lists? Why not a laptop computer or your mobile phone or some other little electronic organiser gizmo? I'd have thought someone as controlled as you would have had everything sorted at the flick of a button."

Phoebe considered for a moment. She wasn't sure she entirely liked the word controlled. "I've tried all that. It doesn't work for me. I suppose it's because I've always physically written things down since I was a child. Years of habit. Unless I'm writing it down it doesn't feel right."

"Yeah, I think I can understand that. I always put my right sock on before my left one. Most people do it the other way round. If I try to force myself to do it in the properly perceived order it feels weird and I'm uncomfortable all day."

"I didn't know that." Phoebe smiled. "So you're closet-OCD as well, then?"

"No way! I just thought I'd share my one little foible with you as a gesture of conciliation."

"Thanks."

"You're welcome."

Now or never, Phoebe thought. "Actually, I suppose you've just given me the perfect opportunity to apologise to you properly."

"No need. We've already sorted that out, haven't we? I was as much to blame — I should have stopped behaving like a prat and told you the truth. Although —" he glanced at her across the table "— it *was* quite amusing, wasn't it?"

"No. But I am sorry. Honestly."

He smiled and said nothing. At least for several minutes. Then he raised his beer bottle again. "What are you planning? Whoops, sorry. Forgot we weren't supposed to talk. Ignore me and carry on writing. I promise not to read it."

As Winchester Road simmered in the heavy evening heat, Phoebe tried. She really tried. She filled in her Twilights appointments, both hairdressing and astrology, made time for meeting up with Clemmie, Amber and Sukie, pencilled in a Sunday visit to her parents, wrote a reminder to herself to let YaYa know about the bank holiday fête and tried to forget that Rocky was even there.

It didn't work.

Rocky, flipping the top off his second bottle of beer, glanced across at her notebook. "Oh, are you studying a foreign language as well? I'm — thanks to a reasonable education and the airline job — pretty OK with most of the European languages, but I don't recognise that one. Although, of course, it's upside down, but even so . . ."

"What? Oh, that, um, it's Romany." Phoebe fought the urge to shield her book with her arms like she had at school. "Well, Romany patois apparently. It's, er, something of Essie's."

"To do with your magic fortune-telling stuff? Right. Yes, I know about all that — not that I understand or believe any of it. She told me about you being a bit of a Russell Grant on the quiet and how the two of you are cooking up some new magical crystal ball stunt. Sounded really interesting, if a bit new-age hippy for a pedant like me. I'm glad you've, well, found something to get into."

"After being jilted, you mean?"

"Well, if you want to be brutal, yes. It's like me and the gardening, I suppose. I wouldn't have known a spade from a hoe before . . ." He stopped. "Do you think Essie was sent to sort out our lives in some way?"

"Like a guardian angel?"

"No, not quite that airy-fairy. I might go along with the gypsy fortune-telling stuff — after all, loads of people swear by it — but I do not believe in angels. No, I mean, like fate. You've admitted that she's made a difference to you and, having had loads of time to think about it when I was in prison, I know that meeting Essie was the catalyst I needed to move my life in a different direction."

"Some catalyst." Phoebe frowned. "If you hadn't met Essie as you did, then you wouldn't have gone to prison and —"

"You have to take the rough with the smooth as my mum always says in her merry clichéd way," Rocky laughed. "And yeah, OK, maybe it was pretty drastic, but before Essie I was unhappy with Mindy, getting bored with my job, couldn't see any way out — and now, I'm my own boss and I sleep well at night and just take each day as it comes along."

Phoebe, still surprised that he hadn't mocked the magical astrology concept, nodded. "She's wonderful, and, yes, you're right, meeting her has changed my life as well. Have you any idea why she's living in Twilights?"

"No, I suppose she had to leave her home for some reason or another. I've never asked and she's never told me."

Phoebe poured another glass of wine. The sky over the tops of the trees was streaked with lilac and gold and pink. "And don't you have any regrets about, well, about what happened?"

"For Essie, yes." Rocky squinted at the sky through his beer bottle. "She should never have had to go through anything like that. No one should. But not for me. I *hated* prison. I was scared most of the time — really scared — and it was truly foul. And afterwards, losing my job, and Mindy's reaction, and my parents cutting me dead and a lot of my friends doing the same . . . But no, I don't regret thumping the yob that hurt and terrified Essie. I never will regret that. He deserved it. And whatever the judge may have thought, we were well matched in size and muscle, and he was far more used to punch-ups than I was." He looked across the table. "Honestly, I've never been a fighter. Ever. Didn't know I had it in me. It was just an instinctive reaction. I was just so angry at what he'd done to her, and the fact that he was jeering and laughing and . . .'"

Phoebe swallowed. She couldn't even begin to imagine what hell Rocky had been through. "Look, I know you probably don't ever want to talk about prison, but if you do, if it would help, I'm a good listener."

"Thanks. That's really kind, and I might take you up on it — one day. At the moment it's easier not to even think about it, and no one I know really wants to discuss it, so I sort of pretend it happened to someone else."

"I know you said your parents have chosen not to have anything to do with you, which I think is pretty disgusting of them actually, but surely your friends understand?"

"The proper ones, yes — another mother cliché coming up — you really do find out who your friends are when things like that happen, don't you?"

"Yes, mine were, and still are, amazing after, well, after the wedding . . ."

"You see —" Rocky smiled gently "— you've been through something just as crappy as me. And you've survived. And you don't cry any more, do you?"

"*What?*"

"Well, you probably do . . . but I used to hear you crying at night, every night, and it ripped me apart." Rocky sighed. "God, listen to me. All we need now is a blast of Joy Division or Morrissey and we'll be fighting one another for the sleeping tablets and a bottle of whisky. Shall we change the subject to, um, oh, go on then, tell me about TOATs."

Slightly wrong-footed knowing that Rocky had heard her heart breaking, Phoebe flicked through the pages of the notebook as a delaying tactic while she composed herself.

"Right, OK — well, I hate the way poor Essie is stuck in Twilights like a, er, prisoner. She's lovely and lively and fit and should be able to live her own life. And so should great people like Lilith and Princess and loads of the others. You know they're not allowed out on their own? And they sit there all day with the telly blaring and the horrible Tugwells dictating their every move. And I think Essie has a bloke she's sweet on — a gentleman friend as she calls him — but I don't think it's another Twilighter, so how is she supposed to get to see him?"

"No idea." Rocky raised his eyebrows. "I hadn't really thought about it, any of it."

"Think about it now. How would you feel if, when you get to seventy or eighty or ninety, you just get shoved away into a home? Because, as far as society is concerned, you've served your useful purpose. Oh, I'm not talking about those who need to be there because they can't look after themselves, or those who are happy there because they enjoy the company. I'm thinking of people like Essie who could have another twenty years of happy life, not pushed into one of those bland rabbit hutches and —"

"OK. Yes, having been in one prison I'd hate to think I'd spend the rest of my life in another. But what can we do? You can't just start rehoming them, Phoebe. They're not like kittens. You can't just get people to pop up to Twilights with a mixed pack of Whiskas and a litter tray and pick the prettiest one."

Phoebe giggled. "I was actually thinking more along the lines of drawing up a rota of interested people that we know, who might or might not have something in common with a particular Twilighter, and just take them out for a while to amuse them or relieve the tedium or, well, anything."

"Nice idea, but would the Tugwells agree? And the council? There's probably some European statute that forbids elderly people being taken out by strangers."

"Well, they wouldn't be strangers," Phoebe insisted, "would they? We could get a scheme going whereby they had introductory get-togethers at Twilights first or something. Oh, I don't know. I just want to help."

"And what does Essie think of this plan?"

"She doesn't know. I'll mention it to her — see what she thinks — before I say anything to Absolute Joy and Tiny Tony, then maybe we could compare notes on dragging in all our mates as escorts. Anyway, what have they got you roped in for at the fête?"

Rocky pulled a face. "White elephant."

"Lucky you!" Phoebe laughed. "The short straw with knobs on. Couldn't you have said no?"

"Doubt it." Rocky stretched lazily. "Anyway, I'd actually do anything for Essie."

"Me too. I'm doing fortune-telling — don't laugh."

"Wouldn't dream of it." Rocky scraped back his chair and stood up.

Phoebe felt a surprising moment of sadness that he was going. She'd enjoyed talking to him. Really enjoyed it. Strange, she thought, he was probably one of the very few men she'd actually ever talked to for any length of time as a friend. It had always been Ben. All her life it had been Ben.

"I'm going to get another beer," Rocky said. "Those didn't even touch the sides really. It's still so damn hot. Would you like one?"

"No thanks," Phoebe said, idiotically delighted that he'd be coming back, "I've still got some wine left although I need more ice cubes. Oh — is that your door bell or mine?"

"Yours." Rocky paused halfway up the outside stairs. "If you've got visitors I'll stay up in my flat."

"No — I mean, there's no need. I'm not expecting anyone. Go and get your beer, I'll drag out some crisps and peanuts, shall I?"

"Fantastic," Rocky shouted back as he disappeared across his balcony. "I love a woman who can rustle up a tasty snack."

Smiling ridiculously, Phoebe padded inside and opened the front door.

"Hi, and don't you look, um, basic." Clemmie grinned. "No hair, no slap — any clothes at all under that shirt?"

Oooh . . . Phoebe groaned. She'd spent ages and ages chatting to Rocky looking like a damn down-and-out. Not, she thought quickly, that it mattered, but . . .

"Lovely to see you, too." She grinned at Clemmie. "Are you coming in?"

194

"Briefly, if that's OK. I was just passing." Clemmie swept into the flat, her long multicoloured ethnic frock flowing. "I've been to the late antenatal appointment at the Dovecote Surgery. I love going back there — having worked there on reception I get treated like royalty."

"I thought they couldn't wait to get rid of you?"

"They soon realised their mistake," Clemmie said airily. "They'd have me back like a shot, if I was available, which —" she patted her belly "— I'm not and never going to be."

"I'm sitting in the garden." Phoebe rattled around in the kitchen for ice cubes, crisps and peanuts. "Would you like a tonic water? Ice and lemon?"

"And olives?" Clemmie said eagerly. "You have got olives, haven't you?"

"Naturally. Not that I'll ever touch them. Here, have them from the jar, one green, one black and a cocktail stick."

"Great, thanks Phoebes." Clemmie clutched everything, continued her swishy flowing trail out of the French doors and settled herself down at the table. "Oooh, your fave notebook. What are you planning now? Can I look?"

"Nothing and no." Phoebe dumped the ice bucket, crisps and peanuts on the table. "Just doing a bit of organising — although you've saved me a phone call because Twilights are having a fête on August bank holiday, and they'd like a firework display. Oh, and you can tell YaYa that they definitely want her to do a cabaret number or two, as well."

"Crikey." Clemmie pulled a face. "Brave of them."

"I've told her to keep it clean."

"Hah, some hope." Clemmie speared several olives at once and chewed with obvious delight. "Oh, wow, great, thanks. Guy'll be happy to do a lovely display for the oldies. I'll tell him to make sure he keeps the date free — even if he's already got something else on he can leave that to Syd and the rest of the pyro crew so that he can be at Twilights. He'd do anything for you, you know that. Sooo, everything going well with your new venture, is it?"

"Great, thanks. I'm loving it. It takes my mind off everything else. The Twilighters are far worse off than I am — honestly. And they enjoy all the astrology stuff and having their hair done and everything. To be honest they just like to see a different face and have someone to talk to. Which is something else I wanted to talk to you about. Do you think you could pop up there — maybe with Suggs because everyone loves him — and sort of adopt one or two of them? I've been thinking —"

"Adopt them? Take them home to Winterbrook, you mean? Have several mad old people living in the spare bedrooms? Bloody hell, Phoebes, you do ask a lot. Of course I'll think about it, but with us, and Suggs and YaYa already in situ, and Guy junior on the way, I'm not sure —"

"Nooo!" Phoebe sprinkled ice cubes into her wine glass. "Just get to know them and then maybe take them out for a drive or to the park or shopping or something."

"Oh, right. What on a regular basis? And do we get to pick one that we like?"

Phoebe giggled, thinking of Rocky's recent rehoming remarks. "Hopefully on a regular basis, yes. So they've got something to look forward to. And as for picking a nice one — well, not exactly, but I'd sort of hoped that the Tugwells would be able to match like-minded people up if at all possible. The Twilighters just need to have a bit more fun in their lives, Clem. We're so lucky — they're not."

Clemmie shovelled up more olives. "Yeah, you're right. That actually sounds a pretty cool thing to do. I'm seeing the other girls later; I'll rope them in as well. It'll be great. It'll be like having adoptive grandparents, only better because you can put them back at night and don't have to listen to endless stories about how great life was in nineteen thirty-five."

Laughing, Phoebe nodded. "Brilliant, thank you."

"Nice to see you've got your appetite back," Clemmie glanced at the heap of crisps and peanuts. "Mind you, that's a bit excessive — even I'd have trouble getting through that lot."

"Some of them are for me." Rocky started to clatter down the staircase. "Hi, I'm Rocky — we've met sort of briefly, haven't we?"

"We have." Clemmie beamed. "I'm Clemmie Devlin."

"Ah, yes —" Rocky slid into the third chair and attacked a packet of crisps "— the one with the gorgeous ferret and the equally gorgeous drag queen mate. They both made me laugh. Oh, and thanks for the food, Phoebe. This is just like being in the best sort of pub."

Casting wide-eyed questioning looks from Rocky to Phoebe and back again, Clemmie then giggled and buried herself in Phoebe's notebook.

"Blimey!" she erupted seconds later. "What in the name of all that's holy is this, Phoebes? What's all this Happy Birthday stuff? And what the heck is the secret magic of birthdays?"

Phoebe blushed. "Oh, um, it's just something I'm doing with Essie at Twilights. Some old gypsy-lore stuff. She's really fantastic on everything to do with astrology — she's forgotten more about -ologys than I've ever known. We're, er, hoping to try it out soon."

Rocky grabbed a handful of peanuts. "Don't say anything — they're both really, really clever with fortune-telling. Essie is like a sort of good witch, and Phoebe, from what I've heard, isn't far behind her."

"Oh, I wouldn't call Phoebes a witch. I'm just really pleased that she's getting back into the astrology — or whatever -ology this is. And as for mocking — no way! I mean, given the amount of various practical magic that goes on in the villages round here, and the fact that I spent for ever discovering the way to develop a magical firework, I'm the last one to cast aspersions." Clemmie beamed at Rocky. "But it's very sweet of you to defend her."

"He wasn't," Phoebe put in quickly. "He was just explaining. Weren't you?"

"I was." Rocky leaned back in his chair and lifted his beer bottle. "Clearly it didn't need any explanation. Just ignore me."

Clemmie sniggered, then speared another mini-kebab of olives and stared down at the notebook again. "Dear Lord — Phoebes! What's this old mumbo-jumbo?

"Happy Birthday chal and chie,
A misto rommerin will be nigh.
Dukker rokker duw not beng
Misto kooshti rommer and rye."

"What the hell does that mean?"

"Put the book down!" Phoebe shook her head. "That's, um, private."

"It's Romany patois," Rocky put in helpfully. "It's linked to the Happy Birthday magic stuff. I think it's something Phoebe might be going to use at the Twilights fête. She's going to be a fortune-teller."

"No way!" Clemmie shrieked with laughter. "Really, Phoebes? You're going to be a kosher Madame Zuleika at last? In public? And do magic? Whoo, I've got a feeling this is one bank holiday fête that no one will ever forget."

CHAPTER
FOURTEEN

It was almost as if the air was throbbing with heat, Essie thought, as ten days later she, Lilith, Princess and Bert, all dressed in their summery best, sat beneath a tree on the edge of Twilights' courtyard, making their personal preparations for Monday's fête.

All around them, Twilighters lolled limply on benches in what scant midday shade there was; the searing temperatures outside being slightly preferable to those in their roomettes.

"If we don't all die of heatstroke before Monday," Bert said happily, "I think this fête is going to be wonderful. So much going on. I can't wait to put the final touches to my origami, and I've dug out some of my early collages, too. I especially like the ones of the Lake District in pearl barley. Mother always used to —"

Essie cut his maternal meanderings short with a kindly smile. "I'm sure your handicrafts stall will be one of the successes of the day, Bert, dear. Now — is everything else we've organised in place?"

"Absolute Joy has finally agreed to let me use the main kitchen, honey," Lilith said, "so I'll be cooking in there and Patience and Prudence are going to ferry the food outside, then the girls from the dining room are acting as servers — so yes, I'm sorted."

"Lovely. Princess?"

"My yoga class have practised a short routine to 'Raindrops Keep Falling on Your Head'. They're inch-perfect. I thought we'd keep it short though, lovie, with easy positions, as they're mostly pushing eighty and any sort of exertion in this heat might prove too much for even the bendiest of my chaps. So, that just leaves you, doesn't it? Are you all sorted out now, too?"

Essie nodded, smiling to herself. She and Phoebe had had a couple more run-throughs of the Happy Birthday magic for their own enjoyment, and each time Essie had become more and more convinced that Phoebe had the gift. And at the Twilights evening astrology sessions, Phoebe, carefully leaving out the Romany chant part of the birthday magic, had become adept at adopting Essie's Five Question method of forecasting birthdays much to the delight of the residents.

"Oh, yes — young Phoebe is going to call herself Madame Zuleika for the day. She'll dress up in full regalia and sit in her tent and be available for all manner of fortune-telling. And I'll be on hand to, um, help out."

Lilith's laugh rumbled across the courtyard. "And can we expect something unexpected, honey?"

"Not at the fête." Essie shook her head. "I'm not going to risk spoiling things by doing anything too, er, 'doubtful', as Absolute Joy would say. And I have warned Phoebe not to use the full birthday-ology."

"Shame, honey. Mind you, young Phoebe has picked it all up really quickly, hasn't she? She's carried on where you left off. And Absolute Joy and Tiny Tony patrol the astrology sessions, thinking that she's just reading straightforward star sign forecasts when, really, she's using all your expertise, isn't she? Not just the birthday stuff. Some of the things she's predicted have come uncannily true almost straight away. She's a big hit, isn't she?"

"She's very talented," Essie agreed. "But I've still warned her to keep it straight at the fête. So far the Tugwells don't realise that she's using my methods and I want to keep it that way."

"Definitely," Princess agreed. "We all love Phoebe to death. Don't want to lose her. Not only can she do our hair lovely like that Teasy-Weasy bloke, but she's uncannily accurate with her forecasting — sometimes it's just like you speaking. Mind, we did laugh when she told Mavis Barrett that she'd come into a fortune, but even Mavis went along with it — right giggle it was. After all, apart from the pittance of leftover pension we get doled out, fortunes here are rarer than polar bears in Clacton. But Phoebe insisted it was what she could see and told Mavis it would happen."

Essie nodded. She remembered every detail of the event very clearly. Phoebe had seemed so absolutely sure. So convinced. It had unnerved even her.

"And then," Bert butted in, "blow me down, a couple of days later Mavis got that letter saying that her premium bond had come up. And they'd been trying to

202

trace her for ages to tell her, and it *was* a fortune, wasn't it?"

Essie nodded. Well, to the Twilighters, twenty-five thousand pounds was riches beyond avarice. And Mavis's windfall had only been the tip of the astrological iceberg. Phoebe, now she had her confidence back and believed in her own abilities, had been eerily correct in all manner of smaller but no less surprising predictions.

It was all going exactly as Essie had planned. After all, the gift may have been passed to her genetically from her grandmother, but she certainly hadn't passed it on to her own daughter in that way, and she saw no reason why it shouldn't be inherited by teaching someone receptive enough to appreciate and accept it.

Essie had known Phoebe was the right person to carry on her work. And now she'd proved it. But the fête was definitely not the place for Phoebe to experiment. Absolutely not.

"Essie! Mrs Rivers!" Absolute Joy's hernia voice sliced through the solid air from Twilights main entrance. "Essie! A moment please."

Princess, Lilith and Bert all stared at Essie.

"What've you done wrong now?" Bert's large eyes blinked moistly.

"Nothing." Essie eased herself to her feet. "Well, not that I can remember. Not that that will stop Absolute Joy having a whinge, will it? See you later, troops."

"Good luck, honey." Lilith flapped the folds of her cerise caftan.

Princess held up crossed fingers on both hands.

Essie took a deep breath — the air scorching her throat — and drifted towards Twilights.

"I'm not sure you should all be sitting out there," Joy, still wearing a hefty blue skirt and a matching nylon button-to-the-neck blouse despite the heat, greeted her. "It's absolutely baking. Wouldn't you all be better in your roomettes?"

"Not without air conditioning, no," Essie said. "And as we can't even open the windows, any air is better than none. Anyway, how can I help you?"

Clearly slightly affronted by the tone of Essie's voice, Joy fluttered. "You have a visitor, Essie. Isn't that lovely?"

"A visitor? Who? Young Phoebe?"

"No, no — although I do need to have a word or two with her. The bigwigs on the council think her idea of Taking Out A Twilighter is an absolutely super one. They've given us the go-ahead, subject to the assigned escorts passing their criminal records checks of course. We'll have that one up and running before you know it. Absolutely wonderful community spirit, the council said, absolutely spot on for PR, and all reflects extremely well on the way me and hubby manage Twilights."

"I'm very pleased for you," Essie said shortly, "and even more pleased for Phoebe whose idea it was, which, of course, you'll publicly acknowledge, won't you? So, if it's not Phoebe come to see me, who is it?"

"No, I'm not going to tell you, but this will come as an absolutely lovely surprise. I've put him in the residents' lounge as no one's in there at present. Come along — no time to dawdle. I'm absolutely up to my eyes in personal damage limitation insurance and bunting and trying to find a pony that doesn't bite."

He? Essie pondered as she strode behind Absolute Joy's sturdy true blue backside. "Oh — is it Rocky? He doesn't do Saturdays usually —"

"And if I'd had my way —" Joy sniffed superciliously over her shoulder "— he wouldn't be doing absolutely any days at all. Yes, I know he's your friend and he's very good and he's very cheap, but he's still a *felon*. Damn fluffy politically correct nonsense. Having to take one's quota of ex-offenders for manual work. Absolute twaddle!"

Essie chuckled to herself. Not Rocky, then. Slo? Surely not. He wouldn't make an appointment, would he? They'd managed to have a couple of outings since the cloak and dagger coffee in Patsy's Pantry, but she really didn't think Slo would make an appointment . . .

"Here we are," Joy said briskly. "You can take him to your roomette if you prefer."

"Not unless he wants to be slow-cooked," Essie muttered, "whoever he is."

Joy pushed the door of the residents' lounge open, stretched her over-pinked lips in a smile at Essie, then smartly goose-stepped away.

Essie peered into the residents' lounge — which was heavily oppressive and seemed strangely quiet without the television blaring — and stopped short.

"Patrick!"

"Hello, Mother."

Patrick had run to fat. It didn't look good on him, Essie thought. He'd always been a chubby child — a bonny baby, they'd said — but now he just looked unhealthily overweight. And he'd lost most of his hair. How had she and Barney ever managed to produce such a cuckoo of a son?

She remained in the doorway. "Don't you 'Hello, Mother' me, my lad. What do you want? Come to see if I'd died and there was anything left over for you?"

"Mum . . ."

"Don't you *dare* call me Mum! So, what do you want?"

"Can't I come and call on my old mum without having a reason?"

"No, you bloody can't," Essie spat. "You haven't been near me since you and Shirley cheated me out of everything and dumped me in this place. Where is your sister, by the way? In the loo? Touching up her latest facelift?"

"I'm on my own." Patrick tried to smile. It got lost in the folds of his sweaty face. "But Shirley sends her love. So do Faye and Nicholas."

"I bet they do," Essie hissed. "Your respective partners were just as keen to see me in here as you were. And no, don't tell me, the grandchildren would have loved to come and see me if only they hadn't been quite so busy."

Patrick, Essie was delighted to noticed, went even more pink and didn't even try to deny it.

"You're looking well, Mum."

"And you're not."

"Come and sit down."

"Why on earth would I want to sit down with you? And your dad and I always taught you to stand up when a lady came into the room, or have you forgotten that along with everything else?"

"Oh, all that manners stuff is old hat now, Mum. Women's lib and all that."

"Do not call me Mum."

They stared at one another for a moment. As always, Essie simply felt nothing. She'd loved him to insanity once, nurtured him, protected him, cared for him, helped him to grow up, and now . . . and now she loathed him. And his sister. Equally.

What sort of awful mother did that make her?

"So, what exactly do you want, Patrick? Don't tell me you've driven the exhausting twenty-odd miles across Berkshire for the first time since I've been in here just to ask after my health?"

"Mum!" Patrick spread damp lamb-shank-sized hands. "This is a wonderful place. Shirley and I saw so many when we looking for somewhere —"

"Somewhere to dump me? Go on, say it!"

"Mum, really, it wasn't like that at all."

"It was *exactly* like that, Patrick, and you know it. Now, I have my friends waiting outside who mean more to me than you or Shirley or your money-grabbing partners and children will ever do. I'm going to join them. I'm sure you'll find your own way out."

"But you haven't heard why I'm here."

"And I don't intend to."

"I've sold the house."

"Really? And I'm supposed to care, am I? The house — my home — was lost to me the minute you and Shirley and your bloody spouses set foot in it. This, sadly, is the only home I'll ever have. I'll die here. Not in my own home, in my own bedroom, in my own bed, as I'd always planned to do. Thanks to you I don't even have all my own things around me, just the few bits I could squeeze into the shoebox they call a bloody roomette. So, why, in God's name, would I care what you've done with my house?"

"*Our* house, Mum." Patrick's voice wheedled. "We grew up there. We loved it, too. It hurt us so much to have to let it go."

"I'll bet it did. But not half as much as it hurt me when you forced me out. Let me remind you. You knew how much I loved that house. You knew your dad and I had that house from when we were first married. Our own council house. So proud of it, we were. Never missed the rent, not once, not even when your dad was on short time. Then when he'd died, and I was finding it hard to make ends meet on my pension, you said it would make sense if you and Shirley moved back in, with your other halves, so I'd always have someone to look after me. Remember this, Patrick?"

Patrick nodded. Several chins swayed from side to side.

"And then," Essie growled, "very, very quickly, one or other of you came up with the bright idea of buying the house from the council, which you were allowed to do as you were residents. Still with me? And you did, and you assured me that as long as the deeds were in

208

your names I'd never have any need to worry about a thing, I'd never have to pay another penny and you'd all be there to look after me in my old age. Still with me?"

Patrick, Essie noted with sorrow, didn't even look slightly uncomfortable.

"And then, out of the blue, you decided that there wasn't room for me any more. That my bedroom would make a nice little office. That I might be getting a bit doddery and need more care. Oh, Patrick, that was cruel — I was fitter than any of you. But it didn't stop you, did it?"

Patrick stared down at his feet. His shoes were dirty, Essie noticed. Barney would have been very cross. He'd always made sure the children had clean shoes.

"And because you lied and made up imaginary falls and forgetfulness on my part and your golfing doctor chums believed you and said it would be better if I went into care, and because I didn't have *anything* in my name, no money, no property, I'd have to go into *local authority* care. I didn't have a say, Patrick, did I? You owned my home. You threw me out. You forced me into Twilights. You and Shirley *stole* my home, my memories, my independence and everything that I ever cared about."

Eventually Patrick cleared his throat. "I don't think it was quite like that."

"It was *exactly* like that. So, have you and Shirley and the others made a fortune by selling my home, and have you all moved on to some tacky mansion in

Maidenhead? Is that what you've come to tell me? Your new address for the Christmas cards? If I ever sent any, which of course I don't and won't and —"

"I've been declared bankrupt."

Essie blinked. She hadn't seen that coming.

Patrick and Shirley had been in business together with their partners, running a small chain of clothes shops. Boutiques, Shirley called them, but they were just old-fashioned outfitters really.

"Just you or all of them?"

"All of us. Suddenly there were all these cheap clothing chains appearing everywhere — Primark and the like — and no one wanted our sort of clothes, the clothes you paid a good price for and that lasted for ever. The disposable society did for us."

Essie smiled. "Good."

"You don't mean that."

"Oh, Patrick, I can assure you I've never meant anything more in my life. So, the house has gone, has it? And the shops? And all your assets?"

Patrick, looking bereft, nodded.

"There is a God," Essie said beaming. "So, where are you living now?"

"Faye and I are renting a small flat. Shirley and Nicholas are in with friends. We're just about scraping by between us, but it's so hard, Mum. We'd all been used to the good things in life and now we're getting too old to start again, even if we could. It'll take six years to clear the bankruptcy by which time we'll be almost pensioners and —"

"Oh, you poor things," Essie mocked happily. "My heart bleeds. Well, if that's all your good news, I'll be off."

"Mum, listen to me, please. We're your flesh and blood. Your children. Surely you wouldn't see us spend the rest of our lives going without, living in cramped, nasty accommodation?"

"Wouldn't I? What do you think I live in, Patrick? And why? And what, exactly, do you think I can do to help you — even if I wanted to, which I don't?"

Patrick had eased himself out of the beige armchair with some difficulty. His breathing was laboured. "We — me and Shirley — thought that, well, being local authority, it can't cost you much to live in here, and pensions have been going up, so even after you've paid the fees you must have a little bit put by, and —"

"Get out of my sight!" Essie howled. "Now! Go, just go! And I never, never, ever, want to see you again!"

Then, to her horror, Essie's eyes filled with tears. Oh, not tears of sorrow that her own children had fallen on hard times, but furious tears of outraged anger and hatred.

She turned in the doorway and blundered out of the residents' lounge, crashing off the walls like some demented pinball machine all the way to Twilights entrance hall in her haste to be as far away from her son as possible.

"Hold up, duck," a familiar voice burred ahead of her. "What's occurring here, then?"

"Slo." Essie sniffed back the tears. "Oh, Slo, get me out of here. Please."

"Mr Motion!" Absolute Joy's ringing tones reverberated in Essie's ears. "This is a surprise. Oh, Lord love us, there hasn't been a death I haven't noticed, has there?"

"Well, one or two of 'em out in the courtyard looks like they haven't moved for a while, but no," Slo said firmly. "I'm here, um, to discuss Mrs Rivers' funeral plan."

"Funeral plan?" Joy shook her head. "First I've heard."

"Saves you money," Slo said, his hand gripping Essie's trembling elbow. "Mrs Rivers wants to put a bit by, see, on instalments like, and make her own final arrangements. Means, should anything untoward happen, Twilights won't be left with the bill. But I needs to take her into 'assocks to sign some papers. All right with you?"

"What? Well, yes of course. Funeral plan. Absolutely good idea. And has your visitor gone, Essie, dear?"

"Don't know and don't care," Essie said. "But probably not. Perhaps you can escort him from the premises. And please, don't let him, or my daughter, or any of my family ever come to see me again."

"Oh, dear," Joy trilled. "Families, eh? Well, whatever you say, Mrs Rivers. Leave it with me. Now, off you pop and sign your papers. I'm sure Mr Motion will look after you very well."

"That I will," Slo said, steering Essie gently down the steps and into the courtyard's blinding sunlight. "That I will."

212

CHAPTER
FIFTEEN

Ten minutes later, in the passenger seat of the elderly Daimler, having poured out the whole distasteful encounter to Slo, Essie finally began to relax.

"Should of let me have a go at 'im, duck," Slo said fiercely as they whizzed round the narrow, dry, dusty lanes of Berkshire. "I'd of showed the young so-and-so right from wrong and no mistake."

"I wouldn't have let you dirty your hands on him, but thank you for the offer all the same. You're a wonderful friend, and —" she glanced across the car "— a pretty wonderful liar. How on earth did you think up something like a funeral plan so quickly?"

"Dunno," Slo said modestly, "it just came to me. I knew if I was going to be allowed to whisk you away, it'd have to be summat that Absolute Joy would jump at. And saving money's allus a goer with 'er, ain't it?"

It was. Essie nodded at his clever quick thinking. She sighed, thinking of porky Patrick. How sad it was — the disgust she felt for him. The revulsion. How very sad. And how terrible to know that she felt far, far more affection and admiration for Phoebe and Rocky than she did for her own children.

"Where are we going?" She turned her head, loving the warm wind that rushed in through the open window and blew her hair into mad tendrils and sent the ends of her scarlet scarves flapping like streamers about her face.

"Nowhere — anywhere — just thought it was best to drive around until you'd calmed down a bit. Is there anywhere you'd like to go?"

"Somewhere where I can have a good long drink or several. I'm so not calm — but even more angry, Slo. So very, very angry."

"I'm not surprised, duck. From what you told me before about how your kids got you out of your 'ome, I wouldn't 'ave thought they could stoop no lower, but that was a right snake-belly trick 'e was trying to pull this morning. Mind —" he glanced across at her "— you look right pretty now, with your colour all up. Matches your outfit. You're my lady in red, and, no, don't fret, duck, I ain't going to sing. Our Constance says my voice'd waken the dead when I leads off on 'The Old Rugged Cross'."

Essie chuckled. "And that'd be dreadful for business, wouldn't it?"

"That's the ticket," Slo gurgled back. "Keep your sense of 'umour, my duck. It'll never let you down."

"Unlike people."

"*Some* people." Slo tried to light a cigarette. It was a tricky manoeuvre as he was driving quite fast and the Daimler's through draught immediately extinguished the flame from his lighter. He gave up with a snort, tossing both unlit cigarette and lighter into the walnut

214

glovebox. "Not all people are rotten, Essie, duck. Most aren't. Thank the Lord."

Essie leaned her head back into the Daimler's soft, worn leather. They'd left the country lanes and were on Hazy Hassocks High Street now, driving slowly because of the tail-back of traffic. Saturday lunchtime on Hassocks High Street. Essie stared greedily at the people languidly wandering along the sycamore-lined road, stopping in the shade to gossip, idly, lethargically drifting in and out of the mishmash of shops and small businesses.

How lovely it would be, she thought wistfully, to be able to just walk out of your own front door and within a few moments be here, with all this life and bustle. How lovely to pop in and out of the shops, to meet up with friends for a coffee and a cake in Patsy's Pantry. Oh, there was so much to do here — and all so close to Twilights, but so far away for her.

She looked longingly at the library, and Jennifer Blessing's beauty salon, and Cut'n'Curl, and the dentist's and the Dovecote Surgery and Big Sava . . . So much going on. So much to do.

"When we gets out of this gridlock," Slo muttered, "shall we drive out to Fiddlesticks and 'ave a drink at the Weasel and Bucket? Or we could go to Bagley and call in at the Barmy Cow. Them old Berkeley Boys there is allus good for a laugh."

"Either would be lovely." Essie fanned her face. The crawl through the town had sent clouds of hot air into the Daimler. "I'm really parched now."

"Me too. Oh, dammit to buggery, them lights has gorn red again. Damn daft idea not making this a one-way when they did the last of traffic planning palaver if you asks me."

Essie glanced across at the row of stationary cars alongside them in the opposite lane and caught her breath. A huge black hearse was practically parallel. She squinted at it. The back was empty. She exhaled — seeing a funeral in all its misery this morning would have been a step too far along the road to depression.

"Bloody 'ell!" Slo exclaimed. "It's our Constance and Perpetua. They must be going to do the weekly shop at Big Sava."

"In the hearse?"

"Ah, we uses the hearse for all sorts. Right handy it is. You can get more'n coffins in the back of there. Daft old bats is in the wrong lane for the car park. Going the wrong way. Keep yer 'ead down, duck and hope they don't spot us."

Too late.

"Slo!" Constance, her whirls and whorls and rolls of much-lacquered hair jerking with indignation, yelled through the window. "What the dickens are you doing? We wondered where the Daimler had gorn. Our Perpetua thought we'd been car-napped. And who is that? You can't use the Daimler as a taxi — you know we was warned about that. No hackney carriage licence — no paying passengers."

Perpetua leaned across from her place in the hearse's passenger seat and waved a skinny grey hand. "Coo-ee . . . Ah, that isn't a passenger, Constance. That's Essie

216

Rivers from up Twilights. You must know her. I've seen her out with Slo several times."

"And you've never told me?"

Perpetua looked a bit scared. "No, I didn't like to. I knew you'd shout. I think he's her sweetheart, our Constance."

"*Sweetheart?*" Constance roared. "What do you mean *sweetheart*? Slo doesn't have sweethearts. None of us has sweethearts. We agreed. Our parents agreed. Sex ruins the business. Slo'll have a sweetheart over my dead body. Sweetheart be buggered! She's nothing but a gold-digger."

"Lights have gone green," Essie whispered, trying not to laugh out loud. "Do a Fangio."

Slo did. The Daimler shuddered and roared, drowning out the remainder of the invective emanating from the hearse and, with several terrifying overtaking manoeuvres, they managed to get ahead of the queue.

"She's trying to reverse and follow us." Essie craned her neck to look over her shoulder. "Not easy with a hearse in the High Street. Oh, everyone's shaking their fists and shouting. Oh, and now she's stalled — right across the road. She's jammed up the entire town."

Slo swept the Daimler away from the High Street and into the narrow back streets.

"Winchester Road?" Essie peered at the nameplate as they tore past. "Isn't this where you —?"

"Live? Yes, duck."

"But surely —" Essie frowned "— this is the first place they'll look? I mean, I know you don't want the

217

confrontation or have to defend our friendship, so why —?"

"One, because I don't think either of us is up to being chased round the blame countryside by our Constance in an 'earse like some damn daft Berkshire version of the *Wacky Races*. And two, because if they comes past here and sees the Daimler —" Slo's tongue protruded through his teeth as he concentrated on easing the car through a just-wide-enough gateway and into the drive of a tall redbricked house "— they'll assumes that I've dropped you off somewhere, and I've come 'ome and they'll go and do their shopping and their chattering to all and sundry like they allus do, and that'll buy me some time to decide what I'm going to say."

Essie shook her head as Slo stopped the car and switched off the engine. "But if they find me here, with you, they're going to be so cross, and the last thing I want is to cause trouble between you and your cousins."

"You let me worry about that, duck." Slo struggled out of the Daimler, and puffed his way round to the passenger side. "There, out you gets, duck. Easy does it."

Essie stepped out into the almost overwhelming heat. She desperately needed a long cool drink more than ever. Tap water would do nicely, and it'd be even better if the Motions kept a stock of ice cubes.

"Blimey, this is getting ridiculous." Slo mopped his brow with the black-edged handkerchief. "Global warming or just a damn 'ot summer — I wish it would bloody rain. Now, are you up to another little walk?"

Ouf . . . Essie groaned. She really didn't think she could walk a step. And where on earth was Slo planning on walking *to*?

"Aren't we going in, then?"

"No, duck. I'm not risking our Connie and Perpetua having a go at you, not after the nasty business you've already 'ad to put up with today. I wants you to be somewhere where you can relax and be among real friends."

"Oh God, you're nor putting me back on the bus to Twilights, are you?"

"Don't you know me better than that?" Slo sounded shocked. "I ain't letting you out of my sight, duck. Come along, only a few more steps, I promise."

Essie trudged slowly along Winchester Road beside Slo, her nose clogged by the stifling scent of hot tarmac, her scalp prickling with heat, her eyes dazzled by the relentless glare of the broiling sun.

"Blame 'ot weather," Slo grizzled. "You think them mad old moon-bayers over at Fiddlesticks would have magicked up a rain dance by now, wouldn't you? Last time they did it, when we had a scorcher like this, it deluged down straight after. Right lovely it was. Didn't stop for days. Mebbe they'll 'ave another go."

Essie frowned. She sincerely hoped not. Not until after Monday's bank holiday fête, anyway. After Monday, a day she'd been so looking forward to, the heavens could open and it could rain for forty days and forty nights for all she cared.

"Here we are," Slo ushered her into the gravelled drive of another tall redbricked house and past a vaguely familiar hatchback car. He rang the doorbell and turned and smiled gently at Essie. "Trust me, Essie, duck. We'll be OK now."

Would they? Would she? Essie felt far too weary to care. It was so suffocatingly hot. She was terribly thirsty. The meeting with Patrick had hurt her emotionally more than she'd care to admit. And it was clear that Slo was scared of his cousins and ashamed of her.

And now she didn't even know where she was.

Oh goodness, she felt an uncharacteristic twinge of self-pity. What was the point of anything? Really, what was the point?

Phoebe pulled the door open and beamed. "Essie! What a lovely surprise. Oh, and Mr Motion, er . . ." What on earth were Essie and Slo Motion doing on her doorstep, Phoebe wondered. Together. How very odd. "No, I mean, it's really nice to see you. When I heard the bell I thought you might be Jehovah's Witnesses."

"I hope we don't come as a disappointment, then, duck," Slo wheezed. "Not God-botherers, just two for the price of one wrinklies, duck, er, we ain't disturbing you, are we?"

"No, not at all. It's my Saturday off, and I was up early to finish my housework and do my washing before the temperature reached boiling point. In fact, I was just about to go through some stuff that Clemmie — that's my madcap friend, Essie, you know, the one I

220

told you about? — has given me for my Madame Zuleika outfit. She always wears lovely boho clothes so there should be something suitable among them. You two can play Trinny and Susannah if you like. Oh, please, come on in."

"Thank you," Essie spoke quietly. "It's very kind of you, but I wouldn't want to be a nuisance."

"You're not a nuisance. I'm delighted to see you. Come on through."

Ushering them through the living room and still rather bemused as to why they were there at all, Phoebe smiled over her shoulder. "Would you like to sit out in the garden? It's nice and cool out there. Much cooler than indoors."

"That'd be right lovely of you, duck." Slo beamed. "And if you could rustle up a glass of cold water that'd be great. Essie needs a drink right badly."

Essie did look rather odd, Phoebe thought. And quiet. She really hoped Essie wasn't ill. This prolonged heat was enough to knock the stuffing out of anyone, let alone a delicate old lady.

"I can do much better than that. You go through to the courtyard, and I'll see what I can rustle up."

"Thank you, dear," Essie said softly. "It's very kind of you. But we honestly don't want to be any trouble. We shouldn't have just turned up unannounced. And what a lovely home you have here."

"Thanks — and for the hundredth time it's great to see you, honestly, and no trouble at all. Just go and sit down — I won't be a second."

Making sure Essie and Slo had found the wrought-iron chairs in the shade of the orange blossom and jasmine, Phoebe hurried into the kitchen.

Right, long cool drinks and something to eat. Essie did look very pale. Maybe she'd been to the doctors. Maybe Slo had been roped in by Absolute Joy and Tiny Tony to rush Essie to the Dovecote Surgery. Maybe Essie had had bad news . . .

Phoebe swallowed quickly. She couldn't bear it if something happened to Essie. She really couldn't bear it.

Quickly assembling tall glasses, lemonade and ice cubes, and emptying crisps and nuts in bowls, Phoebe then sliced a quiche into neat portions and added several tomatoes, broke off some iceberg leaves and a found a hefty chunk of cheese, a jar of pickles, a few bread rolls and a tub of low-fat spread.

There — that looked fine. She just hoped it would be enough for an impromptu lunch for three.

Gathering cutlery and ripping off sheets of kitchen roll, Phoebe carefully carried the loaded tray out into the garden.

Essie and Slo were talking, quietly, their heads together. Aaah. Phoebe looked at them. How lovely. How sweet it was that they were friends. Slo Motion was a kind and eccentric old man and Essie was just the loveliest person she'd ever met. Wouldn't it be just wonderful if they got together?

Phoebe stopped, her mouth dropping open.

Essie's beau. Her gentleman friend. The one with the magic birthday date. It was *Slo Motion*.

Blimey, why on earth hadn't she twigged that before?

Biting back a smile, she placed the tray on the table. "I hope this will be OK. Essie, there's loads more to drink indoors. Is lemonade OK?"

"Nectar." Essie grasped the glass and drank quickly. "Oh, Phoebe, you angel. That's so much better."

"It's better'n better." Slo beamed. "It's better'n the best pub."

Funny, Phoebe thought, Rocky had said the same thing. Maybe the courtyard garden would become a meeting place for the lost and lonely.

Slo whooped with delight. "And you've even got an ashtray!"

"My friend YaYa smokes a lot." Phoebe joined them at the table. "Feel free. Help yourselves to food — there's plenty more."

While Slo and Essie helped themselves amongst murmurs of appreciation and repeated thanks, Phoebe allowed herself to smile. How sweet this was. Third-age love. Was it love? Probably, even if they weren't really aware of it. But even if it wasn't, it was wonderful that two such sweet people had found each other.

Maybe, Phoebe thought sentimentally, when I'm Essie's age I'll meet someone else too. And maybe by the time I'm Essie's age I'll have stopped hurting and started trusting. Maybe . . .

Between mouthfuls, Essie and Slo explained why they were there. As they both spoke at the same time and didn't manage to tell the story in any sort of chronological order, Phoebe was quite confused, but gradually she managed to unravel the threads.

"Oh, Essie, what hateful, nasty children you have. Ooh, sorry, maybe I shouldn't . . ."

"Yes you should," Essie said. "That and more. But it's OK now — I'm feeling much, much better."

And she looked it, Phoebe thought with huge relief. And the picture of Constance and Perpetua blocking Hazy Hassocks High Street with the hearse sent her into fits of giggles. And how funny that Slo was so scared of his cousins.

Essie and Slo, Phoebe thought, were just like any forbidden lovers. Trying to keep their relationship secret, happy with each other, wanting to be together, but knowing no one else would understand.

It was just like *West Side Story* . . . Oooh, no maybe not, Phoebe thought quickly, seeing how that ended. Maybe Rhett and Scarlett — no, that didn't end too well either. Um, Cathy and Heathcliffe? Nah, no good. Lordy — was there any happy couple she could think of . . . Ah, yes — Clemmie and Guy. And Amber and Lewis. And Sukie and Derry. And . . .

"This is blissful," Essie sighed, her plate empty. "What a gorgeous little secret garden. Thank you again, Phoebe. And, oh, is that water I can hear?"

"The Kennet." Phoebe nodded. "It runs right along Winchester Road behind the garden walls. Funny, I thought it would have dried up in this heat."

"Never does. Allus runs full," Slo said, lighting up a cigarette with total pleasure. "Allus has. It's fed from a spring up in the Downs, see. Constantly fills. Our Perpetua hates it. Allus makes her have to run to the lav."

224

They all laughed.

"Look, if you've got time," Phoebe said. "Would you let me try out my Madame Zuleika outfit on you? See what you think?"

"Love to." Essie nodded with enthusiasm. "I'm sure you'll look the part though, dear, whatever you wear."

Once in her pink and frilly bedroom, it only took Phoebe ten minutes to root through the clothes Clemmie had donated, pull on one of the long, multicoloured, layered, swishy skirts, slip into an embroidered, off-the-shoulder, white voile blouse, fasten a triangular scarf over her short blonde hair and add the necessary extras — huge, gold, hooped earrings, several golden necklaces and a jangle of bangles. With plenty of make-up, she thought, posing in front of her mirror, she'd be a perfect fortune-teller on Monday.

She laughed. She was actually looking forward to it. Looking forward to dressing up and being part of the fête. Looking forward to telling fortunes and reading star charts and turning tarots. Blimey, two and half months after the-wedding-that-never-was and thanks to Essie, maybe, just maybe, she was regaining her self-confidence.

"There!" She stepped out of the French doors. "What do you think?"

"Oh, Phoebe." Essie looked as though she was going to cry. "Oh, you look sensational, dear. Absolutely sensational. You'll be perfect."

"Ah, a right bobby-dazzler and no mistake." Slo spoke round his dancing cigarette. "Lovely. Right lovely."

225

Phoebe swirled and twirled.

"Very nice." Rocky's voice echoed down from his balcony. "Very, very nice in fact. Sort of hippie rock chick. It suits you."

Phoebe stopped dancing and blushed as she craned her neck upwards. "Oh! I didn't hear you come in. And this isn't a public performance."

"Hello, Rocky — and no, it's not a public performance, at least until Monday," Essie chuckled, squinting upwards. "It's her Madame Zuleika fortune-telling outfit. Wonderful isn't it? And as well as the sneak preview, Phoebe has treated us to lunch. Isn't she kind?"

"Very. Essie, it's great to see you, oh, and Mr Motion. Um, Phoebe, I don't suppose there's any food left? Enough to feed a hard-working gardener who's generally pretty rubbish in the kitchen and so tired of coming home to an empty flat and yet another microwaved ready meal."

"Save me the sob story." Phoebe smiled. "And there's loads left. Don't tell me you're starving — again."

"Always am these days. Seem to have recovered my appetite. Is that an invitation to join you, then?"

"Yes."

"Great, I'll just go and grab some beers and be down in a minute."

It took less than two minutes for Rocky to clatter down the staircase and pull up another chair.

"Help yourself." Phoebe grinned. "Oh, you already have."

226

She sat back, happily watching Rocky eating and Slo and Essie sipping their drinks and chatting quietly. Three people she'd known for such a short space of time but who now were part of her life. Her new life. Her without-Ben life.

"Fan-bloody-tastic," Rocky sighed after demolishing everything left on the table. "You're a star, Phoebe. Thanks so much. You'll have to let me treat you to one of my microwaved specials in return. Or maybe spag bol — I can cook spag bol. But —" he dropped his voice and nodded his head across the table "— what are they doing here? Together?"

"Sssh." Phoebe shook her head. "Look, why don't you help me clear the table?"

"What? Oh, yeah, right."

They quickly piled all the plates and empty packets on to the tray.

"Just going to make another jug of iced lemonade," Phoebe said as Rocky hefted the tray. "Won't be a minute."

"So, what's going on?" Rocky said, expertly scraping detritus into Phoebe's bin, and removing the crockery and stacking it neatly into the dishwasher — clearly exhibiting all the skills he'd amassed while being a flight attendant. "Why —?"

Quickly, Phoebe told him the whole story.

". . . and, because of the secret magic of birthdays, I know that Slo is right for her. I'm just not sure that he does — yet. Look, wouldn't it be just lovely if they could get together? Spend the rest of their lives together?"

"Great. Yes, of course. But —"

Phoebe grinned. "Well, I thought, as I was dressed as Madame Zuleika, and we have a perfect couple for me to try the Romany secret birthday magic on it would be a shame to waste the opportunity."

"You can't!" Rocky was wide-eyed.

"Why not? If it works, it'll be great — and Essie has already told me that she's done some of the stuff on Slo and he is her perfect partner. And if it doesn't, well, where's the harm?"

"Christ." Rocky exhaled. "I'm not sure . . . I mean, is it safe?"

"Of course it's safe. It's magic, not witchcraft. They just have to be holding hands — I'm not sure how we're going to manage that . . ."

Rocky glanced out into the garden. "Would touching do? They've both nodded off and their fingers are touching on the table."

"Perfect." Phoebe beamed. "So are you coming to watch?"

"Yes, but . . . Blimey this is spooky."

With Rocky following, Phoebe swished into the courtyard. Essie and Slo didn't stir.

She took a deep breath.

"Happy Birthday chal and chie,
A misto rommerin will be nigh.
Dukker rokker duw not beng
Misto kooshti rommer and rye."

Slo made a little coughing noise as he cleared his chest. Essie murmured and smiled. Neither of them woke up.

"Strewth." Rocky shook his head. "So what happens now? How do we know if it worked?"

"No idea," Phoebe whispered. "Although Essie did say that she'd tried it out once and the couples involved immediately pounced on one another and were only forced apart by Absolute Joy throwing Horlicks over them."

"Get away," Rocky laughed. "Old people, you mean? God, I hope they don't wake up and start pawing one another. How embarrassing would that be?"

"Very." Phoebe pulled a face. "But while they're still asleep we'll never know. All we can do now is wait and see what happens . . ."

CHAPTER
SIXTEEN

August Bank Holiday Monday was, as Joy Tugwell said to everyone who would listen, going to be an absolute scorcher.

Phoebe, who'd arrived at Twilights very early and stashed all her Madame Zuleika paraphernalia plus a cool box of bottled water in Essie's roomette, sat out of the simmering heat in the dappled shade of the trees bordering the grounds. The sky was a huge spread of cloudless cornflower blue and the already stifling air was heavy and motionless. Lazily, she watched the manically busy preparations for the fête.

The Tugwells seemed to have called in all their favours, and nearly every person who could be useful to them from within a fifty-mile radius was scurrying about the lawns, putting up stalls, hanging bunting, erecting tents, nailing placards and ferrying non-stop boxes of goodies from Twilights.

The place was teeming with activity, the warm air splintered only by the sound of mallet on stake and fragments of hearty swearing and even heartier laughter.

Watching the activity and wondering, again, if she should be feeling any guilt over practising the Happy

Birthday magic on Slo and Essie, Phoebe examined her conscience and, as previously, found it clear.

Slo and Essie had woken up after their post-prandial doze in the courtyard garden, a little confused about their surroundings and slightly embarrassed at having fallen asleep in company, but had reacted normally to one another with friendly smiles and gentle burred conversation. They'd remained sitting in the cool of the courtyard for the remainder of the afternoon, dozing again, chatting to her and Rocky and each other, and had stayed for tea.

Phoebe had loved it, but was a little disappointed that there hadn't been showers of stars and fanfares of celestial trumpets and a sprinkling of glittering magic dust after the Happy Birthday magic. Maybe she'd got it wrong. Maybe Essie had got it wrong and she, Phoebe, simply didn't have the gift.

She'd discussed it with Rocky later and he'd said, as far as he was concerned, it had just been a relief that Slo and Essie hadn't pounced on one another with cries of unbridled geriatric passion.

No, Phoebe thought, stretching out her bare legs, either the secret magic of birthdays didn't work or it was a slow-burning affair. Either way, she had no regrets at all at experimenting.

As neither she nor Essie had seen Slo since, they weren't sure what sort of reception he'd received from his cousins for his flighty behaviour. Although she wasn't entirely sure she understood the minutia of the Motions' family politics, Phoebe really hoped he'd be a man about it and tell Constance and Perpetua to mind their own damn business.

The fête, like all Berkshire village fêtes, seemed to be developing calmly from apparent chaos. Phoebe watched as a small roped-off arena appeared amid the mayhem, several marquees mushroomed, a trestle stage was erected, stalls formed a circle, and electricians darted about with huge cable reels fixing up the public address system and lighting. Even Guy, Clemmie's husband, and his pyro crew from The Gunpowder Plot, were on site, burying the tubes on the far side of the lawns for the evening's firework display.

"Polly!" Absolute Joy's voice shattered the early-morning bucolic bliss. "Are you looking for a little job to do?"

"Phoebe and, er, no." Phoebe beamed. "I'm, um, just sitting here gathering my karma together in preparation for later."

"Ah, right." Absolute Joy, in a Tory-blue shirtwaister and matching Alice band atop the rigid bouffant, clearly wasn't sure about karma. "Only we need someone to keep an eye on Jezebel McFrewin when she arrives."

"Jezebel *who*?"

"McFrewin. Oh, surely you've heard of her, dear? She's our celeb for the opening ceremony at midday and then she's going to judge the fancy-dress comp. If she arrives at any time before noon then I'd rather she had an aide who had all their faculties and wasn't likely to fall asleep on her or force-feed her custard creams or try to involve her in a hectic session of 'Hands, Knees and Bumps-A-Daisy'. At noon Tony can take over and accompany her to the podium. Can I allocate her to you?"

"Er, well, yes I suppose so — but how will I recognise her? What's she a celeb for? What's she supposed to have done?"

"To tell the truth, I have absolutely no idea." Joy looked flustered. "Tony, my hubby, got her from an agency in the *Yellow Pages*. Very reasonable. I'm sure she'll be absolutely OK. We asked for a popular person, so she's probably a writer or a singer or an actress or something."

More likely a monosyllabic, Z-list, reality-TV-show loser, Phoebe thought gleefully. "Oh dear, I wish I'd known earlier you were looking for a star. I could have asked Joss Benson's — no, of course she's remarried — Joss Fabian's husband, Freddo, to find you someone. He runs an entertainments agency. They live in Bagley-cum-Russet and —"

Absolute Joy sniffed haughtily. "Oh no, I don't think so. I know all about the type of people Freddo Fabian represents. Rock 'n' roll singers and the like — they'd probably be sniffing Ecstasy all round my herbaceous border. No, no — I expect Tony, my hubby, will have come up absolute trumps with, um —"

"Jezebel McFrewin?"

"That's the one."

"Let's hope so — but I still don't know how I'll recognise her."

"Well, for starters she won't be local — and you must know most of those. Use your initiative, Polly.

233

You'll just have to keep an eye open for someone who looks, er, well, who looks absolutely like a celebrity, won't you?"

"Mmm, I'll try. And will the inmates, um, residents be happy with her?"

"God knows. They wanted Vera Lynn. Now must dash — so much to do, so little time."

Jezebel McFrewin? Phoebe pondered. Nope, she'd never heard of her. Still, escorting some airhead bimbo round the fête for a few minutes wouldn't be too much of a problem, surely?

"Hi." Rocky, looking rather stunning in tight jeans and a AC/DC T-shirt and carrying a large cardboard carton, appeared beside her. "As you're clearly not working your fingers to the bone like the rest of us, do you fancy putting your OCD to practical use and giving me a hand?"

"No." Phoebe grinned. "As I've just told Absolute Joy, I'm just sitting here gathering my karma ready for being Madame Zuleika."

"Bollocks. Your karma doesn't need gathering. I *know* you're a witch — so get off your broomstick and use your powers of organisation and come and help me sort this white elephant rubbish into some sort of order."

"OK." Phoebe unpeeled herself from the bench and walked beside him across the sun-drenched lawns. "Oh, have you ever heard of Jezebel McFrewin?"

"No. Oh, um, yes. Didn't she write *Atonement*?"

"That was Ian McEwan."

"Ah, so it was. No then. Why?"

234

"Because she's the celebrity fête-opener and I've got to be her minder but I don't think I'll recognise her and — oh, you've got a great pitch, I *don't* think. Right next to the tea tent. They'll horde out of there, high as kites on fairy cakes, and straight to you. You'll be busy all afternoon — no chance of a skive."

"Thanks." Rocky dumped the carton on the grass. "I'm really looking forward to standing for hours in tropical temperatures, selling a lot of tat back to people who probably donated it in the first place."

"One of the absolute joys of a rural fête" Phoebe delved into the box. "Blimey, what's this? And this? And what the heck would anyone do with this?"

"See what I mean?" Rocky shrugged, grabbing another handful of unlikely objects. "How can I make this lot look enticing?"

Phoebe squinted at the dozens of other stalls all being similarly dressed by little groups of excited Twilighters and their visiting relatives. What a shame, she thought, that Essie had no family here to support her today. Or, on second thoughts, given Essie's family, no it wasn't. Essie was definitely better off without her children.

At least she and Rocky now knew why Essie was incarcerated in Twilights. How truly awful Essie's children had been to her: stealing her home and obviously not even coming to see her after her run-in with the yobs, then only turning up when they wanted to bleed her dry.

The story had made Phoebe more determined than ever to do everything possible to make Essie happy.

"I think," she said, "having done a very quick bit of visual market research, that everyone else is going for the piled and disorganised look with their stalls. Maybe, seeing as you've got all the rubbish that no one else wanted, if I were you I'd try a more orderly approach. At least that way you'll stop mad old bats like the Banding sisters and Gwyneth Wilkins and Big Ida Tomms from Fiddlesticks going in elbow deep and ferreting around. So, if we put all the crockery here . . . and the ornaments this side and then . . ."

"I knew your anal retention would come in handy one day." Rocky grinned at her. "I'm just surprised you haven't drawn up a table-top plan and three lists."

"There's no harm in being methodical." Phoebe poked out her tongue. "You asked for organisation and you're going to get it. Now, before Tiny Tony test-drives the sound system with 'Summer Holiday', and sends us all insane, let's get logical."

On cue, a discordant blast of "The Floral Dance" boomed shakily from the tannoy system. They looked at one another and laughed.

"Now I definitely know I'm at a Berkshire fête." Rocky grinned trying to make the best display possible of two Charles and Diana mugs — chipped — and a Bakelite monkey with one ear. "They always play scratched recordings of typical county tunes. They'll probably whiz through "An English Country Garden" and "Winchester Cathedral" next. There — see — what did I tell you?"

"And you'd have had AC/DC, Led Zep. and Rainbow, would you?"

236

"Now you come to mention it. Oh, and you'd have had Ronan Keating's greatest hits, no doubt?"

"Of course. And never the twain shall meet. Right what shall we do with this? I think it might be an egg cup."

After a further half an hour of delving and dusting, laughing and arranging, the carton was empty and the white elephant stall stocked.

"You know —" Phoebe squinted at it "— if you don't look too closely it looks OK. Quite clever to sort it into categories — jewellery, china, bric-a-brac and, er, crap — even if I say so myself. Nice marketing skills there, Phoebes. But what about prices? Have you got any stickers?"

"No. I just thought I'd let 'em haggle," Rocky said, stretching.

The stretching showed a fair bit of muscle and tanned flesh. Phoebe averted her eyes.

"Right, well, if you've finished with my display talents and classifying expertise," she said briskly, "I'd better go and make sure my fortune-telling tent has two chairs and a table, then I'll go and take Essie up on her offer of a shower before I transform myself into Madame Zuleika. Then I'll be on hand to shield Ms McFrewin from the media glare."

"Will there be any?"

"Bound to be. Absolute Joy and Tiny Tony won't be doing this for the benefit of the Twilighters, will they?"

Rocky shook his head. "Maybe they'll give your TOATs scheme a bit of publicity at the same time then. And all the extra-curriculars that the residents are involved in. It'll all help to improve the image of Twilights as the Berkshire rest home of choice."

"Mmm," Phoebe agreed. "The Tugwells will go for any damage limitation possible after Essie's mugging hit the local headlines, won't they? Good luck with the white elephant then, and I'll see you later."

Rocky bent down to pick up a fallen ET glove puppet with no face and looked at her. "Phoebe, this fortune-telling today. You're not going to do anything, well, pagan, are you?"

She just about managed to stifle her snort of indignation. "*Pagan*? I don't do *pagan*. Sacrificial rituals have no place in Hazy Hassocks."

"I meant the Happy Birthday stuff. I mean, it was OK trying it out on Slo and Essie because it is her, um, magic after all, and you knew they wanted to be together and she'd already tried the first part on Slo, and it obviously didn't work on them, but you can't just *do* it to anyone."

"Of course I can't, and I won't. But does that mean that you're beginning to believe in it?"

"Nah. Course not. Just telling you for your own good — just in case. You know what people are like round here. One whiff that you can make spooky things happen and you'll start a riot."

"Thanks for the warning, but there's no need." Phoebe started to walk away, then she smiled back at him over her shoulder. "I'm well aware that there's a time and a place for the secret magic of birthdays, and it certainly isn't here. See you later."

238

Having managed to avoid Bert's origami stall, and skirting Princess's yoga troupe limbering up haphazardly in the courtyard, and inhaling Lilith's spicy cooking as she passed the kitchen, Phoebe made her way towards Essie's roomette and her transformation into Madame Zuleika.

Essie was standing by her window, watching the frantic activity with detached amusement. "Hello, dear. Goodness you look exhausted already. It's so hot."

Essie, in cream linen trousers and a white shirt, with silver scarves in her hair, looked the epitome of cool chic, Phoebe thought, as damp and sweaty, she wiped beads of moisture from her own upper lip.

"Let's hope this fête doesn't go down in history for the number of heatstroke victims." She nodded towards Essie's bedroom. "Is it OK if I have a quick shower and get dressed now, please?"

"Of course," Essie said, not moving from the window. "Only too pleased to be able to repay your hospitality. Sorry the shower's so very small."

Phoebe pulled a face. Everything in Essie's roomette was very small. It was enough to give a hamster claustrophobia.

"It'll be lovely, thanks." Phoebe grabbed her bags and sidled into the bathroom. "Then I can move my tarots and charts into my tent before I go and do the meeting and greeting of Jezebel McFrewin."

"Yes, of course, dear, but who is —?"

"The fête opener and fancy-dress judger," Phoebe said some minutes later, her voice muffled as she emerged from the miniscule bathroom and changed into her borrowed-from-Clemmie costume. "Some minor celeb from somewhere. Have you ever heard of her?"

"No, dear, I don't think so. Ah, now wait a minute. Didn't she play Miss Marple on television?"

"That was Geraldine McEwan."

"Oh yes, of course it was."

"Er . . ." Phoebe's voice was still muffled as she carefully applied her heavy Madame Zuleika make-up. "Seen anything of Slo?"

"Not since the last time you asked, dear, no."

Bugger, Phoebe thought as she wriggled the embroidered top from her shoulders as low as decency would allow, fastened YaYa's huge hooped earrings and added a ton of bangles. She *must* have done something wrong with the Happy Birthday stuff.

That'd do nicely, though, she smiled at herself in the mirror. It was a very different Phoebe who smiled back from the one who'd looked so woebegone, whey-faced and heart-broken a couple of months earlier. Although inside everything still ached appallingly, at least on the outside she was beginning to make some inroads into the healing process.

Ah, well, she wouldn't think about Ben today. Not today . . .

"Ta-dah!" Making a concerted effort not to look anything but happy, and picking up the handkerchief hems of her skirts and petticoats, she swirled into the living room. "One gypsy fortune-teller at your service."

Essie clapped her hands. "Oh, Phoebe dear, you look lovely — even more lovely than you did at your

240

impromptu dress rehearsal. The make-up is fabulous, dear. Now, are you ready for the rest of it?"

"Yes, I think so. I'm looking forward to it."

"Good. Now, you know what we said — just the straight stuff."

"Exactly what Rocky has just told me. Don't worry, I'll merely use all my years of accumulated astrology knowledge and won't stray anywhere near the Happy Birthday magic. Promise. And I've borrowed a crystal ball from the props department at the am-dram group in Hassocks. Not that I've ever used a crystal ball or read palms, but I'll do whatever anyone wants — except the Happy Birthday thing."

"Good girl." Essie stared out of the window again. "I'll pop down and see how you're getting on later. Oh, I do hope Slo turns up today. He'll enjoy this so much. I hope his cousins don't give him too much of a hard time. We're only friends, after all."

"And would you like to be more?"

"At my age — no, honestly, I wouldn't. Well, not in the way you mean, dear. But I do lo — , like Slo very much. He's been such a perfect gent. And we had such fun together. It would be so nice if only we could . . . No, I'm being foolish. But, oh, Phoebe, dear, I really miss him."

Oh Lordy, Phoebe thought. Essie *was* in love with him. And that was all her fault, wasn't it? And now, because she'd dabbled with the birthday magic, even if she hadn't made them lust after one another as such, she'd made Essie *miss* him — she who knew better than most people how devastatingly awful missing someone was. She missed Ben so much on days like these — well, OK, on days like these and every other day too. But, on silly village occasions they'd always been together. Always — but never again.

Damn — and just when she'd promised herself not to think about Ben.

"I'm sure Slo'll be here," Phoebe said far more brightly than she felt. "He won't let you down."

"He said we should have mobile phones to keep in touch," Essie sighed. "I thought it was a silly idea at the time, but maybe now . . ."

Phoebe swished and jangled across the tiny roomette and hugged her, hoping against hope that Slo wouldn't turn out to be as unreliable as Ben had been.

To a chorus of wolf whistles from the electricians, Phoebe, carrying her case in one hand and the cool box in the other, sashayed across Twilights courtyard towards her pitch. She smiled. It was nice to know a girl could still attract wolf whistles. Wolf whistles, no doubt banned by the EU, the pc brigade and feminist groups everywhere, would fortunately never die out in Hazy Hassocks.

MADAME ZULEIKA — GENUINE ROMANY FORTUNE-TELLER the placard outside the tiny green tent read in rather shaky capital letters. Trade Descriptions anyone? Phoebe thought as she pulled the tent flaps open.

"Ouf! It's like a damn oven!" She pinned the flaps back as far as they'd go. "Blimey, we'll have people keeling over from dehydration before we've got as far as telling them what's going to happen next week if they spend much time in here."

Scrambling around at the foot of the tent, she managed to anchor the sides up to allow at least a little air to circulate. Bugger client privacy, she thought, let's just go for survival.

Quickly setting up the crystal ball, stacking the tarot decks, laying out the star, sun and moon charts on the table and stashing the cool box of bottled water under it, she hurried back outside, where it was almost as hot as inside the tent. This weather was ridiculous, she thought. It'd be fine by the coast with a sea breeze, but in landlocked Berkshire it was no joke at all.

Still, the prolonged heatwave certainly hadn't deterred the locals from turning out in force to make the most of whatever Bank Holiday Monday had to offer in true rural fashion. As Phoebe fanned her face and prayed for rain, the Twilights grounds were filling up quickly. In the distance, the almost-midday sun spiralled from the roofs of multicoloured rows of cars in the parking field, and crowds were already starting to pour in through the gate. It looked like the fête was going to be a rip-roaring success.

Blimey, Phoebe thought seconds later, still staring towards the entrance where a horde of queuing villagers had now parted like the Red Sea to allow a vision in black to pass through, YaYa's early.

She squinted. No, it wasn't YaYa. Not tall enough. Maybe it was one of her other Dancing Queens chums? Foxy, Honey Bunch, Campari, Cinnamon?

Whoever it was, Phoebe thought, she certainly knew how to make an entrance.

Dressed exactly like Olivia Newton-John in the sexy finale scene of *Grease* with sprayed-on black trousers and bustier, a lot of platinum hair and killer heels, the newcomer swayed her way across the lawns.

Every man capable of breathing stopped and stared. Every woman capable of envy did the same.

Ping! Phoebe wanted to laugh out loud as it all fell into place. This had to be Jezebel McFrewin. The fête-opener. Her charge. Well, well, maybe the Tugwells had found a proper celeb after all.

Gathering her skirts, Phoebe pushed her way through the mob. "Ms McFrewin?"

"Do what?" Sadly, the Hollywood image wasn't matched by her voice. The accent was pure Berkshire. "Uh? Oh, yeah."

Close to, Jezebel McFrewin was older than she'd first appeared, but really quite pretty, Phoebe thought. Far too much make-up, and the hair was way out-of-date, and she really wasn't dressed for fête-opening of course, but on the whole, she looked quite, well, celeb-ish.

"Hi, I'm Phoebe Bowler and I'm —"

"I'm looking for Tony Tugwell."

"Yes, I know. They asked me to —"

"He booked me, did Tony Tugwell. I'm only booked for an hour. Don't want to waste time. Time's money." Jezebel flicked a glance at Phoebe. "Where are you from?"

"Er, here, well, not the old people's home, of course. I mean, I do feel really ancient some days, but even I'm not in my dotage yet, er, I mean, I come from Hazy Hassocks."

"What agency?"

"Oh no — no agency. I'm just here to —"

"Bloody freelancers." Jezebel sniffed. "Spoiling it for us professionals. Dunno why we don't have a union. And your costume's pants, love. No one wants that old *Sound of Music* look any more. Done to death on the telly, that was. So, where's Tony Tugwell?"

"Up at the house but they asked me to —"

Jezebel McFrewin marched away. Phoebe, very miffed at the slur on Madame Zuleika, gathered up her skirts and marched after her.

"Ms McFrewin, Jezebel, please," Phoebe panted. "It's too damn hot to be galloping about. Why don't we go and sit under those trees while we wait? I'm sure Tiny Tony, er, Mr Tugwell will be out at any moment. He was going to collect you before midday."

Jezebel shrugged. "OK. I'm bloody hot. I'm OK with sitting an' waiting. So what's occurring here, then?"

"Bank holiday fête." Phoebe steered the pneumatic Jezebel towards the trees. The electricians — damn them — had swapped their allegiance, and now all leered loudly over Jezebel. "Didn't anyone tell you?"

"No one ever says anything." Jezebel frowned. "I just takes me bookings and turns up, does whatever's needed, and buggers off again."

"And, um, are you an impersonator?" Phoebe said brightly. "An Olivia Newton-John tribute act?"

"You mad? I'm whatever I'm asked to be. Today I was just asked to be a popular star. I can be Marilyn Monroe or Lily Allen or anyone in between if I'm paid to be."

"Oh, versatile."

"One word for it I s'pose. Oh." Jezebel suddenly perked up. "Do tell me *that's* Tony Tugwell? Oh, pul-ease. He is hot. Hot, hot, hot. Bloody *on fire*."

"Who?" Phoebe, buffeted by a crowd of oglers, peered. "Oh, God no, that's —"

Too late. Jezebel had peeled off on her killer heels and was unsteadily making her way towards the white elephant stall.

Rocky, who had been attempting to stop a sheaf of 1950s postcards of Hastings slithering to the ground, looked up as Jezebel, with Phoebe in — literally — hot pursuit, arrived in front of him.

"Thank you God." He grinned from one to the other. "All my fantasies rolled into one."

"Tony Tugwell?" Jezebel purred. "I'm your star for a day. Well, for an hour."

"Sadly, much as I'd like to say yes please, and thank you very much," Rocky said, "you've got the wrong man."

"Oh, balls," Jezebel groaned. "I knew I couldn't be that lucky."

Phoebe glared at Rocky. "Don't drool. This is Jezebel McFrewin."

"Who? Oh, the celebrity." Rocky was still grinning in what Phoebe considered an unnecessarily enthusiastic

246

and flirtatious manner. "Tiny Tony clearly struck lucky for once. Not sure what Absolute Joy'll say but —"

Jezebel wrinkled her nose. "Don't suppose you'd be interested in —"

"Dressing up like John Travolta? Nah, not my scene, thanks all the same. Now Bon Scott or Angus Young would be a different matter."

"Who?" Jezebel frowned.

"AC/DC," Phoebe put in crossly. "He's fixated. All leather trousers and very little else. Although I think Angus Young used to dress in school uniform sometimes."

"Excuse me." Jezebel looked affronted. "I don't do pervy."

Rocky chuckled. Phoebe, furious with herself for the shaft of jealousy that had shot through her, glowered at him.

"Polly!" Absolute Joy's less than dulcet tones cut through the tannoy's offering of "I Was Kaiser Bill's Batman". "Polly! It's a few seconds off noon. Where the devil is our celeb — oh!"

Phoebe beamed. "Mrs Tugwell, this is Jezebel McFrewin. Jezebel, I'll hand you over now."

Joy looked Jezebel up and down in some horror but rallied bravely. "Ah, absolutely lovely to meet you, Ms McFrewin. Come along then. The podium's absolutely all ready, and then we'll go straight into the fancy-dress judging. No dawdling — your audience awaits."

"Audience?" Jezebel looked horrified. "I don't do audiences. What sort of place is this?"

"Twilights Rest Home for the Elderly." Absolute Joy went into selling mode. "The absolutely premier home from home for those in their autumnal years. And this is our bank holiday fund-raising fête. As you should know, being as my hubby booked you for the opening ceremony and the fancy-dress judging."

Jezebel looked blank.

"My hubby," Absolute Joy insisted, attempting to steer Jezebel away from Rocky and Phoebe and in the direction of the podium. "Tony Tugwell? Ring any bells, dear? You're our celeb for the opening — and the fancy dress. Tony's waiting for you with the microphone, the ribbon and the scissors. Come along."

"Podium? Mic? Ribbon? Stone me." Jezebel teetered towards Joy, still looking perplexed. "The things a girl has to do to earn a living. And Tony Tugwell is your husband, is he?"

Joy nodded, pulling a "what a bimbo" face at Phoebe.

"Whatever." Jezebel shrugged. "I like an open relationship, me. Mind, it's the first time I've been asked to do a public display."

"Oh, really," Joy sighed. "Trust Tony to get a beginner."

"I ain't no beginner," Jezebel said sharply. "You mind what you're saying. I'll have you know I'm one of the Velvet Pussycat Agency's longest-serving escorts."

248

CHAPTER
SEVENTEEN

". . . and with Pluto rising in your second segment, hovering on the cusp of Libra, you're going to have really exciting news in the next few days."

Phoebe exhaled and took another swig from one of the rapidly depleting stock of water bottles in the cool box. For the umpteenth time she wondered where Essie was. She'd promised to come along and watch. Phoebe hoped Essie was OK, but then again, maybe the heat was just too much for her. It was too much for anyone.

Four hours into the Madame Zuleika act and she must have lost pounds, she reckoned. The tent was like a sauna. And it wasn't only weight she'd lost — it was also the plot and the will to live.

Mind you, she thought, as she trotted out yet another good-news prediction for a florid-faced middle-aged lady from Fiddlesticks with huge arms and an unsuitable sundress, the opening ceremony had been unexpectedly wonderful.

Absolute Joy, absolutely simmering with marital rage, had practically frog-marched Jezebel to the podium. Tony, still blissfully unaware of his faux-pas, had greeted Jezebel with a kiss on the cheek. Joy had hit Tony with her handbag. Tony had fallen over. Joy had screamed about agencies in general and escorts in particular. Jezebel, smiling and — Phoebe had to admit — staying remarkably professional throughout, had breathily declared the fête open without any preamble. As Joy and Tony were still scuffling like badgers behind her, Jezebel — clearly still not totally sure why she was there but determined to do enough to get paid — smiled vacantly for a while, then as no one was giving her any instructions, treated the Twilights audience to a raunchy and sadly off-key rendition of "You're the One That I Want".

Everyone had absolutely loved it. Even the bigwigs from the council had loudly congratulated themselves on appointing a couple of managers who didn't let the rigours of their job grind them down and who were able, despite the heatwave, to provide a touch of slapstick for the residents.

Immediately after Jezebel had finished on the podium, the council bigwigs had fussily ushered her on to the judging of the fancy dress. It was adults only as the Tugwells, mindfully pc, had earlier awarded lollipop prizes to every one of the kiddie entrants in case anyone under fifteen became traumatised by being a loser. Sadly, Jezebel had caused a bit of a hoo-ha when she'd picked out "the scarecrow from *The Wizard of Oz*" as the winner. No one had had the heart to tell her it was a non-participating elderly Twilighter in his Sunday best.

Then, as the Hazy Hassocks Brownies had skipped, out of synch, into the arena to a wheezing version of *The Archers* theme tune, Jezebel had teetered across the lawns, and had last been seen being ushered behind the Bath and Beauty stall by a bevy of electricians.

"And will I get everything that I've asked for?" the big-armed woman asked querulously. "Everything? All of it?"

"Oh, yes. Absolutely everything," Phoebe assured her, not remembering what the woman had actually asked for. "You won't know which way to turn."

"Goody — can't wait to spend 'is bloody insurance money, the tight bastard." The woman nodded greedily, popped her required pound coin into the bucket and, without saying thank you, forced her way outside.

Through the gap in the tent flap, Phoebe could see a queue of wilting fête-goers still waiting to be told that fame, wealth, health, fortune and happiness would be theirs.

"Oh, God," she sighed, fanning her face with her petticoats. "This is ridiculous."

She'd long ago stopped using the astrology charts, and the tarots had been discarded after a couple with seven children had all sneezed on them. The crystal ball was sitting cloudily and ignored to one side.

Phoebe pushed back her chair and poked her head outside. Crikey — Twilights was still heaving. There were crowds round each of the stalls, two ex-policemen dressed as nuns were riding motorbikes round the arena and the tea tent had more or less disappeared under a tidal wave of overheated villagers.

"Right," she addressed Madame Zuleika's sagging straggle, many of whom, being still attired in their fancy dress costumes, were an odd mix of pirates, fairies,

Posh and Becks and a washing machine, "I'm going to be chopping the sessions back to a couple of minutes only. It's too hot in here for anyone to survive any longer than that. If you want a cut-price prediction, then you can cross the gypsy's palm with silver — fifty pence will be more than acceptable — and I'll try my best to give you good news about your future."

Several people muttered and peeled away, but plenty remained. Phoebe took a deep breath of foetid air and plunged back into the gloom.

After a further half an hour of brief but sweatily predictable predictions, there was a surprising and more than welcome interlude of non-fortune-telling visits, the first being from Clemmie bearing dripping ice creams and accompanied by Suggs on his harness and lead.

"We've come to help Guy with the firework display," Clemmie said, after exclaiming over the Madame Zuleika outfit. "And to watch YaYa later too — although having seen the rehearsals for her act I'm still not sure. Oh, and we've met our TOAT. A lovely lady called Lilith who *cooks*."

Phoebe laughed. Clemmie, who had the most voracious appetite of anyone she'd ever met, would be a perfect partner for Lilith.

"And she gave me olives." Clemmie beamed. "Loads of olives. Stuffed with all sorts. And she's going to teach me how to make all sorts of fantastic things. And she and Suggs fell in love at first sight. She's wonderful — you're so clever thinking of the Adopt an Oldie scheme. She's coming up to the boathouse next week. Lord, but this tent is baking, Phoebes, it's not good for someone in my delicate condition — I'm going to have to go. See you later?"

"Definitely. Wouldn't miss YaYa or the fireworks. Bye, Clem. Bye, Suggs."

Clemmie and Suggs were followed almost immediately by Sukie and the divine Derry.

"OK, if we just say hi?" Sukie peered into the tent. "Bloody hell, Phoebes, you looking stunning, but aren't you melting? Thank goodness I'm not can-canning until later. Hopefully it'll be a bit cooler then."

"Hopefully. Oh, Clem's just been in — and have you met your TOAT, too?"

Derry grinned. "We have. Princess. Really outrageous hair and a penchant for yoga. She's as mad as a box of frogs. Sukie's going to introduce her to Topsy Turvey and the rest of the cancan troupe with a view to signing her up."

"Well, why not?" Sukie smiled. "She's more supple than I am and younger than Topsy and we always need more dancers. You will stick around for the show, won't you?"

Minutes after assuring Sukie she wouldn't miss the show for the world, and waving her and Derry au revoir, the tent flap was pulled open again.

"Hiya." Amber, complete with the luscious Lewis and Jem — social worker Lewis's mute and pixielike young-old best friend who had cerebral palsy and a wicked sense of humour and who had lived happily with Amber and Lewis for three years despite the gloom merchants predicting it would all end in tears —

beamed. "Just thought we'd pop in and show some moral support. Christ, Phoebes, you look great, but how can you bear to be stuck in here? Far, far too hot."

"Don't tell me." Phoebe mopped her neck. "I'm really flagging now. Great to see you — all of you — though. Clem and Sukie have already been in. I'm pretty sure there's a bit of a conspiracy and that you're all checking up on me. Making sure I'm not awash with misery."

"Nooo," Amber denied, far too quickly. "Course not. You look better, much better. We're not worried about you at all. So have you been busy? Is Madame Zuleika much in demand?"

"Non-stop. I'd've had no time to wallow in heartbreak, even if I wanted to. Oh, Clem and Sukie both said they've met their TOAT. Have you?"

Lewis nodded. "We have, yeah. Apparently every one of the Twilighters who wanted to has now been matched with someone who will take them out whenever and wherever they want to go. Brilliant idea, Phoebes. Ours is Bert. What a lovely bloke. He and Jem hit it off straight away, didn't you?"

Jem, with his own sign-language, indicated that he was very happy with his new best friend. Phoebe smiled happily. It was lovely to think the TOATs thing was up and running. It would make such a difference to the previously incarcerated Twilighters.

Jem nudged her and, grinning broadly, made some further wildly exaggerated hand signs.

"Sorry, Jem, I'm still pretty useless at this. I'll need an interpreter. Amber?"

"I, um, well, he's telling you that he's really looking forward to our Christmas wedding."

Jem shook his head violently and, grinning, signed again.

Lewis laughed. "He said he's really looking forward to seeing Phoebe as chief bridesmaid at our wedding because if she looks as much of a foxy babe then as she does now he can't wait for the best man's perks."

"First dance, you mean, Jem?" Phoebe smiled innocently. "Of course, no problem. No? What? Oh blimey — even I got the gist of that! Bugger off! You and Lewis clearly spend far too much time reading lad's mags."

They all giggled.

"Not that we want to talk about weddings today," Amber said diplomatically. "Of course."

"It's OK, honestly," Phoebe said, smiling, because it was. Almost. "I'm really looking forward to being your bridesmaid."

Amber hugged her. "Bless you. You'll be fine by then, Phoebes. Trust me. Right, Jem and Lewis both want yet another ice cream, so we'll catch you later?"

Phoebe nodded, waved them all goodbye and slumped back in her chair. It was past five o'clock. Surely the queue would have diminished by now? She peered through the tent flap. Oooh — no chance.

"OK who's next? Two of you? Together? OK, in you come."

Phoebe glanced up at the unprepossessing twenty-something couple now in front of her. Both dressed in vests and cut-off combats, with matching tattoos, they were clearly a match made in heaven.

"Sit down, please — well, not both of you obviously as there's only the one chair. Oh, not the lady? There's equality. Sorry, I'm not doing tarots today. Would you like —?"

"Crystal ball," the girl said abruptly, leaning over the table in a threatening manner. "Tell us the future, if you're a real gypsy — which you ain't."

"It says so on the placard outside doesn't it," Phoebe said through gritted teeth. "Or didn't you read it?"

"No need to snap," the boy said. "We just wants to know if me and Courtenay will be together or if —" he shot his companion a sidelong glance "— she'll go off with that Barry Turnbull again."

Great, Phoebe thought, dragging the crystal ball towards her. Now what sort of nonsense could she conjure up for this pair who really, truly deserved one another.

She wiped the dust and smeary finger marks off the crystal ball. It gave her no inspiration whatsoever, but the wiping looked pretty professional, so she did it again.

"We ain't paying fifty pence for any old rubbish, mind." Courtenay sniffed. "We wants the real stuff. I told Dwayne 'ere there's no way a pretend gypsy can tell whether we're going to stay together."

"An' I said there was," Dwayne rumbled. "An' if you can see her going off with that bloody Barry Turnbull again you gotta tell us, right?"

256

"Oh, yes of course, right." Phoebe gritted her teeth again, staring deep into the crystal. As it was actually perspex it didn't give her any inspirational insight, but the couple were watching closely and looked impressed so she carried on.

"Ah, now, the crystal says I have to ask you some questions. Five questions. I want you to answer them truthfully and accurately. OK?"

They nodded in unison.

Phoebe grinned to herself. Well, why shouldn't she? OK, Essie had instructed her not to dabble with the full Happy Birthday magic, but she hadn't said anything about not asking the Five Questions separately, had she? It couldn't hurt, could it? And surely this was an ideal opportunity to have a little practice, wasn't it?

She eyed up the couple. Possibly not the brightest of Hassocks residents. "The questions are to do with figures — maths, mental arithmetic, addition and subtraction."

"Do what?" Courtenay frowned.

"She means sums," Dwayne said. "Don'tcha?"

"I do," Phoebe agreed. "Sums — so you might need a bit of paper to work them out. Here you are, and a couple of pens."

"We ain't no good at sums." Courtenay frowned. "Are we Dwayne?"

"Nope."

"Just try your best." Phoebe smiled encouragingly. "There's no time limit."

Taking a deep breath and closing her eyes, she remembered to wave her hands over the crystal as she whispered the questions in what she hoped was a suitably husky Romany voice with suitable gaps for Courtenay and Dwayne's obviously shared brain cell to kick in.

"One, add together the days your parents were born on and write it down — like the twenty-first would be two plus one equals three. OK? Now two, add together all the numbers of the year of your birth and write that down. Right — add those numbers together. Three, add together the number of letters in your star sign and write down your answer. Take your time. Done that? Good. Now, four, write down the number of the season of your birth, with winter being number one and add that to your answer to question three. Done that? Thank you. And finally, five, take the second sum from the first and tell me the answer. In your own time . . ."

Scribbling frantically, adding up on their fingers, scratching out their original totals and starting again, eventually, like robots, the couple slowly gave her their answers.

Oddly, as their answers hung on the heavy, stale air, Phoebe felt the gruff Berkshire voices grow faint as cool breezes blew, and the tent was filled with birdsong and the sound of the sea . . .

Shocked and feeling a little peculiar, Phoebe opened her eyes.

"You —" she looked at Courtenay "— were born on December the twenty-seventh. And you, sir, were born on January the third."

Their faces were a picture.

Hah! Right! Phoebe knew she was right! She jiggled a bit inside. This was sooo amazing. They were both Capricorns, born close together, both solid earth signs — should be a good match, but . . .

"How d'ya know that?" Courtenay stared at her, slack-jawed. "That's downright spooky that is."

"You can tell stuff like that just from that old crystal ball?" Dwayne looked totally stunned. "That's magic, like, innit?"

"Very strong Romany magic," Phoebe agreed, trying not to giggle. "Now, let's see what the future holds, shall we?"

Courtenay stopped leaning over Phoebe and leaned across Dwayne instead. They were touching. Touching . . . Phoebe grinned to herself — should she? Well, no of course she shouldn't, she'd promised Essie she wouldn't, but it was far too good an opportunity to miss, and anyway, they'd been really rude to her and . . .

Before she could talk herself out of it, she cleared her throat. "I'm just going to chant a little Romany spell."

"Happy Birthday chal and chie,
A misto rommerin will be nigh.
Dukker rokker duw not beng
Misto kooshti rommer and rye."

There — she'd done it! Too late now to go back.

"Oh, Dwayne, I'm so sorry about Barry." Courtenay stopped scowling and practically simpered as she gave her beloved a slobbery kiss. "Oh, I do love you."

The slobbery kiss, slightly more invasive, was returned. "And I love you, Courtenay. Promise me you'll never look at Barry Turnbull again."

"Never. Never as long as I live. I'll love only you for the rest of my life."

"Let's get married, Courtenay. Let's?"

"Ahem." Phoebe cleared her throat, trying really hard not to jig up and down and scream with glee. "If you're happy, then put your fifty pence in the bucket on the way out."

"Ta, ever so," the girl muttered. "You're the real deal, you are. I feels right funny."

"Me too." Dwayne, the lumpy swain, lumbered to his feet and, touching whatever he could of his bulgy beloved, practically dragged her out of the tent, muttering, "I thinks I needs a drink or twenty — and find a little private place, and then we'll go an' tell ol' Barry Turnbull where to go, eh, Courts?"

"Yessss!" Phoebe punched the air. "It works! The Happy Birthday magic really works! Er —" She stopped punching and grinning and smiled somewhat sheepishly at the next victim, um, customer. "Oh, hello come along in, please."

After that, there was no stopping her. Essie wouldn't really mind, would she? After all, it had been Essie who had taught her, passed on the knowledge, reawakened her own latent skills. What was the point if she was never going to be able to use them?

In for a penny, Phoebe thought cheerfully, and proceeded to use the Five Questions and the Happy

260

Birthday magic on every suitable couple who panted wearily into the tent.

It was a revelation.

In each and every case, the Five Questions gave her accurate answers, and the Romany chant cast its Happy Birthday magic spell.

Phoebe watched in delight as previously unsure couples suddenly discovered undying love for one another and wandered dreamily hand in hand out of the tent.

Well, she thought, it wasn't *wrong*, was it? It wasn't as if she was magically matchmaking unsuitable unions, or dabbling between couples who weren't already together? All she was doing was giving them a little enchanted nudge in the right direction.

Essie had been right — she, Phoebe, *did* have the gift. And she wasn't abusing it. She wasn't. Despite what Essie had said about not using the secret magic of birthdays today, it hadn't done any harm at all, had it? And it had certainly rekindled her own confidence in her powers.

Oh, forget tarots and astrology, she thought cheerfully, that was strictly for amateurs. She was now the Happy Birthday queen. Well, no, that was Essie — which must make her the Happy Birthday princess at least, mustn't it?

"Don't know why you're grinning." Rocky, clutching two pint glasses, appeared in the tent's opening. "Some of us have been standing outside in the equatorial heat for bloody hours, selling rubbish to masses of scarily mad people with straw hats and suncream on their noses and crumbs on their chins."

"Did warn you about the proximity to the tea tent, didn't I?"

"You did but I had no idea it was going to be like that." He flopped down in the chair and pushed a glass across the table. "I'm bloody exhausted. Here, I've brought you an iced cider. I guessed you'd need one."

"Oh, you star, thanks." Phoebe gulped at the cider. "Is there anyone still queuing outside?"

"Nope — they're all taking up their positions by the stage now. And there must be something in the water — it's like a Haight-Ashbury love-in out there. Bloody entwined groping couples everywhere."

Phoebe blushed and fiddled with the crystal ball. Whoops . . .

"So," Rocky asked, "how did it all go?"

"Brilliantly. I've had a, um, crystal ball."

"Ha-ha. And the amorous excesses wouldn't have anything to do with you, would they?"

Phoebe stared at him, wide-eyed and innocent. "*Moi?* Why on earth would you think that?"

Rocky shook his head. "Phoebe, you promised. No, don't deny it — you can't lie can you? And that answer was far too evasive. Blimey — so, it worked?"

"It did." She nodded excitedly. "Like you wouldn't believe."

"Oh, believe me, I'd believe it now. You haven't seen them out there — most of them have taken each other's clothes off . . . But you said you wouldn't."

262

"I know. It just sort of happened. And it wasn't like practising on the wrong people, they were all together anyway, just —"

"Not quite as together as they are now?"

"No, probably not."

They looked at one another and grinned like children sharing a secret.

"The opening ceremony was great too, wasn't it?" Rocky emptied his glass. "Alistair McGowan knocked 'em for six."

"Jezebel McFrewin — and you know damn well what she was called. You were practically panting."

"I was not!"

"Were too!"

Rocky laughed. "I bet Essie loved it. Especially the Tugwell scuffle. Where is she, by the way?"

"I've no idea." Phoebe suddenly stopped chuckling. "Haven't you seen her all afternoon?"

Rocky shook his head. "Not a sign. I assumed she'd be in here with you."

"So did I. She said she would be. Now I'm really worried about her."

"I haven't seen Slo either, and I was sure he'd be here, too. Maybe they just decided it was far too hot and thought they'd give it a miss."

"No." Phoebe shook her head. "I'm sure she was waiting for him to arrive when I got changed. Slo's a tough old bird, and I don't think a little thing like the heat would stop Essie either, she was so looking forward to the fête. Oh, God. You don't think Slo's dumped her, do you?"

"Why would he? And how could he? You'd magicked them."

"Oh Lordy — how do I know? I might have done something wrong. Maybe they were supposed to be awake when I did it. Perhaps they were supposed to *know*. Maybe because they were asleep it's gone into reverse. Oh, sod it — Rocky, what the hell have I done?"

CHAPTER
EIGHTEEN

". . . and you really don't mind missing the fête, duck?" Slo looked at Essie sitting beside him on the soft mossy riverbank; their assorted shoes, socks and sandals abandoned, their trousers rolled up to the knee. "I know how much you were looking forward to it."

"To be honest, no, not at all. Not given this as the alternative." Essie smiled, wriggling her bare toes blissfully in the water. "And we'll still be back in plenty of time for the bit of entertainment and the fireworks, won't we? Mind you, I do regret not being able to give young Phoebe a hand with the fortune-telling. I did say I would."

"She'll be fine. She's a capable lass. She probably hasn't given you — or me — a moment's thought. More champagne?"

Essie chuckled and held out her glass. "Please. I can't remember when I was last so spoiled. This has been wonderful."

Slo refilled Essie's glass and, leaning forwards with a bit of creaking and wheezing, dipped the champagne bottle back into the river, making sure it stayed moored by its string-round-tree-root anchor. Then with a further fair bit of puffing and blowing, sat up again, swishing his feet in the clear water.

Essie raised her glass. "Cheers. Such a shame you could only have one glass with driving. Still, you made fair inroads into the strawberries. What luxury — strawberries and champagne beside the river, and not another soul in sight."

"Ah." Slo nodded. "See, I thought with everyone being up the fête, we'd probably have the place to ourselves all afternoon and into the evening — and we have. It's probably the only cool spot in the county. It's been right lovely, Essie, duck."

They smiled at one another.

Essie sipped her champagne, loving the way the bubbles burst on her tongue and the roof of her mouth, as beneath the canopy of dark-green foliage she idly watched the river winding slowly and gently towards the unseen weir. After it left their dappled hideaway and disappeared from sight, Essie could hear the current gathering speed, slapping at snapping twigs, swishing the trailing willow fronds in its frothy wake.

Here, the early evening heatwave was reduced to a gentle warmth, the town of Winterbrook was hidden from sight and sound, Guy and Clemmie Devlin's boathouse was just around the bend, and in the distance she could hear the rushing and foaming of the weir. Here, on this deserted bit of riverbank it was as if she and Slo were the only people in the world.

Beside her, Slo lit a cigarette and contentedly blew the smoke upwards in a twisting column of shifting blues and greys.

266

"Feet are funny things, aren't they?" Essie squinted down at their feet, side by side beneath the surface of the water. "Especially when you get older. You never notice the changes, do you? You just wake up one morning and they're sort of corrugated with blue veiny knots and you suddenly need a good mate with a hacksaw to cut your toenails, don't you? And legs! They turn all sort of veiny too and go mottled overnight, and then they somehow turn shiny and hairless as you age . . ." She stopped and giggled. "Sorry, it's the champagne talking. Oh, I am enjoying myself."

Slo, his black jacket discarded, the sleeves of his ancient collarless stripy shirt rolled up, gently touched her hand. "Me too, Essie, duck. Me too."

They sighed happily.

Of course, Essie thought, it wasn't going to last. It couldn't last. Not this blissful state of togetherness. Soon, she'd have to return to Twilights like a geriatric Cinderella and Slo would have to go back to Winchester Road to face the wrath of Constance and Perpetua.

Again.

"They were spitting mad, duck," Slo had chuckled throatily when he'd arrived at Twilights that afternoon. "Angry as wet hens that we'd given 'em the runaround on Saturday. Mind, they couldn't work out where we were. According to our Perpetua, once they'd seen the Daimler parked in the drive Constance thought I was indoors, as we'd hoped. She went at it like a dog after a bone. Wouldn't give up. Despite the 'eat, Perpetua said our Connie went barging round the house for hours

267

looking for me like the drugs squad on a dawn raid, only with a paisley frock and big 'air instead of them old stab vests and 'elmets."

"And when you did eventually go home?" Essie had asked tentatively. "After we'd left Phoebe's and you'd dropped me back at Twilights. Did they give you a hard time?"

"Not Perpetua really, she was just all fretty and anxious and just pleased to see me back. Constance had a fair bit to say, but I stood my ground, duck. Long and short being I said I'd have what chums I wanted and it were none of her business."

Essie had been pleased at this. Much as she hated to cause any rift in the Motions household, she was glad Slo had stood up for himself. And her.

"And this afternoon? Do they know?"

"I'm here, duck? No. They don't 'old with fêtes and suchlike — a bit too jolly for them. They're at 'ome Sellotaping up the price lists and scrubbing out the hearse. They didn't ask where I were going an' I didn't tell 'em. One of the reasons I reckoned we'd be better off not staying 'ere though. There'd be plenty of Hassockers who'd be only too pleased to let 'em know we was together. So I've got another little plan . . ."

Which, Essie thought, had momentarily floored her because much as she'd been longing to see Slo, she'd also been looking forward to the fête. But now — she smiled dreamily — she realised that this riverside retreat with Slo, and the strawberries and champagne, was far, far better than any fête.

But it couldn't last.

268

"You know, duck —" Slo flicked his cigarette butt into the river "— I've been thinking. Since last Saturday, summat's been different. With us. You and me. I've felt, well, different."

Essie swished her feet. "Me too. Odd, isn't it?"

Slo wheezed and squeezed her hand a little tighter. "Ah, you could say. Look, I reckons I'd better come clean. I 'ad a exterior motive for this little jaunt this afternoon."

"Did you?" Essie's heart sank. Maybe her feelings weren't reciprocated? Maybe Slo had decided that his loyalty lay with his cousins and not her? Maybe —?

Slo nodded. "Ah, I wanted to tell you — oh, 'ark at me — this is so damn daft." He took a deep breath that rattled and whistled under his ribs. "Right, well, what I feels is, well, I dunno. But I do know I've never felt like this afore. I allus wants to be with you, Essie, duck, an' that's a fact. I counts the minutes until we can be together. There! Now you laugh at me."

"I'm not laughing." Essie turned her head. "It's how I feel too. Crikey, we sound just like lovesick teenagers."

"Lovesick . . . Lovesick. That's it, duck. That's it exactly. I'm right heartfelt lovesick."

Essie exhaled. Both of them! This wasn't what she'd planned, though, was it? She'd known, from that first meeting, that she and Slo were compatible. The Five Questions revealing his birth date had told her so.

But she hadn't worked the Happy Birthday magic on him, had she? How very odd.

And how sad. Because there was no way on earth they could be together, was there? She could hardly move in with Slo's harridan cousins, and there was certainly no cohabiting at Twilights. The twin roomettes were for siblings only like Patience and Prudence, not for elderly couples companionably in love.

Oh bugger.

"So." Slo turned his head and looked at her. "What we going to do about it, Essie, duck? I ain't never been in love afore. You're ahead of me in the love stakes, 'aving been wed, but for me, it's a first and no mistake." He smiled shyly. "It's right lovely though, innit?"

"It is." Essie squeezed his gnarled hand. "But it makes things so difficult. And I still wonder why we never felt like this before Saturday. I mean, I was very fond of you, really enjoyed our friendship, looked forward to seeing you but —"

"Ah, me too. Then it was like — wham! Oh, not right away. Just later that night when I'd had my set-to with our Connie, and I knew I'd leave her and Perpetua and the whole blame business if it meant I could be with you."

Essie swallowed. "You can't do that. You know you can't. We're not youngsters who can cast our fate to the winds and set up home on a shoestring knowing it'll all work out over the years. We don't have the luxury of time or money. I suppose we'll just have to make the most of what we've got."

"It ain't enough," Slo said shortly. "Oh, don't get me wrong, duck. I ain't talking about any old *Karmy Sutra* stuff, but just to spend all our time together, share our lives, share our days having fun and talking and well —"

270

"Being loving friends. Together."

"Exactly." Slo lit another cigarette. "See, I'm just a silly old duffer, but I've given it all some thought and I still can't see any way round it. I knows from what your bloody kids did that you've got no money, and anything I've got is tied up in the business. The 'ouse belongs to all three of us, likewise the business. We've got nothing we can start out with."

"Just our pensions," Essie agreed. "A pittance. We're too old to live on love, too old to find other work, or buy a house or, well, anything."

They sat in silence for a while, listening to the gentle calming swoosh of the river and the leaves rustling overhead. Essie smiled wistfully to herself. They'd just have to make the best of what they had, wouldn't they? It wouldn't be perfect, but they could carry on seeing one another, spending as much time together as possible.

Even if it wasn't what they both wanted?

"Well, now that's all out in the open —" Slo sighed happily as they squeezed hands again "— and you 'aven't laughed at me, I feels a lot better. Now all we have to do is sort out what we have to do."

Essie chuckled. "A proper conundrum. Oh, listen. Is that another car pulling up? A pair of lovers looking for a quiet spot for canoodling?"

"Canoodling. Nice word, duck. We've spent the whole afternoon canoodling, 'aven't we? Yer right though — I thinks there's another lovesick couple's car making its way across the gravel."

"Damn. I don't want anyone else invading our paradise."

"Me neither, duck, but I reckons that's what it's going to be like, though, don't you? Ducking and diving, bobbing and weaving, keeping it all secret and — Bugger me!"

"What?"

"It's the bloody hearse! I'd recognise the sound of that engine anywhere. Quick, duck! Quick!"

With a combined age of over 150, *quick* was a fairly relative word. However, managing to haul their feet from the water, scramble their shoes, clothes, the picnic rug, champagne glasses and assorted debris together, Essie and Slo creaked and hobbled their barefoot way towards the Daimler.

"We'll 'ave to leave the champers bottle," Slo puffed, hurling everything on to the back seat. "Ain't no time to untie it. Still, nearly empty, wasn't it? You get yourself in, duck. All right? All in? Clunk-clicked? Right off we go — hold tight."

With a roar that shattered the rural idyll, the Daimler skidded across the gravel and shot past the hearse as it rolled to a majestic halt. Perpetua, looking rather scared, peered at them.

"Slo!" Constance howled from the open window. "Slo Motion! You come back here this minute! You and your gold-digging floozy! Stop! Now!"

Stopping, Essie thought giddily as the forwards propulsion of an elderly car and an even more elderly driver slammed her back in the passenger seat, was clearly the last thing they were going to do.

272

With Slo hunched over the wheel like a demon, they hurtled into the Winterbrook evening traffic. Essie fought an urge to giggle as, ignoring hooting horns and angry hand gestures, Slo hurled the car through the town centre and the home-going bank holidaymakers. Here we go again, she thought happily. We'll probably spend the rest of our lives being chased across Berkshire by a hearse.

"Dunno 'ow she managed to find us," Slo puffed, "but she ain't going to spoil things. She can say what she likes to me, but she ain't going to 'arrass you, duck. You OK?"

"Perfectly," Essie said faintly as they careered out of Winterbrook and on to the narrow Hassocks road. "It's quite exciting." She cricked her neck round. "Oh, they're still following. Several cars behind, mind you, but some people have gone all good-mannered and are letting them through."

"Bloody 'earse, innit?" Slo muttered. "Most polite buggers stop for an 'earse. Spooks 'em, see. Blimey, these pedals is hard on me feet."

"You're driving barefoot!" Essie shrieked, strands of hair blowing into her eyes and mouth. "Oh, this gets better and better."

And it did, she thought dizzily, as they continued their cat-and-mouse chase. It was wonderfully exhilarating after the months and months of incarceration in Twilights, and so lovely to feel alive again after the attack.

She loved Slo, Slo loved her, and everything else had paled into insignificance.

And now, after the bliss of the strawberries and champagne solitude, this crazy race with Slo, pelting across the countryside like some geriatric Bonnie and Clyde, seemed a perfect ending to the excursion.

"They're still behind." Essie pushed her hair from her eyes and squinted over her shoulder again. "Keep going, Slo! This is brilliant!"

He grinned across at her as the Daimler took a narrow bend on two wheels. "You're a rare 'un, Essie. Most ladies'd be screaming their 'eads orf by now. Hang on, duck. Last sprint coming up."

With surprising agility, Slo had bypassed Hazy Hassocks High Street and was now tearing towards Twilights.

"Crikey." As they arrived in a cloud of dust, Essie squinted at the serried ranks of cars in the fields. "Looks like it's been a wonderful success. So many cars still here. And — oh, look! Over by the stage — crowds and crowds of people . . . Most of them seem to be lying down? Don't you think that's a bit odd? The show must be on, and, oh, where are we going?"

"Not stopping in the car park, that's for sure," Slo hissed. "I'm going to get as far out of sight as possible. We'll leave the car round the back of Twilights and then we'll just mingle with the crowds. OK?"

Essie nodded as, spraying gravel, the Daimler tore towards the tradesman's entrance.

"Right," Slo said breathlessly, "let's get our shoes and socks on, duck, and join the revelry. Constance and Perpetua will 'ave a 'ard job finding us amongst that lot"

274

Essie leaned across and kissed his cheek before reaching for her sandals. "Thank you. I've loved every single minute of today. You've given me back my life."

Slo blushed as he slowly managed to pull on socks and shoes. "And you've done more than that for me, duck. Far more. Right, let's go."

Holding hands, they gradually managed to thread their way through the crowds all sitting round the stage, several dozens deep.

The Bagley-cum-Russet cancan dancers were kicking and screaming their way across the stage in their usual haphazard fashion.

"Should've brought the picnic rug," Slo muttered, "but it looks like we'll 'ave to just sit on the grass. Won't be very comfy, mind. It's fair near burned to a crisp. Give us yer 'and, duck. I'll help you down."

With difficulty and a lot of irritated sideways glances from their neighbours, Essie and Slo eventually managed to sink into the crowd without too much trouble. Slo started clapping along as Sukie, Roo, Joss and the other cancanners attempted to cartwheel to Offenbach's greatest triumph without causing themselves or one another serious injury.

Essie didn't clap.

She stared around her. What on earth was happening here? Everywhere she looked there were couples, well, canoodling, with gay abandon on the tinder-dry grass. Old couples, young couples and all ages in between.

It was exactly like being at a rather low-key rustic orgy.

It was exactly like the night she'd practised the full-blown Happy Birthday magic at Twilights . . .

"Good, ain't they?" Essie's neighbour, a florid man from Bagley, nudged her and nodded towards the stage.

"What? Who? Oh, yes, great."

"You missed the opening act. Really good they were too. Martin Pusey's Hoi-Pollois. You were too late for them."

Thank God for that, Essie thought, still squinting round her at the communal love-in with growing concern.

"Me and our V'ronica thinks they're the business," the florid man continued. "Specially them 'Three Old Maids'."

"'Little'," Essie said automatically noticing with some distaste, that our V'ronica was stroking the florid man's beer belly inside his vest with a soppy smile on her face. "'Three *Little* Maids From School'."

"Ah, that's them," the florid man beerily reciprocated our V'ronica's advances. "Funny voices. Lovely stuff. An' these cancan girls are good, too. Sexy an' that. But not a patch on our V'ronica."

Essie averted her eyes as the canoodling became slightly more frenzied.

These couples, Essie thought, gazing around, probably never even spoke to one another affectionately in public normally, and now they couldn't keep their hands off each other.

Either they'd all been given Sukie Ambrose's love potions or . . .

276

"Bloody hell!" Essie muttered, just as the largest cancanner tumbled from the stage to a rousing cheer. "Phoebe! Phoebe's bloody dabbled with the Happy Birthday magic!"

CHAPTER
NINETEEN

Phoebe, having found Essie's roomette locked and deserted at the end of her fortune-telling stint, was therefore still dressed as Madame Zuleika and feeling more than a bit grubby. Sitting beside Rocky on the periphery of the huge concert crowd and trying not to laugh as the Bagley-cum-Russet cancanners gave yet another less-than-perfect performance, she really hoped she didn't smell.

"Phoebe! Hey, you! Yes, you! Phoebe Thingamabob!"

At the sound of her name, she turned her head away from the performance and tried not to laugh.

Beneath the lilac-, rose- and gold-streaked sky, as twilight softly descended on Twilights, Constance Motion, her curls and whorls of hair nodding like a demented ice-cream cornet, was bearing down on them, high-stepping her way through the entangled couples with very evident distaste.

"Phoebe! Yes, you! Don't move! You stay right there!"

As moving was impossible due to the audience-squash, Phoebe stayed.

Rocky, who had been whistling at the cancanners, stopped and looked first at Constance then at Phoebe.

"What the heck do the Motions want with you? Are you planning your funeral?"

"Not for the next four hundred years, no. I've got a nasty feeling it might be something to do with Slo."

"His disappearance? Or rather Essie's non-appearance this afternoon, which putting two and two together —"

"Which we're not."

"Which putting two and two together, as I said, means the birthday magic has probably worked, and Slo and Essie have eloped, and Slo's nearest and dearest aren't best pleased." Rocky looked smug. "Well, you're on your own there. I know nothing about it."

"Yes you do. You were there when I did it. You didn't stop me."

"As if I'd have dared. You're far too scary when you're practising your witchcraft."

"It's *not* bloody witchcraft. And how can you call me scary? You're the axe murderer."

"Axe murderer?" Rocky frowned. "Oh, Phoebe, I'm cut to the quick. How could you trivialise the severity of my crimes against humanity? I'll have you know that my rural bloodbath mayhem was caused, à la Jason, by serial slaying with a chainsaw."

"Oh, silly me. Of course. I'd forgotten. Anyway, stop splitting hairs. Chainsaw, axe — no difference. You're the only person I know who's been in prison, so I think that scores higher on the shunned-by-polite-society list than being a witch, don't you? And Pauline and everyone at Cut'n'Curl thinks you're an axe murderer, anyway. She told me so. And — oh, God."

They stopped bantering and looked up as Constance loomed over them, blocking out what remained of the sunset.

"What the devil have you done with our cousin?"

"Sorry?" Phoebe feigned innocence. "Which cousin?"

"You know very well which cousin. Where is he?"

"Slo? I've absolutely no idea. Why on earth would I know where he is?"

Perpetua arrived panting behind Constance at that moment and looked worriedly at Phoebe. "He's with that Essie Rivers. We saw them. Again. They're allus together these days. We had a tip-orf from Doreen Prentiss's cousin's lad that they were down by the river in Winterbrook — and they were. And we followed them back here. And now Slo's gorn orf."

"Because he's old? Past his sell-by? Like cheese?" Rocky put in helpfully. "Or bread? Or milk?"

"And even if he is with Mrs Rivers," Phoebe interrupted quickly, pretty sure the Motions wouldn't find Rocky's sense of humour remotely amusing, "what does that have to do with me?"

Constance's reply was lost in a roar as the Bagley-cum-Russet cancanners managed to wreck Orpheus's triumphal return to the underworld by colliding heavily with each other.

"Because," Constance snapped once decorum had been resumed, "we know that you and Essie Rivers are in cahoots. People gossip. We get told lots of things while dealing with the bereaved. It helps 'em to make small talk. Anything to take their minds off their loss. We know that you're up here every minute God sends

280

twiddling about with hair and what have you, and that you and Essie Rivers dabble in all them zodiac-ologys."

"So?"

"And now Essie Rivers has got her claws into our Slo, and we know why."

"Do you? Why?"

"Constance says Essie Rivers thinks Slo's a money-milker." Perpetua chewed her grey lips nervously.

"Cash cow," Constance said shortly. "So, it stands to reason, you must know where Essie Rivers is, which means you know where Slo is."

"I haven't seen him all day," Phoebe said truthfully. "And I haven't seen Essie since before the fête. Tell you what, if I do see them, I'll tell them you're looking for them, shall I?"

"Yes, please," Perpetua fluttered.

"No!" Constance roared. "Tip 'em off more like! But you can tell that Essie Rivers from me that she won't get a penny out of our Slo. Not a damnable penny!"

Phoebe frowned. "I'm sure Essie isn't remotely interested in money. Slo's or anyone else's."

"Why else would she have chummed up with him, then?" Constance sneered. "No one could say Slo was a good catch otherwise, could they? And I says that as one who is mildly fond of him in a family way. But he's scruffy and clumsy and chain-smokes and gets his words wrong —"

Perpetua giggled. "No one could ever call him Rosemary Clooney."

"George," Constance sighed. "*George* Clooney, our Perpetua. But she's right. Slo ain't no oil painting, is he?"

Can't argue with that, Phoebe thought. "Maybe not. But he is kind and funny."

"And perhaps they love each other?" Rocky chipped in.

"Love? *Love?*" Constance turned the same colour as the sky. "Don't be so damned impudent. Love has never been a visitor in the Motion's parlour."

Perpetua smiled sadly. "More's the pity."

There was a roar and riotous applause as the cancanners did a Tiller Girls' exit from the stage, concertinaing into each other stage left, causing Topsy Turvey to scream long and loudly at her raggle-taggle troupe. Princess, Phoebe thought, would fit in really, really well.

"Anyway." Constance frowned when the noise had once again died down. "I'm warning you, Phoebe, you stop encouraging them in this foolish liaison. Essie Rivers will never, never, worm her way into our family, our business, or our bank accounts. Now, I'm off to find Joy Tugwell and tell her just what sort of harlot she's got nestled to her bosom."

"Viper," Rocky said.

"What?"

"Vipers go with bosoms. Not harlots."

Perpetua giggled again. Constance didn't.

"Great," Phoebe sighed as the Motions stomped away. "Now I've not only messed up Essie's life by trying out the Happy Birthday magic, but also caused a family rift for poor old Slo. Do you think we ought to warn them?"

"If we could find them, yes, but as they've managed to escape so far I think it'd be better to leave it. Where would we start looking anyway?"

"Essie's roomette again, maybe? They might have gone back there by now. No, on second thoughts, not together. The Tugwells have probably rigged up some sort of early warning system there that would send out death rays to obliterate suitors. So . . ."

Another round of rural appreciation greeted Tiny Tony and Absolute Joy as they clambered on to the stage and drowned out anything Phoebe might have been going to say. Tony had the beginnings of a black eye and Joy looked anything but joyful. Clearly the earlier Jezebel-fracas had taken its toll on the Tugwell relationship. However, they were attempting to present a united front for the council bigwigs and seemed to have turned into Richard and Judy.

"I'm sure you'll all agree," Tiny Tony screamed into the microphone accompanied by a salvo of feedback, "that both Martin Pusey's Hoi Pollois and Topsy Turvey's cancan dancers have given us a lovely show!"

Everyone cheered their agreement.

"And now —" Absolute Joy snatched the microphone "— before we round off the evening with an absolutely stunning firework display from The Gunpowder Plot, we have the grande finale act here on stage for your delectation!"

There was a moment of unseemly tussling over the microphone. Tony won.

"At vast expense we've secured the talents of the internationally famous Dancing Queens who are going to give us a little cabaret."

The crowd roared their appreciation.

Absolute Joy made a final grab. "I'm absolutely sure you'll give them a rousing Hazy Hassocks welcome."

Everyone roared and clapped and stamped their feet. There was a lot of dust.

Phoebe held her breath and crossed her fingers.

"Oh, shit."

The stage darkened. A recorded voice, in a rather bad German accent, informed the audience that it was Berlin in 1931. Two spotlights illuminated a few ladder-backed chairs and then to stunned silence, YaYa, Foxy, Honey Bunch, Campari and Cinnamon stalked on to the stage wearing bowler hats, skimpy flimsy pre-war corsets, black stockings, suspenders and boots.

"Hi," YaYa cooed throatily into the microphone. "I'm Sally Bowles, your hostess for the evening, and welcome to the Kit Kat Club."

"Good God," Rocky snuffled. "Er, I mean . . ."

"Bloody hell," Phoebe groaned. "I should have known YaYa's interpretation of 'cabaret' was never going to be the same as the Tugwells'."

The Twilights audience was mesmerised. Phoebe winced. Adding the sexually charged stage show to a horde of Happy Birthday loved-up villagers on a steamily hot night was a recipe for disaster of epic proportions.

"They're really good," Rocky hissed as YaYa and co, cleverly improvising Berlin's dark haven of decadence, stomp-danced and pouted provocatively and sat astride the chairs and sang huskily to a backing track. "Bloody sexy."

"And they're all blokes," Phoebe reminded him.

"Oh, bugger. I'd forgotten. Strike that last remark from the records."

"Oh, no. That remark will be stored away to be dragged out in the future and used against you many, many times. Christ, look at the Tugwells."

By the side of the stage, Absolute Joy was watching the shenanigans with a poleaxed expression. Tony was simply goggle-eyed.

The Twilights audience screamed and clapped their approval as YaYa strode to the front of the stage, raised her bowler hat, waved her long cigarette holder in an overtly sensuous manner and growled her way into *Cabaret*'s theme tune. Campari, Cinnamon, Foxy and Honey Bunch, using the chairs to erotic advantage, bumped and ground away in the background.

Twilights went wild.

Amid the communal groping, the audience found time to sing along lustily and whistle their appreciation.

"I hope the St John Ambulance people are ready to deal with mass coronaries," Rocky yelled in Phoebe's ear. "This is triple-X-rated stuff."

It was. It was also really, really good, Phoebe had to admit. Despite the tiny stage and the crackling sound system, the Dancing Queens were absolutely professional. And if she hadn't known their gender, she'd never have guessed they weren't proper showgirls.

"Oh, blimey." She nudged Rocky. "The Motions are bearing down on the Tugwells. There's going to be an almighty collision of outraged dignity and affronted principles at any moment. And, oh — Lord — look!"

As YaYa and co continued to stalk and shimmy, and the audience continued to stare open-mouthed, Slo and Essie had stood up.

"Sitting ducks, well, standing ducks," Rocky sighed. "With everyone else prone, they stick out like nuns in a massage parlour. Oh, too late — Constance has spotted them. C'mon, Phoebe, we'd better warn them."

Without thinking, Phoebe grabbed Rocky's outstretched hand as he hauled her to her feet. Strangely, a sort of tingle zizzed through her fingers. How weird, she thought dizzily, as still hand in hand, they picked their way through the Dancing Queens' gawping audience towards Slo and Essie. Probably just a touch of static, she thought, gazing down at her fingers laced with Rocky's. And how odd — she'd never held another man's hand. Only Ben's. Always Ben's.

"Essie!" She pulled herself together and yelled over YaYa's sexy singing and the audience's cheering. "Essie! Constance is on the warpath and —"

"Sit down and shut up!" The mass groan from the crowd echoed all around them.

Rocky dived away towards the back of the crowd, pulling Phoebe behind him as they jumped over entangled couples on the scrubby grass towards Slo and Essie.

Sadly, the Motions and the Tugwells were hell-bent on heading in exactly the same direction.

286

"Fantastic show, dear," Essie looked quizzically at Phoebe as she and Rocky reached them. "And not just the one on the stage — although that's truly wonderful. But it's like a damned love-in here. You used the Happy Birthday magic in your Madame Zuleika act, didn't you?"

"Yes, but — there's no time —"

"Why did you do it? I did warn you not to for a very good reason. Look what you've done, Phoebe. And this could be simply the start. You know the birthday magic's very powerful and —" She stopped and glanced at them. "Oh, but lovely to see you both — together. And holding hands. You haven't . . .? On each other . . .?"

"No! No way!" Phoebe wriggled her hand from Rocky's grasp. "Look, Essie, I'm sorry about the birthday magic but this is more important right now — listen! The Motions and the Tugwells," Phoebe howled over the raucous raunchiness emanating from the makeshift Kit Kat Club. "On their way! They're gunning for you!"

"Why did you stand up?" Rocky shouted over YaYa. "They'd never have spotted you if you'd stayed on the ground."

"My fault." Slo looked abashed. "When that stunning gel on stage sparked up, I wanted a fag. The people all round us went all po-faced when I got out me Marlboros, not that they'd got any room to talk re moral high ground seeing as they were all mauling one another, but then Essie said I'd probably start a forest fire with the grass being like a tinder-box, so we thought we'd sneak away and —" He glanced across the crowds as his cousins blundered angrily towards them with the Tugwells in hot pursuit. "Everyone's allus said smoking'd be the death of me."

As events at the Kit Kat Club unfurled with further bawdy singing and dancing, none of the rapt audience seemed aware of the other drama taking place on the edge of the field.

"Well!" Constance, purple-faced and breathing heavily, jabbed a finger at Essie and Slo. "Caught red-handed! What have you got to say for yourselves, eh?"

"Yes, absolutely." Joy Tugwell panted to a halt. "If Ms Motion's claims are verified, this is outrageous behaviour, Mrs Rivers. Absolutely outrageous."

"We can not and will not —" Tiny Tony puffed himself out like a small angry sparrow with a black eye "— have residents flouting the rules. We've bent over backwards to make life nicer for you all, especially you, Essie, after your little incident with the muggers, and this is how you repay us, is it? Acting like some damn teenager? Sneaking off behind our backs — no one knowing where you are —"

"Without so much as a by-your-leave," Joy interrupted, clearly reluctant to lose the moral high ground. "On more than one occasion, apparently. Breaking all the rules of your residency. And upsetting the Motion ladies to boot. We can't have this, you know. We absolutely can't condone —"

Then they all started shouting at the same time.

Phoebe shook her head. This wasn't what she'd wanted at all. This certainly wasn't what Slo and Essie deserved. Oh, Lordy, what had she done?

Somewhere amidst the recriminations, accusations and counter-accusations, YaYa and the Dancing Queens had left the stage after four curtain calls and standing ovations. For a second, the whole of Twilights was eerily silent, and then the navy-blue sky was ripped apart by a barrage of multicoloured fireworks.

The crowd, still entwined, scrambled to their feet and, with mass exclamations of delight, tottered across the field towards Guy's Gunpowder Plot pyrotechnic display.

". . . and that's my absolutely final word! Now, hubby and I have to be at the fireworks with the council's safety officers. We absolutely can't waste any more time on this nonsense — oooh!" Joy screamed as a huge rocket exploded in rainbow cushions overhead. "So, you agree to stop seeing Mr Motion, Essie, or you leave Twilights."

"That's not fair," Rocky said angrily. "They're responsible adult human beings. They're not children. You can't dictate to them."

But the Tugwells had already left the fracas, clearly heading for the safety of some very different and less incendiary fireworks.

"She can and has," Constance Motion smirked as one after the other, glorious cushions of colour waxed and waned in the navy-blue sky. "And let's hope that's a lesson to you too, Slo. You'll toe the party line in future and remember where your loyalties lies. With us, your family, not with that old trollop."

"She's no trollop," Slo stuttered. "You apologise for that remark, our Constance. Essie's a proper lady and I loves 'er."

"And I love him." Essie was close to tears. "And I won't stop seeing him."

"Love!" Constance sneered. "You don't love him, Essie Rivers! You only love his bank account. You can see our Slo as a meal ticket out of this place, can't you?"

"Constance!" Slo's voice was quivering with fury. "How dare you! Essie is a kind, decent lady — a real lady, our Constance. And she'd love me with or without my blame money or the blame undertaking business. She's not interested in any of that. She loves *me*, Constance. The first person in all my life who 'as ever loved me."

Perpetua burst into noisy sobs.

"Goodness me," Constance flared. "What soppy nonsense. Love! I've loved you, Slo. Perpetua's loved you. I expect even your parents loved you although they hid it well. We're near in our dotage, boy, an' you talk about love! Pah!"

"But I do," Essie said quietly, clinging to Slo's hand. "Love him. Not your business or his money or anything else. Him. He's a gentle, thoughtful, wonderful man who has shown me how fantastic life can be. And we always want to be together. I don't want to cause any friction between you but —"

"Too damn late for that!" Constance snorted. "You've torn us asunder, Mrs Rivers! We've been together since we was born. The three of us. You've wormed your way in and you've ruined our family! You will stop seeing one another!"

"No we won't," Slo said with dignity. "And you can't make us."

"Maybe I can't," Constance sniffed angrily. "But the Tugwells can. If they throw your so-called sweetheart out of here, then where does that leave you and your silly so-called love affair, may I ask? She won't be moving in with us, not while I've got breath in my body, and you'll not be affording a little so-called love nest will you? Not without being a third of the Motions?"

"We'll find somewhere," Slo managed to remain dignified. "And then it'll be you what 'as ripped the family asunder, our Constance, won't it?"

Perpetua's wails grew louder.

Essie shook her head. "I can't have that. Please, Slo. You can't do that. Yes, I'll carry on seeing you somehow, but if I have to leave Twilights I'll have nowhere to go and —"

"Yes, you will," Phoebe said quickly, impossibly moved by Essie and Slo's obvious devotion, and interrupting Constance's next volley. "Of course you will. You can come and live with me."

Before any of them could say anything else, a manic scream echoed across the field.

"Bloody hell, I'm not sure I can cope with much more emotion." Rocky looked at Phoebe. "That nearly tore me apart. What now?"

"Polly! Ricky! Quickly!" Joy Tugwell, beckoning wildly, her hair awry, stumbled towards them in the dusk. "I need you youngsters! Absolutely quickly."

"Does she mean us, do you think?" Rocky looked amused. "I think I'd hate to be called Ric-kay. It's even worse than Avro. What do you reckon, Polly?"

"I reckon," Phoebe said, near to tears, "that I've done Essie and Slo no favours at all. I should have left the magic well alone. And I also reckon that Absolute Joy, daft cow that she is, clearly needs someone to help her in whatever mess she's landed herself in now."

"Which means, I suppose —" Rocky looked at her "— it's Polly and Ric-kay to the absolute rescue, doesn't it?"

Leaving Essie and the Motions still simmering at one another, Rocky and Phoebe rushed across the dry tussocky grass in the darkness towards Joy. Rushing, Phoebe thought, was pretty difficult, when you were still dressed as a fortune-teller and it was difficult to see and you were wiped out with raw emotion.

"What's the problem?" Rocky reached Joy first. "Has there been an accident?"

"I need help!" Absolute Joy screamed at them. "Now!"

"Is it something wrong with the firework display?" Phoebe staggered to a halt and squinted across the field. As far as she could see, Guy's sky-high explosions were all controlled, gloriously choreographed as always, and drawing the ecstatic "oohs" and "aahs" from the crowd they habitually did.

292

"Follow me — quickly! I need you young people! And of course it's absolutely not the fireworks, you silly, girl. It's sex!"

"Sex?" Rocky queried as they tried to keep up with Joy's strident strides. "Sorry, Mrs T., but you're asking the wrong people here. We've both been dumped, so obviously we're not the best qualified to give you any sort of instruction."

"It's not me!" Absolute Joy panted. "It's absolutely everyone else!"

"Everyone?" Phoebe tried not to listen to Rocky's chuckling. "How do you mean?"

"There!" Joy came to an abrupt halt by the tea marquee. "I only popped in for a bit of leftover lemon drizzle — and, well! You go in there if you absolutely dare."

Phoebe tiptoed to the edge of the tea tent and peered inside. "Well, I know the cakes can sometimes be a bit stale, but — Oh, God."

Every couple, absolutely every unlikely and unlovely couple, that had passed through Madame Zuleika's tent post-Dwayne and Courtenay, were in shadowy humps on the much-trodden grass. In the steamy darkness there was a lot of groaning and small shrieks of pleasure. A trestle table had been upturned in the excitement and the remaining cakes and pastries were adding to the pulsating pandemonium.

"People are copulating!" Joy screamed. "On the WI's fairy cakes!"

"Don't laugh!" Phoebe whispered at Rocky. "If you laugh I will probably have to kill you."

"I'm . . . not . . . laughing . . . But, Joy, honestly, what do you expect us to do?"

"Get in there and stop them before anyone sees them."

"Not a chance." Rocky shook his head, staring at the throbbing blur of flesh. "It's more than my life's worth."

"Where's Tony?" Phoebe, hoping against hope that this really wasn't her doing while knowing full well that it was, looked at Joy. "And, um, surely it would be better if you just left them to it?"

"*Left them to it?*" Absolute Joy's eyes bulged from her head. "*Left them to it?* It's like something from a bloody Bacchanalian revel in there! And we've still got the council people on site! *Left them to it?* If this gets out we'll be an absolute laughing stock not to mention closed down under Health and Safety! Are you mad, girl?"

Tiny Tony crashed across the darkened field at that moment. "I've got one," he panted. "Ah, right, you've found some able-bodied volunteers to join in with me. Now all I need is someone to show me how to work it — are you youngsters au fait with these things?"

Rocky and Phoebe looked at one another in shared astonishment.

"Oh," Phoebe said with some measure of relief, "it's a fire extinguisher! Ah, not a great idea. Oh, look — isn't that one of your council men — over there? No, in the marquee. Under the tea urn?"

Joy gave a little scream.

"With Jezebel McFrewin." Rocky squinted. "I'd recognise that chest anywhere — although sadly we didn't see quite so much of it earlier."

"I didn't do them," Phoebe muttered. "They never came near Madame Zuleika. They're not down to me."

"Oh, good," Rocky chuckled. "One couple out of fifty or so who've managed to leap lustfully on each other without your magicking them. Oh, shit!"

Tiny Tony had managed to remove the safety catch on the fire extinguisher and had rushed into the tea tent like Rambo with all guns blazing.

As Guy's firework display reached its screaming climax, Tony put paid to everyone else's.

"Ooh, now they're all very angry and very foamy." Rocky shook his head. "And naked and not a pretty sight. I think, Polly, if it's all the same to you, I'd like to go home now."

CHAPTER
TWENTY

"Are you completely insane?" Clemmie blinked at Phoebe just over a week later as they sat in Winchester Road's courtyard garden on a hot and sultry September evening. "You can't possibly share this flat with Essie Rivers, no matter how lovely she is."

"Yes, I can." Phoebe stretched her legs out under the table and giggled as Suggs snuffled between her toes. "Why on earth shouldn't I? I'm going to need a lodger in a couple of months, and I can't think of anyone I'd rather share with. She's great, we get on really well and she won't want to borrow my clothes or my make-up or have loud parties or come home completely trollied after a night out or —"

"But she's *ancient*," Clemmie put in. "She'll have the place reeking of Vick or TCP and grizzle if you're watching telly after nine thirty."

Phoebe laughed. "No, she won't. You know Essie's really cool."

"Cool? Then she's the only one in this sodding scorching country who is at the moment," Clemmie fanned her face. "Or are you using the word 'cool' to try to convince me that Essie *gets down wiv the kids i'n't*? Because if you are —"

296

"I'm not. I mean, she's not an *old* person, not in her outlook or her attitude to life. She's laidback and she's my friend."

"OK, that's as maybe, but what about practicalities? You need a lodger for rent, yes? You need your lodger to provide you with enough rent to keep this flat, yes? So tell me exactly how Essie is going to manage to pay said rent?"

Phoebe shrugged. "From her pension, I suppose. We haven't discussed any of that sort of stuff yet, but we'll work it out. I'm not going to be charging her a fortune, Clem. Just enough to make up the rent on this place and keep a roof over my head. It'll be a fair rent, inclusive of all bills and food — I mean, she's hardly likely to eat a lot, is she?"

"God knows — my Granny Coddle ate like a pig right up to the day before she died. Even I couldn't keep up with her. Don't digress, Phoebes. And then there're the other practicalities — what about privacy?"

"She'll have our — my — old bedroom."

"Not her privacy, doughnut! Yours. What if — just say — one day, you meet someone and want to bring them back here and Essie is bustling about in her dressing gown and rollers making Ovaltine and filling her hottie bottle and singing along to Val Doonican's greatest hits. It's hardly likely to get a new relationship off to a good start, is it?"

"There won't be any new relationship," Phoebe said shortly. "We both know that. So that particular scenario isn't going to happen. And actually I think multi-generational sharing is the way forward."

"Bollocks. If that were true you'd still be living with your mum and dad and I'd still be shacked up with Molly and Bill in the Post Office Stores. We leave home to get away from the olds and be independent, don't we?"

Phoebe laughed. "Well, we both hung on longer than most, and getting married was our reason for leaving the nest, successfully in yours if not so in mine, not the fact that we were desperate to abandon the older members of our families. After all, let me remind you, weren't you thinking of adopting Lilith?"

Clemmie shrugged. "That's different. We've got Lilith coming over this evening actually, and we'd have her to stay at the boathouse any time on a temporary basis. But not for ever. Yes, OK, I'll concede that I adore Lilith. And Guy's madly in love with her. Not to mention YaYa and Suggs — you know what they're like about food. She's a genius cook, Phoebes. And she loves the fireworks too. And, yes, OK again, Amber and Sukie and all the others you roped into that TOAT thing are really enjoying their new friendships with their Twilighters, but you still don't have to move yours in."

"I do. I've told you why. Essie's done so much for me and now's my chance to do something in return. Now, can we let it drop, please? I'm too knackered to argue."

Phoebe, still baking in her after-work shorts and vest, leaned back in her chair and stared at what was visible of the simmering solid sky through the trellis-work of dry and dusty branches. Everything was still, the scents from the overblown shrubs were suffocating, and the

298

birds seemed too weary to sing. Even the Kennet's unseen constant tide sounded exhausted and sluggish.

Clemmie drained her glass and rattled the melting ice cubes. "I know you'll yell at me, Phoebes, but I think, as your oldest friend I can just say this. I think that you're using Essie as a substitute. No — don't start denying it. Look, I'm as pleased as anyone that you've got back into your zodiac stuff, and delighted that you've found so much to keep you busy after, well, you know, and of course Essie's brilliant, but you know how obsessive you are. Essie's just filling the gap left by, well . . ."

Phoebe shook her head quickly. "No she isn't. She's not some sort of placebo to keep me happy. Not Phoebe's New Project. I really, really like her. She's made such a difference to my life and we're good friends. Stop being so bloody smug, Clem. Your life is perfect, mine isn't. I'm making the best of what I've got. I'm never going to have a Guy-baby-YaYa-Suggs-Gunpowder Plot-riverside home set up, am I? Yes, OK, Essie came along at a time when I needed to *care*. And caring about her and what happened to her and being able to help her, helped me. And anyway, it's my fault she needs somewhere else to live because I used the Happy Birthday magic on her and Slo."

"But you wouldn't even have *known* about the flipping birthday-ology if Essie hadn't told you about it in the first place. She gave you chapter and verse — not to mention that weird Romany chant thing — didn't she? What the heck did she expect you to do with it?"

"Not use it at the fête," Phoebe sighed. "She did warn me not to do that. And certainly not use it on her and Slo when they didn't — and still don't — know anything about it. Jesus, Clem, it's my fault. If I hadn't made Essie and Slo fall in love they wouldn't be in this mess, would they?"

"Maybe not, although I must admit it was amusing to see everyone else at it like rabbits all over that field after you'd, um, dabbled — although of course, being occupied with the firework display I missed the best bit. YaYa said it was so funny and —"

"It was not funny! Everyone at Cut'n'Curl hasn't talked about anything else all week. Fortunately they just think it was a bit of a village swingers session got out of hand. They don't know it was anything to do with me. But I really, really didn't expect the Happy Birthday-ology to have that sort of effect."

"Why not? You know there's always magic in the air round here, and all sorts of things happen all the time. You must have believed it was going to work or you wouldn't have tried it out."

"I wanted it to work, I admit that. Or at least, I wanted to prove that it did. You know, like you're always saying, scientifically you can't have an experiment without a control — sooo I used, um, Dwayne and Courtenay as my control, and it worked. But that might have just been coincidence, so —"

"So you just went ahead and Happy Birthday love-magicked every poor sod that stumbled innocently into Madame Zuleika's tent."

"It wasn't quite like that, but yes, I agree, I did get a bit carried away — and then so did everyone else, and turned it all into some sort of orgy."

"Honestly, me and Guy were sooo gutted that we missed it. Were they really all fornicating like ferrets as YaYa said?"

"Oh," Phoebe groaned. "It was far, far worse than that. Please don't remind me, Clem. It was total mayhem. I'd never expected anything like that to happen, even though Essie had warned me."

"Did everyone get out alive?"

"Well, the council bloke who was with the lovely Jezebel fetched Tiny Tony a right purler with the fire extinguisher, but yes, I think so. Me and Rocky just legged it."

"Me and Rocky, eh?" Clemmie laughed. "Were you in there as well?"

"No we weren't," Phoebe said quickly as Suggs leaped on to her lap and started nuzzling under her chin. "We were only there because for some reason Absolute Joy thought we could stop it."

Clemmie laughed. "Well, as you started it —"

Phoebe groaned. "Yes, but Joy didn't know that, did she? And hopefully she never will. Fortunately Joy's as thick as a toastie loaf so with any luck she'll never link me with what happened in the tea tent, or to what happened back at Twilights when Essie tried out the birthday-ology for the first time. Anyway, I reckon it's all going to be a bit hushed up because there was more than one of the council bigwigs involved."

"No way! Although lucky for you, I suppose." Clemmie pushed her hands through her hair. "But do the Tugwells really still want Essie out?"

"No, not really. I think that was said to appease the Motions in the heat of the moment, but now it's been said, and Essie and Slo have refused to stop seeing one another, I think they might have to see it through. So, you see? If they do, I've got to have her here."

"No you haven't. And I still don't understand why she and Slo can't just go and live together somewhere else."

"Oh, family politics, lack of money, a million reasons — look, please can we let the whole subject drop now? Again. Do you want another lime juice?"

"Please, Phoebes. Gallons of it. Loads of ice. And olives."

"In the lime juice?"

"In it, round it, separately — you choose." Clemmie fanned her face with the hem of her long skirt. "God, I reckon it's hotter than ever. I can't sleep or get cool anywhere. I wish this bloody awful weather would come to an end."

Phoebe wished so too. She trudged into the kitchen, almost too hot and exhausted to put one foot in front of the other. Since her successes at the fête, the ones people actually knew about, of course, she'd been rushed off her feet with demands for extra astrology and tarot readings, which meant along with the Twilights hairdressing and fortune-telling sessions, this was her first free evening since the bank holiday.

302

Which, she thought as she reached for a fresh glass for Clemmie, was the whole point of the exercise and was bringing in lots of extra cash, but even she hadn't expected it to take off in such a spectacular fashion.

Wearily, she poured pints of iced lime juice into a jug, fresh water into a bowl for Suggs, snatched a couple of stubby bottles of cider from the fridge, piled olives, tacos, nachos, dips, crisps and nuts on to a tray and carefully manoeuvred her way back into the garden.

It truly was unbearably hot. The last couple of days had been sultry and pulsating with heat. The sort of heat that surely could only dissipate in an almighty storm. Phoebe lay awake at night, sweltering, the French doors open, simply praying for the sound of rain.

"Oh great. Thanks, Phoebes." Clemmie reached for her lime juice then stopped and tore open a packet of crisps for Suggs. "There you go, gannet, although you're limited to one packet a day, far too much salt for your little kidneys. Now, let me just dunk these lovely olives in my drink."

"You are disgusting," Phoebe laughed. "That poor child is going to come out pickled in brine and stuffed with pimentos. Oh, was that the door?"

Clemmie nodded. "The gorgeous red-hot Rocky coming home I reckon. Do you want me to go?"

"No. Why would I?"

"Just thought you and he were getting quite pally and three's a crowd."

"There's four of us with Suggs, and, yes, we're friendly, but nothing more. I think . . ."

Phoebe stopped and considered carefully over her cider. What *did* she really think? They were certainly good friends, and he was fabulously good-looking of course, and very funny, and she actually couldn't imagine him not being around . . . And OK, yes, she liked him very much, and, yes, she'd wondered more than once, if it hadn't been for Ben and the-wedding-that-never-was and Mindy-and-prison, if they'd met without the baggage, what might have happened then?

She took a deep breath. "I think we've helped each other quite a lot over the past weeks. We've had some great times together and we get on really well. He's very easy to be with and he's kind and funny and we do make one another laugh and we can talk easily about anything and — What? What?"

"Listen to yourself, Phoebes. Just listen — Oh, hi."

"Hi, Clemmie, hello, Phoebe, oh, and Suggs." Rocky leaned over his balcony. "I was going to have a quick shower and bring my beer down into the garden, but I don't want to interrupt."

"You're not," Clemmie said brightly. "Plenty of room. Not to mention food. And you must be so frazzled after working outside in this heat all day."

"Phoebe?" Rocky looked at her. "OK with you?"

"Fine, yes of course."

"OK — great — be down in a minute."

Clemmie sat back in her chair and grinned.

"Now what?" Phoebe frowned. "Oh, please, Clem — he's just a really nice bloke who's had a really bad time, and we're friends. F-r-i-e-n-d-s — get it?"

"Whatever," Clemmie giggled into her lime juice. "But he's sooo fit. Don't tell me you're not imagining him in the shower right now?"

"No I'm not! You're bloody obsessed. Shut up and choke on your olives!"

Fifteen minutes later, changed into clean jeans and T-shirt, Rocky clattered down the outside staircase and flopped into a chair.

Phoebe pushed the bowls across the table. "Help yourself to food, or have you eaten?"

"Thanks — no, too hot. And I'm meeting up with some mates in Winterbrook later so we'll no doubt get a takeaway on the way home. But are you sure you don't mind sharing this? Next time I really will provide everything — I'm not just a pizza and kebab bloke. I can rustle up a pretty mean spag bol — because I always seem to be eating your food."

"Oh, Phoebes is a real earth mother at heart." Clemmie beamed. "Pernickety to the point of insanity, but she won't see anyone go hungry, or without a roof over their head."

"She's referring to Essie moving in," Phoebe said quickly. "Clemmie thinks I'm mad."

"So do I." Rocky scooped up some guacamole. "Oh, I know why you offered, and it was very kind of you, but why on earth do you want to give up your freedom when you're just coping so well with living alone?"

305

"I need to share with someone in a couple of months. B — Ben paid the rent until November. After that I can't afford it all on my salary alone, not even with the extra cash I'm making from my evening work. And if Essie is thrown out of Twilights it'll be because of me."

"Because of the secret birthday magic stuff?" Rocky frowned and fed nachos and sour cream to a slavering Suggs. "Well, maybe, although you've got a lot more than that to answer for. Everywhere I go it's all anyone wants to talk about: the Twilights tea tent orgy."

"Not funny. I've learned my lesson."

"So have they, I reckon. Never decide to go for a quick roll in the hay when there's a mad rest home manager armed with a fire extinguisher in the vicinity."

"Oh!" Clemmie said again. "I'm so cross I wasn't there!"

Rocky shared a handful of unsalted nuts with Suggs. "Seriously though, Phoebe, I'm still not sure that the Essie and Slo thing was entirely your fault, or that the Tugwells can really evict her from Twilights without all sorts of tribunals and things. And I certainly don't see how having Essie living here will make the Slo situation any easier."

"Why not?"

"Because, if they're in love as they say they are and we think they are, then they'll still want to see one another, won't they? But, if Essie's here, and he's living just a few doors away, he'll still sneak away from his frightening cousins to be with Essie, which means they'll be doing all their geriatric courting here rather than at Twilights or wherever they go now. Have you actually thought about that?"

"No, I haven't. Not in that sort of detail." Phoebe frowned. "But you really like them, don't you? I thought we all got on well and —"

"Of course I like them. I think they're both great. I love it when they're here and I'd do anything in the world for Essie, you know that, but I wouldn't want to share my home with her and Slo billing and cooing."

"Slo won't be living here."

"Don't count on it. You've got a spare double bedroom, so it'll be the perfect solution for them. Cheap as chips rent, so his cousins won't fret about him blowing the family fortune on shacking up with Essie in some millionaire's mansion or whatever it is they imagine she's going to persuade him to do, and he'll still be able to pop back along the road to carry on the undertaking business any time, day or night."

"You're as bad as Clemmie. Neither of you get it, do you?" Phoebe shook her head. "I'm offering Essie a home *because* I know she and Slo want to see one another. If the terrible Tugwells *do* have to kick her out of Twilights she'll be homeless and I can't have that. And I think you're wrong about Slo moving in. He'd have to kill Constance and Perpetua first before he'd be able to leave home. Yes, he may well come and visit her here, and that's fine by me."

"See?" Clemmie raised her eyebrows at Rocky. "Too Pollyanna for her own good. Well, if you're going to talk round in boring circles about the merits and drawbacks of rehoming wrinklies, I'm going to make tracks. Guy's probably collected Lilith from Twilights by now, and she's going to teach YaYa one of her hot 'n' spicy recipes for supper so that's something I can't miss. Lilith reckons hot food makes you cooler because of the sweat. Opens the pores and it, er, pours out."

"Too much information." Phoebe grinned. "Spice, sweat and olives — Guy'll really love you tonight."

"Oh yes, he will, believe me. Now, you try and talk some sense into her, Rocky, for heaven's sake." Clemmie eased herself to her feet and fastened Suggs into his harness and lead. "See you the day after tomorrow, then, Phoebes."

Phoebe frowned. "Will you? Why? Have we arranged something?"

"September the ninth ring any bells? Your birthday? I know you said you didn't want any fuss but —"

"No, honestly, Clem. I meant it. I'm not going anywhere unless it's back to Mum and Dad's for a meal, but even that's doubtful. I really, really don't want any sort of celebration." Phoebe looked imploringly at Clemmie. "Please, you know why."

"Yeah, sure. OK then — I'll just pop round with your card and pressie. But if you change your mind I can always rally the troops for a night of drunken debauchery. No? OK." She bent down and gave Phoebe a hug. "Thanks for the food and drink, Phoebes. See you soon. Have a nice evening children."

CHAPTER
TWENTY-ONE

On the other side of Hazy Hassocks, Essie glared out of the window of her Twilights roomette, and simmered with both heat and anger.

"Damn bloody woman!" she snarled to herself. "Talking to me like I'm some bloody disobedient child! Lord, how I loathe this place!"

Irritably, she moved away from the window and slumped into her chair. The radio played softly in the background. Essie glared at it and the chirpy cheerful voice of the presenter. However, it was preferable to the television. She knew she'd probably shout obscenities at the television.

She'd just had yet another formal meeting with Absolute Joy at her the-lady's-not-for-turning best, and now she couldn't even share the edited version with her friends as they'd all gone out with their Absolutely Lovely New Chums, as Joy called them.

Earlier, Guy Devlin had whisked Lilith away in his ancient BMW for a sumptuous supper at the boathouse; Amber had collected Bert, and he'd left happily hand in hand with Jem who had shown a great aptitude for origami — far greater than Bert's if truth were known; and Sukie had picked up Princess for a jolly night of cancanning and aromatherapy.

"And I'm bloody Cinderella again," Essie groaned. "I wish I'd agreed with Slo about the bloody mobile phones now. At least I'd be able to hear his voice. At least I'd have had someone to talk to. At least I'd know what was going on. Oh, this is such a damn mess."

Since the debacle on Bank Holiday Monday, she hadn't seen Slo and she missed him more than she'd thought possible. Hoping that he hadn't decided enough was enough and abandoned her, she'd waited in vain for him to visit her or contact her in some way.

He *must* have given up on her, Essie thought. After all, blood *was* supposed to be thicker than water, wasn't it? And Constance and Perpetua had been his life for, well, all his life. And what was the point in them even thinking they could have any sort of relationship anyway?

Of course it had been sweet of Phoebe to offer a room in her flat, and very tempting too, given its proximity to Slo's house, but Essie knew it would never work. Much as she loved Phoebe's flat and that gorgeous little courtyard garden; much as she ached to be among the hustle and bustle of Hazy Hassocks village; much as she wanted to see Slo as much as possible, she knew she couldn't impose herself on Phoebe.

Even if she had to leave Twilights and become a rough sleeper, it wouldn't be fair. The poor girl had been through enough and was just starting to rebuild

310

her life. The last thing she needed was Essie cramping her style.

And, of course, it wasn't going to be necessary because the Tugwells had had to back down on their threats. Not, Essie thought bitterly, that that had made her any less keen to leave Twilights. Far from it.

"So, Essie, Mrs Rivers," Absolute Joy had said in her office not half an hour earlier, "you have an official reprieve. Isn't that absolutely wonderful news?"

Essie had said nothing and hoped against hope that Joy's plastic-spray-coated hair would melt in the heat or spontaneously combust or both.

Joy, glistening moistly inside her navy-blue skirt and nylon blouse, had bared her teeth in what passed for a smile. "The council have finally informed Tony and myself that we absolutely can't evict you from Twilights — not," she'd laughed shrilly and unconvincingly, "that we ever wanted to, of course. So much was said in the heat of the moment that evening, if you'll forgive the pun, and regretted later, of course. And we're not unsympathetic to your . . . friendship . . . with Mr Motion, absolutely not. But you can't break the rules and we can't afford to upset the rest of his family, now can we?"

Essie had still remained silent.

"So, what we propose is that we forget my, um, rather hasty declaration that you have to leave Twilights." She'd laughed brightly. "After all, what would we do without you? You're one of our most cherished and, er, interesting residents, Essie, dear, as you know. And you, for your part, must absolutely assure us that any excursions you make in the future are suitably escorted, and arranged and okayed by myself or my hubby beforehand. Oh, and of course, if the Misses Motion really object to you and . . . and . . . Mr Motion being friends for whatever reason, then I'm afraid you'll just have to absolutely abide by that, won't you?"

Essie had simply stared and glared.

Absolute Joy had preened stickily. "Mind you, as Mr Motion hasn't been near us since our absolutely wonderful fête, I think he's made up his own mind on that one, don't you, Essie, dear? All those declarations of undying love that night — ah, so sweet but so false. Men are so absolutely fickle, don't you find, dear?"

Essie had gritted her teeth and clenched her fists but still said nothing.

"So," Joy had concluded, "shall we let bygones be bygones? All friends again? Good. And I'll let little Polly know that her kind offer of accommodation won't be required, when she next visits for the hairdressing or the astrology whichever comes first, shall I? Good. Absolutely great. Right, now Essie, dear, I'm sure we've both got lots of things to do."

And dismissed and still silent, Essie had walked briskly from the office before she committed the cardinal sin of punching a Margaret Thatcher clone in the teeth.

"Oh, God, Slo," she muttered to herself now, staring dismally at the blandness of her roomette. "How sad

312

this is. All that happiness gone in an instant. All that fun we had."

"And can still have, duck," Slo's nicotine-soaked voice croaked through the just-open window, "if only I could find a way to force this blame thing open wide enough to let me get in."

Hoping she wasn't hallucinating and smiling delightedly, Essie quickly pulled herself out of her chair and despair, and hurried to the window.

No, it wasn't a mirage.

Slo, looking extremely summery in baggy khaki slacks and an elderly bottle-green polo shirt, was standing in the wilting bed of ground-cover plants, his head just level with the sill.

"You look very nice." Essie beamed sideways through the narrow gap. "I've never seen you in mufti before."

"I've acome acourting," Slo chuckled, the chuckle disintegrating into a trademark wheezing rasp. "Though, to be honest, it's just got too darn hot today for the black suit. The gels 'ave allus insisted we wear our mourning clothes so as to be ready, if you gets my drift. If someone dies between now and midnight I'll have to go and get changed, but otherwise this is 'ow I'm staying. Oh, Essie, duck, I've right missed you."

"I've missed you, too. I thought you'd decided to call it a day — it's been over a week and —"

"Ah, sorry about that, duck. One thing, we was rushed off our feet with funerals. This heat is knocking people for six all over the region, worse than a cold snap for deaths is hot weather. Good for business, of course, but rough on them as is left behind. And second thing — Oh, look Essie love, can't you open this blooming window?"

She shook her head. "Welded up to stop us escaping."

"So if I can't get in and you can't get out —?"

"We'll have to stay like this."

"Sort of like that blooming onion lady?"

Essie frowned. "Onion lady? No, sorry, don't think I know that one."

"Sat in some locked tower with a little slitty window in olden times. Had to look at 'er boyfriend through a mirror or summat."

"The Lady of Shalott!"

"Ah, shallots, spring onions, scallions. All the same. Like 'er, duck."

"God, I hope not." Essie winced. "That didn't have a very happy ending as I recall, did it? No, we'll just have to be a bit clever, again, won't we? Look, if you keep out of sight of the house and go down to the little spinney where we first met, I'll be with you in about five minutes."

She grinned delightedly to herself as Slo's head disappeared. He still loved her! It was like being a young girl all over again. She'd probably put a gold star in her diary tonight — if she had either gold stars or a diary, of course.

Quickly checking her white trousers and pale-blue top were decent, and pushing some wayward strands of hair back into her blue and white scarves, a rejuvenated Essie giggled at her reflection, and swayed out of the roomette.

314

The bland beige corridors were silent and deserted. Likewise the courtyard as it simmered under the relentless fireball of the evening sun. Despite Rocky's best efforts, the flowers were wilting, the shrubs limp and listless, the grass scorched and parched.

Essie, casting a quick glance over her shoulder and expecting to hear the mandrake scream of Absolute Joy at any minute, hurried across the lawns.

"OK, duck?" Slo took her hands in his and greeted her with a kiss in the blissful shade of the cherry and holly spinney. "No one stop you on route?"

"No one. They're all too exhausted by this heat to move away from the fans in the residents' lounge. And Lilith, Princess and Bert are out, and the Tugwells must be incarcerated in the office counting their money or whatever it is they do in there. So, we have the place to ourselves. Oh, this is a real unexpected pleasure."

"And I didn't come empty handed." Slo grinned and nodded towards an elderly wicker picnic basket. "I knew I'd 'ave to make up for me silence, so sit yerself down. I've made us some sandwiches and whatnot — not as exciting as the strawberries and champers, I'm afraid."

"It'll be lovely. Thank you so much. To be honest, I haven't had much of an appetite this past week." Essie wriggled her hands free and perched on a fallen tree trunk, watching as Slo wrestled with the basket's flaking leather straps. "You do spoil me."

He looked up, his tongue protruding from the corner of his mouth. "Nothing's too much trouble for you, duck. And I felt right down and dunderable with not being able to see you. I hopes you'll understand and forgive me when you hears what's been going on."

Essie stared out across the baked cornfields, misty hazy in the early-evening sun, and noticed sadly that the gently undulating hills were now, like Twilights lawns, scorched brown and withered. Right now, she thought, she'd probably forgive Slo anything at all.

"Orf you goes, then. You dig in." Slo proudly handed her a plate piled high with fat, clumsy sandwiches. "Egg an' cress, cheese an' tomato, and roast beef an' mustard. And I've got lashings of ginger beer for washing it all down with. Like the Famous Five only there's just the two of us."

"Oh, this is wonderful. Again. A feast fit for a . . . an undertaker and a . . ."

"Queen." Slo eased himself down beside her on the tree trunk and helped himself to a wobbling straggly doorstep of egg and cress. "Right, now, duck, you eats yer tea and I'll tell you what's been occurring . . ."

Essie ate and drank and listened to Slo's gentle burring voice as he explained that after the fête, when all hell had broken loose in the tea marquee and taken the edge off Constance's vitriol, he'd returned home to Winchester Road and he and Constance — with several rather insipid interruptions from Perpetua — had had a "gorblimey row what 'ad gorn on nearly orl night."

He'd stood his ground, put his foot down once and for all.

Our Constance had apparently been right bitter, and accused him of "orlsorts", not to mention right

316

blackening Essie's name. Slo had been firm and calm, and the long and short of it was that Slo had convinced his cousins that Essie was no gold-digger, wasn't remotely interested in the Motion's fortune and that he would carry on seeing her no matter what they said and did.

"An' come the next morning, our Constance agreed to go to see the bank, then two days on we 'ad an appointment with our solicitor and then the financial advisor, then next day back to the bank again, and we got all the papers drawn up, dividing the business three ways. We're still trading as Motions, of course. There won't be no noticeable difference outwardly — it's just that now we each own our own shares, have our own profits and what have you, instead of it being in one big account. So, whatever happens to my share of the business, our Constance and our Perpetua will still have theirs. That seems to have mollified both of 'em."

"You went to all that trouble — for me?" Essie blinked back sudden tears. "No one's ever, ever done anything like that for me — but you could have lost your livelihood, not to mention your family, and —"

"No, duck. Although I would of for you, but no . . . Our Constance 'olds family traditions very dear. She wouldn't 'ave let us split up, that's the thing. So, we're still together but separate. See?"

"Yes, I think so." Essie frowned, using both hands to stop her cheese and tomato escaping. "Obviously all this dividing up will take some time, but —"

"It'll all take blame time — just getting it underway 'as taken up the whole blame week, and —" Slo chewed manfully on roast beef"— I didn't want to tell you until it was a fett-a-clumply, which is why I 'aven't been in touch."

"And Constance is happy with that? And with us?"

Slo sucked in his breath. It whistled and rattled like a stiff nor'easter. "I wouldn't go that far. Our Constance is never 'appy as such. But what it does mean is that Constance is now convinced that even if you are after my money, it won't make no difference to her income, 'er security, or damage the business."

Essie exhaled. "So, you've really done this — for me? Oh, heavens, Slo, I'm overwhelmed. I don't know what to say. Honestly I don't."

"No need to say anything at all, Essie, duck. I'm just heartfelt glad we've got it sorted out. We'll just 'ave to let the Tugwells know that we're walking out with the gels' blessing so they don't 'ave any more to say about it and go upsetting you. Mind, there's still one sticking point — more ginger beer, duck?"

"Please. Thank you. Um, what sticking point?"

"Well, the other reason our Constance was so agin you, was that she doesn't want me to split up the family — not just the business, but the three of us being together like we allus 'as been."

"But you wouldn't leave them. Well, not yet . . . I mean, we haven't even discussed it properly — it was only like a pipe dream. I mean, we can't —"

"Bless you, you're blushing. No, but she knows that one day we might want to, well, set up 'ome together, and she'd hate that. Not that I thinks she wants *me* around as much as having a bloke in the 'ouse, you know? Them gels ain't getting any younger, and after what 'appened to you, duck, well, we all knows there's some nasty bastards out there who thinks an older lady is an easy target. Not that I'd be much shakes in a brawl, but I s'pose any bloke is better than none."

"I'm sure you'd be pretty scary if you wanted to be." Essie smiled. "And I can quite understand why Constance and Perpetua don't want to be alone. Although I'd love to be with you all the time —"

"I knows." Slo pulled a face. "I wants to be with you all the time, too. I'd love us to 'ave our own little 'ome and be able to be together night and day. And we will, duck, somehow. I promise you. Still, one step at a time, eh, duck?"

Essie nodded happily. So far so good. It was one small step for Constance, one huge step for her and Slo.

Smiling at one another, they chinked their ginger beer glasses.

"And now you'll be able to tell that little Phoebe that you won't need to take up her offer, won't you? Kind of 'er, though, steppin' in like that. She's a nice lass. And getting herself back on track. I right enjoyed myself that day we spent with her and young Rocky. He's a smashing lad, too. We'll 'ave to do it again — if she'll 'ave us, of course."

"I'm sure she will." Essie sighed as she flicked crumbs from her now-empty plate. "I need to talk to her about something else anyway."

Slo fished out the black-edged handkerchief from the pocket of his khaki slacks and laboriously wiped his mouth and fingers before lighting up a cigarette. "About some of that old magicky stuff?"

"Something like that, yes."

"You know —" Slo drew smoke luxuriously into his lungs "— this is the 'appiest I've ever been in my life. And, smashing as it'd been afore, it all changed for both of us after we'd been to Phoebe's, didn't it?"

"Yes." Essie nodded. "It did. And that's something I really need to talk to her about as soon as possible."

CHAPTER
TWENTY-TWO

Well, as birthdays went, Phoebe thought, it hadn't been one of the best. It could, however, have been a whole lot worse. In fact, she thought, glancing at her pretty birthday-present-from-her-parents watch, she was simply glad it was nearly over.

Another without-Ben milestone almost got through. Only Christmas now, and his birthday, and the anniversary of their first meeting, first date, first kiss, first holiday, first bloody everything they'd ever done together to get through. Easy-peasy . . .

What was it her mum had said? Like bereavement, the first-year anniversaries were the worst, the second not quite so painful, and each year after that was just a little bit easier to bear?

Great, Phoebe thought, sitting in the garden's flickering candlelight. By the time I'm too old to care I might just be getting over the humiliation.

She raised her glass of wine to her invisible companion. "Cheers, Ben, wherever you are. You really knew how to bugger up my life, didn't you?"

Not that she'd been on her own all day. God, no. Anything but.

There had been cards in the morning post, including a glittery one from Essie, with a note saying:

My dear Phoebe, I remember your birth date, dear, from our first meeting. I hope it's a very special magical one for you. A very Happy Birthday, dear — from me and Slo. We will be seeing you soon. And thank you for being such a kind and good friend. I shan't be needing to take you up on your more than generous offer of accommodation, dear. Things have changed. I'll tell you all about it, dear, when I see you. Trust in the secret birthday-ology and make your wish tonight. Your dreams will come true, dear, as mine have. Lots of love, your grateful friend, Essie Rivers xxx

Phoebe had hugged the sparkly teddy bear card. Slo and Essie were still together. And sounding happy. And there must have been a huge change of heart on the Twilights front, too. She couldn't wait to find out what had happened, but at least Rocky and Clemmie would be pleased that Essie wasn't going to be moving into the flat.

Phoebe read the note again and smiled; she definitely wouldn't be making any birthday wishes tonight, but it was a lovely start to a day she'd been dreading.

As soon as she'd arrived at work, Pauline and the Cut'n'Curl girls had showered her with cards and presents, and she'd made the traditional trek to Patsy's Pantry for cream cakes all round. Then, having cancelled all her extra-curricular evening appointments, she'd driven straight from the salon to her parents' semi in Bagley-cum-Russet and had been surprised and rather delighted to find they'd planned a real kiddies' tea party with jelly and ice cream and a birthday cake with pink icing and one huge pink candle.

Mrs Bowler, knowing that Phoebe didn't want to celebrate but also knowing her friends wanted to mark the occasion, had secretly invited Clemmie, YaYa, Amber, Jem, Sukie, Chelsea, Fern and Lulu — all of whom had given her more gifts and cards and joined in the retro birthday party with gusto.

It had been, Phoebe thought now, the best of both worlds and she loved her parents for thinking of it.

And now it was nearly over.

The lights from the open doors and windows in Rocky's flat illuminated the courtyard in a golden swathe and, to a muted backing track of Deep Purple, she could hear him crashing about in the kitchen. The garden was awash with the scents of herbs and red wine, frying onion and garlic, and Phoebe's stomach rumbled. The jelly and ice cream had been a long time ago and she hadn't felt inclined to eat since.

The Kennet splashed noisily behind the wall and, for the first time in ages, a breeze fluttered through the dehydrated leaves. Maybe, Phoebe thought, gazing up at the darkening sky, the weather was going to break at last.

"Er — hi, you're back. Happy birthday." Rocky leaned over the balcony. "Sorry — should have said it earlier, but you were out when I got in and —"

"It's fine. Thank you. You OK?"

"Yep, you?"

"Yes." Phoebe nodded in the darkness. "I think I am. It's been a nice day."

"Good. And, um, are you hungry? Only I was sort of planning to return your generosity and I've been cooking and — is it too late for you to eat?"

"Never too late for me. What time is it, anyway?" Phoebe squinted at her pretty birthday watch. "Oh, it's only just gone eight. It's so dark tonight — I thought it was much later than that."

"That's because of the clouds." Rocky looked up at the heavy blackness of the sky. "Everyone's been saying there's a hell of a storm brewing round the Thames Valley. There was a warning on the radio earlier."

"Bring it on." Phoebe fanned her face. "A nice downpour would be more than welcome — but not until we've eaten, of course."

"So is that a yes to a trial run of my culinary masterpiece?"

"Mmm, please. I'm starving," Phoebe admitted cheerfully. "The smells wafting down here from your food have been driving me mad."

"Great. In that case . . ."

Rocky disappeared again and Phoebe smiled to herself. She'd got him so wrong — and it was lovely to think she wouldn't have to end her birthday sitting alone like the sad dumped singleton she was.

Rocky clattered down the staircase with huge steaming bowls of spag bol, forks, spoons, kitchen roll, parmesan and hunks of ciabatta.

"I know all the celeb chefs say that bread with pasta is a no-no," he said with a grin, after the third trip from the upstairs flat, "but what else do you mop up the juices with?"

"Blimey, yes." Phoebe inhaled greedily. "This all looks superb. And I'm no gastro-foodie, so bread and pasta is more than OK by me. And —" she flourished the bottle of Merlot "— I've even got red wine tonight. Two large bottles. A birthday present from work. Or would you prefer to stick with beer?"

"Beer'd be my first choice, but red wine with spag bol sounds pretty good to me. I'll go and grab another glass then — no, you stay there. This is your birthday treat."

Trying hard not to drool too much over the food, Phoebe leaned back in her chair and stared at the sky again. Perhaps there would be a storm tonight to bring an end to this unbearable heatwave. There were no stars. No moon. Just solid towering banks of cloud. And there was definitely a breeze making the heavy air smell sort of cold and metallic.

"Happy birthday again," Rocky jumped down the last three stairs. "Sorry — not very original."

Phoebe stared at the vast bunch of flowers in every shade of pink in amazement.

"Well, I know you like pink, and I thought roses might be a bit naff, so I sort of improvised."

"Thank you. Oh, they're so gorgeous, but you didn't need to — and I'm so glad you did — and now I think I'm going to cry."

"Oh, God, please don't. I'm out of kitchen roll. I've brought a vase, so let's get them out of the way so we can eat."

Rocky placed the flowers on the table. "There — flowers, candlelight, red wine, food — oh, and music." He sprinted up the stairs again.

Phoebe laughed as the first strains of Westlife's *Greatest Hits* floated across the courtyard.

"One of Mindy's leftovers," Rocky said, returning and eventually sitting down, "which I was going to ceremonially crush with a lot of colourful cursing. I do have to warn you, though, I may well be violently sick long before track four, but even I wouldn't expect you to eat your birthday supper to the strains of an Angus Young marathon guitar solo."

"Oh, I don't know — me and Angus are getting quite used to one another." She picked up her fork and started to twirl spaghetti. "Rocky, seriously, thank you so much. This — all of this — is absolutely out of this world."

"Well," he said, "I know you didn't want any fuss, and I understand why, but —"

"This isn't fuss. This is perfect."

They ate contentedly, pausing only to talk and laugh and refill their glasses.

It was almost magical, Phoebe thought dreamily. The tiny candlelit courtyard, the softly playing music, gorgeous food — and an even more gorgeous companion.

She looked at Rocky in the candle glow, as he regaled her with some outrageous story from one of his

326

gardening contracts. She loved his voice. But he'd changed so much in the last few months, as she had. His face was no longer strained and sad. His eyes were no longer flinty and angry. And the gardening had given him a tan and defined his muscles . . .

She laughed as he reached the punchline and their eyes met across the table.

She looked away first.

Whooo. She blinked suddenly. Too much, Phoebes. Way too much . . .

"More wine?" Rocky covered her confusion, reaching across the empty bowls and scattered crumbs. "Oh, and mercifully Westlife have sung themselves to a standstill."

Phoebe laughed. "You are a fantastic cook. That was the best spag bol I've ever tasted in my life."

"Thanks, but being honest, I think it's what you'd call my signature dish. It's the only thing I can cook that turns out the same every time. Everything else is a bit hit and miss. But I'm glad you enjoyed it. I know how crappy the alone anniversaries can be."

They looked at one another again, understanding, then Rocky raised his glass to her. "Happy birthday, then. And here's to us both managing to survive the next year."

"I'll drink to that," Phoebe giggled, "and to anything else we can think of until the bottles are empty."

And they had, at least until just before ten o'clock when the first fat raindrops had splattered on to the courtyard. The storm seemed to hold its breath for about thirty seconds, then the skies opened, and teeming stair rods had waterfalled non-stop from the clouds, the rain bouncing like pennies from every surface, bowing the leaves on the shrubs, dragging the sweet, damp earthy smells from the baked ground.

Gathering everything together, the wine making them giggle like children in the welcome rain, she and Rocky had eventually cleared the courtyard, shouted their goodnights and dashed for their respective flats.

Now, Phoebe thought blearily, waking some time later to some very strange noises, it was still pouring. It was dark. And cold. And there was a continual roaring sound outside the open French doors. Sleepily, she smiled at Rocky's beautiful bouquet on the bedside table, and pulled the frilly pink duvet closer round her.

Punching the matching pillow, she snuggled down again.

Flipping noise, she thought wearily. When exactly did I fall asleep on a railway station platform? It sounds like a dozen express trains at full pelt, but —

She sat up.

Both the pink frills on her canopied bed and the curtains were billowing wildly. Outside, the rain still fell in heavy, noisy, unrelenting sheets, slapping on the ground, thundering from the wrought-iron staircase, bouncing from the chairs and tables.

And the wind . . . Where had that come from? Gale force, shrieking and moaning, it screamed round the house, rattling the doors and windows.

Phoebe squinted at her alarm clock. Not quite three o'clock — she felt as if she'd only been asleep for about five minutes. Oh, but this was blissfully snug and cosy,

328

not being unbearably hot any more, listening to the storm, feeling safe and so sleepy. She closed her eyes.

Then opened them again.

There was another noise now. Louder than the wind, more insistent than the rain. She blinked drowsily. What on earth —?

There was someone at the front door. Someone hammering at the door and leaning continuously on the doorbell.

Please, please, let it not be Clemmie and YaYa returning from some night out and determined to celebrate the last knockings of her birthday in true WKD Blue style.

Groaning, she stumbled out of bed, pulled her towelling dressing gown over her nakedness and, having wrestled with the locks on her own door, padded barefoot into the communal hall just as Rocky was doing much the same.

He looked gloriously sleep tousled and was also probably naked under his short bathrobe, she thought groggily. Clemmie would have a field day.

"I thought I was dreaming," he said with a yawn, unlocking the door. "Woke up, heard the storm, went back to sleep. Or tried to."

"Me too . . . Must be serious . . . So much noise — oh!"

Rocky had opened the door. The force of the wind nearly knocked them over and the roar of the rain intensified. Two firemen and a police officer stood under the security light, rain streaming from their waterproofs. It was all Clemmie's pre-Guy fantasies rolled into one.

"Sorry to disturb you," the policeman yelled above the relentless clamour of the storm, "but we've got an emergency situation. The Kennet has burst its banks at the lower end of Winchester Road. Some houses are already starting to flood. You should be OK this end because of the incline and the wall between you and the river, but we did have prior warning from the Environment Agency and the Met Office that this was on the cards, so we've got our emergency flood procedure in place. We're organising a mass evacuation of the street just in case."

CHAPTER
TWENTY-THREE

Phoebe blinked. Hearty food, a lot of wine and very little sleep were no aid to lightning-fast thought processes.

"OK," Rocky seemed to grasp the situation reasonably quickly considering. "What can we do to help?"

Phoebe looked at him in admiration. So cool, no panic and offering to help others . . .

"Move everything you can upstairs here first, just in case," one of the firemen said. "Pile anything you can't move up as high as you can. Then switch off your electricity supply and leave. We've got an emergency shelter set up in Hazy Hassocks village hall. If you've got transport, you could help us ferry those without."

The other fireman nodded. "We've dropped sandbags outside all the houses. You'll have to drag 'em through to the back, though. OK?"

"OK," Rocky said. "We'll be out to help as soon as we can."

And the trio moved briskly away to deal with the next house.

Flooded! Phoebe suddenly grasped the full impact. This wasn't just something to be watched vicariously on the television news, feeling sympathy and horror as people waded waist-deep through muddy rivers which had once been their homes. Watching as houses were reduced to stinking shells, possessions were ruined, lifetime memories obliterated, by torrents of untamed and terrifying water.

This was real.

"But how can the Kennet be flooding?" Phoebe frowned. "We've had months and months of drought. And only about five hours of rain. It would take years of torrential downpours for it to overflow, surely?"

"Even though the other river levels have dropped this summer, the Kennet's always running at full pelt." Rocky was grabbing the sandbags. "I can see it from my balcony. I guess with the ground being like concrete and the hills round here being baked solid and not able to soak up the downpour, any rain at all would just rush down here into the Kennet and then overflow."

"Will we flood?"

Rocky shook his head. "We'll be OK, we're at the top of the hill. Don't look so scared. You go and get dressed. I'll grab the sandbags and shove them up against the French doors. Stack your things up high like they said, and I'll get as much of your stuff up into my flat as we can move. The spare bedroom is empty so we'll be able to get everything in there. Then we'll see what we can do for the others."

"Right." Phoebe nodded, calmer now and glad someone else had taken the initiative. "Oh, God, yes, the others. Most of them along here are quite old. Right, yes, I'll make a start."

Pulling on jeans and jumper and a pair of pink Wellington boots, Phoebe found that she was no longer frightened. Angry, yes, because this was her home, and worried for the other residents of the street who weren't young and fit and agile and didn't have Rocky to help them, but not frightened.

They worked well as a team, she thought, as remarkably quickly, Rocky hefted the sandbags, secured the French doors and manhandled all her electrical gadgets, most precious possessions, including her birthday flowers, and moveable furniture upstairs.

"It'll be OK," he assured her as they bumped an armchair up the stairs. "We're lucky being this end of the street. We've got the wall and as these houses were built in the Edwardian era I can't see that crumbling tonight. The people at the bottom end have the Kennet running right through their gardens, don't they?"

"And I was always jealous of them," Phoebe had panted as the chair caught her hand between it and the staircase wall. "Being able to sit out by the water during this bloody hot summer. Not now though — poor things . . . ouch!"

"You OK?"

"Yeah — just a fingernail . . . keep going . . ."

"And so awkward for them trying to shore everything up when there's no back access, too. We'll have to see what we can do as soon as we've finished here." They shoved the chair into Rocky's spare bedroom. "Right. Thank God your obsessive tidiness means you don't live in clutter. Moving your minimalist stuff is a damn sight easier than it could have been. Next?"

They ran downstairs again, and Phoebe helped Rocky move the more bulky things and then tied up curtains, stacked what couldn't be carried upstairs onto high shelves, and made sure nothing perishable was less than six feet off the ground.

"Good God!" Rocky said, peering into her bedroom, his arms full of stereo equipment on the final run. "I know you like pink, but you need sunglasses in here. I'm surprised you get any sleep — and that bed is outrageous. Don't tell me — YaYa was your interior designer?"

Phoebe paused in hurling her favourite books on to the top of the wardrobe and grinned. "Yes — and no doubt your bedroom has pictures of planes and posters of AC/DC and the *Hollyoaks* babes?"

"Is that what you think?" Rocky balanced a couple of CD cases on top of the stereo equipment and headed back upstairs. "You'll have to come and find out sometime, won't you?"

Oh, God . . . Phoebe blushed. So he had read the unguarded message in her eyes over the birthday meal, had he? Despite everything, a little frisson of excitement shuddered through her and she frowned after his retreating figure. Had he actually said that about his bedroom? Did he mean it? Was it an invitation? And if it was, would she?

A sudden volley of howling wind and sheeting rain screamed around the flat. Phoebe dragged herself back from some rather dangerous thoughts. The danger here was far more pressing. The storm was getting worse now. Months and months of rain falling in minutes.

Torrential deluges of rain falling on to concrete-hard ground and into silted-up drains with nowhere to go except over the banks of the Kennet and into the houses.

"Right — we're done," Rocky declared, now having tucked his jeans into his gardening Wellingtons and with a waxed jacket over his T-shirt. "Have you got a decent waterproof coat?"

"No." Phoebe shook her head. Lots of snazzy little showerproof jackets, yes. Something that would withstand an Old Testament Flood, definitely not.

"Here, then." Rocky handed her a second jacket. "Probably smells of compost and bonfire smoke, but it'll keep you dry. OK — I'll switch off the electricity, and we'll go."

They went.

Nothing could have prepared Phoebe for the ferocity of the storm, or the strange sight that greeted her.

Winchester Road had become a war zone.

In the darkness, dozens of distressed people, soaking wet, were running backwards and forwards in and out of their homes, loading things into cars, staggering under the weight of sandbags, using whatever came to hand to try and stem the tide of water that was rushing inexorably towards them from the bottom end of the road.

"Christ." Rocky, his words whipped away by the wind, looked at the torrent now rapidly rising in swirling, dirty waves, where the lowest part of the street had once been. "I had no idea it was this bad."

Phoebe shook her head. This was scary. The sheer force of nature made her feel insignificant and utterly powerless.

"Looks like they need help down there," Rocky shouted, as the rain blew horizontally into their faces. "I'll go and ask the firemen where I'd be best employed. You OK to stay and help out up here?"

Phoebe nodded. She was soaked and cold, her hair hung in rat's tails, the water was almost at the top of her boots. But yes, she was OK.

More firefighters and police had materialised and were wading through the rising water by torchlight, organising people, making sure that anyone with a car got out while they still could.

It was total bedlam.

Phoebe watched as Rocky, head down, fought his way towards the worst-hit part of Winchester Road until he disappeared into the blackness. She didn't want him to leave her — oh, not in a helpless-girlie way, but just because, well, just because . . .

Pulling herself together, she ran quickly into the neighbouring house.

"Anything I can do to help?"

"No, we're fine, love, thanks all the same," Mary Miller, wearing three Rain-mates and a cagoule, shouted back. "Just getting the last few bits and bobs upstairs then we'll be off to the village hall in the Volvo. I've got me mum and dad packed and ready on the drive."

"OK, great." Phoebe frowned. "I'll leave you to it."

She'd always assumed Mary Miller was as old as Methuselah, but clearly she wasn't. The two elderly people sitting, wrapped in Pac-a-Macs in the back of the Volvo and looking quite excited at this sudden turn of events, must be her parents. They waved cheerily at Phoebe as she sped past.

Up and down the street, people from the high-walled end were helping those not so fortunate.

"Hells bells, duck." Slo Motion, drenched and dripping in a trench coat, sploshed his way out of his front drive, loading armfuls of urns into the Daimler. "This is a rum do, innit? Our Perpetua's in floods."

"Aren't we all," Phoebe yelled. "Are you OK, though? Need any help?"

"You could slap our Perpetua's face for us, if yer like, duck. Constance won't let me do it. This is the last load for the Daimler, then we're getting the stuff into the 'earse. Our Connie might be glad of an 'and, duck, being as our Perpetua's about as much use as bacon bap at a bar mitzvah."

Phoebe spat out rain water as another ferocious blast of wind blew the storm straight at her, and pushed her way into the Motions' front room.

Perpetua was wailing in a corner. Phoebe grabbed her hands. "You're OK. Honestly. We'll all be fine this end of the street. Come on. We've got to get out."

Perpetua sobbed and rocked more violently.

"If you could just get her outside." Constance Motion, wearing an ankle-length oilskin and a sou'wester and looking like she ought to be on a tin of pilchards, strode into the room. "I've told her the wall'll stop the worst of the floods down this part of the road. She won't have it. Silly mare."

Phoebe squeezed Perpetua's fingers. "Come along. It'll be great when we all get up to the hall. Warm and dry and safe." She looked at Constance. "Shall I put her in the hearse?"

"Don't tempt me. But yes."

"You could get quite a few people in there, couldn't you? In the back? I mean — if it isn't, um, already occupied by — a — dead person?"

Constance's sou'wester nodded. "Good idea, young Phoebe. I'll just make sure things are hunky-dory here, you get our Perpetua into the hearse, and then start rounding up them as is without transport. Just like the Blitz, all pulling together. Jolly good stuff."

Gently coaxing the trembling Perpetua to her feet, Phoebe led her out into the storm.

"It's OK, really," she shouted as Perpetua whimpered. "I know it's scary. I'm scared, too. Just get into the hearse. No, no — in the front passenger seat . . . There. You're safe now. Safe."

Perpetua, her thin grey lips welded together in terror, her face streaked with tears, nodded briefly. Phoebe leaned inside, trying not to drip too much, and wrapped a tartan car rug round Perpetua's skinny frame.

"There. Nice and snug. Now stay there. I'm just going to find out who else needs us, and then we'll be off to the village hall. I won't be long. All right?"

Perpetua nodded again and Phoebe closed the door.

338

"Good gel," Slo howled. "Blame weather. Can't even light up a fag to calm me nerves. I'm just orf down the bottom to see what I can do. Young Rocky down there, is 'e?"

Phoebe nodded. The strength of the wind nearly toppled her off her feet.

"Good bloke, young Rocky. Essie says —"

But whatever Essie had said was lost in yet another stinging onslaught of rain.

Phoebe, trying to keep her hair out of her eyes and her boots on her feet, slapped and slithered into the stream of water. Along the length of Winchester Road, she stopped everyone and anyone and screamed that if they needed transport to the hall then the hearse was available.

Like the Pied Piper, she sloshed back up the road again with a disparate trail of refugees plodding behind her. They were all carrying bundles of personal possessions. Phoebe could have cried for them.

"Worse down the bottom end, though. We ain't so badly off," an elderly man in a soggy balaclava and too-big galoshes said, scrambling into the back of the hearse. "And I never thought as I'd be saying that when I was riding in the back of here."

One after the other, Phoebe managed to squeeze soaking, frightened people into the hearse until it was choc-a-bloc.

"All in?" Constance strode out into the storm, the rain gushing from the brim of her sou'wester in tiny waterfalls. "Thanks young Phoebe. Maybe you're not as bad as I thought. Right, off we go." She hauled herself into the driving seat. "Hold on tight, folks. This could be the ride of your life."

And with Perpetua trembling beside her, Constance stormed the hearse through the flood water, causing bow waves to rise on either side like some monstrous amphibious vehicle.

"I've given 'em a ring up Twilights to see if they're OK and they are. No problems at all, so I'm driving down the road a bit and getting a few more into the Daimler," Slo shouted. "Then I'll be orf too. You want a lift with me, young Phoebe? Looks like the storm's getting worser."

"No, I'll wait for Rocky, thanks." Phoebe winced as yet more rain hurled itself maniacally from the black sky. "And Slo, I'm really glad you and Essie —"

"Me too, duck. Me too. We'll be round to see you when this nasty old weather changes, you marks my words. See you up the 'all then, duck."

Waving him goodbye, Phoebe wondered if she could get her hatchback out of the drive and even if she could, whether she'd make it through the floods. Probably not. Shoving her way against the gale, and sidestepping the massed emergency services who were doing a sterling job, she splashed towards the lower end of the road.

Rocky, totally saturated, was standing almost up to his knees in water.

"We're all clear down my end," she shouted at him. "What about you?"

"Firefighters seem to be having trouble getting several people to leave, but no idea why." Rocky frowned. "Otherwise, I think this end is evacuated too."

Phoebe peered through the rain. Along the road, several woebegone faces peered out of storm-lashed windows.

"Animals!"

"Christ, Phoebe, that's harsh. Hurling insults at the poor people when they've had such a rotten night. They might be a bit inbred round here, but they're not that bad."

"Nooo!" she yelled. "The people who won't leave their homes must have animals! They wouldn't leave them behind, would they? Um, if you got your van, we could take them, couldn't we?"

"Yeah. Of course. No problem. I'll go and see if I can get the van down here."

"You can't. It's too deep. Just get it out of the drive and I'll bring everyone up to you. Once we're at the hall they can't turn them away, can they? It wouldn't be right. Go on — we can do it."

Rocky leaned towards her and kissed her cheek, then turned and waded away.

Touching her fingers to her face and feeling only rain, Phoebe smiled, took a deep breath and, bent almost double by the screaming wind, slopped her way towards the first obviously occupied house.

It took some doing, but within half an hour, she'd persuaded those Winchester Road residents with animals that the non-human members of the family would be more than welcome at the village hall, and that she'd got transport waiting at the end of the road.

Having wasted precious minutes as the flood waters rose, invading previously pristine living rooms, while grateful, tearful people located cat boxes and dog leads, she eventually rounded them all up.

"Blimey," one of the very-wet and windswept firefighters said grinning at her, "regular little Noah's Ark job you've got there. Clever girl. Of course they wouldn't want to leave their pets behind. I wouldn't leave my Sooty for anything."

"Aaah. Sweet. A black cat?"

"Tarantula."

"Right."

So, with nine cats in carrying cases, two lots of hamsters in perspex globes, three budgies in cages, a bowl of goldfish and seven dogs of assorted sizes wading through the eddying, swirling currents, Phoebe led her last lot of escapees back up the flooded street.

"Jesus." Rocky grinned, having pulled his green gardening van on to the side of the road. "I hope they don't all fight."

"Why would they? They're quite friendly. Know each other well. All go to the bowls club together."

"The dogs, Phoebe, not their owners. Right — let's get you all loaded."

It was a ridiculous squash, but eventually, and with a very large, very wet golden retriever on her lap and a basket of Siamese cats under her feet, Phoebe pulled the passenger door shut on the menagerie.

Rocky started the engine round an inquisitive Jack Russell and with one backwards glance at the filthy, foaming river that had once been a sleepy residential road, pulled the van on its journey towards the village hall.

CHAPTER
TWENTY-FOUR

Hazy Hassocks village hall was a haven of warmth and light. True, the storm still raged unabated outside: the gale battering the windows and doors, screaming under the ancient roof; the rain lashing the building, sheeting down the windows in spattering, rattling torrents. But inside, all was calm.

Well, as calm as anywhere with a mêlée of drenched Hassockers and rescuers, not to mention wet animals and the stalwarts of the WRVS, could be.

"I can't believe it's only four o'clock. I thought we'd been out there all night," Phoebe puffed in the village hall's vestibule, shedding Rocky's borrowed waxed jacket in a deluge of water.

"It certainly felt like it." Rocky removed his own coat and shook rain from his cropped hair. "And you were really great. Thanks so much for all your help."

"No problem. What did you expect? That I'd come over all girlie and flap my hands and scream a lot?"

"No, actually I didn't. I know you far better than that. But it was a scary situation and we worked well as a team, didn't we?"

They had, Phoebe thought. They'd worked like two halves of a proper couple. Each knowing the other's

344

strengths, each complementing the other. With no bickering or shouting or panicking at all. A proper team. Rocky and Phoebe — not Ben and Phoebe. How odd was that? And how even odder that it felt so right?

She nodded. "We did. We do. Although we're lucky. Luckier than a lot of them. At least we've only got a disrupted night to worry about. We know our homes will be OK."

"True. But at least everyone is safe now. And dry. Although those poor sods from the lower end of the road must be frantically worried about their homes —" Rocky stopped as, once they'd stopped shipping water, they felt brave enough to walk into the hall. "Oh, it's OK in here. I thought it would be pretty grim."

"It was for years when no one used it. Mitzi Blessing took it over as one of her Baby Boomer projects a few years ago and gave it back its life. The pretty decoration and heating and lighting are down to her efforts. Oh — it's great to be in the warm." Phoebe laughed. "How weird is that? I've spent the whole of this boiling summer praying for cool rain and now I'm absolutely freezing."

"Shock, tiredness and being wet," Rocky said. "A hot drink and some sleep'll soon sort you out."

"Tea and coffee!" On cue, a slender woman in genteel shades of beige yelled in a carrying voice from behind a huge steaming urn. "Sandwiches, biscuits and fruit cake! Plenty for everyone! Come and form a queue over here! Now!"

"Headmistress," Rocky muttered. "Infant's school. I'd put money on it."

Genteel Beige did another quick recce. "Those with animals, we can provide water and, um, biscuits and cake and, um, bits of ham. Form the animal queue this side of the tea urn! No! No! *This* side!"

Phoebe laughed and, leaning on Rocky, tugged off her Wellington boots. A miniature Niagara Falls gushed from each one. In disgust, she peeled off her sopping socks and wriggled her damp, cold toes.

"I could do with a nice pair of slippers and, oh, Lordy, my jeans are soaked right through. The top half of me's fine, but look at my jeans."

"Take them off," Rocky said. "I won't mind."

Phoebe punched him.

"Right now — listen! Listen everyone! The third queue is for clothing, towels and bedding only!" Genteel Beige screamed imperiously as the Hassockers all sorted themselves out into queues for gathering provisions. "Once you have your food, go and queue over there on the other side of the tea urn and collect your bedding and what have you from Irene. *Other* side, dear! That's the ticket! And the conveniences, for those of you unfamiliar with the village hall, are through the archway to the left — that's *left*, dear — yes, that's the one."

Phoebe giggled.

"Tea or coffee?" Rocky had removed his boots too now, and his jeans, also wringing wet, clung to his legs. "Any food?"

"Coffee, please. And yes, sadly I'd really love a slab of fruit cake. I didn't think I'd be able to eat another

346

thing after the spag bol, but all that exercise has given me an appetite."

"It does that to me, too." Rocky grinned and then threaded his way through the throng of displaced persons.

Phoebe stared after him, trying to ignore the strange tingling inside.

Sod, sod, sod . . . How shallow was she? Less than three months since she'd been jilted. Less than three months since her heart had been irretrievably broken.

Nooo! This couldn't, shouldn't happen.

Especially not with Rocky who never wanted to have a relationship again.

It was just the weird events of tonight, she thought, trying to be rational. Didn't they always say that people hurled themselves into unsuitable liaisons immediately following devastating tragedies as a life-affirming exercise?

That's what it was, she told herself severely, just her body's way of convincing her she was alive and safe, nothing more.

Phew.

And, after all, no two men in the world could be more different than Rocky and Ben, could they? Crikey Moses, she thought, imagine if she and Ben *had* still been together tonight. What a to-do that would have been. Ben would have gone absolutely, completely mad. Ben would have been so angry; only worried about saving his Bang & Olufsen sound system and his white leather sofas and his designer clothes and his laptop and his BlackBerry and other assorted mobile phones and newly decorated walls . . .

"Coffee, cake *and* biscuits." Rocky returned with everything neatly packaged in plastic on a tray. "The ladies over there are brilliant. And loving this. Apparently they practise for just such an emergency all the time but never get to try it out for real."

"Thank goodness for that." Phoebe peered around for a vacant space. "Shall we try and squeeze in over there?"

They squeezed. The floor wasn't the most comfortable place, but it was heaven to be warm and reasonably dry at last. And they were close to a radiator.

"As I said earlier, it's just like the Blitz." Constance Motion on one side of them beamed through a slab of fruit cake. Currants hovered round her chin. "Not that we had much of a Blitz round here, of course, but you get the picture."

Phoebe smiled encouragingly at Perpetua who was now looking a little more cheerful and had both hands wrapped round a plastic cup of tea. Slo was nowhere to be seen.

"Out in the vestibule with his Marlboro," Rocky said, making inroads into a dunked bourbon biscuit. "He's OK."

Phoebe leaned back against the wall and looked at the villagers all doing much the same thing. Wet, shaken and bemused, they'd dredged up some sort of wartime spirit, and were making the best of a bad job. Even the animals had all settled down in their unusual new home

348

with weary resignation. The atmosphere was surprisingly cheerful as neighbours and friends shared horror stories and shed wet clothing with very little inhibition, towelling themselves down and pulling on anything warm and dry that they'd been given.

As most of the donated clothing seemed to be sportswear, they looked like a mob of displaced elderly chavs. One or two were now wearing baseball caps.

"Got your bedding yet?" A stout lady in zip-up bootees stomped to a halt in front of them. "No? Well, don't leave it too long. All the best blankets will have gorn. Here's your lilo. You youngsters may have to help some of the older people with the inflation. We have foot pumps — you won't have to blow. And you should get out of them wet clothes. We don't want you catching a chill. Irene has some nice warm tracksuits over there."

"She's only given us one lilo," Phoebe said as the bootees marched on. "She must think we're, um, well, together."

"We are. For tonight at any rate," Rocky said. "And I'm hardly likely to turn into some sort of Lothario in front of this lot, am I? I may be a bit of an exhibitionist, but I've never performed well in front of an audience. Shall I go and see if there are any suitable bottoms?"

"*What?*" Phoebe mumbled round her fruit cake. "Are you some sort of pervert?"

"Tracksuit bottoms. She's right. We can't spent all night sleeping in wet jeans, can we?"

"Suppose not. OK. Look, you go and grab clothes and bedding and blow up lilos on that side of the hall, and I'll go and help out with anyone who needs a hand with their lilo over here."

By the time all the lilos had been inflated, bedding distributed, and more tea and cake handed out, the Hassockers were growing drowsy. The roars of earlier had dulled to muted, yawning conversations and low muffled laughter.

The Motions on one side of Phoebe, and Mary Miller and her parents on the other, had all changed into warm clothes and were settling down for the night.

"Two pairs of jogging bottoms," Rocky said triumphantly. "Two pillows, one towel and one blanket. You can go first. I'll hold the towel and promise not to peek."

Standing up, with Rocky holding the towel as a modesty screen, Phoebe tugged at her saturated jeans. They wouldn't budge. She wriggled and squirmed, but the wet denim clung like a second-skin.

Rocky grinned. "Sit down and I'll pull them off from the bottom."

"You're bloody obsessed with bottoms," Phoebe muttered, sitting down anyway, wrapping the towel round her and raising her feet. "OK, go on then."

It took five minutes of tugging and giggling and falling over and having to stop to regain composure before Phoebe and her jeans parted company.

"Don't look!" she muttered, grabbing the pale-grey track-suit pants and pulling them on over the damp rest of her. "Oooh, nice." Skintight, they came up to her armpits and dangled off the ends of her feet like flippers. "Your turn. Do you want me to — Oh, no,

350

spoilsport. You're obviously adept at removing your clothing in public." She grinned as Rocky wrapped the towel round his waist and, with seemingly minimal fuss, managed to wriggle out of his own jeans and into his joggers. Then she screamed with laughter. "Ohmigod! Look at you!"

Rocky's tracksuit trousers finished halfway up his legs. His legs though, she had to admit, were rather spectacular: strong, muscled and tanned, like the rest of him.

She dragged her eyes away. "You only need a tartan scarf and you'd be a dead ringer for the Bay City Rollers."

"Hark at you — you look like an anorexic seal."

They looked at one another and laughed again.

"Shush." Constance Motion nodded her hair, flattened unbecomingly by the earlier pressure of the sou'wester. "Some of us are trying to get some shut-eye."

Sleep, it seemed was going to be difficult to come by. All the lights were still on and the emergency workers streamed in and out, snatching much-needed cups of tea and biscuits, bringing up-to-date information on the floods, exchanging cheery banter with the WRVS ladies.

And it seemed that at least two Hassockers needed to use the loo every couple of minutes. And those inveterate smokers, like Slo, puffed and panted their way backwards and forwards to the outside vestibule. And several ladies, calmer now, found it the ideal opportunity to set the village jungle drums a-throbbing and were deep in loudly scurrilous conversations.

"We could play cards," Rocky said as they perched precariously side by side on the lilo, "if we had any cards. I don't suppose you're carrying a handy pack of tarots?"

"Nope."

"Damn. What about your witchy secret magic of birthdays stuff, then?"

"Absolutely not. Not here. Not now. Not ever. Not after the fête."

"Damn again, then. It'd be great. We could get everyone to hold hands while you chanted the Romany magic thing and then stand back and see what happened."

"We know what would happen. Only too well."

"Hmm." Rocky looked round the village hall, where everyone was making the best they could of their temporary beds. "Oh, but think about it — you'd only have to get them to touch, and then you could go into the chant — what was it — ah yes."

"Happy Birthday chal and chie,
A misto rommerin will be nigh.
Dukker rokker duw not beng
Misto kooshti rommer and rye."

"Hush! You can't say that here — but, bloody hell," Phoebe said in amazement. "When did you memorise that?"

352

"Ages ago. You had it written everywhere, every time we were in the garden. I'm quite good at learning stuff like that. I was reasonably good at poetry at school."

"Were you? They didn't do much poetry at Winterbrook Comp. Was yours a posh school, then?"

"Posh-ish. Anyway . . . shall we birthday magic all these people and see what happens?"

"No."

"Shame. OK — what about I Spy?"

"I can do I Spy." Phoebe beamed. "I spy with my little eye something beginning with WP."

"Wet pensioner."

"Bugger."

They giggled again. Perpetua on one side and the trio of Millers on the other were all snoring.

Constance leaned over as Slo trotted off for yet another cigarette break. "As sleep seems to be impossible, I've been wanting to speak to you about our Slo and Essie Rivers."

Phoebe sucked in her breath. "I'm not sure that now's the time."

"Oh, we've sorted it all out, mostly." Constance nodded her flattened hair. The combined efforts of the sou'wester and industrial-strength lacquer made it look as if she was wearing two large pancakes on her head. "At least, she won't be getting her hands on our money in the future. She'll tell you all about it. Why on earth our Slo felt the need to get hisself a lady friend at his age, Lord only knows, but what's done is done."

Phoebe smiled encouragingly, relieved that she wasn't going to have to spend the rest of her life feeling guilty over the Slo and Essie Happy Birthday magic thing. "I'm just pleased that it's all worked out for the best. I think we should all be happy for them — after all, Essie has had a rough time, and living in Twilights can't be easy for her, not when she's been used to having her own home and is so, well, um, not old in her attitudes."

"We've told Slo that he won't be moving her in with us." Constance looked very fierce. "Our parents would be turning in their sarcophagus at the very idea. What I don't want, young Phoebe, is any more encouragement from you on that score. I know you thought you were helping, and I don't object to them coming to visit you, but please don't give them any ideas about living together."

"I haven't! Well, yes I know I said Essie could move in with me but —"

"And don't you think that gave our Slo ideas? Essie living just along the road? He'd be there morning, noon and night."

"Just what I said," Rocky added helpfully.

"But it's not going to happen now, is it?" Phoebe glared at Rocky. "Essie is staying at Twilights, whether she wants to or not, and Slo is staying with you."

"Slo still wants to find them a little place together. I know that. And, although I'd never let him know, I can understand this. But we don't want to lose him either. We need a man, you see. Slo has his heavy duties with the business and at home, and we sleep easier in our beds at night knowing we have a male presence to protect us."

354

Phoebe managed to keep a straight face. Slo versus youthful hoodies didn't seem a very equal battle, but if it kept Constance happy.

"There is a solution," Rocky said, stretching.

"Is there?" Phoebe looked at him. She wished he wouldn't do the stretching thing. And certainly not so close to her. "I can't think of one."

He beamed at Constance. "Slo and Essie can move into Phoebe's flat."

"*What*?" Phoebe screeched. "After everything you said? And I can't — there isn't room."

"I think not." Constance looked scary. "I will not have our Slo cohabitating. I know there are only two bedrooms and if Phoebe is in one then that means, unless my arithmetic is faulty, that Slo and Essie Rivers would be sharing the other one."

"Not if Phoebe shared my flat."

"*What*?" Phoebe screeched again. "You're asking me to move in upstairs? With you?"

Constance tutted at such flagrant flouting of morals in public.

"Not as such, no," Rocky said. "As flatmates. Why not? We're friends, aren't we? We get on really well, my spare bedroom is bigger than yours, and thanks to tonight's, er, extraordinary happenings, most of your stuff is up there now anyway. The rest wouldn't be difficult to shift, would it? I'd even help you paint the room pink."

Phoebe shook her head. Was he mad? Was she mad? Was this really happening?

She looked at him. "Sorry, but exactly when did this little scheme occur to you?"

"Oh, I've been thinking about it for some time. It'd make a lot of sense. Your sofas are much nicer than mine, my telly's bigger than yours, we could pool all our stuff, well, at least what Ben and Mindy left us with and there'd be plenty over to get Essie and Slo off to a good start, wouldn't there? Especially as Essie has no furniture of her own, and obviously all Slo's is part of the family home."

Constance, sensing a money-saving scheme, looked very enthusiastic. "And you youngsters would be on hand to keep an eye on them, wouldn't you? Just in case either of them had a funny turn or something? I think this is sounding like a wonderful idea."

"I'm not sure," Phoebe muttered, completely wrong-footed by the turn of events. "After all, I've just got used to living alone and —"

Rocky grinned. "Look, if you don't want to, then say so. I just thought, as we both wanted to help Essie escape from Twilights, and it would mean Slo would be close to both his cousins and the business, they could have separate rooms too, and be like flatmates. Like us."

Constance nodded. Her hair didn't. "Do you know, young Rocky, the more I'm hearing, the more I'm thinking this is really not such a bad idea at all. I'm not too set in my ways to object to males and females sharing accommodation in a nice decent manner. Separate rooms and what have you. And it'd mean our

Slo would be close to home — even though we'd have to be sleeping without him to protect us."

"Oh," Phoebe said airily, "don't worry about that. I'm sure Rocky has a plan to provide you with some sort of replacement live-in security guard."

"Look," Rocky said, grinning, "if you think it's a lousy idea just say so."

"I think it's a lousy idea. My Take That and your AC/DC. My obsessive tidiness and organisation and your total lack of any sort of planning. Your friends and mine all wanting to visit at the same time. My —"

"OK, forget it. I just thought it would solve all sorts of problems."

And create a whole lot more, Phoebe thought. Living in the same flat as Rocky. Sharing her life with him. Being with him all the time. So near and yet so far. Like sister and brother . . .

She simply couldn't do it. It would be asking far, far too much. Especially when he got over Mindy and started to bring other gorgeous girls home.

She blinked. She'd be jealous. She *would* be jealous. She'd be very, very jealous indeed.

Then again, on the other hand, there was the rent which was looming large in November. And she'd have to share her flat with someone then, wouldn't she? And with Slo and Essie downstairs they'd at least know they wouldn't be having wild parties and trashing the place.

"OK, I'll think about it." Oh, God — she could just imagine what Clemmie and YaYa would make of it. "But I don't think we should mention it to Slo and Essie yet. I'll need to think about it a lot. And then there's our tenancy agreements — we'd have to OK it all with the letting agent and the landlord, wouldn't we?"

"We would." Rocky nodded. "But I'm sure it'll be fine."

"It's absolutely pissing down out there." Slo, very windswept and with raindrops glistening in his hair, traipsed back from his cigarette break leaving squelchy wet footprints across the village hall's nicely polished floor. "And what'll be fine? What've you been cooking up, our Constance?"

"Nothing at all." Constance gave Phoebe and Rocky a huge stage wink. "Absolutely nothing at all. Come along then, I think it's time we all tried to grab a few hours sleep."

Hah! Phoebe thought. No bloody chance of that. Not now. Probably not ever again.

CHAPTER
TWENTY-FIVE

Genteel Beige dimmed the lights. The gossipers had all stopped chatting. The hall-wide snoring had become a gentle hum, like a sleepy, rhythmic relaxation tape.

"Right —" Rocky pushed the pillows side by side "— you get comfy first, then I'll sort of fit in."

"Excuse me?" Phoebe whispered back. "This is a single lilo. Alone, I'll probably fall off it, together, well . . ."

"I promise not to roll on you."

"Stop it. Not funny. Look, Rocky, this flat-sharing thing . . ."

"We'll talk about it tomorrow. The lilo-sharing thing is more pressing — if you'll pardon the expression."

"No — and you're really, really not funny. And I don't want to share a flat with someone who isn't funny."

"Why not? You shared with Ben and he was the most humourless bloke I've ever met."

Phoebe frowned. "He was pretty, um, not funny now you come to mention it. Jilting was probably his idea of a joke. Anyway, as he's off topic until hell freezes over — which won't be that long according to the tabloids

— about this flat-sharing thing . . . Why on earth didn't you mention it to me before?"

"Before blurting it out to all and sundry? Well, because it wasn't really a properly formed plan — just something I'd been thinking about for ages. Ever since you first said about Essie moving in with you, in fact. It seemed like a sensible solution to the problem — and Constance just sort of brought it all out into the open tonight. I'd obviously rather have talked it over with you first. Privately."

"I'd have preferred that too," Phoebe said huffily, trying to wriggle herself down on the lilo. "And there's far too much to think about to make a quick decision and — Jesus! This is just like trying to sleep on a waterbed."

"Not one of my life experiences," Rocky chuckled. "Tell me more."

"No. OK, now I'm sort of settled. You'll just have to sleep sitting up on the floor."

"Why?"

"Because," Phoebe stage-whispered, "I'm not sleeping with you. Not on a single lilo or anywhere else."

Rocky chuckled again.

"What?" Phoebe frowned. "What's so amusing?"

"You. Now — budge over. I'm cold and tired and need to sleep."

"Rocky! Nooo!" Phoebe giggled as he slid alongside her and the lilo slithered to one side. "We can't . . ."

"We can. Just lie still. Right, now I'm going to stretch my legs out and — Oh, sod it."

They both rolled on to the floor, laughing.

"Shush!" the village hall admonished them.

They looked at one another and sniggered.

"Face it," Rocky whispered, "moving into my spare room will be much simpler than this."

"I'm not talking about moving into your spare room," Phoebe panted. "Now get off my lilo."

"*Our* lilo," he corrected. "It's all me-me-me with you, isn't it?"

They giggled again.

"For pity's sake," Constance rasped in the half-light, "shut up and go to sleep."

For some reason they both found this extremely funny.

"Oh, God — right, now I'm going to get on and stretch my legs out," Rocky whispered, sliding on to the edge of the lilo. "Now you do the same your side, at exactly the same time, and hang on. We'll have to sleep back to back and keep a grip."

Keeping a grip, Phoebe thought, was easier said than done. Both literally and metaphorically.

She took a deep breath and eased herself on to the lilo. Far, far too much of her was touching Rocky. Practically all of her in fact.

"Christ, you're a bed-hog," Rocky muttered. "Budge over."

"Can't — look — oh — sod it!" Giggling again, Phoebe tumbled off the lilo.

Rocky leaned across and looked at her. "You know, I've managed to laugh women into bed before, but laughing one out of it is a first for me."

"Don't want to hear about your bloody past conquests," Phoebe muttered, scrambling back on to the lilo. "There, now I'm on and you're on. Keep your back to me and — Where's the blanket?"

"Here. Stay still. There. Comfy now?"

"Nope."

Actually, Phoebe thought, she was. Although it was very, very strange. Being in bed with another man. There had only ever been Ben. Just Ben. And now, she and Rocky Lancaster were back to back, touching flesh and jogging bottoms beneath an army surplus blanket in the company of at least a hundred other people.

She held herself as far away from him as possible, keeping her body rigid. Oh, blimey, this was sheer torture. Every bit of her longed to turn over and slide her arm across Rocky's waist and snuggle in.

She moved her head slightly on the pillow and the lilo lurched.

"Don't move," Rocky hissed. "Not even a millimetre. OK?"

"OK, OK." She smiled in the darkness. "Just don't snore."

"I never snore. What about you?"

"Good Lord, no."

"Good. Goodnight, Phoebe."

"Night."

It was actually amazingly cosy, she thought drowsily. Being warm and snug in the darkness of the hall after the weird events of the night; listening to the steady, vicious moaning of the wind, interspersed with the occasional screaming gust which rattled the windows and whistled through the rafters. And then the rain, which still teemed torrentially, lashing against the windows, drumming on the roof.

Phoebe opened one eye. The rows of makeshift beds were stretched along both sides of the hall. Most people were also asleep now, or at least trying. Some were sitting up, talking softly, others just staring, simply too overtired or overwrought to sleep. The air was warm with damp clothes drying on radiators. And the wonderful WRVS ladies were still on duty, silently still making tea and coffee and providing sustenance for the firemen and policemen and Environment Agency workers who plodded wearily through the door.

She felt safe and secure, like she had as a child on scarily stormy nights, when snug in her bed, she could hear her parents downstairs, contentedly laughing at something on the television, and knowing all was well with her world.

And here she was, with Rocky, in bed. Well, on a lilo. She smiled again into the darkness, and closed her eyes, knowing she'd never be able to sleep in a million years.

"Wakey-wakey," Genteel Beige's dulcet tones echoed through her sleep-fuddled brain. "Rise and shine, campers. It's seven-thirty. We have tea, coffee, scrambled eggs and bacon, toast and marmalade. Form an orderly queue for the ablutions — we have emergency packs of soap and toothpaste — then come and queue this side of the urn where Irene will serve your breakfasts."

Gradually, the hall yawned, scratched, grizzled and stretched itself into wakefulness.

Phoebe opened her eyes. It was daylight and she'd only had three minutes' sleep.

"You do snore," Rocky said directly into her ear, "but only in a pretty girlie way. More like gentle snuffles."

Ohmigod. She'd spent the night with Rocky Lancaster!

She sat up quickly and they both tumbled from the lilo.

"Hi." He grinned at her. "Christ, you look rough in the mornings."

"Thanks. So do you." It wasn't true. Dishevelled and unshaven, he looked fantastic. She quickly ran her fingers through her hair and hopefully wiped any mascara smudges from beneath her eyes. "Oooh, I need coffee and the loo and some toothpaste — and not necessarily in that order."

"Me too, but it looks like we might have to fight a million pensioners for the privilege."

"Easy for you then." Phoebe stretched out her cramped legs and flapped the overhanging jogging bottoms like flippers. "Being as you're the one with an official qualification in fighting. You know, my parents will be so angry that I've spent the night with an ex-con."

"Whereas mine won't be at all surprised that I've slept with a witch. Right, we'll sort out the bathroom stuff first then grab breakfast. Then I guess we'll have to head home and see what the damage is before we go to work."

"Work?" Phoebe squeaked. "*Work?* They can't expect us to go to work after a night like that, can they? I can't go to work. I'll fall asleep on my scissors."

It took another half an hour to manage to get into the loos and pull on their now-stiff-but-dry clothes.

"You do, don't you?" Phoebe paused in doing up her jeans, and watched Rocky instead.

"Do do what?"

"Put your socks on the wrong way round. Well, you know right before left."

He grinned. "You remembered. I'm flattered."

"Don't be," she said airily. "It's all part of my OCD — remembering trivia. What was your name again?"

Rocky threw the blanket at her and they giggled.

Ten minutes later, they were dressed and packed away and joined Genteel Beige's indicated queue for breakfast. Between them they helped the other Winchester Road residents who were too arthritic and too weary to help themselves to food.

"I'm going to make a huge donation to the WRVS," Rocky said, handing out breakfast trays to the Motions and the Millers. "They've been absolutely amazing. Unsung heroines the lot of them."

"They're quite brilliant." Phoebe nodded. "They've worked so hard, and probably haven't had any sleep either. It might be worth mentioning the WRVS to Essie, too. She'd fit in there really well. She loves helping people and — oh, wow — this is the best breakfast I've ever had."

Somewhere in the middle of the communal eating, the local Environment Agency representative made an appearance. The storm, he informed them, had abated and there was no more heavy rain forecast. In fact, it was now quite a pleasant day. Slo nodded confirmation through his spluttered toast and marmalade. Having sneaked out for an early cigarette he'd already informed all and sundry that "The blame rain 'as stopped. The wind 'as dropped. It's all drying out nicely."

The Environment Agency man, plied with tea from Irene, told them that the Kennet had subsided to its normal level. The majority of their houses were absolutely fine and untouched by the floods, and that the firefighters had had several appliances working all night pumping the water away from the others. Winchester Road, he said, was now passable and all but half-a-dozen houses perfectly habitable and those lucky enough not to have been affected could return home immediately.

Those unfortunate enough to have suffered damage would be temporarily rehoused at the Star and Garter Hotel in Winterbrook until their homes could be repaired.

He then read out a list of addresses, all from the lower end of the street, and asked those people to join him afterwards when he'd take them through the full procedure.

As each address was read out a little sob and wail of despair echoed from the depths of the hall. Those luckier Winchester Road residents stopped eating and looked on in deep pity.

"Poor sods," Rocky mumbled through his toast. "I wouldn't even wish that on Mindy."

Gradually, breakfast over, the village hall packed itself up. In between answering a zillion calls on her mobile, as the news had broken on local radio, from her parents, her friends, and Pauline at Cut'n'Curl, and assuring everyone that she was fine and the flat was fine, Phoebe, and several other of the more able-bodied people, helped the WRVS ladies to clear everything away. Rocky, offering his services, became a sort of transport marshal and ushered people and animals into his van, the hearse and the Daimler for the return journey to Winchester Road.

"I'll get my last lot home and settled in, then I'll come back for you," Rocky said, leading the golden retriever with one hand and carrying a cat basket in the other. "You'll just have to be a bit late for work."

"Pauline says I don't need to come in today," Phoebe said happily. "So, once this is done, and we can get home and switch on the electrics and heat the water, I'm going to wash my hair, have a long bath and then go back to bed."

"And move your stuff back downstairs?"

"Well, some of it, yes. The things I'll need at the moment. Look, we'll need to talk about this a lot more, won't we? With Essie and Slo as well. We can't just dive straight in. Think about it, I'd probably drive you mad, tidying things up all the time, and getting anxious if the cushions aren't straight or the candles haven't burned down to exactly the same size, and if we don't have fish for dinner on Friday, or something."

"And I'll irritate the hell out of you." Rocky disentangled himself from the retriever's lead and headed towards the door. "By leaving towels on the bathroom floor and the top off the toothpaste and forgetting which day the bins have to be emptied. But, we've already slept together and that's a start."

Phoebe stared after him, then laughed.

It was, she thought, looking out of Rocky's van at Winchester Road an hour later, as if the storm of last night simply hadn't happened. As if the whole thing had been some huge nightmare. The sky, bright blue and flecked with fluffy white clouds, stretched innocently above the houses, the sun shone and the morning was mild and fresh.

Only wide trails of grey silt and massive splodges of viscous mud along the road, and leaves and branches and other debris banked across the pavements, gave any indication of the previous night's devastation. And, of course, the fire tender still parked at the top of the street, and the dozens of cars, unable to pull into their drives because of the flood, still abandoned along the side of the road.

The Daimler and the hearse were both back in the Motions' driveway. Mary Miller was opening her windows.

All was returning to normal.

"You know," Phoebe said as Rocky pulled the van up outside their flats, "I've been thinking. About the flat-sharing thing. There's another person we could involve here."

"Not YaYa! No way! Much as I love her, I'm not sharing my flat with you and a barking drag queen. One of you, yes. Both, absolutely not."

"Bert."

"Bert?" Rocky frowned at her. "Do I know Bert? Is Bert the sort of bloke I'd pick for a ménage à-trois?"

"Of course you know Bert. Twilighter. Essie's friend. Lovely eyes. Bad origami."

"Ah, yes, Bert. What about him?"

"Well . . ." Phoebe stopped. "Oh, aren't you coming in?"

"I'm going to work. Not for long, but I've just got to finish that job I started yesterday. The man I'm working for lives on that new estate in Winterbrook, the one with the unfashionably huge gardens, and said he'd recommend me to lots of other people — and I'd like to remind him of that. I need all the regulars I can get. It's only a tidying up job, no lawn mowing or anything that the rain would have spoiled. Should only take an hour if that, then we can sort out the small print on the sharing, can't we?"

"Fine." Phoebe nodded. "But about Bert —"

"Go on then — about Bert?"

"Well, I know he desperately misses his mother and his aunts who he lived with until they died recently and then he had to go into Twilights. He's chummed up with Essie and co because he needs to be mothered but he hates it there. Cries himself to sleep every night, poor love. Sooo — if Slo moves in here with Essie, why don't we suggest that Bert moves in with Constance and Perpetua?"

"Why? Oh, yes . . . I see . . . Bert would have his mother substitutes and a proper home, and the Motion ladies would have a man about the house. You're not just a pretty face, Phoebe Bowler, are you?"

"A bit of a munter was what you called me earlier this morning, may I remind you. Anyway, it's quite funny, actually, because I did a tarot reading for Bert ages ago and the cards predicted that he'd find his heart's desire in the most unlikely circumstances. That he'd regain his former happiness and that his life would change for the better in a truly unexpected way."

"Oh well." Rocky grinned. "If the tarots said so, then it must be true. And you can't go against your own predictions, Phoebes, can you?"

Phoebes . . . He'd called her Phoebes. He'd never done that before.

"Er, no. Which means that if I move upstairs to share — and I mean share — with you, and Essie and Slo move into my flat, then we can introduce Bert to Constance and Perpetua and everyone will be happy, won't they?"

"Sounds like it. So, does that mean you're going to move upstairs and catalogue all my books and albums in alphabetical order and date-order the tins in the kitchen cupboard and turn my spare room into a Barbie hell?"

"You know —" Phoebe smiled happily, opening the van's door "— I think it does."

"Thank the Lord for that." Rocky grinned at her. "I thought you'd never see sense. It's going to work out brilliantly, Phoebes, you'll see. We're going to be so happy. I won't be long — then we can make a start."

He leaned across and kissed her very gently on the lips.

They just stared at one another, then, floating, Phoebe smiled some more as she slid from the van. And she was still smiling as she waved Rocky goodbye.

It was going to be brilliant, she thought, touching her lips with her fingertips, as the van disappeared round the corner. Strange, but fun, too. And her obsessive tidiness and Rocky's organised chaos might give rise to some disagreements, but then they'd be able to sort them out, wouldn't they? And laugh about them. They did a lot of laughing. And it would, she thought, still smiling, be wonderful to be with him all the time because —

Oh, God — because she really, really fancied him like mad.

She, sad, jilted Phoebe Bowler, was going to be living with, well, technically at least, the gorgeous red-hot Rocky Lancaster.

And smiling even more, she scrunched up the drive. She was still smiling as she slid her key into the front-door lock. Still smiling as she opened her flat door. Still smiling as she walked into the now partially denuded living room.

Then the smile died. So did everything else.

"Hi, Phoebes. Surprise, surprise, as they say. Where the hell have you been?" Ben said softly from the sofa. "I've been waiting ages for you to come home."

CHAPTER
TWENTY-SIX

"How the hell did you get in here?" Phoebe gripped the door handle to stop herself from falling. "How?"

"Spare key. In the usual place. I reckoned you, being a creature of habit, would still keep it there. Hidden beside the doorstep under the lucky pixie."

Bloody *unlucky* pixie.

She shook her head, feeling violently sick. After all this time, all those early awful sleepless nights of rehearsing what she'd say to Ben if she ever saw him again, Phoebe couldn't manage to utter a word.

She just stared at him.

Neat and tidy — just the same. Short, gelled blond hair — just the same. Chinos and well-ironed shirt — just the same. Shiny shoes and clean fingernails — just the same.

"You've changed a few things in here." Ben looked around the living room. "Got rid of a lot of stuff. Even more minimalist. I like it. Mind, I clearly picked a bad time, didn't I? The firemen told me the street had been flooded last night. We were lucky this end though —"

"We?" Phoebe suddenly found her voice. "We? What the hell do you mean by we? You don't live here any more, Ben, remember? The little matter of a wedding you forgot to attend? The little matter of having arranged to change this flat to a single tenancy *before* you didn't turn up at the church? The little matter of disappearing off the face of the earth for the last three months? The —"

He stood up. "Sorry, Phoebes. So, so sorry. I know I was a bastard for doing it the way that I did. I know everything I did was spineless and cowardly and stupidly cruel, but I never meant to hurt you. I —"

"Don't come near me. Don't even talk to me. Just go."

"I've got to talk to you. I've got to explain."

"No, you haven't. You made a fool of me — deliberately made a public spectacle of me — that says it all."

Ben shook his head. "I wasn't thinking straight."

"Bollocks. You'd planned it right down to the last bloody detail. You knew you weren't going to turn up at the church. You knew —"

"No I didn't. I didn't know what I was going to do. Oh, Christ, Phoebes —"

"Don't call me Phoebes!"

"Yes, OK, I arranged to change the tenancy agreement when I started to get worried about the wedding — No, don't scream at me — please, please listen. I knew that if . . . if . . . I told you I couldn't go through with it, then you'd kick me out and whatever happened, I wanted you to have the flat."

"Nice of you."

"None of it was nice of me. I behaved like a total dick. Look, I've driven all night. Can't we have a cup of coffee or something while we talk?"

"Coffee? Talk? I don't think so. I haven't got anything to say to you."

Phoebe had never been so angry. She wanted to run at Ben and slap him and punch him over and over again, and hurt him the way he'd hurt her. But she also desperately needed caffeine. Pushing past him, she stormed into the kitchen and reached for the kettle.

No kettle.

Where the hell was the kettle? Phoebe blinked round the denuded kitchen. No kettle, no microwave, no toaster . . .

Oh, God — of course. All her electrical stuff was upstairs in Rocky's flat, wasn't it? Carefully stowed away from the flood-that-never-was. And Rocky had gone to work and she didn't have a key and . . .

Great — that was all she needed — no key, no kettle, no coffee . . .

Leaning against the sink, Phoebe tried to stop herself from trembling.

How dare he? How bloody dare Ben come back here? Walk back into the flat as if nothing had happened? Just appear after all this time when she was just starting to get her life back together again? How dare he?

"Still no sugar for me," Ben shouted.

"No coffee for you. No sodding nothing for you," Phoebe, feeling even worse now she couldn't have a caffeine crutch, peeled herself away from the sink and stormed back into the living room. "Just go away."

"We need to talk."

"No we don't." She glared at him. "And what about your parents? Have you seen them yet? Let them know you're back?"

"Not yet. I wanted to see you first. They'll understand."

"I doubt it. They're worried sick. You selfish, selfish bastard — how the hell did you expect them to feel? Why didn't you let them know you were OK?"

He shrugged. "No idea. My head's been all over the place. I had to sort things out."

"Nice that you had the time and opportunity. So, where have you been that was preferable to here?"

"Everywhere. Nowhere for very long. Taking casual jobs, mostly in hotels so I could live in. I needed to sort stuff out in my head. But, Phoebes, you've got to believe me, I never, ever meant to hurt you."

"Well, you did — and don't call me Phoebes."

"Please, just listen to me. I've come back now because I know what I want — and because I really, really missed you. It wasn't you I ran away from, Phoebes, you've got to believe that. It was the wedding — not the marriage. It had all got out of hand. Just one huge circus. You didn't talk about anything else. No one talked about anything else. For over a year it was all lists and charts, wasn't it? Your bloody star signs telling you what was right for us? Dates, times, places — all planned by what the zodiac crap said, remember? It was your friends and your mum, and mine, here all the time, talking about dresses and flowers and venues and menus and photographers — and nothing else. Just like we were preparing for some Royal Variety Performance. Like the wedding mattered more than we did. All those years we'd been together didn't count for anything, it was —"

"Shut up!" Phoebe screamed at him. "I don't believe any of it. You've had time to sort out your story, haven't you? The story that will put you in the best light, and me in the wrong. It's all crap, Ben, and you know it. You could have called a halt at any time if the wedding plans weren't what you wanted. You went along with it quite happily at the time, didn't you? It was a day for both of us to share — Oh, no, but it wasn't, was it? Silly me. I made a solo appearance."

She walked away and stared out of the living-room window. In the September sunshine, Winchester Road was certainly coming back to life. People were sweeping the flood debris from their driveways, chatting over garden fences, laughing about their evacuation to the village hall, nodding sympathetically towards the half-a-dozen devastated houses at the bottom of the road.

How long ago that seemed now. How long since her lovely, laughing birthday meal in the courtyard and the crazily mad night that followed. With Rocky . . .

"Phoebe, look at me."

She didn't turn round.

"Phoebes, please. I know what a prat I've been. How could I just chuck away fifteen years? I've never looked at another girl . . . woman . . . anyone, ever. Just you. It was always us, wasn't it? At school and always."

"Don't play the sympathy card." Phoebe's voice wobbled. She was tired and over-emotional and very, very angry. She really didn't want to cry. Not now. Not ever again. She sniffed. "Do not dredge up the happy memories stuff, Ben. Just don't. Have you any idea what it was like for me? Not just being left at the altar — the horror of that will never go away, believe me. But afterwards? The practical things that your parents and mine had to deal with? The reception — can you imagine what that was like? Oh, no — I didn't go either. I was back at home in Bagley, going out of my mind, with Clemmie and Amber and Sukie and people who really cared. But our parents had to go to the hotel and make the most of it for those people who had travelled miles for our wedding. They cancelled the disco and the fireworks, but the meal went ahead. It was apparently a lot less cheerful than a funeral."

Ben moved towards her. "Christ, Phoebe, I didn't give any of that a thought. None of it. The only thing I thought about was having to be there in front of all those people, dressed up like a bloody dummy, and it all seemed so false."

"It wasn't bloody false!" She swirled round. "It was a ceremony to show our love for and commitment to one another in front of everyone who mattered to us. A traditional celebration, Ben. That's what it was. If you'd wanted a low-key affair with two strangers as witnesses at the register office then you should have said so."

"I always wanted to marry you."

"Then you should have been there."

"I couldn't go through with the pomp-and-circumstance stuff, that's all. I was scared. OK? Scared. Overwhelmed by the fuss. Whatever you want to call it. I never, ever ran away from you."

"Yes, you did, Ben. Like the coward you are. Like a coward, you couldn't tell me to my face, could you? Like a coward, you didn't even get in touch with me afterwards to tell me all this, did you? Didn't even let me or your parents know you were still alive. You were such a coward that you didn't even tell Alan, your best man, what you were planning to do, did you? The poor sod was as nonplussed as the rest of us. You let him go on to the church. Said you were planning a little surprise, and you'd catch him up. Then you rang the vicarage — knowing they wouldn't answer their phone because they'd already be at the church — and, like a gutless wimp, you left a message on the answerphone. Clemmie had to tell me the wedding was off. Can you imagine what that was like?"

"No — no, but I —"

"No, you can't. And you never will. And our families had to return the presents and cancel the honeymoon and a million and one other things."

Ben slumped down on the sofa. "You've got to believe me, Phoebes. I never thought of any of that. I must have been mad. But I'm not now. This time on my own has made me realise that I made a huge mistake — not just by j — j —"

"The word is jilting, Ben. Jilting. Try it out."

He winced. "By not turning up — but also by hurting you so badly. By leaving you. I've missed you every single minute of every single day. All I want now is a chance to make it up to you."

"Really? That's nice. Close the door on the way out."

"I'm back, Phoebe. I'm going to see Mum and Dad after we've sorted things out here, and I'll move back in with them for a while. I've got an appointment with my old boss this afternoon. With any luck, he'll take me back, too. Probably not in my old position, but I gave him fifteen years — that should count for something. So, I'll have a home and a job. I know it'll take time, but we can start again. We can —"

"We can *what?*" Phoebe stalked furiously towards the sofa, staring down at him. "Start again? Are you bloody mad, Ben? Have you listened to anything I've said? Starting again is something we can never do. Even if I wanted to, I'd never trust you again. Never believe a word you said. Never be able to forgive you for the hurt. Just go. I don't care where you'll be living or where you'll be working. I-don't-bloody-care."

"But we can't throw it all away —"

"I didn't. You did. Like I said, close the door on your way out."

She almost ran out of the living room, fumbling blindly with the key to the French doors, and eventually managing to open them, stormed out into the courtyard garden.

The sun was glistening on the tumbling glossy banks of wet leaves and the shrubs had never smelled sweeter in their drenched warmth. The Kennet shushed and rippled and flowed unseen behind the wall, innocent and safe now after its ravages of the previous night. Without thinking, Phoebe picked up the upturned wind-blown chairs and returned them neatly round the wrought-iron tables. Her hands were trembling. Her throat hurt.

How dare he do this to her? How could he come back now?

Oh, God.

She exhaled and tried to stop her hands from shaking, staring up at the sky, trying to compose herself.

How had she felt about him? How did she feel about him now? The first was easy enough — she'd loved him. Adored him. Shared her entire life with him for fifteen years because they'd grown-up together. Trusted him? Yes, implicitly. Wanted to spend the rest of her life with him? Yes, definitely.

And now? Now . . . Phoebe swallowed the tears. It was awful to have to admit it, even to herself, but now — now she didn't love him any more. She simply didn't care.

Love hadn't died just because he'd jilted her, hurt and humiliated her, but because by doing it, he'd made her grow up, stand on her own feet, live her own life, and she realised he'd become a habit, and she no longer needed him. By seeking his own space, Ben had also given her space in which to become a person in her own right.

For the first time since school she'd been Phoebe Bowler, not half of Phoebe-and-Ben.

And this last three months, hideously painful as they'd been to start with, had been mostly OK, hadn't they? After the first shock and hurt had gone of course. There had been so many changes — Twilights and Essie and Slo, the part-time mobile hairdressing, the resurgence of her own astrological powers not to mention the birthday magic stuff, and her friends — and Rocky.

Particularly Rocky.

Definitely Rocky.

She swallowed again. It seemed as if she and Rocky had laughed together, had more fun together, talked together more in the last three months than she and Ben had ever done. As friends, of course. Just good friends.

And Essie, whose knowledge of the Happy Birthday magic she trusted implicitly, had warned her that she and Ben would never have worked, hadn't she? Told her that the marriage would have been a disaster? And Essie had been right. The secret birthday-ology had been right.

Ben had done her a huge favour.

Alone, she'd found what she wanted.

"Phoebes . . ." Ben appeared in the doorway. "Phoebes . . ."

"I thought you'd gone," she said wearily. "There's nothing else to say."

Ben pulled out one of the wrought-iron chairs. The legs scraped loudly and gratingly across the flagstones. He sat down. "I'm just going. I need to see my parents and make my peace with them too. But before I go, just tell me you forgive me?"

She shook her head. Her eyes were gritty from lack of sleep and she was feeling totally drained. "Forgiveness would have to come from someone far, far nicer than me, Ben. I can't forgive you for what you did — either to me or to our families — but I'm prepared to try to forget it. Will that do?"

He shrugged. "It's a start, I suppose. And far more than I deserve. But I promise you one thing, Phoebes, when we're back together properly, I'll spend the rest of my life making it up to you. And in the end you'll forgive me — once I've managed to forgive myself."

"We're not going to be back together," Phoebe said tiredly. "You can come back and live locally, and work at your old firm, and see your old friends, and pick up the threads of your old life — even drink in the Faery Glen — if you've got the balls, which I doubt. And I'll say hello and goodbye if we pass in the street. But as for anything else — forget it."

Ben stood up and grabbed her hands in his. She tried to tug away but he held her fast.

"But I love you, Phoebes. I've always loved you. I always will. I love you."

"How touching," Rocky's voice rang bitterly from the upstairs balcony. "So sorry to interrupt."

"Rocky!" Phoebe slapped Ben's hands away.

"Hi, Rocky." Ben looked upwards. "Nice to see you again. You still upstairs? Been keeping an eye on Phoebes while she's on her own? Nice of you, mate, but no longer necessary. I'm back now."

"So I see." Rocky's dark eyes were flint hard. "I hope you'll be very happy together."

"Yeah, well, there's a lot of stuff to sort out, but when we're back together and I've moved in again, you'll have to come and have a drink with us in the Faery Glen. You and Mindy —"

"Rocky." Phoebe stepped towards the staircase. "Rocky, this isn't — Don't think —"

But he'd gone. And the slamming of his door echoed round the courtyard.

CHAPTER
TWENTY-SEVEN

"I still can't get used to this idea," Essie said happily, fastening the last box in her roomette. "I still think I'm going to wake up and find it's all a dream."

"Well it ain't, duck." Slo beamed at her. "The Daimler awaits to whisk you off to your new 'ome."

"*Our* new home," Essie corrected. "Goodness, I can't believe any of this is happening at last. It's taken so long to get all the legal i's dotted and the t's crossed this end."

"Don't tell me." Slo picked up the roll of Sellotape. "I've been counting the blame days ever since our Constance told me about it, which were the day after the flooding. So, that's a whole thirty-seven of 'em by my reckoning."

"Just over a month? Is that all? It seems so much longer." Essie shook her head. "I was so worried about you that day, when I listened to the local breakfast news on the radio and heard about the floods in Winchester Road. I was frantic, thinking that you were caught up in it, not knowing if you were safe."

"Ah." Slo Selloptaped up the top of the final cardboard box. "But we was fine, duck. And then I was up 'ere sharpish to let you know — an' to tell you what our Constance had arranged with young Rocky and Phoebe about the living arrangements. Right stars, them youngsters were that night. Right stars."

"And all those poor people who were flooded — they're still not back in their homes?"

"Not yet." Slo looked round the room. "But they'll be back in fer Christmas. An' that's summat I'm looking forward to an' all. Us being together for Christmas. Imagine it, Essie duck. Just imagine it."

Essie imagined it and smiled blissfully.

Slo kissed her, then picked up Essie's suitcase in one hand and tucked the final box under his arm. "Right, now is this the lot?"

"I think so. Yes. Oh, I'm so excited, and having to watch Bert go off first this morning was almost too much to bear."

"Ah, the gels gave 'im a right royal welcome I can tell you. Happy as a sandboy is Bert. Got my old room, and the gels fussing over him like nobody's business. And of course, young Amber and Lewis and Jem'll still be round to take 'im out and do 'is blame paper-folding, so all's right there."

And all was more than all right with her and Slo, Essie thought happily. In five minutes, after the final formal farewell from Absolute Joy and Tiny Tony, and a few tears with Lilith and Princess — although she knew she'd probably see them every day — she and Slo would be off to spend the rest of their lives together.

She gave one last glance round her beige, bland roomette and momentarily pitied the next occupant. Whoever they were, she hoped they'd be happier at

Twilights than she'd been. They were probably on their way there now — not knowing what to expect, filled with trepidation at this earth-shattering upheaval so late in their life. As she had been.

She wished them well.

Oh, how she'd hated that move. But not this one. No, this move was what she'd wanted for, ooh, so very, very long.

She locked the door behind her and almost skipped down the beige corridor away from her detested prison cell.

"Essie — Mrs Rivers . . ." Absolute Joy in a blue suit and blouse complete with pussycat bow and massive handbag, extended a hand. "So sorry to see you go, but so absolutely delighted at your good fortune. Tony, my hubby, and I would just like to say we'll miss you. And we do hope you'll be a regular visitor. And of course that you and Mr Motion will find absolute happiness in your, um, new home."

"We will." Essie extricated her hand and beamed from Absolute Joy to Tiny Tony. She'd thought of all manner of caustic things to say at this point but as she was simply delighted to be leaving at last and would want to be allowed back for social visits, she kept them to herself. "And thank you too for making this parting so easy. Goodbye."

"Er, goodbye." The Tugwells clearly weren't sure how to interpret Essie's leaving remark. "And good luck, Mrs Rivers. Good luck."

"I shan't need any damn good luck," Essie muttered as she hurried across the courtyard bathed in bright autumn sunshine. "I've got the Happy Birthday magic on my side, I know I have."

Then she hugged Lilith and Princess amid a flood of tears. "Oh, please don't cry — I'm happy. You're happy. You've got your TOATs friends and you'll be welcome visitors at the flat any time, you know that. And you've got young Phoebe still coming up here on a regular basis for the hairdos and the astrology sessions, haven't you? And Rocky's a permanent fixture as a gardener here now, of course. They'll keep you up to speed — as the youngsters say."

Lilith and Princess mopped their eyes and blew their noses loudly and nodded in unison. Then Essie kissed them both again and, with all the mobile residents of Twilights forming a rather shaky guard of honour, she and Slo drifted hand in hand towards the Daimler.

"Right, duck." Slo helped her into the passenger seat and moved, quite nippily for him, into the driver's seat and urged the Daimler into life. "Off we go, then. Bye-bye Twilights. Hello new life. If I get a shift on, duck, we'll be home in time for a late lunch. Fish an' chips, I thought — as we're celebrating."

"Oh," Essie sighed, leaning her head back against the ancient leather. "That would be heavenly."

"Okey-doke," Pauline said, "that's the last of my perms for this morning. What have you got left?"

"Just doing Mrs Sibley's tidy-up then I'll be finished, too" Phoebe answered, snipping layers carefully against her comb. "And you're quite sure it'll be OK for me to take the whole afternoon off? I mean, Saturday is so busy and —"

"Course I'm sure." Pauline nodded. "You get off as soon as you like. The other girls can double up a bit if we get any last-minute appointments. It's an important day for you, Phoebe. You've waited a long time for this — and a house move is always exciting, isn't it?"

Exciting? Phoebe wasn't sure that was quite the right word. Still, yes, she had waited a long time for this stage of her life. And she was sure it would be wonderful — when they all got used to it.

"There we go." She flourished the mirror for Mrs Sibley to admire her zigzag chop. "Very trendy."

"Smashing, Phoebe, thank you. Now, off you go — I know you're dying to get yourself sorted out at home. It's been the talk of the salon for weeks."

Phoebe chuckled as she removed the strawberry-pink gown and brushed loose hairs from Mrs Sibley's shoulders. Nothing much got past the Cut'n'Curl customers.

"Right then, that's me done. I'll just go and grab my bag and I'll be off. See you on Monday, Pauline — and thanks."

"No need to thank me, dear." Pauline's eyes were moist. "I'm just so pleased that things have worked out OK for you at last. You've had a right rotten time of it this year. Now go on — off you go before I come over all emotional."

Phoebe gave her a quick hug and grabbed her bag and her pink sweatshirt and went.

Walking home along Hazy Hassocks High Street under the colonnade of sycamore trees that were just turning a lovely shade of autumn auburn, her mobile phone rang non-stop. Her parents, Clemmie, YaYa, Amber and Sukie all wishing her luck for the move. She smiled to herself. Goodness knows what it would be like if she was emigrating.

Cutting through the alleyway beside Big Sava and hurrying the last part of the short journey to Winchester Road, Phoebe gave a little skip, looking round guiltily to make sure no one had seen her. Life — almost four months on from the-wedding-that-never-was — was almost perfect.

Almost.

She turned into Winchester Road and heaved a sigh of relief. Slo's Daimler was parked outside. The first part of the move had gone to plan. She could imagine Slo and Essie inside, excitedly prowling round the flat, admiring the changes that had been made for them, arranging their own belongings, getting used to having all that space and privacy.

And even if that was the only good thing that came out of all this, Phoebe thought, unlocking the front door, and then knocking on her own, then it would be good enough.

Slo pulled her door open. "You don't 'ave to knock, duck. This is still your 'ome. But come along in — we're right bedazzled by what you've done for us."

"Phoebe!" Essie emerged from the kitchen. "Oh, Phoebe! I still can't believe this! You've done us proud, dear. It's a little palace. The furnishings are just perfect

— we'll be so spoiled. Oh, and we love the fireplace too, dear, so cosy."

The white free-standing gas fire with its stylish white coals, had been replaced by a mock black-leaded fire with realistic gas logs and old-fashioned tiled surround. To make the living room less minimalist and more suitable for Slo and Essie, the white sofas had been replaced by cushiony wing-backed chairs on either side of the fire and a matching deep-cushioned corner unit — big enough for Slo and Essie to stretch out on and watch television in absolute comfort.

"And my bedroom! All those frills and flounces! Like a pink palace!" Essie clasped her hands together. "I've never seen such a pretty room — and Slo can't believe that you've even put ashtrays in his. He's never been allowed to smoke in his bedroom before. Oh . . ." She hugged Phoebe to her. "We'll never be able to thank you enough. But, are you sure?"

"Of course I'm sure." Phoebe kissed Essie's cheek. "I'm thrilled to bits for you both. Are you managing to find a home for all your things?"

"I am. I'm like a dog with two tails. And now you're going upstairs?"

Phoebe nodded. "Mmm. I think Rocky's got things organised up there, but I'll have to check."

"Good girl — it's a shame —"

"Don't, Essie, please. This is as good as it's going to get. And anyway, knowing that you're out of Twilights and with Slo is more than enough for me."

"I haven't ever said this before, Phoebe, but I know you used the Happy Birthday magic on us. When we were here that first time? I'm not sure how, but —"

"You dozed off in the sun," Phoebe admitted, knowing that it didn't matter any more. "It seemed too good an opportunity to waste. You'd already told me that you'd asked Slo the Five Questions and you knew that he was the right one for you. I could see how happy you were together so I just, um, gave it a little shove in the right direction."

"Thank God you did," Essie said fervently. "You've changed my life. And now you're using the Happy Birthday magic in your sessions, aren't you?"

"Some of them, yes."

Since the lower-key successes at the fête, Phoebe had expanded her tarot readings and astrology evenings and was in great demand throughout the area. Believing in her own talents again, she'd become adept at accurately forecasting her clients' futures. And yes, she'd used the Happy Birthday magic on more than one occasion, but only when the couples had been suitable, of course. And each time it had worked.

But she'd never again risk causing an all-out orgy.

"I want you to carry on with it, you know that. It's lovely for me to know that my knowledge and Romany secrets have been passed on to someone who'll use them properly. Shame you won't use the birthday magic on yourself, though, dear. Not that I'm sure self-magicking works, but it would be worth a try," Essie said softly. "Especially now you know what you want, I mean after —"

"After Ben's reappearance," Phoebe said. "Yes, well, that was pretty awful, but, hey, water under the bridge. Right, now I'll leave you to settle in and go and see what Rocky's up to upstairs."

"An' you'll both join us fer fish an' chips out in the garden later when we're all settled, won't you? It's nice an' warm out there for October." Slo poked his head round his bedroom door. "Our treat so's we can say thank you properly."

"Love to, thanks. See you later, then."

And taking a deep breath, Phoebe ran upstairs to her new home.

That weird day, after the floods, when Ben had turned up like the proverbial bad penny, had certainly been a turning point, she knew now. Not only had Phoebe realised that she was enjoying her new life far more than her old one, and whatever she'd once felt for Ben, she'd never be able to trust him again, and certainly couldn't forgive him, but she had also discovered that she definitely didn't want him back in her life.

Because of Rocky.

And eventually, after Rocky had seen them together in the courtyard and added two and two together to make five hundred, Ben had finally got the message and left. In tears. That had been really awful, Phoebe thought, but sadly unavoidable.

And Phoebe had been left standing in the courtyard, as Ben slammed away, knowing that she'd lost Rocky.

And that had hurt far, far more.

392

According to the Hassocks gossip grapevine, Ben was now back with his parents, back in his old job, and she hoped he'd be happy. But she never wanted to see him again.

"Hi," she called through Rocky's open front door. "Safe to come in?"

Bon Scott was growling his way through some of AC/DC's more doubtful lyrics.

"Yep — I think I'm ready for inspection," Rocky shouted back. "Everything arranged, Poirot-fashion, in nice symmetrical lines, nothing out of place."

Phoebe stepped into the hall. Once they'd agreed that Essie and Slo should have Phoebe's flat and she'd move into the spare bedroom up here, Rocky had become very secretive about some of his redecoration plans, although she'd steered him towards neutral for the spare bedroom so that she could add her own touches, and they'd agreed on gold for the living room as it would go with their accumulated furnishings.

She'd yet to see the final results.

"Wow!" she gazed round the living room, where her sofas and cabinets melded beautifully with Rocky's more eclectic mix of furniture, against the soft golden walls. With gold rugs on the varnished floorboards and her white gas fire reinstalled, it looked both modern and cosy at the same time.

"It's fantastic. Amazing. You've worked so hard . . ."

"To turn it from a squalid bachelor tip into something suitable for a control freak to share?" Rocky grinned at her. "I do hope so. Cushions at the right angle? One single flower in a minimalist vase in the right place? Rugs straight? Spotlights spot on?"

"Absolutely," Phoebe laughed. "Rocky, it's perfect. Thank you."

"My pleasure, although it nearly didn't happen, did it?"

She shook her head. "No, well, you jumped to all the wrong conclusions didn't you? And it took damn ages to convince you that — well —"

"I was more pissed off than you'll ever know." Rocky shrugged. "I was tired, but sort of elated after that really manic night, and so looking forward to seeing you again to sort out the flat-sharing and . . . and then to come home and find you with that prat — after what he'd done to you — and hearing him declaring undying love."

"I wasn't declaring it back."

"No, I know that now. Sorry, Phoebes, I really should have given you more credit. Anyway, slate all wiped clean, you're a free agent, Ben's history, we've all moved on — and Essie and Slo —"

"Have invited us for fish and chips later and are absolutely thrilled to bits with their flat. I'm just amazed the tenancy changes went through without a hitch. And so quickly. Oh, which reminds me, we'll have to sort out my rent book and everything now I'm up here, won't we?"

"Yep — anyway, before we get into all the boring stuff, you'll want to see your room. I've piled all your suitcases and stuff in there, so you can unpack

394

whenever you're ready. It's this one — overlooking the road."

Excitedly, Phoebe peered into her new bedroom. "Oh . . ."

After the magical transformation of the living room, it was nothing like she'd expected it to be. Magnolia, clean and neat, with a divan bed and basic furniture, it had all the soul of a budget hotel room.

"As you suggested, I've left it as a sort of blank canvas. Like you, I moved out of the front bedroom when Mindy left." Rocky leaned against the door jamb. "Like you, I bought a new bed, new furniture, redecorated — made a fresh start. Mine is now at the back of the house, the one that has the French doors on to the balcony."

Well, of course it would be, wouldn't it? She couldn't have expected anything else, could she?

"This is, um, very nice," Phoebe said quickly, not wanting him to see her disappointment and thinking fleetingly of her lovely pink frilly bedroom downstairs. "Lovely — although I may have to add a bit of colour."

"It's yours to do what you want with, of course. However, there's something else we should clear up, as we're going to be sharing."

"Yes, I know — the rent. And we haven't given Essie and Slo their rent books either — and to be honest, I'm not sure if I should have signed new paperwork at the letting agency because —"

"Essie and Slo won't be paying any rent. I'll tell them that later over the fish and chips."

"What? Well, I mean, that's really generous, and of course they haven't got much money, but can we really afford to subsidise them?"

"You won't be paying any rent, either."

"Sorry? Now I'm completely confused — have you won the lottery or something? Or have you registered us all as some sort of waifs and strays charity? Or —?"

"You really didn't read your tenancy agreement very well, did you?"

"Yes, I did! Every word. Just because I'm a hairdresser and a mystic doesn't mean I'm an airhead, you know."

"Phoebes," Rocky laughed. "You're so funny when you get all self-righteous. And I'm not doubting your ability to check small print, but didn't you ever look to see who your landlord was?"

"No, why should I? Who is it?"

"Me."

"*What?*"

"This house was my twenty-first birthday present from my parents. It was already divided into two flats and investing in bricks and mortar, they said, was the only way forwards at that time. So, when I moved in I rented out the ground floor to give me another income, but, yes, the house is paid for. I own it. Outright."

"You own this house?" Phoebe blinked. "And you don't want me to pay rent?"

"Yes. No. We're sharing, Phoebes. We'll divvy up the bills, but that's it. My house is now our home."

Phoebe wanted to kiss him. Properly. Well, she'd wanted to kiss him properly for a very long time. Again she managed not to.

"I honestly don't know what to say. I'm totally stunned. I had no idea. Um . . ."

"Let's just leave it at that, then, shall we?" Rocky grinned at her. "And anyway, my ownership of the house and your rent book wasn't what I wanted to clear up."

"It wasn't?"

"No. There was another little matter of an earlier slur on my character. Come along."

She'd never cast a slur on him, had she? She wouldn't, would she? Oh, well, there was the little misunderstanding about him being a violent criminal and axe murderer, of course, but surely that was all forgotten now, wasn't it?

Her head reeling, Phoebe followed him along the corridor, trying really hard not to drool over his long legs in the denim or his shoulders under the Jimi Hendrix T-shirt, or . . .

"Right," Rocky stopped. "Now as I recall, you accused me of having a room plastered with aeroplane pictures, AC/DC posters, and wall-to-wall Hollyoaks babes, didn't you? So, now see for yourself . . ."

He pushed open the door of the second bedroom.

"Oh." Phoebe caught her breath. "Oh."

With the French doors open on to the balcony and with the white drapes blowing in the warm autumn breeze, the room was suffused in a green and golden light. A room with white walls, scrubbed floorboards, pale limed furniture and the biggest bed Phoebe had ever seen in her life. A vast black iron bed with piles of cushiony white Egyptian cotton linen. And on one of the pale bedside tables was a massive bouquet of tumbled pink flowers . . . and, ohmigod, there was a pale pink ceiling . . .

"Now." Rocky looked at her. "The choice is yours."

"What choice?" Phoebe managed to find something that vaguely resembled her voice. "I'm sure you'll be very happy in the functional front bedroom."

"Not my immediate first choice." Rocky pulled her towards him and kissed her. "Try again . . ."

Ages later, having completely wrecked the neat Egyptian bedlinen, Phoebe moved her head drowsily against the piles of downy, plump pillows and kissed Rocky's naked shoulder.

"So?" He smiled down at her.

"Oh, much nicer than the lilo," she whispered sleepily, her body floating blissfully somewhere just below the pretty pink ceiling.

Rocky laughed softly and kissed her. Again. She knew she'd never get tired of the kissing.

"I was actually going to say — so, do you think you'll be OK with this sort of sharing?"

"I think I could put up with it, yes. But —"

Rocky frowned. "After all that, there's still a but?"

"Mmm — I need to ask you something. Well, Five Somethings actually."

"Oh no, not the old witchcraft stuff. Essie did warn me."

398

"Humour me."

Rocky gave a huge mock sigh. "Oh, very well, as we've got to live together — go on then."

Wrapped in Rocky's arms, Phoebe asked the Five Questions, thinking, knowing, that if the answers were wrong she wouldn't take any notice of them and would give up magic birthday-ology for ever.

Rocky answered them, his voice echoing through her body.

Dazedly working out the formula, she giggled. "Your birthday? Is that really your birthday? Essie didn't prime you?"

"No, it's really my birthday. And don't laugh."

"April the first. I wouldn't dream of it." Phoebe rolled happily towards him. "It means we are totally, absolutely, completely secret Happy Birthday magicked compatible."

"Actually," Rocky murmured, pulling her against him and kissing her, "I didn't have any doubts about that. So, shall we get up now and go and join Essie and Slo for our fish and chips?"

"Tough one," Phoebe whispered into his chest, tracing the outline of his beautiful mouth with her fingertips. "But right now, I think fish and chips can wait, don't you?"